ST. THOMAS PUBLIC LIBRARY
36278008425266

JUN - - 2021

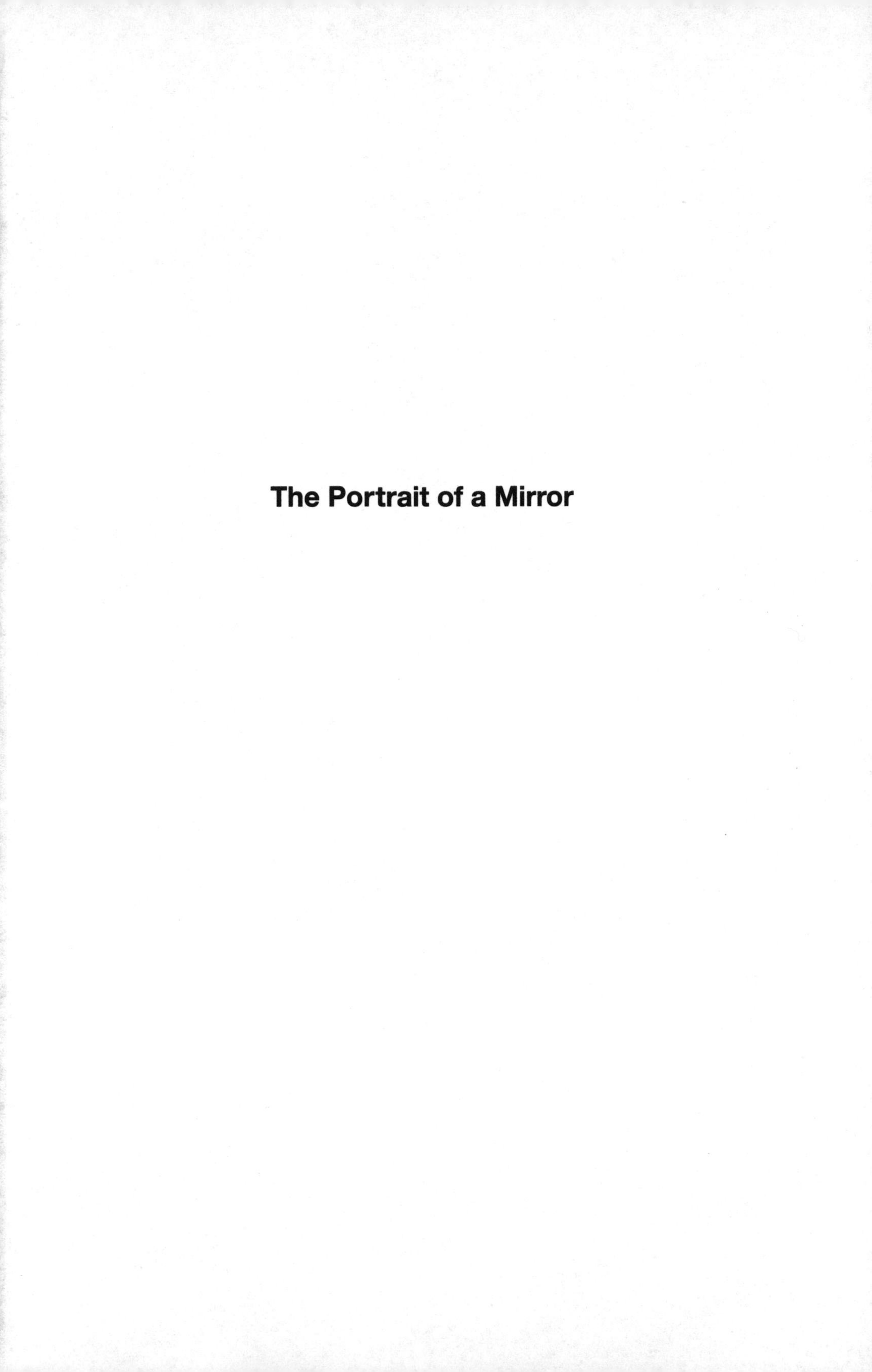

# The Portrait of a Mirror

# The Portrait of a Mirror

A Novel

---

A. Natasha Joukovsky

The Overlook Press, New York

ST. THOMAS PUBLIC LIBRARY

This edition first published in hardcover in 2021 by
The Overlook Press, an imprint of ABRAMS
195 Broadway, 9th floor
New York, NY 10007
www.overlookpress.com

Abrams books are available at special discounts when purchased in quantity
for premiums and promotions as well as fundraising or educational use.
Special editions can also be created to specification. For details,
contact specialsales@abramsbooks.com or the address above.

Copyright © 2021 A. Natasha Joukovsky
Jacket © 2021 Abrams

Pg. 81, song title, "Shake It Off" by Taylor Swift
Music and lyrics by Taylor Swift, Max Martin, and Shellback

Pg. 96, lyric from "Don't You (Forget About Me)" by Simple Minds
Music and lyrics by Keith Forsey and Steve Schiff

Pg. 97, lyric from "Don't Stop Believin'" by Journey
Music and lyrics by Steve Perry, Jonathan Cain, and Neal Schon

Pg. 98, lyric from "Danke Schoen" by Wayne Newton
Music and lyrics by Bert Kaempfert, Kurt Schwabach, and Milt Gabler

Pg. 125, lyric from "Tuesday" by iLoveMakonnen feat. Drake
Music and lyrics by Ousala Aleem, Aubrey Graham, Makonnen Sheran, Sonny Uwaezuoke, and Leland Wayne

Pg. 165, lyric from "Want to Want Me" by Jason Derulo
Music and lyrics by Jason Desrouleaux, Ian Kirkpatrick, Chris Brown, Samuel Denison Martin, Lindy Robbins, and Mitch Allan

Pg. 277, lyric from "It Wasn't Me" by Shaggy, feat. Rickardo "Rikrok" Ducent
Music and lyrics by Shaggy, Rikrok, Brian Thompson, and Shaun Pizzonia

Pg. 299, lyric from "Coming Home" by Diddy–Dirty Money feat. Skylar Grey
Music and lyrics by Shawn Carter, Jermaine Cole, Alexander Grant, and Holly Hafermann

All rights reserved. No part of this publication may be reproduced or transmitted in any form or by any means, electronic or mechanical, including photocopy, recording, or any information storage and retrieval system now known or to be invented, without permission in writing from the publisher, except by a reviewer who wishes to quote brief passages in connection with a review written for inclusion in a magazine, newspaper, or broadcast.

Library of Congress Control Number: 2020944997

Printed and bound in the United States

10 9 8 7 6 5 4 3 2 1

ISBN: 978-1-4197-5216-2

eISBN: 978-1-64700-195-7

*For Evan S. Thomas*
*1979–2018*

O Nature, and O soul of man! how far beyond all utterance are your linked analogies! not the smallest atom stirs or lives in matter, but has its cunning duplicate in mind.

—Herman Melville, *Moby-Dick*

# PART ONE

# I.

There is no greater compliment in this world than being the uncooperative catalyst of another person's misery, if not all-out self-destruction. The critical word here is *uncooperative*. It is easy, lazy, and dishonorable to deliberately distress another human being. But to do so unintentionally, or better yet, unwillingly—for one's mere presence to cause another pain, not by any act of violence, but by the force of the bottomless pool that is unrequited love, that pool that both draws and prevents the other from moving closer—to be loved and not to love back: this is the definition of power.

It's a state of affairs that most privileged, well-educated, self-involved people take great pains to shape in their favor. In the truest mark of artistic mastery, C. Wesley Range IV made it seem effortless.

So highly attractive to women was Wes that, at first glance, for the many (many) girls he had disappointed, it might have been tempting to paint a twenty-first-century Rick Von Sloneker—*tall, rich, good-looking, stupid, dishonest, conceited, a bully, a liar, a drunk and a thief, an egomaniac, and probably psychotic*. In reality, he was only about half of these things, and if Wes was a bit of a devil, he was the kind with whom you'd sympathize. At nearly thirty, Wes was still boyishly handsome, with an Ivy League aesthetic perforating his hipster urbanism, and (85 percent of) a Henley-winning physique. He was kind to children, respectful of the elderly, and attentive to dogs. He rarely drank alcohol, precisely because he knew he had the tendency to overdo it. The lies he told were generally engineered to spare hard feelings, and the main recipient of such lies was himself. With the recent tidy valuation of his tech startup, Ecco, one might have predicted an uptick in ego, but his oldest friends would insist there'd been no change. New acquaintances would scoff that he came from money anyway, until they learned the sorry state of his trust, at which point even Zuccotti Park–populist skeptics had been known to forgive him the suffix and develop a crush. Upon closer inspection, they found Wes could almost pass for self-made—if anything, he spent too much time at work. Factoring in his polite yet straightforward general manner, discretion in sexual encouragement and discouragement, discernment in those choices, and, most especially, his unwavering commitment to (albeit serial) monogamy, it was impossible to brand Wes a womanizer, let alone a rake.

It was a formidable talent, making women feel valued and respected. It shouldn't have been, but it was. Rarely making the first move, even less often a promise, Wes's quiet self-assurance and Sadie Hawkins approach tended to attract the kind of women to whom Wes was most attracted: independently minded and forward thinking enough to proposition a man, confident enough in their own desirability for that man to be him. His real specialty, though, was breakups. Wes's ready willingness to have an uncomfortable thirty-, maybe sixty-minute conversation and be cleanly, respectably done with things starkly broke ranks with long-established practice in male-to-female relationship termination theory. If the great lengths and dramatic unpleasantness his friends accepted to avoid such encounters boggled Wes's mind, his own compassion and transparency shocked the hell out of them. But to Wes, empathetic, definitive communication was a kind of secular Pascal's wager, one of those rare pragmatisms with the added benefit of humanistic appearance. In the absence of ugly breakup mechanics, most women ostensibly bore their post-Wes devastation in ironic nostalgia, if not pride of conquest. Those who did resort to the darker comforts of fiction were hardly believed anyway. Such was the sterling reputation of Charles Wesley Range IV: indelible to the point of immunity, even, on occasion, from the truth.

As the founder and CEO of a company that pinpointed needling errors in vast haystacks of code, Wes would have been the first to admit that with any sufficiently large data set, there are outliers. And as is often the case with outliers, the two women who defied the customary pattern of Rangeian relationship dynamics had a disproportionately large effect. You had to go pretty far back to find the first black swan, a taciturn brunette from—where else—prep school, an upper former two years his senior. It had been an admiration from afar: the obsessive, worshippy sort of lust-love that can only flourish from a distance, but, from a distance, self-perpetuates. Why had he been unable to approach her? Based on the way she'd looked at him a few times, he thought maybe she would approach him. But she never did, and there were always other girls more forwardly demanding of his attentions. Before he knew it, she'd graduated and was gone. Their missed connection was the rare kind of adolescent regret that, with time and maturity, became more rather than less painful. She was now, in his mind, far more than a person. She had come to represent every decision he hadn't made, every opportunity forgone. She was regret personified. One can get over bad decisions, lovers lost. But it is impossible to get over someone you never really had.

The second outlier was just downstairs, the damn incendiary making all that racket: the catalyst of his misery, the love of his life, Diana Whalen. Wes's wife.

Diana took a sip of coffee and set it on the credenza. The mug hit the marble top with an edgy *clink* followed by the hollow little *thud* of full contact. Wes knew she knew he was awake. She was doing that thing where she was pretending to be trying to be quiet, so that if he dared mention her inconsideration, she'd have just enough room to get wide-eyed with hurt, theatrically offended by the affront.

Much like Diana, the loft was built for special occasions and editorial photoshoots, not everyday life—and certainly not sleeping in. "Understated luxury in the heart of the Flatiron District," the listing had said. "Fully renovated prewar building with some of the best views in the city. Whimsical architectural details in a supremely versatile space, dripping with charm and character." And "only" $2.3 million; Wes distinctly remembered the broker calling it "a total steal," and repeating, for the fiftieth time, in his affected, reality-TV accent, "this is New *York*." Later that night, Wes and Diana had found countless, sidesplitting mock applications for this catchphrase, reveling in the reflection of each other's cleverness and the competitive rush of one-upmanship. It remained, to this day, one of their most flexible and reliably funny inside jokes.

The broker had the last laugh. It was a purchase that reflected not who Wes was, but who he wanted to be, who he wanted his friends to think he was. Wes had bought a loft for the formal-living-room version of himself, and was suffering the consequence of having to live in an apartment that was all formal living room. "Whimsical details" meant the bed was exposed and raised practically to the ceiling, photogenic in the abstract, but nearly impossible to make, never made. "Supremely versatile space" stood for one big room with wowing dinner party potential but radically insufficient closet space. On most mornings, including this one, the picked-over remnants of the previous week's wash-n-fold spilled out of gnarled cling wrap on the coffee table, migrating precariously close to a mountain of empty take-out containers. The absolute worst, though, was the "charm and character." Like a former war hero turned flatulent geriatric, the loft was well decorated but involuntarily announced every action of its inhabitants. The price of high ceilings and "industrial chic" was the end of privacy, the reverberating din of your wife at quarter to six when you didn't have to be up until eight.

A late spring sunbeam rose above the window sash, refracting into Wes's eyes through the glass, and this new architectural indignity seemed to be Diana's fault, too. In an indulgence he regretted almost immediately, Wes allowed himself the satisfaction of the tiniest little groan.

Why did he do that? A lapse of self-control with Diana was never worth the dopamine. Self-control was the currency of their marriage, the critical resource in their wars of attrition, and she always seemed to have more of it. Cunning, moreish, and borderline manic-depressive, Diana had a way of teetering on the edge of things, of effortlessly laughing off faux pas or changing the rules to a game midway, never falling herself but leading you off a cliff. She was willful, playful, stubborn, and frank. Coy in her warmth, and sly in her openness. She used her beauty as a weapon and rendered sex a competitive sport. Most concerningly, her spurts of wild ebullience—her utterly outrageous youth—masked a disciplined mind that no one besides Wes seemed able to see. They were all too enamored with the formal living room.

And so as Diana exposed the problem of the apartment, the apartment exposed the problem of Diana. This was a particularly infuriating conundrum for an expert in the resolution of system-compromising infinite loops. Wes's life was unraveling in a manner he was uniquely well equipped to solve, and he was powerless to stop it; he hated the loft for all the reasons he'd bought it, and hated his wife for the reasons he'd married her. His greatest affirmations were drawn from the same well as his personal disappointment, and his brain boiled with the specific kind of regret paradoxically associated with success.

—I'll pretend I didn't hear that.

At mezzo piano, Diana's voice cut through the chirr of her original hardwood steps. As if the loft were in collusion with her and willing to take the fall, the timbre and contrast in volume alone provided evidence of her endeavored consideration, while her words cloaked pettiness in civility, calling him out by allegedly letting it go. This was classic Diana, saying things by saying she wasn't going to say them, attacking in retreat, punishing Wes, yes, but without staining her hands—by making him punish himself.

Had Diana not been Diana, the solution would have been implemented many Mondays and hundreds of *clink-thuds* ago. Wes would have gotten out of bed, gently taken the hands of his hypothetical wife, and lovingly informed her that their marriage was over. He would have weathered the heartfelt hysterics and gasping, blank apologies, maybe even skipping his first appointment of the day to comfort her, taking the time to steady and reinforce the idea in her mind. At a respectable interval, Wes would have had a satisfying rebound fling with Sara Khan, Ecco's attractive Brooklynite CTO, lasting either until he met someone else or the sneaking around lost its excitement and started feeling like an obligation—whichever came first—and at which time Wes and Sara would have had a definitive thirty-to-sixty-minute conversation.

But Diana *was* Diana, and his relationship with her had been so intensely exciting and explosively sexual at first that even as it crystallized into the deep-seated mutual dependence of a far deeper marital entrenchment than its few short years would suggest, there remained a startling kind of urgency to it. They fought about the same things over and over, sure—money, time, sex, tone of voice, what to get for dinner when they were both already hungry; the things almost all couples fight about. But every iteration of the cycle still carried weight. For Wes and Diana's vast disagreements across the banalities of life were never really about their titular controversies: they were about winning.

Her skill in debate was almost the first thing Wes had noticed about Diana, the kind of marvel so attractive it made him want not just to get close, but to enmesh her. They shared the unapologetic pleasure of keeping score, so often observed in those accustomed to victory, and hovering beneath their mutual captivation was undoubtably the sense that in concert with the other's powers, each would become undefeatable. What Wes lacked in natural dialectic ability he more than made up for in competitive drive. Diana was heinously smart, but also lazy, and while it was understood that she was still the superior wit, he was more than good enough to be an uncommonly satisfying sparring partner.

Wes had literally been training for the Olympics when they'd met, and for him, spending time together came to seem like an essential aspect of his training—rowing being, akin to love, a sport of mental as well as physical acuity.

It was hard to pinpoint when the shift happened, when she started keeping score *against him*. Six months or a year into their marriage, maybe, but the trend toward it had been too gradual to say for certain, too multivariable and all in concert with the escalating quotidian practicalities involved in sharing a life. Money could smooth such tensions, but never as evenly as Diana expected. Yes, Wes would receive an ungodly inheritance from his mother via his maternal grandparents—eventually—but he felt guilty even thinking about this sum, considering the circumstances under which he'd get it. His own trust fund had been disgorged as "ill-gotten gains" before he'd ever seen it, along with pretty much everything his parents themselves ever had. Diana made a fine salary, but Wes's current net worth was almost wholly wrapped up in Ecco. They lived a certain lifestyle—the certainly expensive kind—and between Diana's student loans and their mortgage were pretty heavily leveraged.

Poor, poor Wes, with his tony Manhattan apartment and pending hereditary wealth! Every time he laid out their cash-flow problem for Diana, he could feel the justice of his arguments, and he wondered if this wasn't some part of her growing vexation—that he'd narrowed the dialectic gap between them. When she inevitably mounted some blistering rationale for exception, he could often deconstruct precisely how she was trying to manipulate him. And yet, his passionate awe of her mind extended even to her opposition of his; it doggedly followed him from the height of his wrath into fury and cold hate, even into exhaustion and bitterness.

While the terrifying word itself—*divorce*—hovered often in his consciousness, it never, *never*, entered into his lexicon. Too great was Wes's fear, stored in some safer, less accessible part of his brain, that he needed and loved Diana more than she loved and needed him. That if he took her hands and lovingly informed her their marriage was over, she would look up at him, understandingly, maybe even with pity, squeeze back, and say, lovingly, "okay." She'd only cry later. The fuck-you Antigone tears of strong women: persuasive, transcendent, coalition-building tears. The kind that would all but force mutual friends to wholeheartedly take her side and render him a criminal ingrate; not just an asshole, but also a moron. No, unlike every other relationship he'd ever thought about terminating, Wes did not actually want his marriage to end. In a desire so foreign he would have been personally unable to articulate it, what Wes really wanted were those heartfelt hysterics and gasping, blank apologies that with every other woman had just seemed like an inconvenience. He didn't want to divorce Diana, he wanted her to beg him not to.

And so Wes, caught between fighting with and for his wife, vainly endeavored to compute a response to her in the face of mathematically incompatible constraints and inversely correlated decision criteria. His brain overheated and blue screened. He couldn't move, but felt like he was using a lot of energy trying not to, lying in wait until Diana's suitcase bumped toward the door. It opened with a prewar whine.

—Okay, Wes, I'm off. I love you. See you Thursday. Call me tonight?

Diana waited in the doorway for a response. Wes's answer slid down the back of his throat and stuck in his esophagus, expanding like a balloon between his sternum and his lungs. He wanted to tell his wife that he loved her, and yes, he would call her that night, that he hoped she had a safe trip and the hotel was nice, that he missed her during the week and was sorry he hadn't made it to brunch and that once her new project was over maybe they could go on vacation and that he loved her, again. But if Wes kept silent, absolutely silent, he could still present the unconvincing but theoretically possible case that he hadn't heard her at all, that he'd been asleep the whole time. Lots of people groan in their sleep. That was a thing that people did, certainly.

The door shut. Wes could hear the metal latch click, lancing the balloon in his chest, popping it like a festering vesicle. The diffusion of acute pain offered a euphoric moment of relative relief, a self-congratulatory animal delight in the ability to breathe that, as his heartbeat slowed, circulated into a dull tingle at his extremities. His phone vibrated, but it wasn't a text from Diana.

—Hugh Winslow, Anuj Chadha, and 10 others have new photos for you on Instagram!

Wes mentally chastised the cheesy come-on even as he opened the application. There was such a grammatical depravity to exclamation points; they were almost as bad as scare caps. But the pull of an endless scrolling escape from his problems swiftly allayed such objections, and his thumb fell easily into the hypnotic rhythm of its little upward swipes.

Hugh Winslow was in Italy wearing a pale pink suit at a lavish wedding. Anuj Chadha still had an unreasonably good-looking baby of indeterminate sex. Anderson Gregory was in a third-world country doing something vaguely do-goody. He had a stellar tan. Lauren Oleano's bizarre postcollegiate obsession with tattoos and competitive pole dancing featured prominently. Lauren *Coddington* and her husband had closed on a yellow Georgian in Connecticut; they beamed at the camera in matching Patagonia fleeces. It was hard to believe the two Laurens had once been close friends. A video ad for Emirates airline featured a knockout flight attendant sashaying through a first-class cabin with fully reclining seats and French Riviera lighting. Entranced, Wes watched it a second time. He might have watched it for a third, if his phone hadn't buzzed in alert:

—**Save the Date: Ecco All-Staff Tour** *Today at 8:00 AM*

It was seven forty-five.

—Shit, Wes said aloud, scrambling down from the bed as he fumbled with his phone to bring up the details, inadvertently calling on Siri.

She responded condescendingly:

—*I'll pretend I didn't hear that.*

—FUCK! Fuck you, Siri. Fuck *you*.

## II.

**SELECT EMAIL ACTIVITY (RESORTED, CHRONOLOGICAL) OF DALE S. MCBRIDE (ENGAGEMENT MANAGER, PORTMANTEAU STRATEGY, PERSONNEL NUMBER [REDACTED]), FRIDAY, MAY 15, 2015–MONDAY, MAY 18, 2015.**

**From:** McBride, Dale S.
**Date:** Fri, May 15, 2015 at 12:35 PM EDT
**To:** Hashimoto, Eric
**Subject:** Action Required: Introductory Client Brief

Hi Eric,

Great speaking with you this morning and welcome to the Mercury account. Could you please put together an Introductory Client Brief for the rest of the team? Just a few paragraphs on the company's history and our recent work here will suffice. No need to finish it today, early Monday is fine.

Have a great weekend,
Dale

Dale S. McBride
Portmanteau Philadelphia

617.xxx.xxxx
dale.s.mcbride@portmanteau.com

---

**From:** Hashimoto, Eric
**Date:** Mon, May 18, 2015 at 7:42 AM EDT
**To:** Batra, Raj; Childs, Richard C.; Moore, Megan D.; Whalen, Diana W.
**Cc:** Remington, Parker W.; McBride, Dale S.
**Subject:** Introductory Client Brief: Mercury Incorporated

Hi Team,

Please see below for the background information I put together on our client and project. Looking forward to meeting everyone later this morning!

Best regards,
Eric

Eric Hashimoto
Analyst, Portmanteau
w: 202-xxx-xxxx / m: 202-xxx-xxxx
@: eric.hashimoto@portmanteau.com

This message is for the designated recipient only and may contain privileged, proprietary, or otherwise confidential information. If you have received it in error, please notify the sender immediately and delete the original. Any other use is prohibited. Where allowed by local law, electronic communications with Portmanteau and its affiliates may be scanned by our systems for information security purposes and Portmanteau internal policy compliance.

1 attachment
<mercury_brief.docx>

**INTRODUCTORY CLIENT BRIEF:**
**MERCURY INCORPORATED**
By Eric Hashimoto
*Privileged & Confidential. For Internal Use Only.*
*© 2015 Portmanteau*

Mercury Incorporated became a household name in 1995, almost two decades after the landmark *Marquette* decision effectively deregulated the payment card industry. In one of the most successful new product launches in history, CEO Jack Howard introduced the MercuryCard to the world with the "pay like a god" ad during the 1995 Super Bowl, a resounding victory for the San Francisco 49ers over the San Diego Chargers.

The ad featured togaed Greco-Roman gods—Jupiter and his wife Juno, Mars, Venus and Cupid, Neptune, grape-crowned Bacchus, and winged Mercury—all out to dinner, arguing over who would pick up the check at an establishment one can only assume to be the Olive Garden of Mount Olympus.

"Ah, I just *love* this place—dinner's on me!" offers a throaty, neck-cleavaged Venus.

Jupiter shakes his head, lasciviously. "No way, gorgeous—as the king of the gods, I insist."

"You're not paying for *her*," Juno complains, clearly jealous. "I'd rather pick up the tab myself."

"Well, I'm going to kill you all," Mars interjects, played in a stroke of genius by Robert De Niro, who was personally hired by Howard against all advice for an undisclosed but presumably exorbitant sum.

The other gods freeze with their mouths open and eyebrows lifted up. After a moment of silence, De Niro's expression melts into a buttery smile: "Unless you'll let this be my treat."

The tension momentarily lifts, and the unified gods jovially assent—until the camera turns to Mercury, who, half-naked with the wings, looks like a male Victoria's Secret model (objectively speaking). Mercury gives the other gods a roguish look, and, *Accelerati incredibilus*, zips out of and back into the scene in a manner closely resembling the Road Runner getting the better of Wile E. Coyote.

"Too late, my friends," he says, "I already paid with my MercuryCard." He shows them the card. "We're ready to fly."

The authoritative voice-over voice, a swaggering-yet-trustworthy Morgan Freeman baritone, cuts in as we leave the restaurant and follow the various gods through other comical shopping vignettes, now using their own MercuryCards for humorous anachronistic purchases—Neptune buys a surfboard, Jupiter, some naughty lingerie. *Now you, too, can pay with MercuryCard—it's available on Earth wherever credit cards are accepted. Apply today. Pay with MercuryCard.* Dramatic pause. *Pay like a god.*

In the last vignette, the scene cuts to Bob De Niro and Bacchus exiting a bar, arms around some sexy wood nymphs, Bacchus's voice trailing off. "Honestly, Mars," he says, "I was happy to let you pay, but you can't actually *kill* me. Remember? *We're immortal.*" They share a warm, rich belly laugh, shot in silhouette from behind, as De Niro gives Bacchus a friendly straight-arm shove.

The ad was unanimously lauded, receiving numerous creative awards, and the Grand Clio for television. More importantly for Jack Howard, it was obscenely effective. In less than six months, the MercuryCard was Mercury's flagship product. As Clintonomics and the rise of the internet fueled massive industry growth in the ensuing years, MercuryCard further capitalized, gaining more than 40 percent of global market share for combined debit and credit transactions by 2000, benefiting from Silicon Valley's success but escaping the worst of the 2001 tech bubble. Six years later in 2007, with derivative "pay like a god" ads still running strong, Mercury Incorporated had the most successful IPO in US history, opening a new corporate headquarters in the summer of 2008, a sixty-floor reflective-glass monolith towering over Center City Philadelphia, in celebration of the $18B haul. A two-story soaring-ceilinged gourmet corporate café offering 360-degree views through to the Main Line, New Jersey, and Delaware occupies the entirety of the forty-ninth and fiftieth floors. The food is somewhat expensive but quite good—particularly the soft pretzels, a greater Philadelphia culinary staple. The building is reverently named "Olympia."

On September 15, 2008, like almost every other large global financial institution, Mercury Incorporated had a very bad day. As an open-loop payment scheme enterprise, Mercury relies heavily on partnerships with large commercial banks. As those floundered and consumer spending plummeted, MercuryCard applications and transaction volumes did the same. Worse, by the time global markets and economic confidence started to rebound, Silicon Valley and New York startups championing hyper-secure mobile payments, blockchain-based cryptocurrency, and biometrics were starting to threaten the entire payment card ecosystem. Eager to defend his legacy, and not quite ready to pull the cord on his golden parachute, Howard decided to rethink Mercury's strategy from the top, and called up Parker Remington, his college roommate, a renowned partner at Portmanteau.

At the end of the six-week engagement, in October 2012, Remington and Dale McBride, then a promising new MBA graduate fresh out of the Wharton School—and soon to be the Robin to Remington's Batman—advised Mercury to metamorphose, at its core, from a financial services provider into a tech company, vertically integrating across the payment card value chain via multiple acquisitions of midsize payment processors. Wooing startup customer-facing payment apps to contract with Mercury for the capital-intensive, fundamentally requisite but aggressively unsexy work of back-end processing, Mercury would naturally develop the knowledge capital to fast-follow with its own elegant front-end mobile payment solution, ultimately competing in the consumer marketplace with the advantage of singular control over the greater ecosystem. Disruptive startup investors would be indirectly funding their own resubjugation to Mercury, the incumbent competition, the very oligarch they had sought to disrupt. It was an elegant, round stratagem, a clever Trojan horse backed by a kind of divine justice, defending Mercury's preeminence, quite in alignment with the natural order of things. To this end, between 2013 and 2015, Mercury acquired three geographically disparate, midsize payment-processing companies:

2013: Merchantes—*Paris, France*
2014: Pegaswipe—*Saint Petersburg, Russia*
2015: Settlmnt—*San Francisco, USA*

For Portmanteau, this meant a deep well of profitable due-diligence work, all overseen by Remington. McBride served as the lead consultant on the Merchantes deal, then returned the following year as the engagement manager for Pegaswipe.

The success of Mercury's strategic overhaul and acquisitions depends, however, on the right post-merger integration strategy, on this upcoming project, on us. Jack Howard and Mercury's new CIO, Prudence Hyman [sic], seek, per the statement of work, "to integrate their acquisitions into a single, unified operating model and a single, unified technology platform, a centralized underlying hub with localized instances to support country-specific customer requirements and regulations." Spoiler alert: they want to use Pegaswipe's code everywhere, but need our objectivity and a concrete quantitative rationalization for downstream political buy-in. By our powers combined, in these next eight weeks, we must deliver the greatest, most innovative data-driven integrated operating model and technology blueprint the world has ever seen. I am confident we will succeed in this endeavor, my friends: for we are all little engines for data collection, quantifying and prioritizing our wants against the cost of getting them, plotting our entrance past one another's walls.

---

**From:** Remington, Parker W.
**Date:** Mon, May 18, 2015 at 7:48 AM EDT
**To:** McBride, Dale S.
**Cc:** Whalen, Diana W.
**Subject:** FW: Introductory Client Brief: Mercury Incorporated

what the fuck

Sent from my iPhone

---

**From:** Whalen, Diana W.
**Date:** Mon, May 18, 2015 at 7:49 AM EDT
**To:** Remington, Parker W.; McBride, Dale S.
**Subject:** RE: FW: Introductory Client Brief: Mercury Incorporated

Relax, Batman. I'm sure Robin will take care of it.

Diana Whalen
Enterprise Architecture | Portmanteau New York
917.xxx.xxxx | diana.w.whalen@portmanteau.com

---

**From:** McBride, Dale S.
**Date:** Mon, May 18, 2015 at 7:50 AM EDT
**To:** Whalen, Diana W.; Remington, Parker W.
**Subject:** RE: FW: Introductory Client Brief: Mercury Incorporated

Indeed he will. My apologies, Parker.

Dale S. McBride
Portmanteau Philadelphia
617.xxx.xxxx
dale.s.mcbride@portmanteau.com

---

**From:** McBride, Dale S.
**Date:** Mon, May 18, 2015 at 7:52 AM EDT
**To:** Eric Hashimoto
**Subject:** RE: Introductory Client Brief: Mercury Incorporated

Hi Eric,

As much as I may personally appreciate your creativity, we need to discuss what is and is not appropriate in an Introductory Client Brief (and, for that matter, in emails to partners, in emails at work). Please come find me directly when you arrive at Olympia, and **do not send any more emails** until you do.

Thanks,
Dale

Dale S. McBride
Portmanteau Philadelphia
617.xxx.xxxx
dale.s.mcbride@portmanteau.com

---

**From:** Whalen, Diana W.
**Date:** Mon, May 18, 2015 at 8:47 AM EDT
**To:** McBride, Dale S.
**Subject:** FW: RE: FW: Introductory Client Brief:
Mercury Incorporated

Dear Robin, I am downstairs at Olympia security. Told them I was here for Prudence Hyman [sic] and the guard laughed. Is she that new? Please send someone to retrieve me, preferably Eric Hashimoto, as I am absolutely dying to meet him. Facing the exit, I'm on the second bench from the left. My best, Diana

Diana Whalen
Enterprise Architecture | Portmanteau New York
917.xxx.xxxx | diana.w.whalen@portmanteau.com

---

**From:** McBride, Dale S.
**Date:** Mon, May 18, 2015 at 8:49 AM EDT
**To:** Whalen, Diana W.
**Subject:** RE: FW: RE: FW: Introductory Client Brief: Mercury Incorporated

Regrettably, the Joker is still en route from DC, so you'll have to make do with me.

Dale S. McBride
Portmanteau Philadelphia
617.xxx.xxxx
dale.s.mcbride@portmanteau.com

---

**From:** Whalen, Diana W.
**Date:** Mon, May 18, 2015 at 8:50 AM EDT
**To:** McBride, Dale S.
**Subject:** RE: FW: RE: FW: Introductory Client Brief: Mercury Incorporated

Fine, but you better take me to the two-story, soaring-ceilinged corporate cafe with the breathtaking views of scenic New Jersey. I hear the food is somewhat expensive but quite good, and have never been more in the mood for a gourmet pretzel.

Diana Whalen
Enterprise Architecture | Portmanteau New York
917.xxx.xxxx | diana.w.whalen@portmanteau.com

## III.

Wes range left his Uber and briskly ascended the steps of the Metropolitan Museum of Art, squinting at his growing reflection in the glass of the revolving door. His simple button-down was resemblant in both pattern and texture a fine Japanese graph paper, and peeked out from under the variegated silver-gray shawl collar and cuffs of his cashmere pullover, falling past the hem in the deliberate nonchalance of a quarter tuck. Cypress chinos—slim, weathered, and at least half an inch too short—exposed some sinewy bare ankle above his Nikes, which were lightly worn, but still by New York standards white. Correcting his windblown hair with his left hand, his image did the same with its right. His ring and delicate gold watch, his father's, caught the early sun. The comparative darkness blinded him briefly as he entered the Great Hall.

—Excuse me sir, a voice intoned, sans modulation, without even the hint of a verbal comma between "me" and "sir." Museum's not open till nine.

It was a tired, abstract voice, the kind you heed but don't acknowledge; equanimous in apathy, too well practiced in routing rowdy schoolboys and Zenned-out backpackers, Midwestern dadbods, European metrosexuals, and Asian tour groups looking like they stepped out of a 1985 Ralph Lauren catalogue and decided to rob RadioShack; unflappable by ingenues, presidents, and bums, rainbow-coiffed art students and skinny-jeaned Brooklynites, chinless Upper East Side tuxedos escorting mink-topped ladies, and privileged, well-educated, self-involved technocrats running twenty minutes late.

Wes turned to address the security guard with a warm, apologetic smile. The incongruity of her garish makeup and nails against the forced professionalism of her ill-fitting uniform stirred in Wes an uncomfortable mixture of pity and remorse. He'd already been kinder to *her* this morning than to his wife, Wes thought. The emphatic italics (his) felt horrible and snobby even in his mind, and Wes unfairly resented the guard for precipitating his own unfair judgment of her.

—Sorry . . . er, I'm just a bit late for a private tour.

His face pled institutional ignorance and contrition for haste. He rubbed the back of his neck bashfully.

—Just check in for me at security, hun, and I'll escort you, she said.

Her response had a sudden pleasance, a rich, varied timbre—almost, if he wasn't imagining it, like a tonal atonement.

He got his badge and followed the guard through the Greco-Roman wing. She left him with a warmer nod than he deserved at the entrance to the exhibition, a soaring black wall heralding in enormous, floor-to-ceiling white sans serif:

ART &
MYTH:
OVID'S
HEIRS

A few feet to the right he found the prologue:

*"My intention is to tell of bodies changed*
*To different forms . . ."*
OVID, *METAMORPHOSES*

Art, in its broadest sense, is perhaps our only real chance for apotheosis. It is not through life, but rather its mimesis, its artistic mirror, that we glimpse the possibility of living forever. This idea originates with Homer, whose heroes perform glorious acts in the hope of being immortalized in song, but is perfected in Ovid's *Metamorphoses*, an epic tribute to transformation—and fundamentally, to art itself. First published in A.D. 8, *Metamorphoses* ambitiously chronicles the history of the world from creation to the deification of Julius Caesar by weaving together transformational stories from the canon of Classical Mythology. Tales of boys turning into flowers, of men into stone—many of them already well-established in Ovid's day—build toward the most alluring transformation of all: of a human being into a god.

Renaissance author Leon Battista Alberti held mythic Narcissus, lovingly transfixed by his own image, to be "the father of painting"; Medusa might be similarly deemed the original sculptor. Her foil is Pygmalion, whose Ovidian rendition is curiously similar to anecdotes of the historical, if legendary, realist prodigies Zeuxis, Giotto, and Bernini. It is then, perhaps, no surprise that Ovid's epic has become one of the most influential works of Western art: the *Metamorphoses* not only deifies Caesar, it deifies Ovid. It provides a successful, unabashedly derivative road map to artistic apotheosis, and an ideal source for subsequent derivation. "Art & Myth: Ovid's Heirs" is one small slice of this story, a single chapter in this connective narrative of connection. The late Renaissance, with its innovative, transformational underpinnings (and its kindred consequent movements of ebullient Classicism and celebration of individual achievement), provided particularly fertile ground not only for the depiction of metamorphic mythic artists—Medusa, Pygmalion, Narcissus—but specifically for Ovid's description of them; for meta-metamorphic, expressly recursive Ovidian visual art.

The exhibition is made possible by
Mercury Incorporated.
It was organized in conjunction with
The Philadelphia Museum of Art.

It positively reeked of Julian. There was something of a bard in Wes's chief operating officer, a fundamental humanism underneath his exaggerated intellectual hauteur and comically abject elitism. And "expressly recursive"? How could Julian resist. *To understand recursion, you have to understand recursion*, he told anyone who asked what he did for a living. And he was always on the lookout for ways to aggrandize Ecco's cultural significance. This kind of self-promotion, rife with lay metaphor, had always had an icky lubricity for Wes, the aerie perspective of someone who, with a knack for finding people like Julian only too happy to do it for him, never had any need of it. The name Ecco itself had been Julian's too, of course—and it was he who had insisted on the two c's so that the second might be vertically reflected. Any graphic designer worth their bacon would connect them almost intuitively into the symbol for infinity then break it—which was exactly what their graphic designer did, cutely rendering a near-palindrome by going all lowercase. It was so, too, almost offensively literal—obnoxiously clever. But it was the kind of reduction that put corporate procurement departments at maximal ease, the kind of reduction Julian was a genius at. Wes wondered sometimes, not infrequently, if he relied on him a little too much. Julian was, besides his COO, his sounding board, frequently his personal psychologist, and probably also his best friend.

Wes turned the corner, passing through a corridor before making a left into the main room of the exhibition. There, at the back of the group: Julian Pappas-Fidicia, dressed like a parody of Julian Pappas-Fidicia. Madras shirt, fuchsia pants; a navy blazer with golden-fleece-emblazoned brass buttons draped consciously over his fleshy shoulder. Julian stood upright, one hand in his pants pocket but sans contrapposto, top-heavily well fed but not obese. A monogrammed L.L.Bean canvas tote bag—known by Wes to be one of Julian's "dress" tote bags—occupied his other hand, falling past his slightly knocked knees and almost to his velvet smoking slippers. His hair, well-combed and parted to the side, partially obscured the extent to which it had started running away from his face—which was spotless, clean shaven, and as youthful as a face over the age of thirty wearing horned-rim glasses can be. The overall effect was somewhere in the neighborhood of Paddington Bear at a gay club in Palm Beach.

—*Love* the pants, Wes whispered, smiling wickedly, sneaking up behind him.

—You're fucking late, Julian quipped, so you can shut the fuck up.

—Are they new?

—Yes, actually—custom Paul Stuart. I picked them up yesterday after the brunch you missed, just like the first half of the tour.

—So, five-hundred-dollar pink pants.

—They were six hundred, and they are fuchsia. It was one of those situations where I went too far down the procurement path before asking how much they cost and it was too late to back out. But they do fit very well, and I like them very much.

—I pay you too much.

—Just be glad I'm not wearing the monocle.

—Saving that for your gentlemen callers?

Julian inhaled theatrically in mock offense, widening his eyes, jutting his jaw forward as he turned his head in slow motion, for the first time visually acknowledging Wes.

—I'm going to file an HR complaint.

—You'd never make more paperwork for yourself.

Pursing his lips, tilting his head like a pug, Julian considered it.

—That is actually a rather good point.

Wes rocked back onto his heels.

—Hm, sounds like you aren't doing your job. I'd like to file an HR complaint.

—Most of you are probably familiar with the myth of Narcissus, the curator was saying.

—Will you shut the fuck up and listen to the lecture? Julian hissed. She's talking about you.

Wes mouthed a *hah-hah* but started paying attention, listening to the curator, looking up at the painting—it had been hung unusually high—and assumed the absorbed, craning body language of one who is seriously considering it.

—Narcissus, the beautiful boy who falls in love with his own image. It's a creation story for the eponymous flower perhaps better known in the US as a daffodil and the original source of our English word *narcissism*, meaning vanity or inordinate self-obsession. It's a story that has long held a particular fascination for painters. There are literally thousands of depictions of Narcissus in the history of art, and we have two of the finest ever here in this exhibition—we'll take a look at Poussin's in a few minutes—but this one painted by Caravaggio just before the turn of the sixteen century is, in my mind, the most quintessentially Ovidian.

The heads in front of Wes nodded as the curator paused briefly. She had one of those highish, gently lilting voices that seem feminine and soft even when clearly projecting. Allowing her audience to get as close as possible to the painting, she was standing off to the side and hidden behind six-foot-seven Joel Francis, a junior programmer at Ecco fresh off the Stanford basketball team. Wes couldn't see her face.

—Ovid's version of the tale describes *a pool, silver with shining water to which no shepherds came, no goats, no cattle, whose glass no bird, no beast, no falling leaf had ever troubled.* You can feel this absolute stillness, the total calm of Ovid's scene in the painting, in the surface of the water and the pitch-black shadows. We call this dramatic, low-fi-filter-like technique *tenebroso*, and many art historians posit that Caravaggio invented it. Then there's the position of his body in the light, forming a circle as his hands meet his reflection's, the left one disappearing as he *dips in his arms to embrace the boy he sees there*. And look at the craning of his neck and how his lips part—you can see that he's about to try, again in Ovid's words, *to kiss the image in the water*. Caravaggio even foreshadows the tale's conclusion with those voluminous, almost petally white shirtsleeves surrounding the dramatically foreshortened knee. If you squint, you can almost see Narcissus's transformation into *a flower with a yellow center surrounded with white petals*. That knee, guys, I've got to tell you. If Narcissus here were alive, he'd have to get it insured by Lloyds of London. You would not believe how many scholarly articles have been written about that knee. If you're ever in London, incidentally, you can go and see the work of a professional Caravaggio-knee appreciator by the name of Salvador Dalí. His *Metamorphosis of Narcissus* is in the Tate Modern, and owes a very heavy debt to the painting that you see.

Julian nudged him, indicating that Wes should mentally file this as a Really Excellent Thing for Them to Do the Next Time They Were in London Together. Several of Ecco's other employees seemed to have had the same thought as Julian and gave short, seizury nods to one another in that *yes let's go see that painting together but let's talk about it later because an expert is talking and I'm actually into an expert lecture for once and, honestly, neither of us are likely to follow through because let's be real going on a trip to London to see a painting with your best friend from work is one of those ideas that sounds good for, approximately, four seconds before it sounds like lunacy—but yeah, if I go to London someday and happen to go to the Tate Modern, in that scenario there is a nonzero chance I will actively look out for that painting, and if I do end up seeing it, then I will think of you* sort of way. You know, those silent, tacit, wistful plans that are immediately backtracked and forgotten.

—He's a pretty handsome guy, right?

The curator asked this, to more eyebrowish smiles and nods—Joel Francis was *really* enjoying himself. The curator must be pretty, Wes thought.

—But don't let Caravaggio's pretty surfaces fool you, said the curator. At its depth, this is perhaps his most violent painting. Narcissus is caught here between pleasure and pain, desire and anguish. We have to remember that at the end of Ovid's tale Narcissus begs the gods for death, he pleads to be forcibly released from the image he loves too much to voluntarily escape. By painting Narcissus, Caravaggio indefinitely prolongs this tension and pain, denying him transformation, capturing him at the pivotal moment he is captured by himself, as he *looks in wonder, charmed by himself, spellbound, and no more moving than any marble statue*. Those are the words Ovid uses, *no more moving* than *any marble statue*. Medusa might make you afraid to turn around—but *Narcissus*, when you think about it, is the more frightening image. Here the fear is in *not* turning around—and not, by the way, because you literally can't, but because you don't want to, because *you don't want to* to the point that you're willing to accept any and all consequences of continuing to look. Caravaggio wanted this painting to be as seductively beautiful to you as the pool is to Narcissus. And the painting is as far beyond your reach as the viewer as the image in the pool is for Narcissus within it. It's really rather cruel. Caravaggio is again, as he did with his Medusa, trying to turn us into stone, into sculptures—into art. He's again asking us to question our reality in favor of his, to override our self-interest, if not our very humanity. He wants us to fall in, to our detriment. But this time he's asking us to ask for it. It's a power move in a painting.

She paused, letting that one sink in. There were appreciative "ahs" and chuckles. Wes kind of wished he hadn't missed the first half of the tour.

—But there's someone here I haven't even mentioned yet, someone I believe this group in particular will have a special affinity with—yes, that's right, Echo, the pretty nymph who could only repeat the last thing said to her, who fell hopelessly in love with Narcissus and bore his callous rejection. Now before you say, "wait a minute, I don't see a pretty nymph anywhere in this painting," let's go back to Ovid. When he describes Echo's metamorphosis, Ovid says that *she frets and pines, becomes all gaunt and haggard, her body dries and shrivels till voice only and bones remain, and then she is voice only for the bones are turned to stone.*

The curator paused.

—*For the bones are turned to stone*, she reiterated. So, where is Echo in the paint—

—She's us! interrupted Joel Francis. We're the Echo! And *we're Ecco*!

He smiled like a maniac. Julian inhaled deeply, wide-eyed with embarrassment. He looked at Wes as if he expected him to do something.

—Right, that's right! the curator replied with a laugh, not seeming to mind in the slightest, if anything delighted by Joel's enthusiasm. And that Echo is itself an echo, too: an echo of Narcissus—*no more moving than any marble statue*; an echo of Ovid's words in paint; an echo of Caravaggio's own *Medusa* painted two years earlier; and today, as you say, an echo of Ecco with two c's. There are Echoes in echoes; Eccos all over the place. It can get rather confusing, actually—although today I realize I'm lecturing to a group of experts on the subject, so I'm sure you all will be able to keep them straighter than I.

—Yeah, but even the highest-IQ human brains can only process like six, maybe seven levels of recursion before meaning is rendered unstable, Joel Francis explained, trying to humbly offset the compliment and failing, in a tone that suggested he felt he'd already developed a deep personal rapport with the curator over the course of the tour.

Julian seemed to be frantically searching for a prefrontal cortical fire extinguisher. Wes squeezed his shoulder firmly, reassuring him it was all right.

The curator herself seemed unfazed by the interruption:

—Well, you may need all of those levels today, because I have another one for you. If you haven't already fallen too deeply into the painting, would you please turn around.

On the back wall in parallel opposition to the Caravaggio she had installed a gargantuan, floor-to-ceiling, wall-to-wall, Versailles-style mirror, at least sixteen feet square. Joel Francis's face lit up with game-show-contestant-level overenthusiasm. It became evident why *Narcissus* was hung so unusually high. The effect was breathtaking, reflecting the object and its admirers together—most prominently, as the stage had reversed, Wes, Julian, Joel, and—

—Vivien Floris? Wes whispered aloud, looking at Julian, who seemed confused by his confusion.

It was definitely her. All pencil-skirted and official-looking, blushing a bit in the glow of her audience's admiration.

How could the curator be Vivien Floris? Shy, quiet, self-conscious Vivien Floris? Wes realized that despite the wealth of material in his long-dormant-but-much-cherished Mental Catalogue of Images of Vivien Floris he had almost never heard her speak. He'd rarely even *seen* her speak to someone else—she had been, truly, that shy. And unapproachable. Really almost painfully pretty, vaguely out of the Jennifer Connelly–Megan Fox school, with freezing pale blue eyes and freckles, moody lips, and delicate features.

Many of the Ecco employees, to Julian's obvious dismay, had already taken out their cell phones and started posing, snapping mirror selfies of themselves with the painting.

—You can relax, Julian, Vivien said warmly, smiling coyly as if they knew each other (in a new expression promptly added to the Mental Catalogue)—I wanted people to take pictures—please, yes, don't be shy—take a selfie! Just no flash, please! And if you're posting to Twitter, Facebook, or Instagram make sure to tag and follow the exhibition too—@imetovidsheirs. We're reposting our favorites.

The lecture all but disbanded as Wes's employees diplomatically jousted for position at the mirror. Joel asked Vivien if she would get in his selfie and she graciously indulged him, smiling for the camera, her long hair exactly as Wes remembered it, falling in a smooth dark sheet as she leaned to the side. There was a flash of jealousy.

—No flash, please!

—How do you know her? Wes demanded as Julian got out his phone and dragged Wes to an unoccupied corner of the mirror for a selfie.

—Um, she went to Penn with me. Could you please try to make a less-pained facial expression right now? I know you can get away with that sort of thing, but be warned, I am posting this to Instagram. Oh my god, wait, no, don't stop, wait you *really* look like him. Turn your head down and to the side. Oh my god, brilliant.

—She was two years ahead of me at Sill.

—Ugh, I should have known you were boarding school friends. The one percent is such a small place. Tell me, was there a single unattractive person who attended that school? Did you have to submit a headshot with your application?

—I wouldn't say we were friends, really. I mean, she was older. I had no idea she lived in New York.

—She doesn't. She's a visiting curator from the Philadelphia Museum. This is the kind of thing you would know if you ever showed up on time for anything.

—Oh, Wes said, with a tinge of disappointment, but also, for some reason, relief.

Wes couldn't stop looking at her, at how adulthood and mastery and professional success and confidence had and had not changed her. He studied the angles of her face, and noticed they'd sharpened with age. If anything, she was even better-looking now.

—Well, we'll be getting dinner tonight so I suppose I must invite you, Julian sighed.

The idea that there was such a thing as a future tense broke Wes's reverie.

—What? No—I'm not sure she would even remember me.

Vivien's didactic "okay" with an extended "a" cut through the din of collective narcissism, indicating the group should regather in front of the Poussin. Most people continued taking photos, gradually recoalescing with Vivien's playful derision:

—*Why try to catch an always fleeting image, poor credulous youngster? What you seek is nowhere, and if you turn away, you will take with you the boy you love. The vision is only shadow, only reflection, lacking any substance. It comes with you, it stays with you, it goes away with you, if you can go away.*

It was all from memory, Wes realized as he watched her talk.

## IV.

**SELECT WEB BROWSER ACTIVITY (RESORTED, CHRONOLOGICAL) OF DALE S. MCBRIDE (ENGAGEMENT MANAGER, PORTMANTEAU STRATEGY, PERSONNEL NUMBER [REDACTED]), MONDAY, MAY 18, 2015.**

7:53 AM EDT - https://www.google.com/
[Search Criteria 'Diana W. Whalen LinkedIn']
About 198,670 results (0.69 seconds)

[FIRST RESULT]
Diana Whalen | LinkedIn
https://www.linkedin.com/in/diana-w-whalen-6312xxxx
Greater New York City Area - Enterprise Architect at Portmanteau - Portmanteau

Diana Whalen · 2nd
Enterprise Architect at Portmanteau
Greater New York City Area | Management Consulting
Current: Portmanteau
Previous: Portmanteau
Education: University of Virginia

**Summary**

System of systems engineer specializing in machine learning and dynamically adaptable enterprise architecture at Portmanteau, mainly in the high-tech space.

(I help tech companies solve IT logic puzzles with insufficient clues and where those insufficient clues keep changing.)

**Experience**

Engagement Manager - Enterprise Architecture
Portmanteau
December 2014—present (6 months) | New York, NY

Consultant - Enterprise Architecture
Portmanteau
December 2013—December 2014 (1 year) | New York, NY

Analyst - Enterprise Architecture
Portmanteau
October 2012—December 2013 (1 year, 2 months) | New York, NY

**Education**

University of Virginia
Bachelor of Science (BS), Systems Engineering and Bachelor of Arts (BA), Philosophy
2008—2012

George Washington High School for Science and Technology
2004—2008

**Skills**
Enterprise Architecture (30 recommendations)
Systems Engineering (27 recommendations)
IT Strategy (26 recommendations)
Programming (15 recommendations)
Machine Learning (9 recommendations)
Information Technology (8 recommendations)
Strategy (7 recommendations)
Computability Theory (2 recommendations)

[BACK]

[SECOND RESULT]
Diana Whalen and Charles Range IV — Weddings — The New . . .
http://www.nytimes.com/09/22/fashion/weddings/diana-whalen-and-charles-range-iv-weddings.html
[Article, *New York Times*, "The Best Kind of Gratification? Delayed Gratification"]

## *The Best Kind of Gratification? Delayed Gratification*

by Ramsay Smith Blake
September 22, 2013

<media_photo.jpeg>

Diana Witt Whalen and Charles Wesley Range IV were married on Saturday, September 21, 2013, at the Woodland Country Club in Charlottesville, Virginia. Julian Pappas-Fidicia, a friend of the couple who became a Universal Life minister for the event, officiated.

Ms. Whalen, 23, who is keeping her name, is an enterprise architect at the New York office of Portmanteau, a global management consulting firm. She received a joint B.A./B.S. with Highest Distinction from the University of Virginia.

She is the daughter of Regina Witt and Richard Whalen of Washington, DC. The bride's parents are both professors at Georgetown University: her mother in systems engineering, her father in philosophy.

Mr. Range, 27, who is known as Wes, is the founder and CEO of Ecco, a start-up company providing specialized algorithm diagnostics and reprogramming services to other companies. He graduated magna cum laude from Princeton University and holds an M.B.A. from the Darden School at the University of Virginia.

He is the son of Agatha Young Range and the late Charles W. Range III of New York. His mother is a philanthropist and sits on the board of the Metropolitan Museum of Art.

The groom is the maternal great-grandson of shipping magnate Cortland R. Young Jr. [link].

The couple met in the Patrick Henry Society, a literary and debating club at the University of Virginia, in the fall of 2010 when the bride, already a member, conducted the groom's interview. Interviewees are permitted to choose their topics, and Mr. Range left the encounter astonished by Ms. Whalen's repartee on everything from John Nash to John Keats and cyborgs to coxswain. "I'd never met someone with her particular kind of mental acuity. At the time, I don't believe she'd ever even been to a regatta, but based on our conversation you'd have thought she'd rowed in Henley herself," he said. Mr. Range was the captain of Princeton's decorated 2009 varsity crew and competed in the 2012 London Olympics [link].

The groom was so impressed, in fact, that he preemptively

ended his current relationship later that day—even before his admission into the Society as a probationary member ("It felt disingenuous not to," he said).

They were fast friends, loaning each other books and casually going out to eat, where the conversation often turned to mathematical logic and computability theory, a shared interest. Ms. Whalen, however, was initially more reticent for things to turn romantic. "I just needed a few more data points," she said. "Plus, delayed gratification is the best kind of gratification, am I right?"

Just as Mr. Range was beginning to lose hope, Ms. Whalen asked him to her sorority's end-of-semester formal event, a black-tie soiree held at Woodland Country Club, the future venue of the couple's wedding. When he arrived to pick her up, she revealed a computer program she had written, an algorithm that predicted the success of other algorithms. Mr. Range was so taken with it that they missed the event entirely. "I guess we're making up for that now," the groom said. "Consider this our first date."

[BACK]

8:10 AM EDT - https://www.google.com/
[Search Criteria 'Wes Range']
About 7,000,000 results (0.76 seconds)

8:10 AM EDT - https://www.google.com/
[Search Criteria 'Wes Range CEO Ecco']
About 965,000 results (0.73 seconds)

[FIRST RESULT]
Wes Range - Wikipedia
https://en.wikipedia.org/wiki/Wes_Range
[Article, Wikipedia, 'Wes Range']

**Wes Range**

<image.jpeg>
Range at TechCrunch in 2014

| | |
|---|---|
| **Born** | Charles Wesley Range IV January 1, 1986 (age 29) New York City, New York [link], United States |
| **Nationality** | American |
| **Alma mater** | Princeton University [link], University of Virginia [link] |
| **Occupation** | Entrepreneur |
| **Known For** | CEO of Ecco [link] |
| **Spouse(s)** | Diana Whalen (2013–present) |
| **Relatives** | Charles Wesley Range III (father) [link], Agatha Young Range (mother), Cortland R. Young Jr. (great-grandfather) [link] |
| **Website** | www.ecco.com/wes |

**Charles Wesley "Wes" Range IV** is an American entrepreneur and Olympic rower, competing in the men's eight at the 2012 London games. He is the founder and chief executive officer of Ecco, a business-to-business (B2B) technology company specializing in resolving system-critical infinite loop [link] errors in enterprise systems.

**Contents** [hide]
1. Life and education [link]
2. Career [link]

3. Awards and Recognition [link]
4. References [link]

**Life and education** [edit]
Range grew up in New York City, the son of the late former YW Capital Management [link] co-founder Charles Wesley Range III [link], and Young Industries [link] heiress Agatha Young Range. He is the great-grandson of Cortland R. Young Jr. [link] He married Diana Witt Whalen in 2013. [reference]

Range received his A.B. in Mathematics from Princeton University in 2009. At Princeton, he was a member of the varsity crew and Tiger Inn [link] eating club. He earned an M.B.A. from the University of Virginia Darden School of Business in 2012.

**Career** [edit]
Range founded Ecco in 2011 while a business school student at the University of Virginia [link], inspired by an algorithm [link] that evaluated other algorithms built in 2010 by his future wife [reference]. The company provides specialty algorithm analytics services leveraging a proprietary diagnostic algorithm that identifies, at a >99% efficacy rate, recursive anomalies—in particular, system-compromising circular references and infinite loops [link] (See also: recursion [link]).

. . .

[EMBEDDED LINK]

**Recursion** occurs when a thing is defined in terms of itself or of its type and may broadly refer to any form of self-similar embedded repetition. Its reach transcends academic disciplines, is likewise discernible in art and nature, and may be the fundamental linguistic and even cognitive function that differentiates human from animal existence. Its propensity toward complexity and infinity quickly defies comprehension. For instance, when the surfaces of two mirrors are exactly parallel with each other, the nested images that occur are a form of infinite recursion [link], even though practically speaking we can perceive only the first few instances. According to one study, the average human being with a score of 145–160 on the Stanford-Binet Intelligence Scale ("Very gifted or highly advanced") was able to cognitively process 6.3 embedded layers before encountering instability of meaning. [citation needed]

**Contents** [hide]

1. In mathematics [link]
    - 1.1. Recursively defined sets [link]
        - 1.1.1. Fibonacci numbers [link]
        - 1.1.2. Factorials [link]
        - 1.1.3. The golden ratio [link]
    - 1.2. Proof involving recursive definitions [link]
    - 1.3. Recursive optimization [link]
2. In computer science [link]
    - 2.1. Computability theory (Recursion theory) [link]
    - 2.2. Recursive functions and algorithms [link]
        - 2.2.1. Turing computability [link]
        - 2.2.2. Infinite loops [link]
3. In nature [link]
    - 3.1. Fractals [link]
    - 3.2. Biological networks [link]
        - 3.2.1. Circulatory systems [link]
        - 3.2.2. Mammalian reproduction [link]
    - 3.3. Social networks [link]
4. In economics [link]
    - 4.1. Recursive economics [link]
    - 4.2. In game theory [link]

- 4.2.1. Metagames [link]
- 4.2.2. Pooling games [link]

5. In art [link]
   - 5.1. In visual art [link]
     - 5.1.1. The Droste Effect [link]
     - 5.1.2. Matryoshka dolls [link]
     - 5.1.3. Mise en abyme [link]
   - 5.2. In literature [link]
     - 5.2.1. Frame stories [link]
     - 5.2.2. Story within a story [link]
     - 5.2.3. The Portrait of a Mirror [link]
6. Recursive humor [link]
   - 6.1. See also: Recursive humor [link]
7. See also [link]
8. Notes [link]
9. References [link]
10. External links [link]
11. . . .

# V.

The Olympia lobby felt like a futuristic Vitruvian airport, with a long check-in desk flanked by security gates on either side, east and west. In the center of the glass foyer a spiral staircase yawned chasmically, leading down to a food court known as the "Underworld." Six white Chesterfield benches arced around the staircase's circumference, facing the desk. Diana Whalen sat on the second from the left, looking intensely at something on her phone and absently eating what appeared to be a Doritos Locos Taco.

It was a disorienting jolt into reality for Dale, the idea that the Diana Witt Whalen of recent digital acquaintance and *New York Times* Style section notoriety was a real human being who physically had to eat, the pretzel in her email having seemed more like a metaphor. This reality along with the violent blond dye job and shoulder-length chop that clearly postdated the stunning photographs of her online rendered the real Diana less objectively beautiful yet somehow more attractive. Her dress was simple but obviously expensive, one of those shortish, high-necked shapeless things that, in no more than an afterthought, maybe highlighted the legs. Over it, in a flagrant affront to professionalism, she wore what seemed to be a man's hunter-green ski fleece with a little white Vail logo on the left side. In the spectrum of possible female ensembles, hers looked almost, to borrow a turn of phrase from Eric Hashimoto, *aggressively unsexy*. It was as if she were actively working to subvert her beauty, and her inability to do so highlighted it all the more. Or maybe she knew that. Maybe she did it on purpose, maybe she was showing off, throwing her beauty into relief by poor dress: a literal, physical humblebrag. She was declaring herself "ordinary and unimportant," yes—but in the manner of Eva Perón. It didn't even look like she was wearing makeup—and not in the way that skillfully applied makeup successfully achieves "the natural look." It looked like she was *actually* not wearing makeup. Dale had lived with a woman long enough to know the difference.

In the elevator he had tried out various introductory lines, from the simple, *oh hi, you must be Diana, I'm Dale*, to replacing *Dale* with *Robin*, to really going for it with a *Robin at your service*, to pathetic, tortured attempts to cast her as Catwoman that were immediately discarded, to finding some new portion of Eric's Brief to satirically appropriate. *Spoiler alert: I'm Dale.* A Prudence Hyman joke, in Olympian open air, was radically bold but far too dangerous. He'd pretty much settled on *spoiler alert* until he saw the Doritos Locos Taco, which more or less required direct commentary. *I thought you wanted a pretzel* was the obvious choice here, but *you're ruining your appetite for our forty-ninth-slash-fiftieth-floor date* was, he reasoned, more expressly confident.

Dale was less clear on why he was so intent on impressing her. Diana was married. In what should have felt like a "more importantly comma" sort of thought, in less than four months, he would be too. Dale's fiancée was beautiful, well educated, professionally successful, and sexually unselfish, with an affable temperament and lovely family vacation homes in Breckenridge and Spring Lake. He had no intention of letting her go. His intention made no difference. He wanted to impress Diana anyway.

—Oh, hi there. Spoiler alert: I'm Diana.

She struggled to free a hand for him to shake and he fumbled to help her, disoriented by the impression that she was capable of reading his mind. Up close, she looked ludicrously young, all eyebrows and pointy features in that small-woodland-creature kind of way. There was an almost blinding quality to the whites of her eyes, he noticed.

She was too young to be a manager, and way too young to have such an imposing, heirloomy pair of rings perched on her third left finger. Dale chastised himself for even noticing them. And yet, even though he had just met her, he couldn't rattle the feeling that he wished she wasn't married. The thought that she should belong to someone who was not him, regardless of his own availability, seemed like a grave mistake. That she belonged to someone with both the lineage and taste to present her with a ring like that illogically made this mistake all the more egregious.

Dale could feel the transfer of orange Dorito dust onto his fingers, and he didn't even mind.

—What's this? he asked, nodding at the taco. I thought you wanted a pretzel.

—Well, I do—for second breakfast.

—Second breakfast?

—We've only just met and you're already second-chairing my eating habits? Don't second-guess second breakfast. There are exactly two Taco Bells south of Ninety-Seventh Street in New York City, and neither of them are in travel-type locations where I'm inclined to lift my personal day-to-day regular-life ban on fluorescent cheese-like products. It was a measured decision, and I don't regret it. In fact, I have to say, I almost feel like you're angling for a bite.

Dale was surprised and delighted by the lilt in her voice as she said this. There was something distinctly coquettish in her faux self-righteous didacticism. It was the auditory equivalent to a wink, deliberate and provocative, the "already second-chairing" foreshadowing some kind of guaranteed intimacy, a tacit indication, almost an order, that they were going to become good, probably very good, maybe best friends. Dale had the strangest feeling that he already knew Diana from somewhere, and already admired her. This illusory sensation presented itself like a question to which Dale knew he should readily remember the answer but always forgot, like the definition of *teleology* versus *ontology*, or whether cheese was supposed to be pasteurized. *Maybe through Julian*, Dale thought. Never had a gay man had such exquisite taste in women.

Dale left guest passes for the rest of the team at the desk and they walked through the right security gate to the elevator bank, falling into easy chitchat. How had Diana's journey been? Her journey had been uneventful. Wasn't 30th Street Station an architectural respite from the subterranean labyrinth of Penn Station? The only catch with 30th Street was, of course, that once one left the station, one was in Philadelphia. Dale had attended the University of Pennsylvania for undergraduate as well as graduate school and was well-nigh a local now, and he assured Diana that once he'd understood which blocks to avoid (they required some swerving navigation) he had ceased to think of it as the poor man's Boston, the city from which he originally hailed. She was staying at the Sheraton; did he think she would be all right? So long as she'd brought her own toiletries. Dale did not have a working hypothesis for what the Sheraton shampoo was, but he was fairly certain it wasn't shampoo. Not that this was by any means a Philadelphia-specific problem. He had come to find a certain appeal to the City of Brotherly Love. Dale now lived in an 1,800-square-foot, four-story brownstone less than a block off Rittenhouse Square. A Flywheel class here was only twenty-five dollars and one might easily keep a car. The grocery-store-slash-strip-club wasteland by the river was odd, yes, but there were two Whole Foods and a Trader Joe's in walking distance and, unlike in their New York counterparts, at most hours one was able to physically move in them. Dale had been to Eataly, though. Yes, that was very close to Diana's apartment.

They dropped off her suitcase on the fifty-second floor and returned to the elevator. Mercury was, as far as clients went, a rather good one, Dale told her. Jack Howard was a force of nature, and Prudence Hyman's stern earnestness was mostly comical. Yes, that was really her real name, and Diana should practice saying it in the mirror without laughing. She (Prudence Hyman, coded PH) had the chiseled personality, Dale explained, of someone who grew up with a name as unforgivably bad as Prudence Hyman. While many women might have gone by Pru or Dennie, or assumed a new name in marriage or something, Prudence resolutely rejected every opportunity to soften or forgo her moniker. She might even have been accused of deliberately flaunting it. She baited displays of immaturity and toyed with those who took them, all through Socratic lines of questioning so resolute they effectively precluded retaliation.

—And she keeps editing my slides to abbreviate "Standards" to "STDs."

—Oh, I can totally see it, Diana gestured expansively, "Promoting the Deep Penetration of Global STDs."

PH was in a tough position at Mercury, though, and with less than a year under her belt had very recently, as in the last three or four weeks, acquired a—Dale dropped his voice, almost requiring Diana to lip-read—*service animal*. It was a very small dog that could only be for some kind of nonphysical ailment, presumably depression or anxiety. Diana howled in disbelief. This project was getting better by the minute.

Yes, she went to Vail fairly often. Dale went to Breckenridge. Each had frequented the other's mountain home base and had complimentary things to say. Diana would be spending the long weekend in Nantucket. Dale loved Nantucket. Several of his childhood friends' parents had places there, but this weekend he would be in Spring Lake. Spring Lake was in New Jersey, but in, you know, the nice part of New Jersey. Both of both of their parents were professors. Dale's taught law at Boston College, but he had majored in English. He'd done his thesis on Milton. *Very serious*, he intoned in a pompous Britishy accent meant to self-deprecate in proportional compensation for his vanity. Diana's second major had been philosophy. How unusual in the consulting world. They had both been attracted to the profession because it preserved optionality. No one ever gave humanities students enough credit for common sense.

Dale insisted on buying her pretzel (and latte) on the forty-ninth-slash-fiftieth floor. Diana congratulated him on paying *like a god*. She was shockingly decent at imitating the authoritative Morgan Freeman–ish accent. He accepted her offer to, in return, get lunch. The sushi up here was, for corporate cafeteria sushi, really remarkably good, but was even better at Circle 2shi in the Underworld. Both Dale and Diana, it was discovered, greatly enjoyed sushi but often ordered sashimi instead, not so much for its gastronomic purity as American restaurants' near-total inability to properly prepare the rice. They had both seen that documentary . . . what was it called? *Jiro Dreams of Sushi.* Yes, right. It took years to learn how to prepare the rice. Sushi was, truly, just not the same outside Japan. They agreed that the 800 yen omakase at Narita Airport's best counter might well be preferable—in terms of sheer fish-and-rice quality itself, stripping away all thoughts of decor and ambience—to even, say, Nobu or Morimoto. There was something charming about the gruff passage of each single perfect piece of sushi from the hands that made it, anyway. Really, you know, *authentic*, right?

The authentic Morimoto was, by the way, in Philadelphia, Dale said, not defensively, but not not defensively. The New York location was derivative. Dale had been to both locations, but Diana had only been to the one in New York. The one in Philadelphia was like a whitewashed Pueblo structure that opened into a purple neon cave, she learned. It had a local art gallery with soaring gothic windows above it. Dale knew the owner, a former housepainter, very unpretentious. Diana's childhood friend Georgia Wimberly's older sister, Audrey, had gone to Penn and interned at a local Philadelphia gallery, but she wasn't sure which one. Dale knew Audrey Wimberly well. They both followed her on Instagram and agreed she might post fewer pictures of her coffee.

It was at best a half-turn away from the kind of pompous, fundamentally solipsistic conversation Diana and Dale would have enjoyed eviscerating if they overheard, or floundered to carry on out of politeness with someone else. But with each other, every turn of phrase took on an inexpressible deeper meaning, like a permanent double entendre had been embedded into the English language itself. They were talking so fast and so excitedly and had so much in common that Dale was afraid he might start losing track of what he'd read about Diana versus what she'd told him herself. He had definitely lost track of time. They discarded the remnants of second breakfast and made their way to the elevator.

—Well, if you know Audrey Wimberly, you must know the one and only Julian Pappas-Fidicia, Dale ventured with the confidence of already knowing the answer.

—Oh, you know Julian, do you? I just had brunch with him yesterday. I see quite a lot of him, actually. We were in the same debating society—when I was an undergrad and he was at Darden. He works with my husband now.

She said the last sentence quietly but distinctly. Dale realized that up to this point he had been subconsciously steering the conversation away from any mention of spouses, but now felt a sudden, pressing need to let Diana know he was engaged and happy.

—Yes, my future wife actually knows Julian better than I do, but we're all friends from Penn.

Diana looked very directly into his eyes, almost as if she could see through them, smiling wickedly, like she'd been wanting him to mention his fiancée and was gloating in her victory. There was something almost supernatural about the expressiveness of her face, in the range of emotion she could project and transform from second to second. He found it borderline disconcerting, and was eager to be further disconcerted. Those were freeze-in-tracks eyes. Lethal eyebrows.

—Oh, you're getting married? Well, I guess I should give you my congratulations, and very best wishes to your bride.

She *guessed she should*, but she didn't.

It was ultimately a loaded declaration that formed a silent pact. That feelings might be alluded to but never spoken, that lines might be bent but not crossed, that all truly important conversations would be restricted to hypothetical and metaphor and negative space. There was to be a fundamental honesty in their joint self-deception. Even if they couldn't tell each other exactly the truth, lying was not permissible either. All's fair in love and war, but there are steadfast rules for dead-end mutual flattery.

—So, what's her name?

—Prudence Hyman.

The elevator stopped on fifty-two. Diana laughed as the door opened—genuinely, and recklessly loud.

—Kidding! I'm kidding, he whispered. It's Vivien.

# VI.

In the well-established rumor hierarchy of the Sill School gossip network ("Sill Mill"), the 2004 news of Wes's father threatened the creation of a new categorical apogee. The least valuable still-Sill Mill-worthy news was anything positive—college acceptances, belated loss of virginity, outrageously phenomenal birthday/holiday presents (cars were not permitted on campus, but wraithlike status symbols nevertheless)—anything, essentially, that portended greater social clout to the subject of the story than its narrator fell into this category. Next came minor misfortunes or infractions: injuries to star athletes, low-grade infidelity, illegal intervisitation charges for an established couple, other nonexpellable disciplinary infractions, other objectively dumb behavior (e.g., mercury poisoning from extreme overconsumption of dining hall tuna). The expulsion or withdrawal of a far-fringe/little-known student/under former for upper formers would fit here as well, the key criterion being a high ratio of narrative schadenfreude to narrator consequence. The third tier included most other expulsion and/or withdrawal cases, heavy drug/alcohol use, sexual rampages, high-grade infidelity, stealthily aborted pregnancies, consensual student-teacher relationships, low-grade self-harming attempts for attention, and creative combinations of multiple misdemeanors. The major definitional exception to categories two and three was eating disorders. Confirmed ones, while certainly not "minor" misfortunes, were tier-two gossip—more depressing than salacious—while debatable eating disorders (very often perpetuated by envy and not eating disorders at all) fell, at their recounted height, firmly in tier three.

Things got tricky in the fourth tier, as major scandals often approached or simply were actual tragedies, requiring dissembling gossip-transmission mechanisms, for narratives to be well warmed in the cloak of concern. Particularly egregious expulsion/withdrawal situations (a cool sixth former mistaking, in a 3:00 a.m. drunken stupor, a teacher's apartment carpet for the bathroom urinal), high-grade self-harming attempts not for attention, abject sexual abuse, and the death of a student, teacher, parent, or sibling fell in this category.

But when, on a crisp, clear October day, an afternoon resplendent in its perfect, autumnal Connecticutness, the varsity cross country coach pulls the popular senior prefect aside and sends him to the headmaster's house—not office, but *house*; when he does so not so much in a "you're in big trouble, mister" kind of way, but almost with an apology; when Coach doesn't provide any explanation, but, as the prefect turns to run past the club fields, squeezes his shoulder more than a few seconds longer than anyone has ever seen Coach squeeze anyone's shoulder before; when Father Griffin opens the door with an expression that fails categorization, florid forehead wrinkling, as if unsure of the face he is supposed to make; when (as it was later discovered) the prefect's father, Charles Wesley Range III, has been indicted on three counts of insider trading and promptly shot himself on the second floor of their East Seventy-Fourth Street town house—well, there just wasn't really a gossip category for that.

Dean Kennedy was tasked with retrieving some personal items from his dormitory and driving him into the city. That Wes was immediately whisked off campus, directly from the headmaster's house before sports ended—that was in and of itself a solid tier-three situation, full of tantalizingly unanswered questions and prone to rampant speculation. By Formal Dinner, there were essentially two leading theories. The first was that Wes had been quietly found to be on some kind of academic performance-enhancing drug and Sill, to avoid a reputational scandal with its darling boys' prefect, had allowed him to atone in the form of medical treatment. (Wes had, it was known, at least on rare occasion purchased Adderall from Kate Manningham's highly profitable personal prescription.) Proponents of the second theory argued that no way, Wes was already into like half the Ivy League on full athletic scholarships. His grades no longer really mattered, they reasoned, before venturing in a respectful hush that *it had to be something worse.*

It was posited that Marnie Davenport, whose father worked at a hedge fund in the same building as YW Capital Management, was the first to learn something close to the full story later that night. It turned out that the new tier-five category of information was of an almost nuclear-bomb variety in that it was something one wanted to be known to have possession of, but not publicly heard—even in care-cloaked words—to be disseminating. Marnie made rather a big show of holding back, saying simply that it was unspeakably awful and not Wes's fault and they all had to be unfailingly kind to him and it was the sort of thing that Wes should be allowed to share and talk about on his own terms (but perhaps making an exception for Ainsley Cooper, as Wes's girlfriend, who in turn may have needed one or two or three shoulders to cry on). By the next morning, when Charlie Range's indictment-suicide was also the cover story of the *New York Post* (BANKER BLOWS BRAINS IN $23M BROWNSTONE [salacious photo]), the Sill administration was forced to make a school-wide announcement at morning meeting to dispel rumors that, particularly among the under formers, were, seemingly impossibly, far *more* indecent than the truth. Dean Kennedy delivered the full set of facts. Wes would be gone for at least a week and a half. This was a personal tragedy for a strong leader of the Sill community. It was not Wes's fault, and it was every student's obligation to be unfailingly kind to him. It was, she explained, the sort of thing that Wes should be allowed to share and talk about on his own terms (though Lauren Coddington later overheard her telling the modern European history teacher Mr. Bern that the sorry affair was *not* an *un*expected byproduct of the Bush administration's unconscionable lack of governmental financial oversight).

Once Dean Kennedy lifted the taboo from the school and internal gossip lost its appeal amid fact and transparency, the Sill Mill alumni network was more than fair game. Recent graduates of all types weighed the news from current-student friends and siblings against the story in the *Post* before regaling all the sordid details to their college mates. It was in this round of dissemination that Sebastian Floris (Sill '08) informed his older sister, then a sophomore at the University of Pennsylvania majoring in the history of art.

Though he had been two years her junior, Vivien Floris most certainly remembered Wesley Range. For the majority of her time at Sill, Vivien had been terrifically homesick, agonizingly shy, and really, in retrospect, far too intimidated by the New York–New England old money, grander even than the old money she grew up with on the Philadelphia Main Line. Despite being younger, Wes had been a total embodiment of this kind of stratospherically prestigious pedigree. He was all shaggy hair and perpetual tan and gracefully frayed khakis that didn't quite fit, but didn't quite fit in just the right way. Vivien's family had three homes, yes, but Wes's had at least five, and *home* wasn't really the noun one would use to describe any of them. He flew private, obviously. As a human being, she thought, he was reminiscent of a work of art: a well-valued one, prominently displayed in an exclusive gallery, so obviously expensive she wouldn't even dream of asking the price. Rejection was bad enough, but rejection from an under former? Unthinkable shame; unimaginable risk. She was barely a fringe member of her year's cool-girl group (semi-affectionately/semi-offensively dubbed the "Sillian Rails"). It was a precarious, fraught social position, one of which, at the time, Vivien had been acutely aware and intensely protective.

And so, even less than two years out of Sill, before the general impression of her prep school years had donned the fuzzy veneer of nostalgia; before her memories had permanently set into the wide-angle tableaux of brick colonnades and rolling fields and crisply delineated seasons; before, in short, the oeuvre of her memories from Sill was reduced to the preview of a movie she remembered seeing and being touched by, but for which she couldn't quite remember the plot—even then Wes had occupied the privileged glamour of distanced abstraction, and a far larger, rosier corner of her mind than to which he had any right.

The idea that Wes had experienced such a great personal tragedy touched Vivien deeply, and made him somehow more approachable, despite the distance between them. On more than one occasion she considered sourcing his telephone number or email address. But what would she say? *Hey, I know we've never really spoken, but I felt like we shared some pretty loaded gazes a couple of years ago and, hey, I'm really sorry about your dad, and if you're ever in Philadelphia it would be great to see you. Oh, yeah, sorry, this is Vivien. No, Vivien Floris.* Disaster. There was a nonzero chance he would not even remember her. Being close to home again and slightly more mature and really excelling in her college coursework, Vivien had started to, as they say, "come out of her shell," but she was not that brave, not yet. She told Sebastian to give Wes her condolences only if the appropriate situation presented itself. They never spoke of it again. Presumably, the appropriate situation had never arrived. But when the boys at Penn asked her out she still caught herself thinking about Wes while rendering her decisions, and when, weeks after he would have received his college email address, Wes still had not friended her on Facebook, Vivien felt a very real pang of phantom rejection.

It was not until she met Dale McBride in a comparative literature senior seminar on the nineteenth-century Russian novel that Wes was fully relegated to the subconscious depths of her mind. What he lacked in wealth and lineage Dale made up for in sophistication—a more valuable social attribute in intellectually focused undergraduate circles anyway. His parents were academics first and attorneys second. They were both philosophically minded, and he'd grown up listening to them argue passionately about the law in its relation to the categorical imperative and Rawlsian veil of ignorance and utilitarian pleasure monsters and Heidegger—if Heidegger made any sense at all if you didn't read him in the original German (consensus was no). Because his parents had the summers off, Dale had traveled extensively; instead of buying a place on the Cape or the Islands, which many of his friends' families had anyway, they got a lovely one in Nice for a fraction of the price. As a result, Dale spoke very good French—better, certainly, than Vivien. He knew how to sail, was above average at golf and tennis, genuinely enjoyed going to the opera, and even played the violin. Brookline High School wasn't Sill or anything, but it was nothing to sneer at, surely. There was no shortage of other girls invidiously consternated by the news that Vivien Floris was dating Dale S. McBride.

But it was still a surprise to her, the way they fell in love. It wasn't in grand gestures and glances, but little by little, in more of an auditory than a visual way. He was good-looking, certainly, but what she really loved about him was the way he talked about books and ideas. He had a fervent, almost reverent belief in the power of literature to affect the world in a very real way. He was impressed that she'd applied to PhD programs to continue her studies in Northern Renaissance art, and absolutely understood "the tremendous appeal of very-exact cheese." No, he was not making fun of her idealism—he wanted to be a novelist himself—and the cheese was a metaphor, yes, clearly, for order and control in a transient world of relentless precarity. She shouldn't care, he assured her, if Grace Cho, who was also applying to PhD programs, thought realistic figurative still lifes were boring and overstudied and unlikely to lead to tenure-track positions. Grace Cho, Dale told Vivien, probably thought a metaphor was a Spanish bullfighter. They started having sex. For her birthday, in December, in what turned out to be one of those small but genuinely life-changing kinds of gifts, Dale got Vivien Ovid's *Metamorphoses*—the beautiful little red Loeb set, bifurcated in

Latin and English (though she went on, literarily speaking, to prefer Humphries's poetry translation). For his birthday, in March, she gave him a poster of Goya's *Portrait of Pedro Romero*, the artist's favorite matador. He was tickled to the core: she'd given him a metaphor. She proceeded to show him, in wonderfully explicit physical terms, what exactly it was a metaphor for.

If Vivien had been almost anyone else, she might have done well to listen to Grace Cho. Operating without regard for industry trends and market forces by getting a PhD in art history was the Ivy League equivalent of getting a neck tattoo: a tacit renunciation of the professional job market in either an ostentatious display of privilege or absurdly self-confident risk. It was a recipe destined for either spectacular success or spectacular failure. It decidedly did *not* "preserve optionality." You were either going to end up a rock star or utterly unemployable, and far more likely the latter.

But Vivien Floris *had* been Vivien Floris. Her mother was on the board of half the cultural institutions in Philadelphia, and she'd been the immediate darling of the Art History department. Not shy, just *reserved.* Plenty of other young women (and one or two young men) had similarly stellar marks (and perhaps better foreign-language skills), but none could match Vivien's poise and taste and maturity. She had that rare undergraduate ability to engage with her professors politely and yet still as actual people. There was just a hint of sweetness to her, not too much, like a natural flavor. It has to be said that Vivien had the right—*exactly* the right—look for a budding art historian. Primly polished without being overaccessorized. Pretty. Thin. Classically sophisticated. Her recommenders had been essentially the same as the doctoral selection committee, and her acceptance into the UPenn PhD program had been almost a foregone conclusion.

She hadn't gotten in anywhere else, but Penn was a top program. Besides, she only needed one. It was kind of nice having decisions made for you sometimes, so long as they were decisions that you liked. Dale had been thrilled for her, and terribly proud of his own encouragement. It took real self-control to accomplish a long-term goal like that; Dale liked that in a person. He'd gotten into a few MFA programs himself; the best one was in the Midwest. She tried to be as excited for him as he was for her, but while she didn't want to be responsible for him not going, the truth was she didn't want him to go. He had also managed to land one of those crazy high-paying entry-level consulting jobs, the kind that all the Wharton undergrads drooled over. It was based in Philadelphia.

Both of them knew the underlying decision he was making, and Dale had struggled with it rather more than Vivien would have liked. When he gave her what should have been the good news, she found herself instead resenting his struggle with a pang of compunction. Dale had rearranged his life for her. Did she owe him something now? She loved him, yes, but it wasn't like she was sure if he was *the one*. Another name hovered disturbingly in her mind.

The 2012 rumor (ultimately true, prone to exaggeration) that Charles Wesley Range IV was engaged to be married ravaged the Sill Mill faster, if anything, than the news of his father had eight years earlier. The story was of that special variety of disappointing gossip that spreads, perversely, not because people want to know it, but precisely because they don't. The only anecdote for such misery is its further diffusion, like the old *misery loves company* cliché but even more irresistible, whereby one finds comfort in one's own festering scab through its comparison to a raw, open wound. The news of Wes's engagement was so traumatic for much of the Sill '02–'08 heterosexual alumna population as to require endless fresh meat, which in turn generated a whole new kind of meta-disappointment when one expected the satisfaction of a relative disappointment differential only to discover one's audience already had the same scab. Misery didn't love company then.

Margot Coddington (Sill '06) happened to be in Nantucket the weekend of the engagement and ran into the happy couple at Black-Eyed

Susan's brunch. The bride-to-be had great hair and an enormous vocabulary, and Wes seemed devastatingly smitten. They were staying at his grandparents' estate in Polpis. He had proposed on a postprandial sunset stroll. As soon as the initial elation and tears and everything wore off, she had been terrifically afraid of accidentally dropping the ring in the shallows. The ring was described by Margot Coddington to be a 7-carat (actually 4.3) emerald-cut diamond with elongated side baguettes and fully annular pavé. Margot immediately called her sister Lauren, who, in devastation, sent a deluge of texts to most of Sill '05, including Kate Manningham, the epicenter of the Sill Mill's New York chapter. By the time the rumor reached Gillian Whitaker (Sill '08), the female market was utterly saturated, and in desperation, Gilly turned to the gays. This included Vinny Kim, now the roommate of Sebastian Floris, who—thanks largely to his older sister's long-term boyfriend—had just started his new job as an analyst at Portmanteau in New York and *most definitely* recognized the bride-to-be's name from his hiring class there.

Vivien never would have connected the events in her mind, but within a week of learning that "like, the cleverest, hottest girl" from Sebastian's analyst class was marrying Charles Wesley Range IV, Vivien finally agreed to, at least unofficially, move in with Dale, keeping her old apartment strictly for purposes of storage and appearance.

## VII.

Even before he said anything, there was a physical sincerity to Eric Hashimoto's contrition. You could feel it in his footfalls as he paced the south window bank of the fifty-second-floor conference room, in the sweat curling over the collar of his new Harris tweed. His designy, wire-framed *I-got-new-glasses-for-my-first-real-job* glasses sat cockeyed; his tufty coif had been anxiously mussed. Even at six feet he had this underfed hedgehog-like put-him-in-your-pocket adorableness that awoke in both Dale and Diana an almost parental instinct to protect.

—Dale?

Eric called to him, moving his lips as little as possible, as if terrified Dale would prove to be someone else. He looked relieved when proven correct, and briefly seemed to relax until registering the girl standing next to him, introduced as Diana Whalen but who, Eric thought, could not possibly be Diana Whalen because Diana Whalen was an enterprise architecture manager. Eric Hashimoto was new to Portmanteau—Mercury Incorporated being, in fact, his very first client and this, his very first project—but he clearly had it on good authority that enterprise architecture managers were not supposed to look like that. His eyes darted from Diana to Dale and back again, trying to spot a ruse that wasn't there before remembering his current predicament and the unpleasant reality of the moment.

—Dale, I want you to know, you have to know . . . you have to *understand*. I am so so *so, so sorry*. Like, *so sorry*. But you *have to help me*. Please. *Please*.

This kind of overreaction was almost the hallmark of a good analyst, the natural result of a lifelong will to overachievement combined with deep professional naivete. Diana shot Dale a look to *go easy on him* and he returned a mask of mock offense that she would even have to ask. There was no need to be so upset, Dale assured him; it was just an internal email. A good learning experience. Partially even Dale's fault. He should have given Eric more instruction, an example of a strong Introductory Client Br—

—No no no no no. Not *that*.

Eric dismissed Dale's sympathies with haste, his nose-wrinkling expression of impatience bordering on condescension. The gesture would've probably seemed hubristic and maybe even insolent coming from someone else, but Eric's innocent, blinky hedgehog face allowed him to walk the line in a way that Diana seemed to recognize and appreciate in its primitive reminiscence of her own wiles. Eric Hashimoto continued his defense, arguing that the ICB was pretty well written, in his own personal opinion, before remembering himself once again and, crestfallen, admitting that the transgression to which he was referring was much, much, much worse.

Dale meanwhile was half-smiling, both trying to suppress his entertainment and preparing mental popcorn. He was somewhat looking forward to learning whatever trifle was so vexing poor Eric, and very looking forward to its retrospective with Diana over lunch.

Eric took a deep breath, doubling down on what seemed like a Herculean effort not to cry. He motioned for Dale and Diana to follow him to the far-east window bank of the conference room and gestured to the carpet, illuminated like an altar in the morning sunshine. Dale's halt was so abrupt that Diana crashed into him, knocking his left shoulder with her right at the very same moment that he saw what was on the floor.

—Oh my god, Horace, said Dale.

Voluminously splayed, in a pitiful orange heap, was either a dead or a thoroughly comatose Pomeranian. Diana did not have to ask. She knew who Horace was. But Eric was obviously beside himself at the receipt of such a human-sounding name, and demanded the subsidiary details of Horace's identity.

Dale closed his eyes hard, opening them slowly, as if the creature might, by some act of mercy, stand up and be gone. He moved his middle fingers up his temples, trying to think.

—Horace, Dale sighed, grinning maniacally at Eric in spite of himself, is our client Prudence Hyman's service animal.

Eric Hashimoto was suddenly in full-on self-preservation mode.

—It wasn't my fault! Please, I'm sorry, *please*, it wasn't my fault! Are you going to fire me? Oh my god, you're going to fire me. I only left to go to the bathroom for like, one minute! *One minute.* I wasn't even here when it happened. And, how was I supposed to know our client had a *dog*? *What was he doing* roaming around up here anyway? And . . . *excuse me?* . . . this dog—this dog *cannot possibly* be a *service* animal. It's the kind of dog a girl would carry in her purse. Um, no offense, Diana.

—Oh, certainly not, she said, deadpan.

—What happened?

—Did something fall on him?

—Um, I think he ate this, Eric said.

He pulled from his back pocket a gnarled chewing-gum-style packet of pills and surrendered it to Diana. Four or five of them were missing. It was Eric's sleeping medication, more or less requisite for post-traumatic tiger-mother helicopter overparented anxiety disorder, he explained. He'd left it in the open front pocket of his backpack, next to Horace on the floor. Dale knelt beside the orange puff and put his hand first on his bony chest, then in front of his mouth. He could feel Horace's tiny little body under all that fur; it felt a lot less like a stuffed animal than Dale would have imagined. Horace was still warm, but Dale couldn't ascertain whether or not he was breathing. Diana quietly removed her iPhone from her pocket and fiddled with it intensely for a few seconds before bringing the device to her ear, ambulating mechanically to the other side of the room the way people do when it's ringing on the other side of the line.

—Okay, Dale thought out loud, trying to control his panic, so when did you find him? Right before we arrived? Say, five, maybe ten minutes ago?

—Um, more like half an hour . . . Eric trailed off.

—*Half an hour?* Why didn't you call me? Email me? What were you thinking?

—But *you* said not to! *You* said **do not send any more emails** until I found you in person. And I couldn't very well, like, leave *him* here and go looking for you!

—You didn't think that the possible murder of our client's service animal might, I don't know, constitute an exception?

—I had no idea whose dog it was! Look, Dale, I know you're, like, really really *really* mad, and you *totally* have a right to be—but I am reasonably confident this doesn't qualify as murder. First of all, I don't think you can be charged with murder when it's a dog, even—and I'm going to put like a ninety-five percent confidence interval on this—even if it is a service dog—a title, by the way, the applicability of which I personally remain dubious in this instance. And, American Disability Act compliance aside, would you really have wanted me to, like, *document* this? Not to say there's anything untoward going on here. This was purely an accident! Put the blame on luck, not crime. What crime is there in error? Accidental death is manslaughter not murder anyway, right? Oh my god. *Shit!* Does *manslaughter* extend to a *dog* . . . ?

—Eric, Diana said, hanging up the phone. Calm yourself.

She put her hand on Dale's arm, silently instructing him to do the same, but having to know it would have precisely the opposite effect. He could still feel his shoulder trembling where she'd run into him, but under this new level of intentionality his arm's erratic pulsation seemed like an emergency everyone should stop and attend to prior to Horace. Diana had called a vet on Arch Street. She was instructing Eric to empty her bag, to unload all her stuff into his and Dale's. Eric crouched to help her, participating in the invasion of Diana's personal artifacts into the territories of their attachés, but reticent to touch her things directly, preferring to hold open the bags for Dale and Diana to fill. Dale transferred an expensive-looking monogrammed black wallet from one of those slick anticonsumerism luxury consumer brands that self-consciously fails to self-identify on its wares. He wasn't sure which one, and felt a disconcerting stroke of socioeconomic insecurity that made it hard to put down without closer examination. Then there was a brand-new ultra-thin yet fairly seriously cracked iPad. The bottom of her bag was an intriguingly disorganized collection of tampons and cheap hotel pens and bottles plural of Maximum Strength Visine that neither of the men felt comfortable touching but Diana transferred with only a dash of personal embarrassment and no recognition of their own. Finally a battered glasses case emerged from the front pocket, inspiring a startlingly vivid pornographic overlay of Diana qua librarian. *Even without a bra, those were remarkably perky tits.* Dale's reverie was interrupted by Diana's request for his home address and cell phone number.

—My address?

—Yes, in Philadelphia. We have to use Eric's name because of the medication, but your address for the forms. It'll make sense in a second. Eric? *Eric?* Pay attention. I need you to look me in the eye. You and I have an emergency appointment at Best Friends veterinary clinic for our dog, whose name is Dale—got that? Not Horace, Dale. And sorry, human Dale, it was just the first name I thought of on the phone.

Dale could not decide whether to be consciously offended or subconsciously flattered. Diana continued:

—Eric, we're a couple who just recently moved to Philadelphia, finally reunited after years of long-distance. We haven't fully unpacked yet and just as we were about to head out the door for work this morning we saw our darling dog Dale collapse and realized he'd gotten into a box that included your pills. You'll have to bring them along with you—do you have the packet? Good. This part we need to be fully honest about, obviously, so they know how to treat him. Are you following me?

Eric was following, if in a kind of frozen awe. Diana adjusted her rings as she spoke, dispassionately moving her wedding band over to her right hand.

—We've only recently gotten engaged, so nothing is set yet for the wedding. We don't have a date or a venue or anything.

—Huh?

—Just trust me, someone will ask. You proposed to me last Friday night in our new house—er—

Diana threw human Dale an eyebrow.

*—just off Rittenhouse Square.*

Diana studied the address and phone number Dale had written down, reading it aloud to Eric before safeguarding it in an interior zippered pocket of her fleece.

—Okay, purse is empty then? Hold it open.

Eric's hands were shaking as Diana lifted Horace, hoisting him up in a manner so perfunctory it nearly suggested she'd accidentally knocked out a client's service animal before, like a person who knew how to put out a fire precisely because she was a practiced arsonist. Horace's foxy little snout separated, his tongue languishing pathetically to the side as his head rocked back. Dale moved to help her, directing Horace's enormously fluffy tail, which kept ostentatiously curling over the side. Tactilely, Horace fell somewhere, the three of them decided, between a human baby and luxuriant fashion accessory—one, Dale thought out of habit, that Vivien might quite like. Once tucked inside, one had to admit that if Horace was in fact dead, the black leather tote made a rather elegant shroud.

Diana stood up, positioning the bag on her shoulder. She looked up at Dale expectantly.

—Don't worry, ass covering is my specialty, he grinned, handing her back her wallet and feeling a new, strange sense of serenity. Just go. As Horace himself once said: *Even as we speak, time speeds swiftly away.*

—Dude, what are you talking about? said Eric. I am so confused right now. Horace is a dog.

—But also a Roman poet, Diana told Eric, before turning back to Dale. Very clever, there. You might also start calling local shelters and pet stores. What you want to ask for is an "adult orange Pomeranian with black points and subtle white markings on the snout and chest." We need a backup plan in case Horace doesn't make it.

—You don't think she'll be able to tell if it's a different dog?

—I think it doesn't matter, so long as nobody else can. Hopefully it won't come to that. But really, think about it, what kind of lunatic would rave that her dog's been replaced with another one that looks exactly like him? She'll look crazy if she says anything, so she won't. No dog at all will be a much, much bigger problem for us. Oh—do make sure Horace 2.0 is male, though. I'll text you updates.

She looped her arm tightly through Eric's, as he looked just about ready to faint. Unless Dale was imagining it, in an almost direct invitation to jealousy, Diana gave him an actual wink, suggestively mouthing "bye" as Parker Remington walked through the door. If he caught Diana by surprise, she barely showed it.

—Oh hi, Parker. Lovely to see you, glad you're here. This is Eric Hashimoto. We have to head out for a bit. Rather urgent *medical* issue; private. Do you want anything from the Underworld on our way back?

She passed him, Eric in tow, with a smile and introductory wave, but briskly and without waiting for a response, leaving Remington frozen, mouth ajar, looking quizzically at their backs. It was a virtuoso performance, Dale thought, precisely because it wasn't a performance at all. She had spun fiction out of facts, a deception without deceit. And she knew Parker well, clearly—a lover of creative solutions, but also a steadfast follower of rules. He would never, ever take the chance of creating even the hint of an appearance of an iota of a smidgeon of a HIPAA violation. Remington turned his eyes to Dale.

—Parker, Dale said, how was your weekend?

## VIII.

In retrospect Vivien would develop a clear explanation for herself as to why it happened, how many (many) years of resisting what she wanted to *do* in favor of what she wanted to *have done* had, far from building up a tolerance, reached some kind of maximum capacity in her, some outer-bound limit to human restraint. It wasn't a departure from her character, she came to believe, but rather an inevitability precisely *because of* her character: her oversaturation in the present perfect tense had left her perversely, cruelly vulnerable in the face of a perfect present. And Julian hadn't helped.

Sill Mill gossip notwithstanding, Vivien had never really pictured Wesley Range as a tech CEO. Her impression of him was built on the kind of emotional truth impervious to fact, and she could only conceive of his adulthood as the creative class ideal: an endless extension of ultra-privileged adolescence, of ambiguous job but definitive lifestyle. He'd be perpetually at the epicenter of the universe, conspicuously at leisure whatever the season. Summers in Nantucket that rounded into a Telluride September. Autumnal New England culminating in a traditional Connecticut Christmas before skiing in Adelboden or Chamonix. A "real" vacation in January or February—St. Barths or Nevis, something remote and lush and invariably involving a yacht. There'd be at least one extended, more exotic self-discovery sort of sojourn each year: Rajasthan, Machu Picchu, Marrakech . . . By Vivien's intuitive calendrical expectations, Wes should have been in Cannes this week.

And yet he was here, in New York, at her exhibition—and supremely complimentary of it. He lived in the Flatiron District. It was a loft, he told her, right on Broadway. It sounded exactly like the kind of place she pictured him owning, the kind of place she'd like to live in herself. When he made it a point to say that his wife was out of town, Vivien's chest contracted with the implication she read in it. There was a jarring, teenage quality to her embarrassment then; it was laced with the same strain of underlying danger and excitement she might have felt fifteen years earlier if he'd said the same thing of his parents.

Dinner was scheduled for eight. After Wes and Julian left and her heartbeat slowed, as raw shock and delight gave way to postmortem social replay and analysis, Vivien couldn't help but resent Julian for the surprise, for failing to make the connection, for failing to prepare her adequately. Had she struck the right balance between pleasure and indifference to Wes's encomia? Seemed too eager for him to join them that evening? She tried to beat back her annoyance with qualifiers—that she had forgone an early night to prepare extra-thoroughly in the hope of impressing *Julian*; that the tour had objectively gone well; that Wes was married; that she was engaged; that, while yes, she would have probably opted for a different outfit had she known (something a bit less starchly professional, a touch more "downtown"), she should *always* be sartorially prepared for this kind of thing. Preparation was, after all, an attribute that Vivien deeply prided herself on; it was an attribute that made Vivien Vivien. How embarrassing, to be caught off guard in the Internet Age.

Vivien threw the rest of her day into ensuring she would not be caught off guard again. When Raffaela, the Renaissance curatorial department's teeny Italian secretary, so old-fashioned she herself seemed Baroque, complained to her that the private school girls on her morning commute were wearing obscenely short skirts without nylons, Vivien fought the urge to engage, avoiding a lengthy debate on twenty-first-century norms and allowing her to finish most of the day's administrative work before noon. In lieu of lunch, Vivien signed up for a last-minute barre class. She called Dale on her way to the studio, loosely conscious, on some level, of ringing him now so as not to be obliged to later. While she told him the truth—that she was going to dinner with Julian and one of his business school friends—Vivien could not entirely shield herself from the sense that somehow, the truth here had a lie-like quality. She'd never spoken to Dale in that specific tone before; it was the tone she used on authority figures with whom she intended only to superficially comply. This alone seemed to forge a little cleft between them, and she was relieved when they hung up and the isometric pelvic thrusts commenced.

Vivien grabbed a chopped salad on her way back to the Met that she ate at her desk in the company of Ecco's website. This led her to flattering articles about Wes and photographs of his wife, which she indulged in for a time until she couldn't stand it anymore and sought digital reassurance in Pinterest. The images, so rhythmically haphazard as to be obviously staged, had that comforting blend of surprise and predictability perfected by *Law & Order*, Vivien's all-time favorite show. The perfectly torn jeans and Delpozo gowns and delicate lace details and suntanned shoulders and Grace Kelly portraits and Euclidean beach umbrellas—they offered an escape that felt like self-improvement without any of the work actually required to move toward it, the Ideal Vivien. It was pleasurable research that she could even, to some extent, bill to herself as work-related—curatorial. Sometimes it seemed the pictures might go so far as to diffuse through her ocular mucous membranes, instantly transforming her very being into a better one, a more enviable one, just by looking; as if she were at least partially absorbing their glamour and cool. Sometimes, if she looked long enough, it almost felt as if she were the one in the picture, like she could somehow feel her own gaze admiring her transformed self, like she'd bested Narcissus. *Oh, Vivien—excellent work*, she could almost hear herself say, *excellent work*.

After her 3:00 p.m. public lecture, Vivien resisted the temptation to linger and bask in the layup questions and flattering compliments of the well-educated yoga moms and retirees in attendance, instead clocking some face time with the head curator so she might duck out early and scout something to wear. She needed to look like she hadn't given the dinner a moment's thought, and this would take time.

Vivien found the dress at Vince, across from her hotel at Madison and Seventy-Sixth. It was a simple shift, deliriously soft and just the right length, as in a bit too short but seemingly accidentally so, as if she were a touch taller and thinner than the intended model. It was effortless without being sloppy, editorial but in no way dressed up. With her low-tops and denim jacket, it would hit the right note, showing her off without her showing off. If the dress had come only in black, or only in navy, she would have gladly, almost thoughtlessly, purchased either. But unfortunately it came in both. She spent over half an hour in the dressing room switching between them, examining herself, posing, evaluating the implications, agonizing over the decision. It was amazing how the same dress in only slightly different colors could seem so different. But then again, nothing highlights difference quite like homogeneity. The black was so stark, so purely minimal. Very now, very New York. The navy would have seemed the same in isolation, but by contrast it almost felt like a grown-up version of something she might have worn at Penn or even Sill. Comparatively, it paid homage to prep without being preppy, developing a latent infusion of nostalgia and youth. She wanted to prefer the black. Reason told her to go for the black. In a movie, she'd definitely wear a black dress. But viscerally, physically, she felt lighter, looked younger in the navy. It made her feel how she wanted to feel in the black. Even if she bought both, she could wear only one. Vivien had to choose.

Back in her hotel room, she performed her ablutions slowly, using as little product as possible. She showered and dried her hair upside down, infusing its natural order with a little chaos to make it look more natural. At various points in the evening she might nonchalantly reassess the side of her part. She plucked two or three microscopic strays below her eyebrows, resisting the urge to pick at the tiny pimple on her chin. She moisturized her cuticles. The dress looked as good as she'd thought it would with the denim jacket and sneakers, and she tried to prevent herself from second-guessing the color. She decided to skip a bag, stuffing her hotel key, ID, and a credit card into the pocket of her jacket. No jewelry either, aside from her everyday studs. The only thing she added was sunglasses, classic Ray-Ban Clubmasters. She hooked them onto the neck of her dress, letting them pull the fabric slightly, revealing its heft. Like she'd been out enjoying the city and hadn't even bothered to stop back at her hotel. Like she'd changed right after work without thinking about it at all.

The restaurant was in the West Village on Bedford, about half an hour by cab. Timing was always iffy with such gatherings—especially in New York. No one wanted to be the first to arrive, waiting awkwardly at the table, worse at the bar, worse still by the host stand. Being on time was always too early. It gave an impression of overeagerness, that one wasn't adequately pressed for time (busyness being, to a far greater extent in New York than Philadelphia, a prime signifier of social clout). But no one wanted to be visibly last either, to be the one holding up the party from being seated. Anything past fifteenish minutes late was rude and disrespectful of everyone else's busyness. It signaled either that you were trying too hard or that you had an equally uncool total lack of self-awareness. It was important to minimize the chance of either scenario. Vivien intended to arrive at 8:08.

It was a lovely little restaurant. One of those upscale, neighborhoody gems full of exposed brick and tattooed staff that hit just the right balance between social open-mindedness and economic exclusivity. Thankfully, Julian was already at the bar, sipping an Old-Fashioned garnished with a geometric orange peel and single oversized cube of ice.

He'd changed since the tour that morning, and now sported dark jeans and a quilted Barbour vest over a muted plaid shirt of the genre that looks truly appropriate only when carrying a dead duck you yourself recently terminated. Ferragamo loafers and a lightly scuffed L.L.Bean tote, known by Vivien to be one of his "everyday" tote bags, completed the ensemble.

—Kind of you to join me, you look lovely, Julian said, looking at his watch, only slightly annoyed. Fucking Wes is always fucking late. And *he* lives the closest to this place. It's ridiculous. Oh, well, there he is. *Finally.* At least you two have given me adequate time to peruse the menu. I hate being rushed into an order. Did you see that the special is *blanquette de veau*? I'm positively giddy.

—Hi, sorry to have kept you both waiting, Wes said with a smile, pressing his cheek to Vivien's and shaking Julian's hand as the hostess showed them to an interior table, much to Julian's irritation.

Wes had obviously showered. His skin still had that just-showered warmth and humidity. He'd likewise changed into jeans (but more fashion-forward, butt-hugging ones) and a plaid shirt that he tucked under the same silver-gray pullover he'd worn on the tour.

They exchanged the various customary pleasantries; Julian complained again about the table. Wes ordered what Julian was drinking and Vivien opted for a Moscow Mule. Julian ordered another round, as well as a Diet Coke and a club soda with lime. It was hardly unusual for Julian to order three or even four different beverages at a time with meals, but Wes and Vivien affectionately ganged up on him about it anyway, the way old friends tend to do with one another's eccentricities. The server confirmed all the drinks were to everyone's liking and prepared to take down their food orders.

—The roasted Brussels sprouts to start, please, Vivien said. And what would you recommend between the *moules frites* and the duck?

—Ooh, impossible. They are both so good—it just totally depends on your mood. Are you super-hungry? The duck is a ton of food. The mussels are definitely on the lighter side.

Vivien was ravenous.

—Let's go with the mussels, then.

—I'll have the quail to start, and the filet, please, said Wes.

—And the *foie gras* and *blanquette de veau* for me.

—I'm *so* sorry, the server cringed, dragging the "o." We literally *just* ran out of the *blanquette de veau.*

—You're out of the *blanquette de veau*? Are you shitting me?

The server was not, as it turned out, shitting Julian, and he begrudgingly—chiding the server not to rush his order—compromised on the roast chicken.

—Ugh, we should have gone to the Yale Club, Julian said when the server was almost out of earshot. This is what you get for going to dinner below Twenty-Third Street.

It was the kind of interchange both Wes and Vivien understood Julian to relish, an opportunity to comically overreact to a minor grievance for social effect. This episode launched a foray into past quintessential-Julian grievance-overreaction folklore (a rich, nuanced genre) that had Wes and Vivien alternating in sidesplitting laughter over the well-established antics of their mutual friend. Julian was all too delighted to fan the flame, hilariously rearticulating, defending, and even embellishing every far-fetched behavioral rationale. To Vivien, Wes's deep knowledge and understanding of Julian felt almost like a knowledge and understanding of her. On top of their Sill connection, it was easy to mistake similar memories for shared ones, for their separate personal histories to elicit the impression of a long-standing intimacy that did not exist.

Their appetizers arrived, and they ordered another round. For the entrées, everyone switched to wine.

—Has Julian ever told you about Audrey Wimberly, Wes?

—No, I don't believe so—a former girlfriend, Julian?

—Not quite, Vivien said, to a roll of Julian's eyes. She's a friend of mine—a close friend, actually—from our "Art Since 1945" class sophomore year. One day after class, I happened to mention I had brunch plans with Julian. It was a casual, offhand comment, you know; I thought she liked him. But Audrey was flabbergasted. "Are you *sure* you want to do that, Vivien?" she said. "Don't you know that he rubs people the wrong way?" Julian overheard her and went ballistic.

—Well, and why wouldn't I? First of all, I rub plenty of people the right way—

—Yes, so you said! said Vivien, turning again to Wes. And then he proceeded to offer himself as a reference *for himself.*

Wes was laughing so hard he was nearly in tears. Though he still managed to thank the server clearing their plates, Vivien noticed.

—I couldn't fathom why he'd been so deeply offended, she continued, returning to Julian. You know not everyone understands your jokes.

—It wasn't like Audrey understood "Art Since 1945" either.

—Don't be an idiot, Julian. Audrey works for Larry Gagosian. Anyway, Wes, it gets better. He ultimately threatened that if she "ever, *ever* uttered another word critiquing his esteemed personage again," he would "sell her into slavery for twenty-four dollars in expired Applebee's gift certificates."

—In retrospect, perhaps not the best turn of phrase for the situation, Julian admitted, abruptly changing his tone and readjusting his glasses, sliding them up the bridge of his nose.

—*Why*, Wes wailed, now fully crying, that's *amazing*.

—Well, because Vivien forgot to mention that Audrey Wimberly is Black.

—Jesus Christ, Julian, Wes coughed, making a valiant effort to stop laughing. Vivien, this is why I'm going prematurely gray. *This* is my head of HR.

—Oh please, Julian rejoined imperiously. I am the paragon of minority acceptance. I campaigned very hard, if you'll recall, for us to have MLK Day off.

—You also campaigned for Columbus Day.

Julian waved him off, trying to catch the server's attention, making an ultra-exaggerated version of the universal American "I'd like the check, please" face.

—So soon? Wes said. I was hoping for another round.

—Um, seriously? My bowels are going to be in an uproar tomorrow as it is, said Julian. But don't let me stop you.

Vivien casually reassessed her part, the mass of her locks tumbling over the alternate shoulder:

—I could have another.

# IX.

**SELECT INCOMING AND OUTGOING SMS TEXT MESSAGE ACTIVITY (RESORTED, BY CONTACT, CHRONOLOGICAL) OF DIANA W. WHALEN (SPRINT NETWORK, WIRELESS NUMBER 917-XXX-XXXX), MONDAY, MAY 18, 2015.**

**[CONTACT NAME(S): "McBride, Dale"]**

**Monday 11:43 AM**

Important question for you

Diana?

Correct
On a scale of 1 to 10
How much does Parker remind you of Alec Baldwin?

How are you only just now texting me
I've sent you two emails
Didn't have your cell
Is Horace ok?
What are we dealing with?
7.5/10

No way

No way he's not ok or no way 7.5/10?

Oh sorry
Yes that was ambiguous
No way 7.5
It's at least a 9
Did you factor in that they both hawk credit cards?

Jesus Diana

And manage to look distinguished AF in spite of it?

He's looking more pissed than distinguished right now
Because he can't ask why you're gone
Clever, with the "medical" bit BTW
Raj and Megan's flight was delayed
They are stuck at ORD
So it's just Parker and Richard ("Rich") and Me

What is "Rich" like?

Brosef
Ex-johns Hopkins lax
He's already mentioned cross fit twice

Nice

Enough with the suspense
Are you trying to put me in the hospital too?

Relax
Canicide averted
Horace is going to be fine
He's hooked up to an IV
Little dope fiend just needs to detox
I'm more worried about Eric TBH
Hyperhidrosis issue I think
And he's not a very good actor

You know who else is having hyperhidrosis issues right now?
ME
FOR REASONS I THINK MAY BE FAIRLY OBVIOUS

Scare caps are never the answer, Dale
Control your passion, for unless it obeys, it commands you.
-Horace

Hah
When fools shun one fault they run into the opposite one
-Horace

Well played
Ok I'm sorry for the anxiety

I am only accepting this apology because he's alive

Naturally, I understand
Horace is more or less the lifeblood of our friendship
Definitely worth the $5K this is costing me

Wait what
. . . $5K?!

You are lucky I have a rich husband

Oh am I?

Money is a handmaiden if you know how
to use it

. . . but a mistress if you don't.
(nice try there)

Pretty good mistress IMO

Fidelity is the sister of justice.

Horace?

Horace.

The lofty pine is oftenest shaken by the winds
-Horace

Shake it off
-Taylor Swift

Tis not sufficient to combine
Well-chosen words in a well-ordered line

None knows the reason why this curse
Was sent on him, this love of making verse.

Have you done anything since I left besides google
Horace quotes?

In peace, a wise man makes suitable preparation for war.

[fire emoji; 100 emoji]

It's not like you haven't kept up valiantly

Woof woof
Woof woof woof
-Horace

Lol

For real
He just woke up
You can stop calling shelters

What?
I already stopped . . .
When you said he was going to be ok

Well, we are now fully out of the woods

(I see what you did there)

(Did you see what I did there?)
Damnit!

So how are we going to get him back up here
Diana?
Going to lunch with Remington and Rich . . . you want anything from Circle 2shi?

**Monday 2:46 PM**

. . .
Hello?

Hi hi hi
You worry too much

It is your concern when your neighbor's wall is on fire

Lol
Ok
Sorry
But I was in with prudence human
Hyman
And we are now best friends

Of course you are

I also have a pretty good understanding of what she's looking for from us
Work wise I mean

Of course you do
So what happened?

Smuggled him back in my bag
He was still drowsy, thankfully

Waited for an empty elevator
Took him out once safely inside
Fluffed him up a bit
Told the floor admin we found him just lying around by himself

Technically not untrue

PH was beside herself with gratitude
Insisted on buying us lunch immediately
#win
Gourmet pretzels have dramatically improved Eric's overall sell being Asian
Wellbeing again!
Not Asian!
Ducking autocorrect

Hahahaha

I give up
Coming up now

**Monday 11:55 PM**

Did you find your way back from the bar all right?

Yes
Thanks

Thanks for everything you did today
I'm fairly certain Eric is head over heels in love with you

Bah
Doubtful
I think I nearly gave him a heart attack

And Horace is one lucky dog

And a wise little fucker
All I did was follow his advice . . .
Carpe diem

How did we both miss that one earlier today?

Pretty unbelievable

You're pretty unbelievable
Hah

Why do you laugh?
Change only the name and this story is about you

Horace?

Yas

[CONTACT NAME(S): "Pappas-Fidicia, Julian"]

**Monday 11:48 AM**

I'm currently at a Philadelphia veterinary office because one of the analysts almost killed our client's service dog

No fucking way

I swear to god
Orange pomeranian
I thought this might amuse you
Also I thought about you this morning bc I had taco bell

Glory of glories!
You are too kind to the analyst

You'd throw him under the bus?

Indubitably
One of my favorite things is throwing people under the bus

How about Wes?
Jk
He's not answering my texts though
Could you pls ask him to call me?

Sure
He's kind of in a mood today
Showed up half an hour late this morning
So fucking annoying
But did you see my Instagram?
Priceless

[CONTACT NAME(S): "Range, Wes"]

**Monday 8:31 AM**

Arrived in Philly safely
What time do you wanna talk tonight

**Monday 11:45 AM**

Cool that works for me too

Hi sorry
Phone was off
Glad you got there ok
Will text when I get out of this mtg

**Monday 1:10 PM**

What is this large purchase alert I just got from Best Friends Philadelphia?
Did you lose your credit card?

No
Legitimate transaction

What?
Holy shit, five thousaand dollars??!?!
What is this for?
Is this one of your jokes?

Can't talk now

This is not okay
When can you talk?
Hello?

**Monday 2:48 PM**

Sorry client lunch
No joke
Sorry

Sorry?
Are you fucking kidding me?

There was an accident at work

What kind of accident?
Are you getting reimbursed?

I'd say gratitude is a kind of reimbursement, wouldn't you?

I'm not falling for that
What the fuck happened?

Honestly, you're making me not want to tell you

Call me now

Calm down
It's not that big a deal

Don't tell me to calm down
That's a lot of money Diana
We've been through this

Like you've never thrown money at a problem
To make it go away

We're not talking about me right now

We never do!
I don't want to hear it
It was a life or death situation
Client's service animal almost died
I have team dinner at 8
Want to talk at 11?

I have a dinner too
Don't know how late it will go

Who is your dinner with?

And don't think you can just change the subject like that
I see what you are trying to do

Does 11 work for you?

It won't work

Why not?
WTF

**Monday 3:17 PM**

Can you talk now?

**Monday 7:22 PM**

Hello?

What do you want me to say
I don't have time for your games and excuses right now

I'm calling you
Did you just send me to voicemail?
Unbelievable

You are the one who is unbelievable

Stop texting me

# X.

It was Vivien's idea to go to Lord Henry's. Wes reminded himself of this fact over and over. Before Julian left, it was already turning into one of those magical, instant-classic sorts of evenings, the kind that you hope will never end, that you mythologize and reminisce about even as they're happening. Wes and Vivien had already stayed for two drinks past "another round" at the restaurant, the conversation seamlessly oscillating between personal histories and cultural recommendations, the waitstaff's hints growing increasingly less subtle that they'd like to close down. Until she'd mentioned Harry's, Wes had grown, it seemed, permanently affixed to his chair—as if so long as he didn't move, time couldn't either. But Lord Henry's offered something better: the ability to go back. *Just like old times*, Vivien had said. Harry's was on Eighty-Fourth and Second—yes, totally out of the way for Wes, but no, no, of course he didn't mind. He loved Harry's. It was the only possible place to go.

Lord Henry's Restaurant and Bar—Harry's to those on the in—was a New York institution and the long-standing St. Elmo's–style hangout of several elite New England preparatory schools. Rare was the Sill graduate who had never presented a fake ID at its doors, danced to Hall and Oates in its famed back room, or tested consumption limits around its red-and-white checkered-cloth tables. Rarer still was one who had not heard its mantra, superimposed on the giant, mirrored backsplash behind the bar:

**THERE IS NO SUCH THING AS A MORAL OR IMMORAL BAR.**
**BARS ARE WELL STOCKED OR BADLY STOCKED.**
**THAT IS ALL.**

The place was so thoroughly imbued with adolescent excess and tales of charmingly inconsequent bad decisions that it already had an air of nostalgia by college, when plans to meet the Old Sill Crew at Harry's after Thanksgiving or over Easter Weekend were made well in advance and hotly anticipated. By the time "everyone" returned to the city for jobs after graduation, it was a thoroughly legendary location. Well into Wes's twenties, nights there still invariably struck that poetic balance between promise and stasis, surprise and predictability. It was a place where you met new people, but no one with whom you didn't share a few Facebook friends. It was a place where you did old things and felt young.

More than once after a long, enchanting night at Harry's, Wes's heavily compromised senses had been so firmly embedded in the past that he'd accidentally walked to the Seventy-Fourth Street town house, fully remembering only when he got to the door—no longer a dark wood but a brilliant vermilion—that it had been seized and sold. It was a painful reorientation, looping back uptown to his grandparents' apartment on Fifth. But it was a melancholy, wistful pain; a pain that was not only bearable, but secretly irresistible; a pain to be subconsciously baited and cherished and lingered in, one that validated the sentimentality Wes felt toward himself as the wholly sympathetic tragic hero of his own life.

And that was part of the problem, wasn't it? The pleasure of the pain? Wes's genuine devastation at the time of his father's suicide had been swiftly, uncomfortably quelled by the startling material benefits it mobilized. He'd been anxious about returning to Sill after his father's funeral; Wes knew the satisfaction others got out of watching the mighty fall. But his roommate had welcomed him with a hug so warm and affectionate as to qualify for some kind of award in adolescent male bravery, and Jack Dorset—just an acquaintance, really—stopped by to tell Wes how sorry he was, and did Wes and his mom want to join his family in Aspen for Thanksgiving? At the Senior Council meeting, Marnie Davenport insinuated that if Ainsley was not adequately comforting Wes in his time of need, he might count on her instead, if he knew what she meant, and Kate Manningham borrowed Ingrid Cheng's phone after lights-out to imply the same. The whispers he overheard about himself didn't include so much as a whiff of derision. His father's crimes hadn't damaged Wes's golden-boy reputation—if anything, they'd made it impossible to resent him for it. Wes suddenly understood why, in the winter of their fourth form year, Portia McLaughlin had lied and told everyone she had cancer. There was a seductive, asymmetric quality to sympathy: so many reasons you might need it, yet such a narrow moral purview for eliciting the real, true, genuine thing.

The chilling thought had infiltrated the manor of his mind like a bloated rat squeezing through an impossibly tiny crack, violating the memory of his father, the pain of his loss, the concern for his mother, the kindness of his teachers and friends, the mature appropriateness of his own behavior: *No one would be asking him to Aspen if his father was out on bail from Riker's Island.* Only Diana—years later—had fully, unnervingly understood this: that in very real, measurable ways, Wes had been fortunate his father committed suicide. Charlie Range had bequeathed his son something far more valuable than his lost inheritance: he'd bequeathed him a sympathetic story. It was not a coincidence, that he'd married the only person who had ever seen this clearly—who had loved him not because of, but in spite of it. But it was also an exhilarating cognitive pleasure to indulge, on occasion, in the great myth of himself, and tonight Vivien Floris was divinely alight with his personal narrative momentum.

How enticing, even in the happiest of times: to experience the smooth, varnished version of yourself, to control it like a video game, watching your simulacrum perform with such uncanny fidelity you can almost believe it's the real you. And yet, on a different *tonight*, Wes would've enjoyed this sensation without latching on to it; he would have savored his final drink and walked summarily home. His heightened susceptibility to Vivien's version of himself on this particular evening could be drawn back to Diana, of course, but not due to some remarkable singularity in the day. No, their interactions had been all too characteristic of their fundamental stalemate. Recall that it was not some grand catalyst or a rogue bad decision, but many (many) tiny compounding ones, systemically incentivized and magnified and reinforced, that ultimately allowed a nuclear reactor to blow at Chernobyl.

Wes hailed a cab and helped Vivien in, forgetting, somehow, that he was supposed to subsequently let go of her hand. It was polite to help her in, and helping her in had required holding her hand, and it wasn't like she'd exactly remembered to let go either, but upon the realization he blushed and reclaimed it, rubbing the back of his neck bashfully. Vivien responded by tossing her hair from right to left and turning her gaze to the window, exposing her profile in a manner Wes instinctively felt to be designed for his benefit. What a benefit it was! The streetlights fell on her cheekbones and jawline and fingers and kneecaps in rapid succession—now, *there* were some knees that belonged in a museum, he thought. He just watched her for a while, his heartbeat quickening. *It was Vivien's idea to go to Lord Henry's.* Wes slyly poked the knee closest to him.

—These little things look cold.

—Oh, do they?

—Yes, frozen. I'm legitimately concerned.

Wes furrowed his eyebrows in exaggerated alarm, poking her knees from several new angles, examining them in mock examination. They were cool and smooth and perfect. Vivien twittered with delight, and Wes felt further emboldened. Suddenly locking her eyes in alarm, he wrapped his hand around her right knee with a dramatic gasp.

—Are these insured by Lloyd's of London?

—No, she laughed. State Farm.

Now they were laughing together. He let his hand slightly—as if accidentally—travel half an inch north, giving her knee-thigh a squeeze that could technically be defended as playful and friendly but it probably wouldn't hold up in court. Vivien didn't move. Her inaction felt almost like a dare. Wes held her gaze, but removed his hand slowly, almost extravagantly, intensely analyzing her face. He wasn't imagining it. She wanted him, certainly. He knew it. Precisely the way he wanted her.

—Do you want my sweater? Here. It's not your fault, he said lightly. I've heard Sillian Rails are frequently chilly. According to legend, it's due to their metallically icy hearts.

—Oh please, said Vivien, I was never really one of those girls.

Wes grinned, preparing himself to confess.

—Sure you were, he said. You were always my favorite one of those girls, actually . . . I had a pretty massive crush on you back in the day.

—What? No you didn't.

—Sure I did.

—Um, *I* had a crush on *you*.

—I didn't even think you knew who I was.

—Well, I did.

—Come on, no you didn't.

—I did!

It was all so clumsy and trite and exactly what he'd hoped she'd say. The whole interchange felt a bit like a scene from the undiscovered sequel to a John Hughes movie, and he was dying to go back and watch the original. He stopped laughing and looked away for a second before meeting her eyes again with renewed purpose.

—Why didn't you ever say anything?

—I was shy, Vivien said. You?

—Uh, you were *you*.

—What does that mean?

—You know perfectly well what it means.

He knew she did. Perfect understanding was transparently written on her face. But she wanted to hear him say it. It was exhilarating, having the power to deny her the pleasure.

—You're going to have to be more specific, she said.

—Specifically . . . trailed Wes, returning to levity, helping her out of the car. Specifically, I would like another drink.

—How decadent! she said with a silly little accent, taking his hand.

—*Darling*, he said, this is New *York*.

For a Monday, Harry's was packed. It was commencement week at both Columbia and NYU, and several loosely organized groups of euphoric red-faced graduates in seersucker shorts and white sundresses, frat tanks, and plastic neon-armed "Class of 2015" sunglasses dominated the scene, with a few Upper East Side private school kids and predatory hedge-fund types filling in around the edges. Vivien managed to squeeze to the front of the bar, returning with two beers and an abandoned pair of NYU shades that she promptly donned, giving Wes a victorious look in the mirrored backsplash before turning and making her way back to him.

He told her she looked like bad news. She laughed and moved to give the glasses to him, but he stopped her—no, she couldn't possibly take them off, he said, coaxing the Ray-Bans from her neck as a consolation prize, knowing the style suited him brilliantly. *Hey, hey, hey, hey!* the back room called. *Ooooooooooooo-ooh-ooo-oo-ooehoo-owhoa.* Vivien grabbed Wes's hand excitedly, pulling him through the crowd toward the music with a practiced impulsiveness. *Won't you come see about me—I'll be alone, danc-ing—you know it, ba-by.*

—*Tell me your troubles and doubts. Giving me everything*—they sang to each other, peeking over the rims of their shades, the room plenty dark enough without them.

It wasn't just that song. The entire set list that night was steeped in timeless adolescent longing. Cult movie soundtracks. Journey. All the something-"Girl" songs—"Jessie's Girl," "Rich Girl," "Uptown Girl," "American Girl," "Yesterday Girl," "My Girl." Wes and Vivien both knew almost all of the words to almost all of the songs, and whatever song was playing seemed to have been written specifically for them. Any contradictory lyrical narrative underpinnings were rendered entirely irrelevant. What mattered was the chorus. *Don't stop believin'. 'Cause you know it don't matter anyway. Don't, don't, don't, don't—don't you forget about me.*

Like everyone else there, they danced in that vaguely eighties collegial way that involves a lot of jumping around and emphatic arm movements. The battle for "best dancer" in the back room at Harry's was one of those baffling unofficial social contests to which everyone implicitly understands the rules despite their making no logical sense. For the "best dancer" at Harry's was almost always actually the *worst* dancer; that is to say, whichever very bad dancer gave the fewest fucks about being a bad dancer and danced with reckless abandon anyway. The "winner" that night had already been crowned: an overweight fellow wearing a printed orange bow tie and light blue Columbia College shades. He had an astonishingly bad "Lawnmower," a jump split bordering on grotesque, and deeply reminded Wes and Vivien of at least two different characters from Sill. But then, everyone there that evening seemed like someone else, some ghost of Harry's past—including themselves. It didn't matter that in all the nights they had each spent at Lord Henry's, it was actually only the second or third time they'd ever been there on the same one. Their fond recollections folded together and tangled and combined, implying—no, insisting—that two similar pasts were actually a single shared one, augmenting each other's importance to the other's life in a way that seemed to fully, unequivocally justify the present. Alcohol and nostalgia make for a pretty toxic concoction; the surgeon general doesn't warn you about that. Wes could feel the anachronic webbing cloud his mind—until he couldn't. Until the web began to hide the webbing. Nothing makes sense except paradox, Lord Henry seemed to say. *Exult in bad news.* Don't *means only, quite emphatically,* do. Vivien was Diana. She was the absolute worst.

The room regressed a couple of decades further as "Danke Schoen" started to play. Wes presented his hand and led Vivien in a loose, ballroomy swing, lip-synching theatrically. As the song's intensity and tempo built though, they both strangely, strangely intuitively, slowed down. He took off Vivien's sunglasses, and lifted the NYU ones away from her face. Her eyes were expectant; her face, dewy with exertion. It was the most radiant she'd ever looked to him, but the Mental Catalogue was not open for business, its equipment having been redirected to processing live-action video. When the brass entered in full force, he pulled her closer—dangerously close. She'd long abandoned her denim jacket, as he had his sweater, and the arcs and turns of her body that the dress hid from his eyes were immediately visible to the touch. She felt totally impossible: relaxed but tight, hard and soft. *Danke schoen, oh darling, danke schoen.* He realized he was already kissing her before he realized he was going to. Like it hadn't even been a choice. Or rather, like he'd affirmatively made the *opposite* choice, but thinking so hard about *not* kissing her made him precisely more likely to do it. Wes pulled back quickly—wide-eyed, shocked by his own nerve—and almost started to apologize. But there was no need. She was already dancing again, lip-synching with charming pizazz, almost as if it hadn't happened. Had that *not* just happened? No, it had, it definitely had. He could still taste it. *Danke schoen—auf weidersehen—danke schoen.*

They stayed for two more songs, "Twist and Shout" and "Summer of '69," dancing furiously, with such joy it almost hurt. But timing was always iffy leaving Harry's. You wanted to walk out the door precisely at the party's apex. Leave too early and sure, you'd miss out on a bit of the fun. But leave too late, and you risked breaking the spell entirely, of having to walk that depressing musicless halogen exit, surrounded by the other people who'd gotten as bombed as you, or were, very deep down, too sad and lonely to pull themselves away sooner, like you. It had been Vivien's idea to go to Lord Henry's, but it was Wes's idea to leave. He was just sober enough to be deeply invested in propelling the magic outside. It was late. He should walk her back to her hotel.

The air outside was misty and wonderful. For the first couple of blocks they reveled in its cool humidity, singing aloud, still wobbly twirling. As their lungs adjusted and the pace slowed, Vivien started hugging her arms together. Wes draped his sweater over her shoulders and his arm managed to remain. She reached up, pulling his hand into hers, and they walked slowly like that, in more of a "mosey" than a "walk" really, saying absolutely nothing, holding on to the moment, savoring it, willing it to last. At the entrance to the Carlyle, she didn't let go. She didn't let go again at the elevator bank or inside the manned elevator. The gentleman smiled pleasantly at him, the way you smile at an attractive young husband who is clearly still very in love with his attractive young wife. For a brief second Wes felt strange and uncomfortable, like maybe he should retrieve his hand, but then they stepped off the elevator and the sensation dissipated.

She led him to her room, still not letting go of his hand but spinning to face him, as if guarding the door behind her. For a few seconds they just looked at each other, considering each other seriously, like one might examine a painting. But then, oh my god and then they were kissing like Wes only ever wanted to kiss, the way that made him certain he was being fully appreciated for the exceptional lover he knew himself to be. With urgency and passion and tension and thirst. With instinctive deliberation and transcendental physicality. At some point, Wes noticed, the door had opened and closed behind them and it was very dark and his shirt was unbuttoned and there was a maddening unfastening motion happening at the top of his jeans. He inhaled deeply and ran his hands up the insides of her arms, pinning them back to the door above her head, holding them there with one hand and exploring her body with the other. She made a wonderful little noise that fell somewhere between disgruntled compliment and satisfied complaint, and he pressed into her harder still, wrapping his free hand into the crease of her taut little thigh-butt border, inching up her dress, then releasing her arms and turning his entire attention to the effort. He lingered in the exercise, deliberately tormenting her, and himself. Her skin felt like hot ice—familiar yet unfamiliar, exquisite and unsatisfying, surprising and predictable. It responded to everything he did the way he wanted it to respond, and his own body responded to the response.

The second time she went for his jeans, he let her, only marginally hindering her progress, gnawing her neck and shoulders and chest, working the inside of her thigh, investigating the delicate lace first with his fingers, then lips and tongue. She pushed him onto the bed. He would have sought a dresser or table instead, but it was dark, he didn't entirely trust his own coordination, and experience told him he would probably most enjoy whatever it was she most wanted to do—which turned out to be climbing on top of him and torturing him to the point he could no longer resist ripping off her underwear and fucking her.

Over time, sex with the same person always settles into an orange you peel yourself and divide on the natural membrane. Still delicious, of course, but contained. It had been a long time since he'd tasted the smooth surface of interior fruit, cut with an extrasharp knife. It was oozing and juicy. Not just ignoring the membrane, but somehow spiting it.

# PART TWO

## XI.

The single greatest innovation in modern workplace sexual politics was the holy union of invention and practical application that is the fully corporate-sanctioned Enterprise Instant Messenger (E-IM). Here, the technical capability of internet-wide GUI-based messaging à la PowWow, ICQ, and—most nostalgically from a Millennial perspective, that ancient maker and breaker of reputations and hearts—the AOL Instant Messenger met a user base essentially trapped for eight-plus hours per day at a computer, supposed to be doing things that they didn't especially want to do.

It is almost painfully easy to imagine the power of the original pitch, full of words like *speed* and *productivity gains* and *The* capital T F *Future* and *email reduction* and *employee mobility*. What was perhaps underestimated was the timeless, universal compulsion of human beings—even without, like, a tailor-made mechanism for it—to complain and scheme and procrastinate and flirt. The kicker here was not just that there was an almost infinitely elastic new way to waste time, but that idle pinging suddenly looked exactly like working. From behind the curtain of a laptop privacy screen, the modern professional servant might easily gossip about a colleague or undermine a political decision or try to get laid *all while the boss was watching*. It was a paper bag sort of open container arrangement, a calculated cease-fire from both sides. Statistical data on the subject is scarce, but anecdotal evidence suggests that the leading use case of E-IM, running diametrically counter to its intention to support swift, remote corporate communications, was in fact the conduction of pseudo-to-outright-non-business matters from within the same room. Nowhere was this use case more palpably irresistible than in those wretched, infamous black holes of corporate time, those infuriating cesspools of egotism and rhetoric, those bitter traps of white-collar adulthood: *meetings*.

Diana was sitting across from Dale in one now, wearing another short, shapeless dress, only marginally different from the one she'd worn yesterday, slouching slightly in a pose so relaxed it bordered on unprofessional, one knee draped over the other lazily. She was a greedy online conversationalist—fond of bypassing greetings and transitions, frequently jumping between threads of discourse in a manner that might have been hard to follow except for the fact that she neurotically numbered them. Their texting had felt fraught with meaning the day before, but this new element, of being physically with her in the same room, able to trace and analyze the micro-metamorphoses in her face from word to word—it was as if the Wi-Fi connection between them had grown a visible cable, directly linking their human operating systems. The little blue bubbles elicited almost programmatic physical manifestations: redirected half-smiles, goose pimples, neck rubbing. The public nature of their environment only enhanced its smiting intimacy.

Within seconds of his arrival online that morning, Diana had plunged straight into one of her neat little lists:

1. *Clogged with yesterday's excess, does the body drag the mind down with it?*
2. *What are we having for lunch?*
3. *You are going to love me.*

Number one was addressable. Number two, a false anchor: one of those cognitive illusions so powerful that even piercing awareness of it fails to counter its effects. She'd thrown in a banality just to highlight the audacity of number three. Dale knew Diana was being deliberately, cruelly provocative here, revving him up to some anticlimax. That she'd scored free Phillies tickets, maybe, or extracted a toothsome chunk of gossip out of another member of the team. She'd already demonstrated herself an expert in plausible deniability. But she also hadn't lied, quite explicitly. There was an underlying truth fixed in everything she said, and no small pleasure watching it refract into blistering shards of irony. It hardly mattered what they were literally talking about. The specter of number three was always there, the shadow conversation of their shadow conversation. Every topical thread pulled and wrapped around its slippery fulcrum of negative space. Oh, the unsaid known!—or, rather, the unsaid *almost* known. Few things are more alluring: that final sliver of uncertainty and danger and risk fanning your desire for more more more as you wade like Tantalus, knee-deep and dying of thirst for approval from someone you very much approve.

The E-IM medium deftly accommodated this kind of reverie, and played much to Dale's strengths re: the return exhibition of cleverness. In live-action conversation, he was forever thinking of the perfect thing to say thirty seconds too late. When instant messaging, however, Dale had just the right touch. He googled a Horatian rejoinder, taking his time, knowing the interval served only to enhance his response. He wanted Diana to feel the absence of his attention—for her to feel it sharply, her pleasure comingling with pain. Only when he saw a trace of disappointment—only then did he hit send, monitoring her face intensely, mesmerized by her change of expression, like he was witnessing a work of art come to life. *1. It is the false claim of fools to try to conceal wounds that have not healed*, he typed, watching Diana's brain wrap around the farthest corners of his double entendre, oscillating over the ripple between self-deprecation and adversarial slight. *1. The greatest lesson in life is to know that even fools are sometimes right*, she'd sent back in no time, almost as if she'd known the quotation he was going to choose. Like she'd actively wanted to be cast as the fool all along.

They made plans for lunch. *But how to escalate things?* Dale ached to push beyond the prosaic here with original material—a natural impulse of those inclined to woo—but all the poetic schemata traditionally designed for wooing were categorically inappropriate, and even if they hadn't been, would have felt maudlin and embarrassing. No, there was only one form of love poem that couldn't possibly be construed as one:

*There once was a poor dog named Horace*
*Who caused quite a kerfuffle for us*
*Just give me some ale,*
*And I'll tell you the tale,*
*Supported in full by the chorus*
*(That's you, Diana, you're the chorus)*

There was something grossly immodest about the way she had looked at him then. Something unapologetic, even wickedly self-satisfied, as if accepting a challenge she'd already won. The little blue bubbles flew faster now, addictive, unsatisfying, ever accelerating his need for the next blue bubble:

*There once was a fellow named Dale*
*Whose limericks were shockingly stale*
*So why was he failin'?*
*He needed a Whalen.*
*To make it a whale of a tale.*

The meeting ended, and the Portmanteau team returned to the fifty-second floor to drop their laptops. Diana went to the bathroom, and Dale urged the rest of them to go ahead and grab something to eat—he'd wait for her. Everyone (but especially Eric Hashimoto) was still fairly hungover and hungry and welcomed the suggestion. When Diana returned to find Dale alone, she beamed viciously.

—You never responded to number three.

—What?

—Do you want to know why you're going to love me or not?

For a moment Dale had the fervent wish to be again constrained by a meeting, as if his swashbuckling boldness were trapped in his laptop. The power of speaking out loud, of physical mobility—there was something awkward in it, a separate kind of pressure, harder to push back against. Freedom seemed to Dale to possess its own new set of constraints, and his disadvantaged mind threatened to drag his body down with it.

—Only lawyers ask questions they already know the answers to, said Dale.

—Oh, but I don't *know* the answer. I only almost know it.

—Let's hear your hypothesis, then.

They exited the elevator and walked through security, slowly approaching the Underworld's staircase. At the top of it Diana turned toward him.

—Fine, she said smugly, passing him. I've already finished ninety-two percent of the tech blueprint.

The bob of her little blond ponytail descending the steps felt distinctly imperious to him, and he rushed to catch up.

—That's a rough estimate, I take it.

—Eric's brief was right-on about one thing: they want to use the Russian company as a platform.

—Pegaswipe? Yeah, I wonder who supplied him with that information.

—You? Then why did you guys sell them a *blueprint*? If they're just going to scale Pegaswipe, they already have a blueprint. *Pegaswipe* is the blueprint. Diana laughed. You strategy people just love the word *blueprint*, I think. It's one of those pretty little words you use to ensure you're never actually responsible for *doing* anything.

—Your job should be pretty easy, then. Sounds like you are the one who should love me.

Dale grinned like Mephistopheles, ready to collect her soul. He could feel the cadence of their easy conversation from yesterday returning, the cloudy haze of E-IM melting away. They reached Panwich, the Underworld's gourmet deli, and he gestured for Diana to order first.

—Hi, yes, thanks, I'll have the Napoleon, please, she said to the chef.

Dale read the menu. *The Napoleon: Roasted turkey, Normandie Brie, caramelized onions, fig jam, 7-grain roll.*

—Ooh, good choice. I'll have the Napoleon, too, thank you.

Diana's glare was white-hot.

—Can there really be two Napoleons?

They walked around the corner toward the pickup counter, prattling on about Napoleon and thinking about conquering each other until their sandwiches arrived. Diana paid while Dale scouted a relatively isolated corner of the food court. They sat down.

—Not to rubber-stamp the historically less-than-airtight strategy of Russian campaigns, said Dale, but if PH wants to use Pegaswipe and that's that, shouldn't the blueprint be, like, a hundred percent done?

Diana looked at him like a schoolteacher pleased by a precocious student, and Dale was momentarily incapacitated by hot librarian vibes again.

—Obviously Mercury *wants* to use Pegaswipe, she said. I mean, it makes sense from a labor arbitrage perspective alone, right? But they can't. At least not as is. Weren't you paying attention in *any* of the meetings this morning?

—I may have been a touch distracted.

Diana smiled wryly.

—Pegaswipe has an Achilles' heel, she said.

—What?

—*Fraud.*

—*What?* Dale whispered in disbelief, twisting it into a new word. No *way*. Nothing like that came up in the due diligence. Does Jack Howard know about this? I audited their books myself—they were totally clean. This could invalidate the acquisi—

Diana took an enormous bite of her Napoleon that only marginally impeded her ability to dismiss his anxiety. Dale felt silly for misunderstanding. It was the first piece of evidence he'd garnered thus far against their mutual telepathy, and in a strange way it stung.

—No, no—not fraud *in* their business, fraud *as* their business, she said in between wolfy, inelegant bites. As in Pegaswipe's ability to detect credit card fraud for their customers. The missing piece of the blueprint boils down to a security issue. Their fraud-detection technology is woefully inadequate for US standards, let alone European regulatory requirements. Mercury can't scale Pegaswipe as is. And no, Jack Howard does not know. I think PH actually hired us just so she didn't have to tell him. Can you imagine—spending millions of dollars to avoid an uncomfortable thirty-minute conversation?

—Sure. It's one of the main reasons people hire consultants, don't you think?

Diana reluctantly conceded in a nose scrunch.

—It makes sense now why Merchantes and Settlmnt have been so recalcitrant, Dale continued a moment later, inhaling audibly. Without a tenable fraud solution, Pegaswipe's platform can't replace theirs—

—and Pegaswipe's employees can't replace them.

—Correct.

—Eric—or should I say, you—had the rest of it backward. Our project doesn't give Mercury political buy-in, getting political buy-in is our project. Mercury needs Merchantes or Settlmnt to play ball with Pegaswipe to build a tenable fraud solution. They're holding out mutually for respective survival. We can't complete the blueprint, or the operating model for that matter, without finding some way to get one of them to capitulate.

—The question is, how do we shift the incentives?

Diana put down her sandwich abruptly and leaned back in her chair, crossing her arms and narrowing her eyes. In an apparent non sequitur, she asked if he'd ever been to the University of Virginia.

—Unless you count Florida, I've never been south of the Mason-Dixon line.

—That is such a snobby Bostonian thing to say, Diana chastised him, rolling her eyes. It's beautiful—UVA, I mean. Sympathetic red brick, glistening white colonnades, Palladian symmetry. The whole Academical Village is a UNESCO World Heritage Site.

—Not to discount your educational utopia, but I don't believe that *academical* is the preferred adjectival variant.

Diana ignored him.

—The prettiest part is the Lawn, though. At the north end is the Rotunda, which is basically the university's profile picture. It's flanked by ten pavilions and fifty-four individual student rooms evenly distributed along the east and west colonnades. These things are, like, dripping in charm. I mean, each one has its own fireplace.

—Sounds desirable.

—So you'd think. Except that it's actually a pain in the ass of a place to live. The rooms have sinks, but no toilets. It's legitimately an outhouse situation. Perhaps worse, there's no air-conditioning. As newer dorms and off-campus housing with, like, twentieth-century amenities built up in the fifties and sixties, living on the Lawn started to decline in popularity. Pretty soon, no one wanted to live there—thousands of students, and the university couldn't sign up fifty-four. Now, these are precious, very early nineteenth-century buildings designed by Thomas Fucking Jefferson. The university couldn't afford for them to be empty. So how do you think they filled them?

—By letting in women?

Diana erupted in laughter.

—No, but really not a bad guess! Increasing supply would be the more logical way to compensate. But no, no; the university actually did just the opposite.

—They restricted demand? Dale was tracking.

—Exactly. They turned it into a competition. Drew up an elaborate application process. Lots of barriers to entry. They made it "prestigious." Called it an "honor." They pitted the students against one another; made it seem like you were "winning" a slot.

—And it worked, then?

Well, they didn't have to resort to Chapter 11. I lived there.

—And did it feel like an honor at 3:00 a.m. when you had to pee?

—Honestly? I just slept at Wes's apartment most nights—but, um, that isn't the point.

It was the first time Diana had mentioned her husband by name in Dale's presence. Instinctively it irritated him, but she didn't look like she'd been trying to spur his jealousy. If anything, her face betrayed the regret of having made some sort of rare miscalibration, a human sort of technical error. She started fumbling in her bag, as if to hide that she was avoiding eye contact. The muscles in his face relaxed. It was a startling, almost heartwarming possibility to him, that Diana might be capable of insecurity.

She pulled out a bottle of Maximum Strength Visine. Dale felt the need to rescue her.

—You're saying we set up a competition, between Settlmnt and Merchantes, he circled back, to her visible relief.

—May the best fraud win.

—It doesn't even matter who the winner is, actually, Dale clarified. We just have to get them to earnestly apply, for the Russians to learn what they need to learn.

Diana blinked as the clear round droplets hit her eyes. When she met his gaze, their white borders were blinding. It was ferociously penetrating.

—That sounds like an elegant, round stratagem to me, Diana said.

—But is it a clever Trojan horse, backed by divine justice?

—Divine justice doesn't come cheap.

—Well, there are some things money can't buy.

—But for everything else, there's MercuryCard.

# XII.

Of all the dangers in life, there is perhaps none more treacherous than getting precisely what you want. As it has been said, the mistakes we male and female mortals make when we have our own way persist in raising wonder at our fondness of it. For unbought dresses can never be stained. Uneaten food doesn't make you fat, and unconsumed alcohol won't give you a hangover. Only unwritten novels are perfect.

Most relevant to Vivien Floris on the morning of Tuesday, May 19, 2015, was this: no one, not even a prehistoric-looking woman in brown polyester pants pushing a walker with tennis-balled feet, could—by accident or otherwise—take a watery shit in your *unhung* exhibition. But Vivien had managed in only her third year post-PhD to stage a diplomatically and logistically challenging show as a visiting curator at the Metropolitan Museum of Art, and such realized success today entailed physically guarding *Narcissus* and his other admirers from the human fecal matter between her feet, taunting her in the Versailles-style mirror. She tried to remain calm, instructing one guard to alert facilities while another escorted the poor woman to the closest restroom. This kind of thing actually happens in museums more often than you might imagine, and Vivien was well versed in the canon of Visitor Horror Stories and knew all the protocols, but experiencing one firsthand and with a hangover was nevertheless sensually alarming and sufficiently horrible. Let this be said of portraits and mirrors: as often as they are objects of devotion, they are vessels of ridicule.

*Art and Myth: Ovid's Heirs* was closed to the public a good two hours for obvious health-code-type reasons, during which time Vivien washed her hands with Lady Macbeth–level fervor before walking to Eighty-Sixth Street to buy a new pair of shoes, little desert boots that she wore out of the store. She spent the rest of the morning at her desk, compulsively checking her phone, uncertain of what, exactly, she should expect it to herald. The prior evening's enchantment had been so powerful that she'd awoken still feeling the lingering effects of it, marveling at the persuasive force her person had impressed on Charles Wesley Range IV. He wasn't the type to act lightly in such matters; neither, of course, was she. The anomalous nature of their actions lent them an extra weight and velocity—an unspoken and unearned but viscerally propulsive quality. That they'd done what they'd done seemed to carry a deterministic significance. It would be messy and painful, for a time, unwinding and rearchitecting their lives, but the broader narrative arc gave such a satisfying roundness to the story of her life, and Vivien didn't mind a little dramatic conflict—so long as she could see where it was leading.

Only in the aftermath of straddling someone else's shit did Vivien's illusions begin to unravel, slowly at first, almost invisibly, as if a moth had nipped a single thread, creating a weakness, a vulnerability, but not yet quite a hole. *Was it possible the route to drastic action was a bit more circuitous? That first came a thorough, extended affair?* This had its advantages, too, basking in the magic for a while longer, delaying the inevitable unpleasantness—and yet—

Vivien had never had an illicit tryst before, and her first whiff of anxiety found its foothold in her unfamiliarity with the proprieties of her impropriety. For there *were* proper ways to manage things, surely; there was a right way and a wrong way to have an affair. Vivien always wanted to follow the rules, even for how to break them. How would they choose the most suitable course? And—what of the wedding? *A logistical snag, for sure—but they'd figure it out together.* They'd both, she reminded herself, have to deal with their partner's devastation. So . . . was Wes going to text her? Or call to minimize the data trail? *No, calling was even more suspicious.* No one called anyone anymore. But, if Wes did call—what would he say? What would she? What was she *supposed* to say to him? When—where—would they meet next? Vivien racked her brain for guiding examples of stylish affairs, but her mind only drifted to Emma Bovary and Anna Karenina. This seemed the crux of the problem. Her experience of adultery was so remote as to rest on fictional women from the nineteenth century who didn't exactly inspire confidence.

She took another field trip, this time to Dean & DeLuca for lunch. Vivien ate at her desk with care after another obsessive hand-washing session, but with every bite, a new stray thread of concern caught in her teeth. They seemed to wrench and pull with Raffaela's blathering, as she recounted every episode involving bodily fluids she could remember from her twenty-seven-year history at the Met. Unfortunately, she had an excellent memory.

—This is reminding me, Vivien, did I tell you my sister is planning to kill Mike Tyson?

Vivien ignored her, looking down at her lifeless phone.

—Because of his pigeons.

Raffaela raised her precision-painted eyebrows, her eyes seeking Vivien's, nodding with latent meaning. She was wearing an ancient yellow skirt suit, half a size too small and with borderline-hostile shoulder pads, which made her resemble an overstuffed steak fry.

—A few years ago, Mike Tyson moved to Phoenix, right near where my sister lives, and he brought his pet pigeons, and some of them, they escaped. Now they are out of control. They have been pooping all over my sister's gazebo and in her pool. My brother-in-law is fit to be tied.

—Are you comparing the woman in the exhibition today to the pigeons who poop in your sister's pool? Vivien asked her absently.

—You know, I don't know, but I just thought to tell you, because he has a reality television show, Mike Tyson, about him and his pigeons, in case you were interested.

—I'm interested, the head curator said playfully, surprising Vivien from behind.

Victor Barlett, the Cortland R. Young Jr. Curator of European Paintings, had come over to thank Vivien for her Highly Professional Behavior in Such an Undeniably Difficult Situation that morning, and proceeded to recount a similar story from years ago that Raffaela had already told. This time Vivien listened to it with expressive interest, rewarded in the form of a request for her to attend a mid-level donor reception in his stead that evening. Donor receptions in general were the purgatorial babysitting jobs of curatorships, sure to spoil your after-school plans and likely to involve a fair amount of ass wiping. But mid-level donors were unquestionably the worst: rich enough to make statistically significant gifts on an individual basis, not so rich that such gifts were personally inconsequential to them. This was insecure, hard-earned upper-middle-class Protestant-work-ethic-type money you were going after, rarely separated from its type-A producers without engendering heavy expectations and feelings of entitlement to some sort of remuneration (institutional lexical insistence on *gift* notwithstanding). Compensatory benefits were usually payable in the form of unlimited alcohol and a conversation at an evening reception with someone like Vivien, whose reflective glow validated their sense of their own cultural refinement and social importance. Such indirect purchase of obsequious flummery was undeniably the more common method for shitting on a curator.

—Of course, I'd be delighted to go, she said.

It was after 11:00 p.m. by the time Vivien unlocked the door to her hotel room and was forced to fully confront the treachery of another precisely fulfilled want. She had forgotten to remove the "Do Not Disturb" tag from the door—stupidly—and the unretouched space now possessed a *preserved* sort of quality, less like a museum than a crime-scene cliché. Articles of clothing littered the floor. The sheets, settled in specific rumpledness, looked dirty and cold. For Vivien, normally emphatically neat, one of those people for whom cleanliness is well-nigh a moral issue, the tableau was not only jarring, it was a judgment. Surrounded by the evidence of her success, she felt nefarious and ashamed, and not in a Bond villain or sireny hot mess kind of way. Her offense suddenly had all the wrong aesthetics. The price of the hotel couldn't hide the tacky averageness of her actions. What had she been expecting? For Wes to be sitting there in a silk robe and Moroccan slippers, awash in tenebrific light? He hadn't even stayed until morning. She checked her phone again, then chastised herself for checking it, her anxieties now unraveling rapidly. How could she have allowed herself to be surprised by such predictability? While the idea of losing Wes came as a devastating blow, she could have handled and perhaps even reveled in being the victim of some kind of cruel, grandiose tragedy. But Wes hadn't cared enough even to deliberately wound her, and without him in the picture, their rendezvous fell out of high art. It became the generic backstory from some episode of *Law & Order: SVU.*

This was the primary humiliation—not the categorical presence of their affair, but the inability of its visuals to support Vivien's romantic narrative of it. The scene design had screwed up her inner monologue, and the death knell of her illusions rang. There was a fine line but an essential difference between an *illicit tryst* and *cheating*, and a steep downward slope from *ease* to *easy*. It was a lexical rift with devastating emotional implications, and an association it was hard to unsee. When she tried to reclaim proprietorship of the former argot she found it razed by pathetic pretension worse even, somehow, than honest vulgarity. *This is all the room's fault*, she thought. If only she could fix the room. Vivien closed her eyes, trying to remember how it had looked, how orderly and inviting, on Sunday night when she'd first walked in. She took a deep breath, then opened her eyes and set to work with Marie Kondo diligence.

She tackled the clothes first—sorting, hanging, folding. She threw the offending underwear in the sink, and the navy dress, stained and reeking of beer, into the designated hotel laundry bag. She fanned the magazines and arranged the desk. She made the bed, charily turning over the pillows, tidied the towels, wiped down the bathroom countertop, and organized her toiletries. At this juncture, she briefly considered requesting off-hour maid service, but decided against it. No one ever asks for housekeeping at midnight when *everything is, like, totally all right.* Abnormal behavior was a form of admission, a maid a credible attestant to her shame. She only slightly more seriously considered a personal expedition to CVS or something for Lysol and Febreze. But the closest drugstore was on Second Avenue, and a French bath wasn't going to cut it on those sheets anyway. A hot shower was tabled for similar reasons, and Vivien was forced to admit that, at this particular juncture, she had done the very best she could reasonably do.

Vivien undressed and performed her nightly ablutions with all of her customary fastidiousness. The room looked undeniably better now—lived in, yes, but hardly sordid. Still, as she approached the bed, Vivien found herself unable to lift the covers. Thankfully there was an extra blanket in the closet, a sateen-bordered lightweight quilted down topper that Vivien willed herself to assume had been seldom used by prior patrons. Wrapping herself up in it, she settled on top of the coverlet, lying prone, staring at her phone forlornly. She had checked it dozens, maybe hundreds of times that day, but this was the first in which it occurred to her that Wes Range was not the only person from whom she had no report.

It was exceedingly unlike Dale not to call when she hadn't, not to text her at the very least. *No*, she thought, attempting to head off the question: *Could he possibly know?* Vivien frantically examined her memory for witnesses and evidentiary cracks. *Could Julian have said something to him?* No, there hadn't been any real impropriety at dinner, certainly none before Julian left. *Someone at Lord Henry's, then?* But for all of the night's supporting doppelgängers, neither Vivien nor Wes had run into a single acquaintance there. Some unseen pro-Dale lurker seemed preposterous. Nearly all of her fiancé's friends in New York were aggressively married Whartonites—parents of newborns or pregnant or nearly pregnant—the sort who ran marathons and hired night nurses and went to bed before ten. Vivien briefly indulged in outright paranoia—*the Uber driver? The bellhop?* She knew she was venturing into Ms. Scarlet in the Library with the Candlestick territory, and willed herself to cease and desist. A tip could only have come from someone so tangential and unreliable that Dale would've been, if anything, *more* inclined than usual to call. *Yes, that's right, he would have demanded an explanation.* She felt better for a brief moment. *Unless there was a picture!* Lord Henry's back room. *There was a kiss.* And an inherent validity to photographs, to images generally. Vivien tried to channel the force of reason that had neutralized Clue in the direction of *Gossip Girl* (*really, Vivien? Prep school paparazzi?*). But it was too late. The recollection of pleasure had already transformed into the luxury of self-reproach; she'd waded into the possibility that Dale's love might fall short of unconditional, and found the silver pool quicksand. Unconditional love only ever really comes up when people behave very, very badly, Vivien thought. When she gazed into her phone, her old life seemed trapped behind its glass.

There are few emotions that can obfuscate shame, but one of them is fear. Vivien had become so comfortable in Dale's affection, so well accustomed to being the doggedly pursued, the beloved, the in-power party, that she hadn't even considered double abandonment a possible outcome. Her concern, her entire concern, had been winning over Wes—but only because Dale had been a given, an expectation. It sounded horrible, but he'd been a kind of backup, a safety school of sorts, allowing her to be bolder and more ambitious than she ever would have been alone. Wes had presented the possibility of breaking off her engagement to Dale, but the idea that Dale might break off his engagement to Vivien—? It was unthinkably ghastly, an unfinishable sentence. She imagined having to explain it to her brother, her parents—worst, her friends—*their* friends. She saw superior eyes, mired in faux concern, moving to comfort her dryly, itching to get away and relay the tale. She herself looked so—what was it? *Unenviable.* Alone. Like her unhappily single friends, except not quite as sympathetic. Vivien thumbed at her engagement ring anxiously. She might have passed for twenty-five, but Vivien was thirty-one. For all of her education, she had never really grown up. Or maybe it was precisely because of her education, that immersion in well-preserved images, that she hadn't ever had to; her identity had been so wrapped up in being the precocious child that she'd turned into an inept adult. Regardless, the idea that decisions could have such perilous consequences was an iconoclasm that smarted mercilessly. The notion that Dale was a losable person increased his value to her exponentially, and Vivien started to cry.

The human brain may be a lazy economist, but it is an absolutely outstanding lawyer, capable of persuasive argument and shrewd cross-examination. It can render damning evidence inadmissible and plead out your conscience, often without any time served. Indeed, the greater the threat to feeling good about yourself, the more of a shark it becomes. As Vivien's self-piteous tears gained momentum, drifting toward those huge, round sobs that preclude access to one's analytic faculties, her subconscious mounted an increasingly resilient defense in the case of *McBride v. Floris*. It considered an insanity plea, then near-insanity (i.e., "passion"); it tested the construction of factual boundaries and flirted with honest supplication for sentence reduction.

When Vivien awoke in her sateen-bordered cocoon the following morning, she felt slightly better somehow—even before discovering an early morning logistical email from their wedding photographer to which Dale had already promptly and unremarkably replied. Preliminary relief coursed through her veins. *He's just busy with work.* Dale didn't know anything; she was still getting married. She didn't trust herself to call him yet, but a long shower further improved her mood, and two well-received tours encouraged her further still. She took a yoga class at lunch, and felt lithe, if still a bit heavy. When Raffaela told her she was looking awfully tired around four, Vivien skillfully leveraged the slight, playing up a touch of malaise, just enough to warrant heading out of the office on the early side.

It was a few minutes after five when Vivien unlocked the door to her hotel room again, finding it bathed in clean ivory light. The navy dress hung in the closet, neatly pressed. The bed looked fluffy and layered and crisp, like a buttery biscuit. As she slid between the sheets—starkly white, almost radiant—the defense floated into her consciousness so softly it didn't even feel like a defense, merely a corrected misunderstanding. Every bride was entitled to a bachelorette party, a hall pass from premarital judgment and consequence. Hers had gotten a little out of hand, yes, but that was all part of the tradition—an indicator, even, of success. Vivien thought of Alfred Molina in *Chocolat*, waking up to the horror of his Lenten gluttony, but forgiven, a better man for tasting the forbidden fruit, even if he'd overindulged. If there was a moral lesson here, surely it was that she'd denied herself too strictly.

There was a mental tug, a dwindling twinkle of conscience. But it was an insecure, hard-earned, upper-middle-class Protestant-work-ethic-type conscience, no match for the competing will to protect her sense of her cultural refinement and social importance. It was easily ignorable against the buzz of a phone, its reflective glow.

Vivien was so glad that Dale had called—she disagreed vehemently with his logistical instructions to the photographer. And surely this was the most important part of the wedding, right? There was such an inherent validity to photographs.

## XIII.

Diana would not have minded so much if he'd answered an incoming call, but that he would proactively choose, however briefly, to excuse himself to phone his fiancée—well, she had either misread her influence entirely, or Dale McBride was a better-skilled adversary than Diana had originally thought.

There were some consulting projects that became a part of your life and others that caused a fissure, where Diana felt like a different person Monday through Thursday than she did over the weekend. She could already tell which type Mercury would be. The bonds of tribal unity had started to envelop the team; she could sense everyone's one-on-one interactions building a familial network and feel the burgeoning halo of collective bond and group identity around it. There is a special closeness born from relationships of short duration but high intensity, a way they tend to overcome barriers and escalate rapidly so that it's possible to live whole lives in the span of weeks. Such projects, microcosmic and insular, felt like high-stakes summer camp or some über-bougie adaptation of *The Real World. This is the story of seven strangers, picked to advise corporate executives and get drunk on expense accounts. Parker. Eric. Raj. Megan. Rich. Diana. Dale.* On such projects, you almost always got to find out what happened when people stopped being polite and started getting real.

And so it was unsurprising that Diana would feel a betrayal in Dale's elective absence on Wednesday evening. He was breaking an inchoate normative code, voluntarily violating the freshly circumscribed sphere of MercuryTime. Outside life was to be dealt with, certainly, if outside life came to you. But seeking it out was another matter entirely. Diana would have felt the same twinge of self-righteous disappointment if it had been Eric or Megan. She would have, wouldn't she? Particularly at this moment, during a celebratory dinner. Everyone was there save Parker, who had left for another client right after they presented the fraud competition approach to Prudence Hyman. It was decided that the teams from Merchantes and Settlmnt would be given a few weeks to prepare detailed pitches for a global MercuryCard fraud solution prior to an in-person exposé and multi-day workshop. The prize would be obvious if never explicitly stated: *leading the transition effort* was a pretty transparent euphemism for saving your job from offshore arbitrage.

Prudence Hyman had gone for the idea immediately. It allowed her to give concrete orders that had an air of excitement and potential; it was a unified directive that structurally protected the mothership from mutiny. Neither of the acquired companies could afford not to seize perhaps their only chance to truly remedy their employment situation as opposed to merely delaying the inevitable. And it preserved optionality for Hyman: she could choose—or delay in choosing—a winner on entirely her own terms. Dale had spent the remainder of the day delicately finagling logistics so the workshop would be separately bankrolled by Mercury on top of existing fees, include the entire Portmanteau team, and take place in Paris—*the clear, obvious, pragmatic choice* given that you had to cover a geographic spread from San Francisco to Saint Petersburg. They could work out of the Merchantes offices. The Pegaswipe engineers would walk in through the front door with everyone else—welcomed like a Trojan horse.

Diana had watched Dale attentively throughout this negotiation process and been amazed by the way he could make administrative issues disappear when he wanted something badly. Except for two, of course. That she had a husband, and that he had an almost-wife.

—Apologies for that, Dale said, returning to the table.

—When is the wedding? Megan asked politely, trying to smooth over the rift in conversation.

—Labor Day weekend.

Diana rolled her eyes mockingly, half-behind his back in that way expressly designed for the person you are mock-excluding. It was considered if not rude then at least presumptuous to schedule your wedding on a summer holiday weekend. Dale pointedly focused his attention on Megan, joking that the process had seemed strangely familiar to him—weddings being the personal version of corporate M&A: high-stress and expensive unions, both of them, with rabid stakeholders and limitless potential for dramatic conflict.

—Hope you've done your due diligence this time, Dale, said Raj with a friendly elbow to his ribs.

—Indeed, Diana said, curling her lips. Because, trust me, postmerger integration is the hardest part.

She blinked, and Dale blinked back, like twin basilisks lying in wait, circling, studying each other, watching at all times, even when they didn't appear to be looking, as if through transparent, panoptical lids and eyes.

—Hence the honeymoon in Paris, said Dale.

—I, like, still can*not* believe we're going to Paris! said Megan, wide-eyed.

Even Eric knew that Paris was an uncommonly desirable consulting destination—that you were far more likely to end up in Atlanta or Dayton, Ohio, or . . . Philadelphia—but Megan was looking at Diana to validate her exclamation anyway. Megan was already submerged in that envy-neutralizing heterosexual-female-to-heterosexual-female sorority pull, a loyal attraction born out of esteem and resulting in the desire for association and proximity, as if some of Diana's personal magic might rub off on her.

—Oh, I know, Diana cooed. They say that when good Americans die, they go to Paris.

—What about bad Americans? asked Eric.

—I believe the joke is they go to America, said Dale.

—Since we're already there, Raj cut in, let's make the most of it. Who wants to go out?

—*Club goin' up on a Tuesday*, said Rich.

Dale shook his head.

—Sorry, but there comes a time in life when you no longer want to go anywhere involving a velvet rope.

—I think this is it for me, too, Diana followed swiftly, raising her glass. Go on ahead, have fun—I'll take care of the check.

Diana gave the waiter her corporate card and topped up on Maximum Strength Visine. Once the rest of the team had gone, she turned to Dale with renewed confidence and energy.

—In the absence of any velvet ropes, would you want to get another drink?

—I thought that was understood, he said.

His boldness surprised her, and she noticed him flush briefly at his own confidence. They strolled south a couple of blocks to a nondescript bar Dale knew. He hoped she would not be offended by the averageness of the place. There was an inverse relationship between the necessity of interesting places and interesting people, Dale explained. If you had to have a drink with your mother-in-law or something, an interesting place was essential. However, with the best kinds of company, the key was to minimize distraction. The ideal bar for ideal company was just full enough that you'd never notice it seeming empty. It had unmemorable drinks and still less memorable music. The background stayed in the background; it faded away around the person you were with. He wanted to be able to hear Diana speak. She ordered an IPA and looked unconvinced.

—Why did you fight so hard for the workshop to be in Paris, then? Because you know you'll be bored with us all in a month and in dire need of spectacular scenery?

—No, of course not. I'm hideously cultured and want to show off my French.

—You're hideously something, but I don't buy it. Background interest acts more like an accelerant to foreground interest, I think. Compelling music makes average moments seem special and special ones extraordinary. Can you really imagine a sound designer saying, "No, cut the Simon and Garfunkel—there's enough interesting stuff going on here already"? I mean, maybe you can. Maybe Simon and Garfunkel aren't *cultured* enough for you. But what about, like, something highbrow? Like that really famous opera guy?

—There's more than one.

—You know the one I mean.

—Pavarotti?

—Thank you.

—I think if you were only watching your life, you'd probably be right. But you also want to live it, don't you?

—All right, answer me this, then—think about the most interesting person you know. Your fiancée, right? Otherwise I assume you wouldn't be marrying her. Do you seek out boring places with her so she can more fully consume your foreground focus?

Diana cocked her head defiantly. It was a limit-testing sort of question. Dale had to either admit argumentative defeat or declare his fiancée on some level inferior to present company.

—No, but she's a different sort of person than we are.

A tacit declaration, Diana thought, but a declaration nonetheless. There was a whisper of restraint on Dale's face. Diana recognized this genre of discourse. There was a very specific socially acceptable way to criticize one's spouse, one that revealed your partner's genuine shortcomings, but under a flattering unidirectional light source. The effect amounted more or less to a relationship-based humblebrag. Diana itched to trounce it, but instead decided to play. Attractively bad-mouthing your spouse was a marvelous cover for heavy flirtation, and mannered honesty was Diana's A-game.

—What, *exactly*, does that mean, Dale? she said with faux-aristocratic elocution, knowing full well what he meant. What *sort of person* is she? What *sort of person* are *we*?

—In many ways Vivien's greatest depths are rooted in material things. She's an art historian, grew up in a wealthy family—what she sees in objects, the way she reacts to backgrounds—that's part of her foreground interest. This is going to sound kind of douchey, and you're probably going to eviscerate me for it, but you—me? I think we're fundamentally more interested in ideas than things.

Diana said nothing, motionless save another ophidian blink.

—This isn't to say she's not smart, of course, he continued. Vivien's a curator, an academic doctor—she's exceptionally bright. But her professional love of fine objects bleeds seamlessly into the personal acquisition of five-hundred-dollar shoes. Growing up, I thought a fifty-dollar pair of shoes was expensive, so at first this blew my mind a bit. There's definitely a superficial streak to it—to the well-curated life.

Talking about money had become so taboo that flatly doing so exhibited its own kind of nonchalance, a rebel disrespect for convention that Diana enjoyed and admired. She smiled wryly and nodded in the direction of the floor.

—Aren't those loafers Gucci?

—Hah! Yes, but they were a gift from Vivien.

It was a slick move, twisting hypocrisy into a case in point, and Diana felt the need to one-up him.

—When I met Wes, it wasn't so much the five-hundred-dollar shoes that shocked me; those I knew were out there. It was the five-thousand-dollar shoes, and the ten-thousand-dollar bathrobe. I'm not exaggerating—Wes's mother owns a ten-thousand-dollar bathrobe. It's from Loro Piana and made of vicuña, which, I have since learned, is some rarefied South American mega-soft camel species that can only be shorn every three years. I mean, I'd known about diamonds and rubies, minks and cashmeres, but these were luxuries in the context of special occasions, even for the wealthy—or so I thought—things you'd bring out for a black-tie gala, a state dinner maybe, or a society wedding. But a ten-thousand-dollar bathrobe suggests an exponential nature to banalities. Once you can conceptualize that there's a ten-thousand-dollar bathrobe, that such a thing can possibly exist, you just *know* that somewhere out there, there is a hundred-thousand-dollar bathrobe, a million-dollar one even.

—Thanks to my future wife, I've had dinner with enough experts in sixteenth-century Chinese textiles to know that million-dollar bathrobes do, in fact, exist.

—None of this bothered me initially—just the opposite, if I'm being honest. I mean, I was sort of awed by it all, you know?

It was another confession formed less for its specific content than the desire to illustrate an unusually incisive capacity for confession—and implicitly, to beg its reciprocation.

—She doesn't have one, but Vivien would definitely want a ten-thousand-dollar vicuña bathrobe, Dale said with gratifying bluntness. It's on her radar, I'm sure. If you met her—well—I'm afraid you might find her a bit of a . . . a bit of a basic bitch.

—Oh—no. She sounds like a pretty advanced bitch to me.

Dale laughed.

—Come on—you know what I mean. Don't act like you don't. Over-educated, expensively dressed, no body fat, "natural"-looking in the way that requires a lot of upkeep. Important job, fulfilling marriage—near-marriage anyway—and still manages to get to SoulCycle or barre every day. I'll bet your house looks like a Restoration Hardware catalogue—sophisticated palette, quixotic elephant sculptures and shit. I'll bet it's always clean. And when you get married she'll bear you like four children and run them like a little corporation and still manage to do all the things she did beforehand without ever looking haggard or stressed or anything. I don't mean for any of this to sound critical, let alone cruel. If it does, that's only because I'm jealous of her. I'm jealous of all of them. I've been conditioned to want all of those things too, and even as I disdain them, I want them. I do.

—Alas, the litany of advanced bitch accomplishments is hard-fought, Dale admitted. Quixotic elephant sculptures are the subject of terrific anxiety in my household, I assure you.

Diana narrowed her eyes, trying to calm her craving for Maximum Strength Visine.

—It doesn't always *seem* hard-fought, though, not from the outside. When I first met Wes, this was the intoxicating thing about him, much more so than the presence of quixotic elephants.

—Accomplishing difficult feats with ease and all that?

—Sort of, though you don't make it to the Olympics without at least some willingness to expose your efforts. It was more as if, to go back to our original argument, his foreground self was enhanced by an ultra-deluxe background, yet also somehow unencumbered by it. I wanted him because of this, but I also wanted to *be* him. Sorry, that probably sounds super-creepy.

She thought about telling the story of Wes's father here, the irony of how well it had all played out for him, but decided against it. At face value it was the ultimate pathos-generating narrative, and she wanted Dale to save up all of his sympathy. Besides, she already had his undivided attention. Dale wasn't looking at her so much as staring, studying her almost, as if trying to relearn the rules to a game he loved but hadn't played in a while. Diana tilted her head at what she imagined would be a particularly obliging angle, rolling her shoulders so that her collarbones popped. They sat in silence for a few deliciously awkward seconds before he invited her to continue.

—What I'm trying to say is, Wes just had this *thing* about him—the not-actually-a-thing thing that people always seem to think they're going to achieve by buying certain shit and doing certain things, but never seem to be able to. You know—you know the special effect some people give off that seems materially imitable, but just isn't? He had that. Do you know what I mean?

The manner in which Diana said this rather emphasized the unsaid: the tacit implication that Dale was also one of those instantly intoxicating people—and, perhaps more importantly, so was she.

—I think the term you're looking for is *self-actualization*, he offered.

—Sure, fine, whatever you want to call it—self-actualization, self-assurance, ease, nonchalance, *thing*—the point is, I wanted it too. Violently. For a while, even though I was working very hard and miserable and exhausted from all the SoulCycling, I could sense that people were under the impression that I'd actually achieved it, like they thought *I* lived in a magazine or something. Our wedding, certainly, would have yielded this impression—although by now you must realize what a ruse that particular illusion to be.

—But illusion or not, you have to know you *still* give off that impression—of quirky feminine perfection and whatnot. Stop fishing for compliments, Diana, it's unseemly.

—I swear I'm not fishing—

She was, though, and Diana paused, feeling preemptive embarrassment for what she was about to say in proof of her innocence to this accusation. At this moment more than at any other point leading up to it, she wanted to seem raw and uncut and real, to lay bare her feelings with such forthrightness that the stunning bravery of unmitigated personal exposure would overshadow any question in his mind. She needed to paint marriage a more dismal landscape than she actually felt it to be, and was fully prepared to self-humiliate in order to achieve her desired effect.

—Something fundamental changed for me. I'm not sure whether it happened before or after the wedding, it was such a sneaky slip—at some point, I realized that our self-actualized selves, that special *thing* everyone else now saw in both of us—not only had I never had it, not really—I no longer saw it in Wes, either. He was encumbered with something now. He was encumbered, I think, with me. I feel like you must know what I mean.

—Yes, of course I do, because you're describing any long-term relationship. There's always an inflection point, a point where you slip into that intimacy-killing sort of intimacy. Achieving the insatiable closeness you initially crave inevitably satiates the craving. You said it yourself tonight—*postmerger integration is the hardest part.* If you want to stay with one person, you have to find a way to live on the memory of it; to be able to occasionally rechannel and bring it back. Because honestly, think about it: there's an appeal to stability, too. It's nice knowing you have someone to go to weddings with, someone who already knows all your foibles and friends. Can you imagine what your life would actually be like—how shaky and chaotic—if you were always passionately in love?

—What is so wrong with wanting that? Diana exclaimed, almost yelling. Call me naive, but that's what I want. Why wouldn't you want every moment to be movie-caliber? Or better yet, like the preview? I want my life to be packed with that kind of incessant intensity—which, by the way, I am aware is fully incompatible with the patient dedication it takes to achieve advanced bitchdom. But just because I know these things are illusory and impossible doesn't stop me from wanting them. This realization—this is what has been my recent undoing. I had an experience that extinguished the sliver of hope embedded in my illusions, the great illusion of illusion itself: that somewhere in there, some small part of it has to be real.

At this moment Diana's phone, which was sitting on the bar faceup, started to ring. The name Wes was clearly visible for Dale to see. Diana looked down at the phone, then up at Dale, deliberately. Yes, her speech had had the intended effect. She held his gaze as, with the tiniest flick of her eyebrow—so small as to be almost imperceptible—she silenced her phone. It was a haughty sort of showmanship, but she made sure not to overdo it, turning her attention swiftly thereafter to the inside of her bag. She had not yet forgiven Dale for his pragmatic approach to passion. It felt like the defense of something she didn't want him to want to defend. And yet, the way he had defied her wishes somehow made her respect him in a way that harkened to an even deeper kinship. The first bottle of Maximum Strength Visine she tried was empty, and she fished around for a second. He ordered another round as the tetrahydrozoline hydrochloride flooded her eyes.

—What? I have allergies, she said.

—Nothing—nothing at all. Go on; tell me about your recent experience, please.

—On my last project, someone googled me and found our wedding announcement from the *New York Times*.

Dale had been mid-sip as she said this, and promptly aspirated on his Stella Artois.

—Are you okay?

He nodded and waved her off.

—The team couldn't get enough of it; there was even a dramatic reading at dinner one evening. Are you sure you're okay?

—Yes, yes—okay, he managed to say.

—It had been ages since I'd thought about the article, and it'd reclaimed the ability to surprise me—you know, like a movie you haven't seen since you were a little kid. There it was, the most public, permanent record of my life, saying everything I could ever want it to say—and I didn't recognize myself in it. All the facts about us, the story of how we met—it was all technically true, of course, but it wasn't *the truth*, if you know what I mean. The part at the end, especially. They make it sound like we missed this big social function because Wes was super-interested in an algorithm I built. What actually happened is he was so late coming to pick me up it didn't seem worth the effort to go, and we decided to stay in. He played with the algorithm for most of the night, yes, but on and off, and not with some blazing enchantment. It wasn't until months later that he connected it to a few other ideas he'd been working on with Julian in the ideation phase of Ecco. You see? The unvarnished reality was messy and inelegant. But the way the *Times* tells it, spinning the story into a eureka moment—it makes our whole relationship, our whole lives, even, like glow in the dark or something. Like we're these lovable geniuses. All of the plodding, interim work that built Ecco—hell, that built our relationship—that gets totally lost. The facts are presented in such a way as to render their collective narrative fictitious.

—But that's precisely why everyone loves those things, Diana! The *New York Times* Style section is just analog Instagram. It's a vehicle built explicitly for the exposition of your best self.

—I know you're right, but I'm telling you, this went beyond a filter. It didn't even seem like me in there. Like, I was *actively jealous* of the girl in the article—jealous of myself! The girl in the article seemed like the luckiest fucking human being in the entire fucking world. Now she had that *thing*. I'm telling you, aspiring to my fictional self and empirically knowing that she wasn't and could never be real—it was mind bending and ego shattering and dehumanizing and *bleak*. You don't realize how important that sliver of hope is until you've lost it, I think.

—Perhaps not, he said, blushing . . . but it does explain why you've colored your hair.

Diana burst into a rich guffaw. *It was the only possible thing for him to say.* She would have been disappointed if he'd overindulged her melodrama, but she would have been likewise so if he'd lacked interest in it. Dale had read the damn article. He was interested, all right. She grinned at him with her entire body.

—Yes. Guilty.

—Pretty cliché response to such a profound revelation, I'd say, he gently teased.

—Oh, don't worry, that's just one part of my recent experiment. I've also fired our housekeeper and removed the Instagram app from my phone. I've been letting go of little things I love but are bad for me.

I've been seeing how it feels, how I handle it. It's my natural approach to decision-making, I guess.

Diana trailed off, biting her lip and blinking, the background fading behind him.

—What are you trying to decide?

—Isn't it obvious? Whether or not to leave Wes.

Her words hung in the air as if suspended in front of her face between them, waiting to see whether Dale would breathe them in or blow them away.

## XIV.

It was the Friday before Memorial Day. Wes was supposed to have met Diana at noon, and it was nearly half-past. He could see her waiting for him in front of their building, head back, laying into the Visine. *She uses way too much of that shit*, he thought with a shiver, bracing himself to face the whites of her eyes as he crossed the street.

She'd returned from Philadelphia the previous evening in such an icy mood that the little mechanisms Wes had built to solve for the problem of Vivien Floris froze on the spot.

He'd started erecting them even in the wee hours of Tuesday morning, when Wes had had the good subconscious sense to make his way home. Waking up alone in his own bed did nothing for his hangover, but it significantly expanded the options for self-deception. There was no disputing the *who*, the *what*, the *where*—these images were too vivid, and hardly outside Wes's moral boundaries in and of themselves. It all boiled down to a problem of *when*. Change the date and the whole affair was not only aboveboard, it was a memory to revel in. A *distant* memory. He'd had too much to drink at dinner, come home, and dreamed of another night—a real night, yes, but one years in the past. This version of the events had much to recommend it. He'd had sex with Vivien, but it wasn't adultery. How could it have been? When it had happened, Wes hadn't even been an adult.

He'd repeated this story to himself over and over in the days that followed, but it couldn't hold up to the reality of Diana's presence. As is so often the case with truth, it wasn't dead but merely hibernating. The shames of his crime hung upside down in his mind, like sleeping bats, and every word and action that passed between Wes and his wife shot through him the terror they'd awaken.

—Hi, he said, gingerly, navigating the curb with a cautious step, rubbing the back of his neck with his hand.

—You're late, Diana snapped.

Almost all of Wes and Diana's arguments followed a similar arc, with every new row like the outermost shell for a growing matryoshka doll of past disagreements. Even on the Friday before a holiday weekend, when the Uber surge was unreasonable, the traffic flow to JFK ossifying, and both Wes and Diana in frantic need of lunch, her objections to him running behind, he knew, would have little to do with whether they made their flight. The specific transgression would become an exemplar of some systemic issue like "spending too much time at work," which they'd argue about in escalating cycles until one of them objected to the other's "tone." The natural response here was that there was no "tone," or, if there really obviously was a "tone," that this "tone" was merely in proportionate reaction to the tone accuser's "tone." It was generally during the "tone" debate—usually five, maybe six argumentative layers deep—that the instability of their dispute began to manifest, and either Wes or Diana would didactically instruct the other to "calm down," a request that was received, invariably, as the single most inflammatory and uncalming thing it was possible to say. Any remaining pretense to debate would devolve into irresolvable bickering over whether the accused party was or was not in fact calm, who was calmer, &c., and ultimately deteriorate into the ever-infuriating were-they-or-were-they-not-presently-capable-of-having-an-argument argument about—*what was the original argument about?*

Wes was keen to avoid this series of events, and managed not to respond. He disliked squabbling with Diana in front of third parties in the best of circumstances, and their Uber driver, Raoul M., was pulling up now.

Raoul M. had an adolescently sparse mustache and the nonleather interior of his Toyota Highlander harbored the lingering plasticized-gluten smell of a Subway sandwich. Wes was abashed, thinking this way about poor Raoul M., but consoled himself that developing an unflattering mental portrait of him at least recognized his humanity. Many of his friends treated their Uber drivers like the central processing units of autonomous vehicles, he told himself. And to be fair to his friends, eventually they probably would be—autonomous vehicles, that is. But not yet, not Raoul M. Wes wondered whether Raoul M. ever used Uber on his days off. Something told him probably not. *Ultimately that's the problem with the sharing economy: not everyone gets to share in it.* Wes imagined himself delivering this line in a TED Talk, and tried out a few subtle variations. It was a gratifying image. There is nothing like abstract righteousness to distract from one's concrete personal failings.

Traffic was indeed bad, but Diana became engrossed in texting someone, and Wes was able to maintain a wary near-silence all the way to JFK. They breezed through PreCheck, and once it became clear there would be enough time to buy snacks, Diana defrosted a bit. By boarding time and down half a bag of Chex Mix, he would have classified her temper somewhere between impassive and resting-grouchy. Not his favorite Diana, but well within her normal emotive range. She was still young and pretty enough to be broadly forgiven by the world for both sour attitude and questionable diet.

As usual, the plane to Nantucket was one of those dated puddle jumpers with no real first class and two seats on either side of the aircraft. Wes and Diana generally had an unspoken understanding that on all forms of commercial and public transportation she took the interior seat and he the aisle. It was an arrangement that tended to work well for both of them, and made total physical sense, but to which Diana occasionally objected vehemently on spurious grounds of sexism, only to dramatically concede, deliberately reverse-engineering an example of her magnanimity for leverage in subsequent disputes. Wes was duly relieved when she shuffled toward the window unceremoniously and fell asleep before takeoff. As they soared away from the big city, he polished off the Chex Mix, glanced at the nutrition facts and immediately hated himself for it, queued up a podcast, and tried to ignore Diana. The way her mouth half-opened in sleep made this difficult. It was unattractive, and yet there was something endearingly defenseless about it, childlike almost. This impression didn't wholly dissipate when she woke a few minutes before landing. He watched her peer serenely out the window, transfixed on the island below, almost like she was empathizing with it.

Nantucket! Go on Google Maps and look at it. See what an incredible corner of the world it occupies; how it stands there, away off shore, basking in the benefit of a little distance. Look at it—a storied hillock, and keenly conserved elbow of sand; a manicured wild, the ultimate background. Now double click, switch to satellite, then Street View—yes, zoom in. See the cedar shingles, cobblestones, and brick. Mosey down the Straight Wharf and examine its boats, the houses on stilts. Visit the Whaling Museum and learn of its history, how Nantucketers conquered the watery world like so many Alexanders. Is it any wonder, then, that now so many Alexanders of our watery world seek to conquer Nantucket?

Wes's uncle Cort, his mother's younger brother, picked them up from the airport in his obligatory doorless Jeep, clapping Wes on the back and bear-hugging Diana—who suddenly radiated warmth and sunshine, as if she'd been saving up all her good humor specifically for him. Exaggerated kindness to others was one of Wes's least-favorite tactics in their marital war arsenal, mainly because Diana was better at it. Witnessing her charm someone else was far more punishing than universal gloom or petulance. There was something chastely perfidious about it—the relative demeanor differential, its wide expanse—like she was systematically excluding Wes from the essence of her winning Diana-ness he most wanted to singly trounce and possess. He watched Cort bask in her expressive, sly joviality, the things she did to please, that high-decibel laugh ripping into the wind. Little wisps of hair escaped her ponytail as she turned toward him or threw her head back in peals, like Cort was the most interesting man in the world.

Cort *was* interesting. A sea hermit of sorts, with a tinkering, handy sort of intellect, Cort, fifty-three, lived on the island year-round. Like Wes, Cort had rowed for Sill and then Princeton, but dropped out the summer following his freshman year, the summer after he moved into his parents' guesthouse in Polpis and fell violently in love—with fishing. It was like rowing minus all the yelling and other people and physical agony. It was like boating for pleasure, but with a purpose. There was something cyclical about it without being repetitive, a surprising sort of predictability. He loved the weather, the exposure to the elements, the misty predawn, the torrential sun glittering on the waves, the Crayola pastels, the gray cumulonimbus; he loved the speed, the salty wind, the way it smelled and tasted; he loved what he caught—that tasted even better—and the unbelievable self-sufficiency of it. He loved the solitude. He loved being so profoundly alone and yet amorphously, indelibly connected. Cort had found himself in the darkened seas. It was the image of the ungraspable phantom of life; and this was the key to it all.

Wes's grandparents were not, strictly speaking, *pleased* about the whole not-returning-to-college situation, but they didn't panic either, figuring a winter in Nantucket would shatter some illusions and Cort could return the following year. When he phoned them shortly before Memorial Day in 1982, saying he had news he wanted to deliver in person, this indeed was the news they expected to hear. He'd made a reservation for them all at a new restaurant in town called Tashtego's. It was not until his mother declared her scallops *divine* that Cort revealed he'd borrowed against his trust fund to buy the restaurant. In the ensuing years it flourished, and he bought two others, becoming the preeminent restaurateur on the island. If you saw "Cort's Catch" on the menu at any of his establishments, it meant he'd had a good morning on the water. Cort had never married. In what was probably the only circumstance under which it was cool to be in your middle fifties and living with your parents, he still occupied the guesthouse.

The Jeep circled up to the estate and Cort went to go fix drinks, giving Wes and Diana plenty of time to unpack—but when she fleetingly dropped her bag and returned to Cort, Wes followed suit. The sound of her mirth tinkling upstairs in his absence would have been worse, somehow, than its full thrust in the same room. Wes's mother, Agatha Young Range, put on her customary show of making everyone else wait twenty minutes for her appearance before entering like a reluctant sovereign, graciously prepared to receive tribute in spite of a feigned disregard for pomp. Her measured response to Diana's ovations, while warm and polite, felt faintly retributive, and Wes sensed a subtle shift on the terrace. Cort handed Wes a mint julep and took a seat to the right of Agatha.

Seeing Agatha and Cort together sometimes felt like an anthropological study, the way you could precisely follow and compare the forces of nature and nurture at work shaping them. You could almost see his shaggy-dog hair hiding under her expertly processed lob. Both had the same fine bone structure and cerulean eyes. Their joint tendency to carry a little extra weight conveyed similar commitments to pleasure with different environmental manifestations. Cort was heavyish-set in the hard, muscular way that often settles in the midsection and indicates gastronomic overindulgence tempered by plenty of physical activity. Combined with his dermal patina—a variegated, dark red-brown that had a damaged sort of youth to it—he was the picture of rustic gentility. By contrast, Agatha had aged in an indoor cat sort of way. There was a seared-fois-gras texture to her plumpness, the result of resolute inactivity on top of too much Fancy Feast. It was a deceptive softness, however, encasing a shrewd woman: observant and seriously minded for a socialite. Like Cort, in her cool self-possession Agatha exuded the glamour and cool of someone far more physically attractive. She had navigated her husband's demise with a grace and maturity that, counterintuitively, is rarely witnessed in full-blown adults. A little cellulite was not going to unravel her.

Plenty of people disliked Diana, often for her sheer likability, but Agatha was the only person Wes had found to be Diana-immune on arrival. *She's nice*—that was what his mother said after their first meeting, which was more or less her reaction to all the girls he introduced. Initially this had driven Wes bananas, frustrated by his own inability to explain Diana's singularity and the wild attraction he found so patently self-evident. He'd felt vindicated when, over time, Diana weaseled into Agatha's affections, winning her love, if not entirely her respect—but Wes had also come to appreciate the limits to this in-law kinship, that there was at least one person who he could confidently tell himself unequivocally preferred his company to his wife's. His mother smiled at him, as if to confirm this. Because on the whole Agatha smiled seldom, when she did, it had the feel of a benediction. A ship launched from his chest, down to the sunless sea. For the first time in hours he felt he could breathe, the salty wet air clinging to the inside of his lungs like life itself.

As his mother nestled deeper into her chair, listening to Diana tell a story—one Wes had heard before, but which, he had to admit, brimmed with hilarity—she gave him her secret nonverbal analysis: solid content, garish style. Cort's body, meanwhile, heaved in waves of laughter Wes found contagious in spite of himself. At the climax of her chronicle, Diana surprised Wes, grabbing his hand in the emphasis of some point, letting it linger there, turning her head toward him in the kind of tease that made him forget everything he didn't like about her. As her thumb pressed into his skin, a tender feeling collided with his latent shame and he thought that maybe he should tell her what happened, that she would understand. Yes, confession would absolve his sins. Wes inhaled, trying to make space, letting the affection wash over him, squeezing Diana's hand. She smiled at him, and it was easy to mistake his intention to tell her for the sense that she'd already forgiven him. Wes's mother told an anecdote from his childhood with an adoring look. Cort handed him another mint julep. The dam broke, and he overflowed with fondness for all of them.

And so Wes tentatively allowed himself to burrow into the familial routines of Nantucket—a Xanadu that, on weekends like this, when his grandparents weren't there, felt a great deal like home. Mornings on the boat with Cort, lunch by the pool, sunny spots of greenery blossoming with the last of the daffodils. The *Velvet Underground & Nico* album on infinite loop. A solid row on the erg machine. Outdoor showers, crisply warm. A Whale's Tale Pale Ale, maybe rounding into a nap. Drinks on the terrace and retold stories, Diana's walloping laugh echoing beneath the waxing moon. Some nights Cort would have one of his chefs stop by to cook up the daily catch; on others Cort would do it himself. Either way everything was fresh and simply prepared and paired well with the wine. Wes almost always slept brilliantly up here, with nothing but the blankets between Diana's snugness and the cold breeze of the outer air. Whatever vague guestly best-behavior-type discomfort Wes felt around his grandparents, he had to admire their taste in duvets.

Sunday morning, Diana joined them on the boat, bedecked in the sunwashed regalia of a true Nantucketer, hand-me-downs from Wes himself, found who knows where. The ratty polo dated back to Sill. Weather-wise, it was a textbook perfect day: warmly cool, clear sun, breezy. And yet there was something too bright about it, something raw and overexposed. The water reflected everything like a mirror, almost blindingly, as the spangling sun shifted like a living opal in the blue morning sea. Climbing aboard, Wes nearly fell off the gangplank.

—You better watch your step! Diana said, coming toward him.

Her presence there on his uncle's boat, wearing his own old clothes, so wholly submerged in his life—there was a graphic discomfort to it, a knottiness that, yes, recalled their legal union, but also another, far deeper bond; the true fusion of selves of which that societal transaction is symbolic but imperfectly correlated. He felt reason slipping away from him, seeing their division grow together. It almost felt like, looking at her, he was looking at his own reflection, not just at his wife or even his partner but an image utterly inseparable from himself—a phoenix of his own ashes, the heroine in his blood.

There was a sudden clarity and congruence to Wes's predicament. He understood, quite abruptly, why his friends always made such messes of their relationships. Perversely, it was because those relationships mattered to them, mattered deeply. It was easy to break up with girls who had been little more to him than pleasurable fashion accessories. It was easy to take them out, treat them with respect, and politely set them aside. Things got messy only when women were no longer interchangeable, when they were an inextricable part of oneself. Many (many) women were lovable on their best day. Only Diana was lovable to him on her worst, through endless circular arguments and maddening mind games. Wes and Diana were unhappy. They were both terribly unhappy together, he knew—but he could not even conceptualize her absence: it amounted to a sort of suicide. His infidelity was the twisted explosion not of cruelty or apathy but of an overdeveloped sort of love: a sick, needy adulation borne of his very inability to let her go. Wes loved Diana furiously, possessively, even though their marriage didn't really work.

The epiphany's shame reduced him to terror, his head bobbing and weaving with the swells as the boat made for open water. Oh, how he loved Diana! What had he done? Gone looking for something he wanted to seek but didn't actually want to find. And for what? The thrill of the chase? Some orgastic, receding green light? Wes wished it had eluded him. He had outrun his own self; he had dove in after an idol, and drowned for a mere mirage. For the first time he saw in Vivien a plain art, that primordial temptress of Woman the history of the world makes it so very hard to discredit. It was all deeply unsettling. But in this world, it is not so easy to settle these plain things. Plain things are the knottiest of all.

—Is something wrong, Wes? Diana called from across the deck, as if she could see his mind.

His stomach reeled with the boat. How could he have thought he could tell her? It had been a selfish impulse to want to unburden himself. What would hurting her accomplish? That night had been merely a symptom of the disease that was all the other days of their marriage. No, he was going to fix the presuppositions and resentments, the circular fights, those sticky, toxic communication patterns. He was going to clean up after himself and close the bathroom door. He was going to be a good husband, the charming person he'd been with Vivien. Putting in the daily work—that would be harder than confessing, he assured himself.

—It's nothing at all, he said.

There was a splash in the midground off to starboard. A mighty fountain forced itself up in a swift half-intermitted burst, followed by a threshing flail.

—Oh my god! Is that, like, a whale?

—Very like a whale, Cort admitted, grinning at her.

—Look, there's another! Or maybe it's the same one.

This time Diana had her phone ready, and succeeded in capturing its fanning tail.

—Here, get one of me, would you please? she asked Wes.

She handed him her phone and backed up against the railing. They were pretty far out now and cruising at a fair clip. It was getting choppy and he struggled to frame her properly on the screen.

—Too much boat and not enough ocean, she complained. Ugh, half of these are blurry.

Diana tried another pose, and then another. Normally Wes had a limited tolerance for playing photographer, but he obliged her every instruction and angle. Still dissatisfied, she tried moving closer to the stern, one leg out to sea, throwing her hands up in an off-kilter V, giving

Wes a whiplash girlchild wave, clowning around as if she'd won something. The boat hit a swell and lurched abruptly. There was a splash in the foreground off to starboard, then the shadow of a dome floating midway on the waves.

—Oh my god, Di—! Cort—*Cort*—stop the boat! Stop the boat *now*!

Diana's ego bore the largest brunt of her fall; they fished her out and counted only a couple of minor bruises. Cort was furious at first, but by the time they got home and were no longer wet and chilly, the episode was allowed to become one of those legitimately terrifying situations that is roaringly funny in retrospect. Wes had captured such a sensational shot of the fall, or the imminent pre-fall, rather, that it prompted Diana to redownload Instagram. She posted the picture captioned solely with the hashtag *#ACK*. Even for Diana, it got a shocking number of likes.

# XV.

Is it possible to be more than one person at the same time, to cast ourselves in multiple roles and to play them all well? When Diana reviewed the month between Nantucket and Paris in her mind, it possessed an undeniable montage quality, even as it lacked the technique's customary power of synthesis. It was, rather, like a montage of montages, as if a film student had spliced together several individually coherent mosaics from different movies entirely. Days at Olympia and nights of overindulgence oscillated between *Rudy*-esque determination and *Push It to the Limit* hedonism in the mold of *Scarface*—unless Dale was in the scene, at which point painfully abstinent *Hungry Eyes* yearning took over for *Dirty Dancing*: E-IM edition. On lighter workdays Diana would try to burn off her sexual energy in a run, literally ascending the Philadelphia Museum of Art steps like the great hero of montage himself. Intensity built on intensity in a shaky, indecisive kind of way. She was Rudy and Tony and Baby and Rocky.

The Tuesday following her return from Nantucket it occurred to Diana that perhaps Dale was slightly less good-looking than she'd appraised him the previous week, but also that she somehow liked him, this week, even better. In describing all the pleasures of her weekend to him, she realized there had been something missing in it, and was strangely glad to be back in Philadelphia. After work, without quite knowing why, she made a stop at Sephora.

• • •

At team dinner a week later, Dale gave an astonishingly accessible critical introduction to *Anna Karenina* for an audience who, with the exception of Raj, had never read the novel. Privately, Dale encouraged Diana to rectify this grave inadequacy in her literary education post-haste. When she made a show of downloading the Kindle edition on the spot, Dale beamed.

—Excellent; you can read it on the train, he said. Wait, wait a minute, did you get the right translation?

His smugness knew no end. He really was intolerably likable.

The next day produced a third consecutive Wednesday tête-à-tête at "their" backgroundless bar. Diana and Dale talked for hours, closing the place down, wandering around the city after that. She liked immensely being alone with him. There was an awkward, prolonged goodbye in front of the Sheraton this time. Finally Diana backed through the doors, achingly alone. It was well after 3:00 a.m., and it took almost another hour for her heart rate to slow to the point of sleep. When Diana woke the next morning, she was seeing double. Needless to say, this required an obscene quantity of Maximum Strength Visine.

On Monday, June 8, Dale and Diana went out for sushi together in Old City after happy hour, and opted for the sake tasting. When the little rows of ceramic glasses arrived, Dale swished the sake around in his mouth like a connoisseur, wearing a mask of faux pretension that did not entirely cover his genuine pretentiousness.

—*Well, my, my—Ms. Whalen, here we have a fine vintage, a very fine vintage indeed—hits the tongue with an imperial mélange of orange peel and cellophane balanced by an—*sniff—*Instagrammed coffee aroma. Notes of questionable decisions, old newspapers, and desiccated Sea-Monkeys. The aftertaste? A smooth oil, quite ready to lubricate some raw fish.*

Diana tittered and preened, very like a good date, before launching into a little mock review of her own. The backgroundless bar could not wait for Wednesday. They were drinking in unprecedented quantities, she realized, not out of any sort of social anxiety—being in each other's company was almost terrifyingly easy and natural—but as a pretext to spend time together in the first place. There was nothing improper about *grabbing drinks with a coworker*, even if it evolved into *grabbing a bite*. So long as alcohol was involved in a public place, Dale and Diana might safely be alone together.

The ensuing Wednesday, the team went to karaoke. Dale asked Diana to indulge him and sing something from *Evita*, but Diana had never heard of it and excused herself to the stage before he could rectify this deficiency. She had a voice that demanded to be seen, bopping around on the stage in her mod little shift. That she chose "It's the End of the World as We Know It"—truly the K2 of karaoke songs, second in height to Whitney Houston, but on certain technical metrics more challenging—put a definitive end to every side conversation. The entire bar started whooping and hollering, cheering her on. Dale only half-smiled, standing out in the crowd not for his enthusiasm, but his relative motionlessness, as she positively brought down the house.

This was the same week that Dale started referring to all sorts of things as being *Whalenesque*. She wondered if he might feel something more than self-satisfied intellectual lust for her, if maybe he had for a while. One has to apply a certain pressure, a certain force on another human being in order to cross the grammatical line from noun into adjective.

The team met with Prudence Hyman on Tuesday, June 16, to review their latest versions of the operating model and blueprint—the latter being the deck Diana had put together in the first week of the project and basically sat on since. (She was not entirely sure how Dale was functioning from, like, a physical, sleep-deprivation perspective; he actually had work to do most days, unlike Diana, whose primary job at the moment was merely to appear busy, passing any actual assignments on to the all-too-willing Eric Hashimoto.) PH's unequivocal approval of their interim deliverables meant dinner would be a blowout, followed by drinks at the team's now go-to establishment, a Center City lounge and taproom called Clock, where Diana regularly commandeered the jukebox. That night everyone—including Parker Remington—got sufficiently obliterated and took it to the dance floor. From a pelvic-gyration perspective, Diana was the least inappropriate member of the team that night, she assured herself. But when she went over to the jukebox to choose the next song, she dropped a quarter. Dale picked it up.

The coin twisted in his hand, then it became unclear whose hand it was in. It was impossible to say who was the instigator, who had crossed the line first and admitted, if only in the language of brushing thumbs and hungry eyes, that there were feelings on both sides far in excess of friendship. There was grasping and staring and clutching. "The World Is Yours," the universe whispered—for only twenty-five cents. Suggestive half-smiles morphed, in slow motion almost, into euphoric, toothy grins, then settled into rapt gravity. His every expression and emotion, she was sure, perfectly mirrored hers, the sea of activity around them buzzing in counterweight to their stillness. The entire exchange lasted maybe twenty-seven seconds. What were the best twenty-seven seconds of your life? When you took the field in blue and gold? When you blindly called out *Adriannnn*—and she called back? The answer should have been easy for Diana, and it should have had something to do with Wes. Their first kiss, maybe, or the one at the altar. When he'd proposed on the beach, or their racy pool-house rendezvous after. But in that particular twenty-seven seconds, it was as if all of her other once-vivid memories were drained of their color. None could match the searing passion of restraint.

Twenty-seven perfect seconds. The kind you replay in your head over and over. Isn't that what most of us live for, anyway? The reason we wake up and go to work or whatever it is we do, day after day; the reason we sit through the long, unedited scenes of our lives—all those endless meetings—inevitably destined for memorial montage? The anticipation of an unforgettable twenty-seven seconds in time—isn't this the reason that we try? Why we sign up again and again to get the shit kicked out of us, only to stand up again and ask for more? Whether it takes the form of a stadium screaming your name or the extrasensory silence of a single person, we all yearn for some connection to the universe, for some indication that the universe, too, is trying; that it wants to grasp us back, that it *wants* to fulfill our desires, even if it can't; even if our desires are doomed.

Diana was facing the jukebox, quite unsure of how she got there. Dale had gone to the bar for another round. Regaining self-possession, she searched for the right song. Yes, there it was—yes. Diana offered Dale an eyebrow in exchange for the beer, and pressed PLAY.

Dale and Diana had officially become adversaries in a game of chicken, barreling toward each other with vehicular fury. Both wanted, desperately, for the other to swerve, to have the distinct pleasure of being the one to do the rejecting, to be the responsible person and the unresponsible party, the champion of self-control, and even more importantly, the object of the other's weakness, so personally desirable as to incite the other into welcoming a miserable spiral of consequences while maintaining the moral and ethical high ground of resistance, avoiding any unpleasantness on his or her own home front. The challenge of orchestrating such an outcome—of extracting the world's greatest compliment from such a privileged, well-educated, self-involved adversary—was, naturally, irresistible.

And so when neither acknowledged the truth, their silvery banter remained a euphoric sort of drug, rapturous and addictive. When he was inappropriately bold or complimentary, she thrilled in brushing off his affections. When she started in on eyebrow-laden hypotheticals, he relished delivering disappointment, claiming the morally superior side to every debate. And, on the rare occasions when they both tangentially admitted attraction and guilt—however technically correct their behavior—they blamed each other bitterly, eager to prove the more uncooperative body. Thus their interactions hardened into a guerrilla war of wills over who would be the blameless image in the pool, and who would fall in.

*Why, really though*, Diana asked herself, was she so intent on resisting him? That she was physically able to stop herself—was this marker enough that she was not actually as enamored as she seemed to herself? That what she really loved was the deeply flattering attention he paid to her? *Perhaps.* Was the sense of duty she bore for Wes indicative of a superior, if latent, love? *Perhaps again.* It wouldn't be worth arguing with him absent the remnants of their former flame. Was her longing for Dale really, then, a longing for Wes, like some kind of referred pain? Or was that a cop-out, too—a way to justify sunk costs and choices? Dale and Diana were fundamentally, materially, philosophically compatible—not only theoretically, as lovers, but as people. Was it possible she loved Dale so sincerely, so selflessly, that even if she could stand to ruin her own life, she could not risk bearing the responsibility for ruining his? She recoiled at this provincial notion of infidelity as "ruinous" and the possibility it was some bourgeois moral squeamishness holding them back. The idea that middle-class sexual taboo had any power whatsoever to shape her decision-making contrasted sharply with Diana's image of herself—but this was precisely the image she'd crafted in Wes's reflection. How unfair, that the only moral exemption she sought was the one that threatened her social claim to moral exemption! It was too deeply unflattering to be the explanation in her predicament with Dale. And yet she could not help but think that things might have been different if only one of them had been in a serious relationship, that either of them in full pursuit would have toppled the other without even much difficulty. But as it stood, both wanted the other person to be *that* person, to have the clear choice and moral high ground and security of ending up with someone. To *preserve optionality*. The more successful her resistance, the more powerful her yearning for him became—and yet the more intensely she aspired to resist. Delayed gratification might be especially gratifying, but power is the ultimate aphrodisiac.

There was, also, the formerly isolated problem of Wes and that other montage of Diana's present life, the seminal black-and-white breakfast serial that so closely mirrored her weekends. *It was a marriage like any other marriage.* What Diana told Dale that first night in their no-background bar was overdramatized, yes, but fundamentally true: she had tentatively intended on leaving Wes that summer already. Nantucket had offered a jolt of marital concord and nostalgia and temporarily weakened her resolution, but by the following Thursday, Wes had reverted to his Wellesian performance of unreadable moods and last-minute cancellations and obsession with Ecco (*Really, Charles!*). After that, the problem had been finding a plausible weekend. She could not identify a slot that wouldn't spoil some prearranged plan that Diana herself was rather looking forward to: weddings, trips to Nantucket, Hamptons shares with friends. It turned out that divorce was an extremely inconvenient item on one's to-do list, and she kept putting it off, even as the fissure between her two lives developed into a chasm.

If Diana was being honest, there were other considerations about this chasm giving her pause, aside from the logistics: the perception of her looming decision weighed heavily on the dense little group of ideas that Diana had about herself. For Diana's internal calculation of her own image was less one of actual social rebellion than the impression of it, and the outward narrative implications of her prospective classification as a divorced person played no small role in her mind. There had been, in certain lights, a modern romance to it: to fierce, uncompromising independence; to the implicit confidence of exercising her power with remorselessness. She imagined stoically rising above conventional gossip, overhearing intelligent critics calling her "brave" and "interesting." This imprint was closely tied to the idea that, in renouncing a spouse such as Wes, she could only be destined for something greater.

And yet, when "something greater" had presented itself—as her longing for Dale deepened, and the inappropriate relationship underlying their appropriate behavior morphed into a kind of weekday marriage, it had strangely shifted this mental calculus. It no longer even mattered that, quite independently, Wes misread her every move, that every argument with him devolved into a grotesque marital retrospective avoidable only by icy silence. If Diana left him *now*, it would be impossible to divorce her decision from Dale's existential presence. Leaving your husband for irreconcilable differences was, perhaps, brave. Leaving him for another man? That was betrayal. Wes's ire would be perfectly justified. The Haemonic madness of the reasonable: persuasive, transcendent, coalition-building wrath. The kind that would all but force mutual friends to wholeheartedly take his side and render her a criminal ingrate; not just an asshole, but also a moron. She saw Agatha's disdain, Cort shaking his head in disappointment. *Ruinous.* Dale was a more suitable match for her, there was little doubt of that. But the world at large would not make the same assessment, and this extrinsic analysis played too great a role in Diana's evaluation of herself. If Dale would even have her, over his own fiancée! This note of failure, of self-doubt and uncertainty, combined with the self-preserving sense that it was rather glamorous to be acerbically dissatisfied with a husband such as Wes. The idea of playing this sort of dissatisfied wealthy wife character was perversely appealing in Diana's mind, encouraged by the likes of Cate Blanchett. Such women were always beautiful in their misery—self-conscious and critical with themselves for it, deeply glamorous even in (because of?) their vanity. No, she did not want to divorce Wes. She wanted the right of indignation. She wanted the chorus advocating on her behalf—and an unimpeachable marital severance package. In a desire so foreign to her she would have been personally unable to articulate it, what Diana really wanted was for *Wes* to divorce *her*.

And so Diana read the newspaper at breakfast in subconscious protest of his failure to capitulate, exceedingly miserable for someone in such assiduous avoidance of misery. Inaction is, after all, its own form of decision. People forget that.

On the train back to New York on the evening of Thursday, June 25, Diana continued reading *Anna Karenina* (McBride-approved Pevear and Volokhonsky translation). She had reached the part of the novel where Anna is likewise reading a novel on a train, but finds it unpleasant to read because she wants too much to live herself. The hero of Anna's novel was beginning to achieve his English happiness, a baronetcy and an estate, and Anna wants to go with him to this estate, when suddenly she feels that he must be ashamed and realizes she is ashamed of the same thing—and Diana could tell that she, too, was supposed to feel ashamed here. She had seen the preview of the Keira Knightly movie version two or three years ago, and could guess where all this was headed for Anna—to bed with that Vronsky fellow, for sure.

What a cheeky book recommendation! *You can read it on the train*, indeed. Diana could not decide what was more dangerous, Dale's physical presence or the very idea of him. But surely they were past the risk of an actual affair now, weren't they? An affair would never be enough, so there was no point in being an asshole in service of one. So, then, what was she ashamed of? *What am I ashamed of?* she asked herself in offended astonishment. She put down the book and leaned back in the seat, clutching her Kindle with both hands.

Diana sat there very quietly for several minutes until, in an unwelcome leftward whirr, a southbound train came roaring past.

# XVI.

## SELECT TELEPHONE ACTIVITY (TRANSCRIBED, CHRONOLOGICAL), OFFICE OF C. WESLEY RANGE IV, CEO, ECCO LLC (TIME WARNER CABLE, WIRELINE NUMBERS 212-XXX-XXXX, EXT. 2233 & 2234), FRIDAY, JUNE 26, 2015.

**[9:05 AM INCOMING CALL FROM: PAPPAS-FIDICIA, JULIAN (INTERNAL EXTENSION 2235), 3 minutes]**

RANGE: --ot it, Cassie. Hello, Julian.

PAPPAS-FIDICIA: Oh, shit, why did you answer?

RANGE: This may shock you, but . . . because you called me?

PAPPAS-FIDICIA: Well, this is awkward. You've entirely thwarted my prank call.

RANGE: By all means, please proceed. Far be it from me to ruin your fun at my expense.

PAPPAS-FIDICIA: Too late, you've already ruined it.

RANGE: Have it your way, that foiled look on your face is satisfying enough. You look like some maniacal cartoon villain.

PAPPAS-FIDICIA: Goddamn it! I hate these fucking glass offices. They make me never want to see you again. What are you doing this weekend?

RANGE: Stuck in the city for some horrible wedding. One of Diana's friends. I'm not going to know anyone. And Diana's a bridesmaid, so I'm sure to be promptly abandoned.

PAPPAS-FIDICIA: Just download an e-book to your phone. Have you read *Brideshead Revisited* yet? Actually, don't tell me. You've already ignored that particular recommendation an embarrassing number of times, so I don't want to know. Where is the wedding? Not in Brooklyn or anything, I hope.

RANGE: Actually yes. The Brooklyn Botanical Garden, I think.

PAPPAS-FIDICIA: Oh, no! Not *that* den of iniquity! Well prepare yourself: it is sure to involve multiple fire hazards and unsatisfying food. This is assuming massaged baby kale and vegan cake count as food at all. Take care to avoid any sort of "signature cocktail." It's like they are programmed to give you the runs. Come to think of it, I would stay away from anything served in a mason jar. Don't go near the sparklers either. Some drunk person angling for a photo is liable to whack you with one. And be careful getting home! I'm exceedingly wary of Prospect Park. Its primary prospect, as far as I'm concerned, is murder in the first degree.

RANGE: You're being ridiculous. It's no more dangerous than Central Park is.

PAPPAS-FIDICIA: I'm not advocating a wedding in Central Park, either. Taking a few photos there would be okay, I guess. But what exactly is wrong with the Yale Club?

RANGE: Why are you so prejudiced against Brooklyn?

PAPPAS-FIDICIA: Oh, I've got all kinds of prejudices, don't worry. Is there some Bed-Stuy brunch on Sunday featuring a band you've never heard of and bottomless kombucha? Or do you and Diana want to go to Café Croix with me?

RANGE: We should be good for Sunday.

PAPPAS-FIDICIA: I'll confirm with your wife--

RANGE: That's very kind of you.

PAPPAS-FIDICIA: --for her sake, I want to be clear.

RANGE: Yeah, yeah, yeah.

PAPPAS-FIDICIA: Okay, well ta-ta.

RANGE: Later.

**[9:07 AM INCOMING CALL FROM: PAPPAS-FIDICIA, JULIAN (INTERNAL EXTENSION 2235), 2 minutes]**

RANGE: Yes?

PAPPAS-FIDICIA: Don't you want to know what *I'm* doing this weekend?

RANGE: Not especially.

PAPPAS-FIDICIA: Dick. Just for that, you're getting the detailed version. I have a lengthy personal to-do list. First priority is Taco Bell. I have been dreaming of a Cheesy Gordita Crunch all week. Also, I am going to Paul Stuart. I need to buy white flannel pants. Actually, I haven't decided between flannel and gabardine, but the point is, I want a nice drape. Anuj Chadha, by the way, is having a dinner party tomorrow night that you weren't invited to; sorry, I bet you didn't know that. I'm looking forward to it: his wife is an excellent cook. Ooh, and I hope their son is still up so I can read advanced books to him--

RANGE: So the Chadha baby's a boy! Thanks, I've actually been meaning to ask you that. I could never tell from his Instagram.

PAPPAS-FIDICIA: Ugh, you're so racist!

RANGE: What? No I'm not! What are you talking about?

PAPPAS-FIDICIA: That reminds me, I tore a pocket in my blue blazer. I'll have to get the Koreans to stitch it up.

RANGE: Oh my god. What you have to do is stop saying things like that.

PAPPAS-FIDICIA: Why? I have strong racial preferences when it comes to dry cleaners.

RANGE: Jesus, Julian. You don't even mean that. You never mean anything you say

PAPPAS-FIDICIA: Excuse me, but Mr. and Mrs. Kim are extremely professional and I've come to rely on their sage counsel in matters of sartorial repair.

RANGE: Only you would render a compliment that offensive.

PAPPAS-FIDICIA: And only you would predicate your compliments on how they reflect upon you.

RANGE: That would sting more if you didn't look so pleased with yourself for saying it.

PAPPAS-FIDICIA: Goddamn it! Cassie? Can you order me blinds?

**[4:32 PM INCOMING CALL FROM: PAPPAS-FIDICIA, JULIAN (INTERNAL EXTENSION 2235), 1 minute]**

RANGE: Yes?

PAPPAS-FIDICIA: I want to fire Joel Francis.

RANGE: No. We need more programmers, not fewer. Did you like that guy Sara interviewed this afternoon?

PAPPAS-FIDICIA: How can you even ask that? He was wearing a green shirt with a green tie for a job interview. He didn't even bother to shave.

RANGE: So?

PAPPAS-FIDICIA: So he looked like a Macy's elf at an off-season audition for *Duck Dynasty*! I swear, it's like your eyes otherwise cease to function when Sara Khan is ar--

RANGE: Shit, Julian, I have to g--

**[4:33 PM INCOMING CALL FROM: HOWARD, JACK (WIRELESS NUMBER 215-XXX-XXXX), 6 minutes]**

ECCO ADMIN: Wes Range's office, this is Cassie, how may I help you?

HOWARD: Hi, Cassie, this is Jack Howard. I'm the CEO of Mercury Incorporated. I'm hoping to have a quick chat with Wes if he's around.

*{Background rustling.}*

ECCO ADMIN: Um, yes, Mr. Howard, absolutely, let me transfer you. One moment, please.

*{Pause for transfer.}*

RANGE: Wes Range.

HOWARD: Wes, this is Jack Howard from Mercury. How are you? I hope you're not working too hard on this Friday afternoon.

RANGE: Hey, Jack, good to talk to you. I'm fine, thanks. Just wrapping up a few things before the weekend. How about you?

HOWARD: My wife and I are headed to our place in Cape May for the weekend, and I'm determined to get in a round at Wildwood.

RANGE: Oh, very nice! Such a great course. How's the weather looking?

HOWARD: You've played it?

RANGE: I've been very fortunate.

HOWARD: Sounds like you've also been making some pretty exciting things happen for yourself. I read that piece in *Forbes* last week. Ecco's all over my Twitter feed. Congrats.

RANGE: Ah, thanks. Things are going pretty well. We have a great team.

HOWARD: Your modesty does you credit, Wes, but I'm more interested in your ambition. We have a lot of big goals at Mercury right now. I want us to become a technology-first company, one that just happens to operate in the payments space rather than the other way around. We've bought a few mid-sized processors recently--perhaps you've seen this in the *Journal*. In the middle of integrating them now. You probably know where I'm going here. Every technical integration has a few hiccups.

RANGE: Well, Fortune 500 hiccups are our specialty. But, I have to tell you, Jack, the CEO isn't usually the person calling me personally to retain our services.

HOWARD: No, I would imagine not. And I am already up to my eyeballs in consultants, believe me. You're perfectly right, I called with a bigger question in mind. Do you have a clear picture of what you want to do with your company?

RANGE: Right now it's all about controlled growth and keeping our options open--

HOWARD: Mhm.

RANGE: --but things are moving quickly. Things can change. Sometimes a good decision is worth more than preserving optionality.

HOWARD: Ah ha, thank you for saying that. Do you know--I met with my CIO this morning, and she used the exact same phrase? *Preserving optionality.* I must have skipped the wrong article in *HBR* last month. Anyway, I'll cut to the chase: have you given any thought specifically to selling? Is that one of the options on ioo for you?

RANGE: Sure, I've thought about it. It would have to be the right fit, you know, the right deal.

HOWARD: Sure. But it is something you're open to exploring, as a possibility?

RANGE: Yes, definitely, yes.

HOWARD: Okay, well, that's great news in my book. Listen, I'm in Europe next week, but I'll be coming to Now York tho following Thursday--Thursday, July 9, I believe. We're one of the sponsors for a big event at the Met. Most of our executive team should be there. It would be great if you could join us too. It'll be a nice time. Bring your wife.

RANGE: Ironically, my wife will be in Philadelphia--but I'd be delighted.

HOWARD: Okay--well, bring your number two, then. Maybe that's even better. We can all get to know each other. See if it's "the right fit." We can test the waters.

RANGE: Sounds great, Jack.

HOWARD: I'll have my assistant call Cassie with the details, if that works for you.

RANGE: It does. Looking forward to it.

HOWARD: Likewise. Enjoy the weekend. Bye, now.

RANGE: Bye, Jack.

**[4:40 PM OUTGOING CALL TO: PAPPAS-FIDICIA, JULIAN (INTERNAL EXTENSION 2235), 1 minute]**

PAPPAS-FIDICIA: Hello, asshole.

RANGE: Julian!

PAPPAS-FIDICIA: What?

RANGE: I fucking love you! Come to my office.

*{Laughter. Music playing in background.}*

PAPPAS-FIDICIA: What is going on over there?

*{Singing.}*

RANGE: *--you're the one--I want--to--want me--*

PAPPAS-FIDICIA: I am severely concern--

RANGE: Get over here!

PAPPAS-FIDICIA: Fine, but I'm bringing a straitjacket.

**[6:53 PM INCOMING CALL FROM: WHALEN, DIANA (WIRELESS NUMBER 917-XXX-XXXX), 1 minute]**

RANGE: Hi.

WHALEN: You're still at the office?

RANGE: Yeah.

WHALEN: Seriously? The rehearsal dinner starts at seven fifteen.

RANGE: Oh--shit. Okay, okay--I'm leaving. I'll see you there.

WHALEN: Fine, whatever.

RANGE: What? I said I'll see you there. I'll be there.

WHALEN: And I said fine!

RANGE: Yeah, but you're obviously upset. I can hear it in your tone.

WHALEN: I don't have a tone!

RANGE: You d--

WHALEN: I'll talk to you later. *You* have to go.

**[6:55 PM OUTGOING CALL TO: PAPPAS-FIDICIA, JULIAN (WIRELESS NUMBER 917-XXX-XXXX), 2 minutes]**

PAPPAS-FIDICIA: I'm glad you called. I am at Taco Bell, and having second thoughts on the Cheesy Gordita Crunch. Should I get a Chalupa or--

RANGE: Sorry, I really can't talk--running late.

PAPPAS-FIDICIA: Oh, *I'm* sorry. I was under the impression that *you* called *me*. You know how I feel about interruptions involving food.

RANGE: I know, I know--I'm sorry. Forgot to tell you not to mention anything to anyone about Mercury or the Met event, okay? Including--er--your friend that works there--and . . . even Diana, okay?

PAPPAS-FIDICIA: And with such a fishy request, no less! And not even, by the way, of an edible kind.

RANGE: Look, there's nothing "fishy" about it. I just don't want Diana getting her hopes up. Like, it's still so early, you know? What if their offer sucks? I just--I just don't want her getting her hopes up. Look, I really have to go. Just please do this for me, okay?

PAPPAS-FIDICIA: Fine. But that doesn't quite explain why you wouldn't want me to tell Vivien. Not anything about the deal, just that we'll be at the event. I was planning to go anyway, and she'll definitely be there, you know. And why did you just call her *my* friend? You seemed pretty chummy if I recall. Technically, you've known her longer.

RANGE: Yes, no, yes--I mean--there's no big reason why. She's . . . great. I just don't want *anyone* to know and thought--only because she works there and all--that you might tell her specifically. Look, I just don't want anyone at all to know, okay? It could be construed as inside information. I'm not being unreasonable here. And I really have to go.

PAPPAS-FIDICIA: Okay, okay, yadda, I get it. I won't say anything. Go have a lovely evening.

RANGE: Thanks. Careful not to get Chalupa on your new white pants.

PAPPAS-FIDICIA: I hate you. See you Sunday.

## XVII.

SUNDAY IN THE WEST VILLAGE WAS UNSEASONABLY COOL WITH AN intermittent light drizzle, the kind of weather, Diana knew, that encouraged the realization of Julian Pappas-Fidicia's most profound sartorial fantasies. There—see him in front of Café Croix, teetering in his wellies and reading a book, an extravagantly hooked umbrella curled over his left forearm like a dormant scepter. Upon closer inspection there are several competing tartans at play, broken up by a moody mélange of waxed cotton and weathered leather. With the threadbare canvas tote bag—known to Diana to be one of Julian's "rustical" tote bags—he yielded the overall impression of Lord Grantham going antiquing in mid-coast Maine.

Diana hollered a *good morning* from across the street and rushed ahead of Wes to give him a hug, which he only sparingly tolerated, and she relished in flaunting her exemption. Wes shook Julian's hand and asked what he was reading. Julian proudly displayed the book for inspection, as if he were advertising it on the Home Shopping Network. As Wes read the title aloud, it took the form of a question:

—*Paid For: My Journey Through Prostitution*?

—I stole it from the Yale Club. Their checkout system is incomprehensible.

Wes grabbed the book playfully and skimmed the back.

—Seriously? You were that keen to read the memoirs of a prostitute?

—Maybe I'm considering a career change because my boss is a dick.

—Mm, I see. Because prostitution is the logical choice when you are looking to encounter fewer d—

—Oh, all right! You win this round, Julian bristled.

Wes released a roguish grin, the kind that still had the power to captivate Diana. How charming and funny he was around everyone else!

—Can we backtrack for a second? Diana cut in. You *stole* a book called *Paid For*?

—I am aware of the irony in this particular detail.

—We'll make sure he pays for it now, Wes said to his wife with a wink, flopping the book into Julian's tartan stomach casually, drawing a mock-offended hiss.

—Well. Aren't you two just the Bonnie and Clyde of my dignity. Is this like foreplay for you? It has a compelling narrative and I could not put it down! Can we go inside now? I haven't eaten in almost two hours.

Café Croix on Twelfth Street was a midsize establishment beloved to the New York alumni of the Patrick Henry Society that compensated for terrible service with excessive crown molding, Parisianly striped waitstaff, and sensational food. They did not take reservations for brunch, and refused to seat incomplete parties, relying instead on a handwritten clipboard list, protectively wielded by unwashed American Apparel–model-type hostesses like a squad of sexy Saint Peters with the keys to the kingdom of heaven.

—Paypass—er—Paypass FedutchEEah, party of three? One of the hostesses called out the door.

—Oh, thank god—it is pronounced Pahpahs-FihDEEchia, but yes, that is us, said Julian.

The hostess looked at her list warily, as if she suspected Julian of trying to screw over poor Mr. Paypass, clearly ahead of them in line. When no one else came forward and Julian pursed his lips in that universal *I told you so* look of wide-eyed exasperation, she relented, showing them to a table past the bar.

Menus were unnecessary. They would all order the same thing: the Breakfast Club Sandwich. If brunch was their religion and Café Croix their chapel, if literature their doctrine and debate their dogma, then the Breakfast Club Sandwich was a holy sacrament indeed. Crispy toast encasing crispy bacon, lettuce, tomato, and avocado, with an ambrosial spicy mayo and perfectly fried egg—all carefully balanced and aesthetically sliced on the diagonal, providing visual confirmation of the layered presence of every flavor in every bite. Thin, delicate fries, piping hot, with swirly little Edenic tubs of ketchup and more spicy mayo provided the ideal complement. The aroma of other parishioners' orders hung in the air, delivered tantalizingly to other placemats.

—Aren't you off to Paris tomorrow? Julian asked Diana. Where are you eating there? Hopefully the service will be better than it is here, though I wouldn't count on it. Lousy service is the Frenchiest thing about this place.

—I'm going tonight on the red-eye. The food will be conference-room fare for the most part, sadly. Oh, except Thursday. We decided not to fly out until Friday morning so we could have a big night out—

Diana blushed at her offhand use of the first-person plural—

—As a team, I mean, she continued. Then I'm flying to Nantucket Friday morning—to meet Wes.

She smiled unconvincingly and asked Julian what he was doing for the Fourth.

—Montauk share house, with a group from Penn, said Julian.

*With Dale, you mean*, Diana thought with a galling surge of jealousy, followed shortly by self-reproach. She struggled to keep her gaze trained politely at Julian while her brain focused on the periphery, at Wes, shifting in his seat. He looked—what was it? *Wary, maybe. Circumspect? Uncomfortable for sure.* Did he—was it possible that he suspected her of something? *Of what, exactly?* And—what did it matter if he did? She had done nothing wrong. She had painstakingly, expressly violated her every desire and impulse precisely in order to have done nothing wrong—precisely to avoid the very guilt she was beset with anyway. Perhaps she should proactively mention her "nice colleague" Dale McBride; she could prove through casual admission that there was nothing to admit. But she'd already reddened at the mention of staying in Paris for an extra night, and remembering it made her blush again. *You don't have to prove anything,* Diana reminded herself.

—How fun, Julian; I love Montauk, she said.

—I am probably going to have to share a room with someone repellent, but I am guaranteed a seafood dinner at the Lobster Roll. It is amazing what I am willing to put up with for excellent food and the air of exclusivity. Speaking of which, where the hell is our server?

They ordered their Breakfast Club Sandwiches and Bloody Marys. Julian added a couple of other sundry drinks and, as usual, a side of "limp" bacon.

—What? Why are you looking at me like that, Julian demanded, more in a statement than a question. We have been over this. That is how I like it.

—Prostitution may not be the field for you after all, Diana remarked.

—Don't bet on it, said Julian. People have all sorts of perversions. Would you prefer if I ordered it flaccid?

—There has to be a better way.

—If there was, I dare say I would have found it. I'm a very articulate person; I think we can all agree on that.

The Bloody Marys arrived and the conversation shifted with commensurate morbidity. The new topic was the long-form pseudo-documentary podcast *Serial.*

In the spring-summer of 2015, nothing had captured the post-post-collegiate creative-professional Sunday-brunching American psyche quite like Sarah Koenig's Peabody Award–winning "story told week by week" about the 1999 murder of Hae Min Lee, a high school student in Baltimore County, and Adnan Syed, her ex-boyfriend convicted of the crime. It was a factual drama of debatable facts, a real-world tale of love and death and justice and truth repackaged in the rhetoric of highbrow fiction and presented through the aesthetic metanarrative lens of Koenig's personal investigative discovery fifteen years later. Koenig was *Serial*'s journalist, but also a new kind of self-consciously unreliable narrator, opining on "secret assignations" and packaging "tendrils of truth" like a particularly literary personal acquaintance. Listening, it often felt like she was there in the room with you, that crescendo of dissonant percussive chopsticks and automaton introduction like a knock at your door: *This is a Global Tel-link prepaid call from* [Adnan Syed], *an inmate at a Maryland correctional facility.* It had the emotional intrigue of a Shakespearean drama wrapped in the titillating frame story of an Agatha Christie novel. There was a sense of desperation and immediacy, yes, but also a detached archaeological quality, allowing for endless debate and analysis. Above all, it carried a high ratio of narrative schadenfreude to narrator consequence. It was bloody fucking seductive.

—I'm sorry, but he's guilty.

This was Julian speaking.

—You're missing the point, said Wes. It isn't about guilt. What matters here is *beyond a reasonable doubt*. The state's case was never strong enough to warrant a conviction. No physical evidence, conflicting accounts, a single unreliable witness . . .

—I think we can all agree there wasn't enough evidence for a conviction, Diana said. It's the question of truth that—

—Excuse me, but we cannot all agree that there wasn't enough for a conviction, Julian interrupted, adjusting his glasses on the bridge of his nose. Other than Sarah Koenig's poetics, this is a story of the United States Criminal Justice System at work. Adnan Syed had legal representation and received due process. The prosecution and the defense presented their arguments, and a jury of his peers found him guilty. Because, hello, *he is guilty*. There is a preponderance of evidence.

—It wasn't a civil trial, said Wes, and the last time I checked, in this country defendants are presumed innocent. Adnan may have had a jury of his peers, but they were hopelessly bias—

—Oh my god, please tell me you are not about to say something like "the only thing Adnan is quote unquote 'guilty' of here is being Muslim," Julian said loudly, rolling his eyes.

—Do you honestly think that you or I would have been convicted on the same evidence, Julian? Wes said. At the absolute minimum, there was unconscious bias at play. And yes, potentially outright bigotry.

—Oh, this is rich! Charles Wesley Range the Fourth, ladies and gentlemen, Julian slow-clapped, drawing the attention of tables nearby. Defender of the downtrodden, paradigm of political correctness. Is that why everyone is so enamored of this case? Because it provides the opportunity to show off their finely tuned liberal morals? I cannot fathom any other reason why this has so captured the public imagination.

—Maybe if you hadn't interrupted me, you would, Diana quipped. *Serial* is revolutionary as a medium because the metanarrative overpowers the actual one. There is the question of whether Adnan is guilty or innocent, sure. But the question we really want to know the answer to is whether Sarah will find out. It's more a story about the reporter's relationship to the crime than the crime itself. She's been pulled so far in, she's become part of the story. The teenage love triangle helps, of course, but it's Koenig's internal conflict with the truth's unknowability, of what actually happened that day—that's what makes *Serial* so interesting.

—Oh my god, are you serious right now, Diana? Julian said, finding a new target for his indignation. What actually happened that day is *he did it.* Sarah Koenig's intimations of innocence rest on, like, Adnan's "big brown eyes."

Diana could feel herself getting heated:

—But she admits her own thoughts are prejudicial! Koenig's personal discomfort with the way she's feeling, the way she works to counteract her own bias, wondering if she's overcompensating—it's fascinating.

It's one of those stories where the narrator turns out to be the most interesting character.

—I guess I'll give you that she's a character, said Julian, because she certainly isn't a journalist.

Wes wrinkled his brow:

—A teenage girl was murdered, and a teenage boy was sentenced to life in prison on scanty evidence, and you think the most interesting person here is the privileged white woman winning awards for being, like, really, really interested in it?

Diana had mistaken Wes's individual conflict with Julian as a unified front, and her husband's accusatory rhetoric came as a hard surprise. As she studied him more closely, though, she began to sense that Wes's fervor really sprung from his own growing discomfort with the arguments he was making—that, eager to disprove Julian's ad hominem attacks, he had wandered into a position in which he knew he was supposed to but probably did not quite believe. It was cowardly, and she looked at him coldly.

—Sarah Koenig is using her position to get at the truth, and yes, I find it both interesting and admirable that she would personally embed herself in such an effort. Sorry if I forgot to apologize for her privilege, Wes. Ugh, women are supposed to apologize for everything! I refuse to apologize. Stop using us to offload your own liberal guilt.

In the self-serving competition of *who was better at recognizing and apologizing for his or her own privilege*, the insinuation of sexism was an outright declaration of war. Diana could see the onslaught of Wes's objections hanging on his lips with a rising personal exigency:

—Calm down, Diana, he susurrated. None of this is about guilt. I'm just trying to keep the focus on what's important in *Serial*: the faulty legal proceedings, the conviction of a man without the evidence necessary—a shit ton of reasonable doubt. You need to relax. Liberal guilt doesn't land you in jail.

—I'm not *un*calm! All of your self-righteous posturing, Wes, and you don't even care whether or not Adnan actually did it. He should be free only if he's truly innocent. If he's guilty, he belongs right where he is. Stop leaning on some abstract accusation of privilege to obfuscate the real moral dilemma here.

—Can someone please explain to me what exactly is so horrible about privilege? Julian asked. I, for one, enjoy it immensely.

—You don't mean that, Julian, Wes said.

—Sure he does, countered Diana. We all enjoy it.

—How can you say that? The very problem with privilege is that not everyone has it, Wes intoned didactically.

—I meant the three of us. Jesus, Wes. It's like you're intentionally misunderstanding me. And I'm not saying that privilege isn't a moral dilemma, by the way, I'm just saying it's not the primary moral dilemma at issue in *Serial*.

—Oh thank god, the food is here, Julian said. Moral dilemmas make me hungry.

The Breakfast Club Sandwiches temporarily put a halt to the conversation, if not the tension around the table, as they all fell into worship at the altars of their plates. A few minutes later Diana broke the silence, picking up where she left off with her mouth still half full of food:

—Do you think it's better to be guilty, and thought to be innocent—or innocent, and thought to be guilty?

Wes studied his water glass.

—That is a false dichotomy, Julian stated obliviously. You left out the other two options. You could also be innocent and thought to be innocent, or guilty and thought to be guilty—like Adnan Syed. It's a two-by-two matrix.

—Yes, but both of those other outcomes are rational and just. The whole point of the hypothetical is which *in*justice you'd choose if you had to, rejoined Diana. Whether you ultimately care more about reality or appearance, truth or facade. Whether you would rather have peace of mind, or peace of matter.

—You're either guilty or innocent of something, Wes said, so your "truth" axis is fixed. The question comes down to appearance. And what rational actor would choose anything but the appearance of innocence either way?

—Clearly you have never read *Crime and Punishm—*

Julian cut her off with vigor:

—Are we seriously still arguing about *Serial* at brunch in the West Village? Sorry, I need to step away from this parody of my life. I'm going to Patagonia. They're having a sale.

He deposited a wad of crumpled cash on the table theatrically.

—Wow, Diana said, why do you have so many ones?

—What are you implying? Julian rejoined. That I made a lot of money stripping this weekend? Small bills are useful at food trucks and coat checks and Taco Bell when their payment interface crashes on Friday night, not that I owe you any explanation.

Wes and Diana unanimously laughed at this, and the tone of the table neutralized.

—No need to be ashamed of stripping, Wes grinned. I'm sure you'll get used to it in your new line of work.

—Excuse me, but I do not think you understand the nature of shame. And I quote, "Shame does not ebb away slowly over time; it sometimes hides its face for a while, seeming to slink out of sight, only to stride purposefully back out of the shadows and onto the center-stage of your life, as real and alive as it was the first day you saw it."

He paused dramatically, clearly enjoying Wes and Diana's astonishment. Julian shook his head and smiled, breaking the character of himself for a brief second before standing up and retrieving his tote bag.

—I'll let you sit back and marvel at that, he said, deftly playing himself once again.

—What's it from? asked Wes.

—*Paid For: My Journey Through Prostitution*, Julian said. Why do you look so surprised? I told you, it's an excellent book.

## XVIII.

SHE STOOD IN LINE AT LA MAISON PAUL IN A CONTRAPPOSTO SLOUCH, an elbow draped crudely over the handle of her luggage, her attention vacillating between the boulangerie's vaulted menu and a glossy disposable gift bag, mint-green in color, hanging over her other elbow, from which she extracted macaron after macaron.

*She* was Diana Whalen in Charles de Gaulle Airport Terminal 2F. Dale McBride had the long-standing tendency to record his memories in novel form like this, like a pending mental draft of his life that one of these days he would finally find the time to type out and dramatize. Back when he was putting together applications to MFA programs as a college senior, Dale had mustered enough self-awareness and insight into the modus operandi of graduate school admissions not to submit some story about himself, to write instead about the abduction of an underprivileged woman in South Boston that demonstrated all of the appropriate intersectional sensibilities. He'd genuinely believed in the outraged moralism of his own story, of course, but he also had to admit he'd only written it to satisfy the canon-balancing bloodlust of a few purple-pen-wielding deans. Dale was unusually capable of genuine empathy for a handsome young man, and especially when genuine empathy was much to his own benefit, but the true subject of his writerly interest fundamentally boiled down to himself.

Turning down those modest-yet-prestigious MFA stipends for commonplace big money at Portmanteau was a decision that Dale had, over the years, spent a great deal of time reminding himself how much he did not regret. His initial plan had been to defer acceptance for one year—just long enough to cement his relationship with Vivien and earn the Portmanteau signing bonus—but then he got promoted early and was slated to make even more money and *didn't it perhaps make most sense to defer again?* He deferred again. A few weeks later, the economy collapsed. Pandemic uncertainty swept across the upwardly mobile young-professional landscape, and it started to look like he had dodged a real professional bullet. The next summer his friends with newly minted MFAs—even top ones—were by and large forced to accept teaching positions at third-rate institutions or even low-paying noncreative jobs to support their writing on the side. When Dale met up with them, the most innocuous conversations often exposed the sharp divergence of their material circumstances. His friends were envious and embarrassed by their envy, which embarrassed Dale, too—even as it pleased him, and made his friends ashamed of embarrassing him, and Dale ashamed of his perverse pleasure. It was all so obvious, and yet sedulously unsaid. American liberal politeness required the forceful denunciation of inequalities in the abstract while pretending not to notice them between friends. You assured yourself they didn't exist, even as you jostled for position. How could Dale say no when Portmanteau offered to pay for his MBA? He couldn't. He had already gone through the thwarted do-gooder cycle of failing to change and becoming, as a result, increasingly focused on his own comfort. In truth, the salary that had sounded enormous coming out of undergrad had failed to keep pace with his—or Vivien's—expectations. After all, his banker friends in New York made far more.

Everything had worked out so well for him. He'd gone to *Wharton*. And yet, the mind is its own place, and Dale had never quite been able to quash his road-not-traveled regret. It was at small-talk-heavy parties with Vivien, where it was difficult to briefly convey his singularity and prestige, but everyone oohed and ahhed at the Philadelphia Museum of Art—let alone now the Met. It was after the economy recovered a bit, and Dale found out on Facebook that one of his once-envious writer friends had sold his debut novel for six figures. A flattering professional portrait of this friend, delicately composed to suggest a down-to-earth intellectual coolness, front-lined an article in the *Times*. It was exactly the sort of authorial portrait that Dale, much to his own annoyance, could not prevent himself from thinking he would rather like himself.

It took three weeks for Dale to fully grasp the real reason why Diana Whalen had seemed so immediately familiar to him, so inherently trustworthy. How could he have failed to see it sooner? At the nondescript bar, she'd practically said so. They were both tormented by a compounding series of voluntary decisions, a controlled spiral of ceded control. They were connected, if at first only subconsciously, by the memory of a freedom surrendered for well-appointed captivity. There was an underground Kerouac in both of them, dying to hit the road.

He hesitated for a moment, watching her with prickling anticipation. The skin under her eyes was puffy and bluish from inadequate sleep. But the polar whites of them glowed. Like heartless voids and immensities of the universe, blank and full of meaning, operating without medium upon matter in the morning light.

Nowhere did Dale's misgivings envelop him more painfully than when he saw Diana like this, proximate and far away, dissatisfied, placid, and tumultuous, a too-human array of contradictions and appetites that perfectly mirrored his own. It was when Diana was at her most artless, when the unattractive realities of her humanness seeped to the surface, that Dale was most inclined to deify her in symbolic worship. In harboring her own parallel spiral of regret, Diana had become the embodiment of his. She was every MFA acceptance he'd turned down and deferred and watched lapse, every risk he'd successfully avoided but wished he hadn't. She was all the nights he'd gone to bed early, and all the girls he hadn't fucked. Diana Whalen was the protean face of his own fictional pasts, all the butterfly versions of his life that he yearned to grasp.

He approached her slyly, poking just below her elbow, the mint-green, glossy-bag-laden one.

—Let me in on those macarons, he smiled—and second breakfast is on me.

—Oh, hi! Yes, please have some—and yes please!

Her excitement to see him was so palpable, it was almost possible to forget why they were here. He wanted to say: *Let's hop a train to Nice. Yes, I'm serious. Yes, right now. My parents have a place there. Fuck Mercury. Fuck Portmanteau. Fuck Wes, and fuck Vivien. I'll take you all around the Riviera—or—let's just move there, permanently. Economize, but like kings, on baguettes and fresh pasta. Don't you see what I'm trying to say? It doesn't even matter, so long as I'm with you. Let's go, now-now. I don't want to analyze it or rationalize it or develop a list of pros and cons or build a fucking issue tree. For once in our lives can we please please please not think and just do?* It was what the fearless character of himself in his unwritten novel would say.

But Dale didn't say it. He didn't say it for the same reason he didn't do any of the other totally unacceptable things it occurred to him at various points that he would like to do—the same reason that he didn't take his pants off in hot weather or ask Vivien's friend Grace Cho if she'd gotten a boob job. Because invariably, exerting your freedom to do this kind of thing precluded your ability to exert it. You *could* beg your married coworker to run away with you—but only until you actually *did.* And Dale wanted the inchoate possibility of indulging his whims more than he wanted to actually indulge them.

He made an exception and did indulge in a macaron, however, extracting one with unflinching eye contact. He made another for postmortem analysis—and rationalization, pro-con list development, and issue-tree building—second-guessing and reaffirming and second-guessing every aspect of his inaction in an agonizing loop of regret and relief.

For the taxonomy of Dale's feelings for Diana Whalen was not mutually exclusive and collectively exhaustive. It both was and was not that old, remote worship of a woman, characterized precisely by her proximity out of reach. Dale had, by this time, become acutely acquainted with Diana's flaws, and it was impossible to reduce his admiration to glamoured abstraction. Indeed, in their strange friendship Dale and Diana had developed that deep, variegated intellectual-emotional intimacy rarely found outside of marriage, the kind that generates expectations and obligations and too human familiarities. The kind that tends to shatter the illusions of courtship. Diana was manipulative and balky and loud and erratic. She drank too much and overused profanity. There was a scar on her forehead that, once he noticed it, Dale had been surprised he hadn't seen sooner. Her second toes protruded slightly past her big ones in that way he otherwise found rampantly unappealing. The bewitching nature of her eyes was manufactured by fucking Johnson & Johnson. Her youth, even, was not entirely without its drawbacks. While in general Diana's shrewd practicality yielded the impression of maturity, there were moments when this effect fell away and it felt more like he was chatting to a precocious adolescent than a woman—like she was a teenager catfishing him from her parents' basement. The clear white light shone unforgivingly on the things Dale didn't like about Diana, the things he found unattractive, the things, even, that did not compare very favorably to Vivien. But it didn't matter. It was not the velvet paw he loved so much as the remorseless fang.

And yet Diana's remaining remoteness—her tantalizing unavailability—was an undeniable aspect of his fascination, her resistance augmenting her irresistibility. Naturally his body yearned madly for that one great intimacy, the one that supposedly compensates for all the rest. But he also wasn't sure if anything could be hotter than *not* having sex with Diana. Dale was hardly insensible to the pull of the world's greatest compliment and his desire to overpower her in the game they were playing. But there were timeworn contradictions in his imaginative demands, and his sensations of inferiority and superiority traced their origins back to the same source. Dale would have been hard pressed to articulate it as such, but the unseen presence of Charles Wesley Range IV was a curious part of Diana's appeal. It made him feel important to have such a competitor for her affections, even in his jealousy, and especially in his resistance. As if what was good enough for Wes Range, "entrepreneur and Olympic rower," was not *quite* good enough for Dale McBride: amateur athlete, sure, but *real* intellectual. Dale ordered their coffee and croissants, and the airport barista, doubtlessly fluent in English, responded to his French in French, as if in direct support of this position.

There was then, too, something honorable in Diana's loyalty to her failing marriage, and she would have lost some of her halo in willing infidelity to her husband. The moments, in fact, when Dale felt Diana's conjugal resolve cracking were those in which she became least attractive to him—needy, desperate—and Dale found himself, often to his own surprise, the half-hypocritical guardian of fidelity, putting forth passionate arguments on his rival's behalf. When Diana spoke of Wes fondly, however, or regaled the team with jaunty tales of her weekend life, Dale privately burned with the shame of a cuckold, quite as if she'd been Vivien. If only he could have resurrected all of Diana's spousal dissatisfactions then! He wanted to hurl her own secrets back at her, to watch the very arguments that erstwhile brought Dale to Wes's defense explode gloriously in her face. That Dale knew this shame to be misplaced only exacerbated his pain. If anything, the shame of his misplaced shame, this meta-shame, was even worse. He blamed Diana for precipitating his feelings and felt guilty for blaming her. He hated himself for wanting her, and more for wanting to hurt her. The dominos of his thoughts and feelings were set up in a circle, and he resented her most at the apex of his lust.

Dale McBride was teetering on the edge of this annularity just now, as Eric Hashimoto had arrived with a rollicking "Sup," interrupting their pointed lack of conversation with the sort of personal chitchat inevitable to elicit some soft mention of Wes. Dale already knew Wes and Diana had gone to a wedding in Brooklyn over the weekend; having to share her attention with Eric in the process of hearing about it only served to rile Dale doubly. Her latte arrived and they turned toward the exit.

—Oh, it was just like every other wedding these days, Diana was saying. Elaborately orchestrated into elegant simplicity. I'm sure Dale's will be just like it.

She said that last sentence as a jocose slight, toeing the line between backhanded compliment and fronthanded complaint. Diana was abusing Vivien's specialness in a tacit declaration of jealousy, needling at Dale's marital reticence precisely by gratifying his ego with her own displeasure. Her air of nonchalance had been partially pulled back to expose the edge of something darker. As they joined the taxi line, she pointedly turned to Eric.

—Macaron?

—Yeah. Thanks, Mom, Eric said casually, taking two at once, but carefully, visibly mindful of his shirt cuff.

Over the past six weeks, Eric Hashimoto had undergone that particular metamorphosis of self-assurance often discernible in smart new analysts granted blanket psychological safety. Social inclusion combined with praise for his (undeniably) high-quality work and personal preciousness had systematically invigorated Eric's fragile confidence a bit too far in the other direction. This was partially Dale's own fault, he knew—though it was mostly Diana's. Her tutelage was like a NICU for the gifted novice, and she had gotten Eric milk-drunk on his own future promise. It wasn't that he was "different" now so much as just extra-emphatically himself. Eric's genuine eccentricities had been exaggerated with positive reinforcement in the same way that laughing even once when a four-year-old says "fuck" will incline him to say it again—except louder the second time, and to a larger audience. That was the problem with incentives, though—not that they didn't work, but that they worked only too well. Diana and Dale had made all of the well-meaning mistakes of parents anxious to ensure their child's success, and having helped Eric shed his cocoon with too great an ease, it occasionally became necessary to thrust him back into it.

—Eric, you have to stop calling us "Mom" and "Dad" before you accidentally do it in front of the client, said Dale.

—Come on, Dad, you know I wouldn't do that.

—I'm serious, he added, doing his best to look serious.

This time Eric appealed nonverbally, blinking his eyes in that exaggeratedly innocent "who me" face of his. His *new* new glasses—not the new ones he started the project with, but a slightly heavier, more sophisticated set—somehow accentuated this motion. Even Eric's precious blinky hedgehogness had undergone a subtle change, one characterized specifically by his awareness and cultivation of it. There was a temerity embedded in his timidity now, a well-acted quality to his affectionate insubordination. Eric Hashimoto was officially in on the joke of himself, and eager for everyone to hear it.

At first Diana managed to repress her laugh, but when it got the better of her, Dale too smiled in spite of himself, shaking his head in resignation.

—Your notes from all the workshop sessions better be flawless today, he bartered.

—Oh, absolutely, Dad—I promise you, I promise you they will be.

—Here, let me give you a head start, Diana cut in with a look Dale registered as exceptionally mischievous. Don't get sidetracked by all the rousing welcome speeches about "innovation" and "agility"—the main thing you need to get down today is the participants' names and roles and home organizations and personal anecdotes. Calling people by their names, showing them that you listened to and remembered their little stories—these tiny kindnesses build trust and rapport, and trust and rapport incline people to share things that they weren't intending to share. Maybe even things that they shouldn't. *Right, Dale?*

—That tactic tends to be most effective when the other person doesn't know that you're employing it, he said wryly. *Bonjour Monsieur, nous voudrions aller à la Rue de Richelieu près du Palais Royal . . . oui, deux ou trois blocs au nord, ça marche.*

—*I* know, said Eric with offense, oblivious to Dale's conversation with the driver. The whole workshop is predicated on deception. That's kind of the point of a Trojan horse.

Dale would not have been so annoyed if Eric hadn't been right. They had all been calling the fraud workshop a *Trojan horse* as a clever sort of compliment to the deceptive blur of its deception. Diana had perhaps brought up trust and rapport for its more private relevance, but Monday's introductions and pleasantries *were* a ploy to build false trust. The fraud presentations scheduled for Tuesday were likewise pretext and Wednesday's "small-group work" was a daylong euphemism for underhanded knowledge transfer to Pegaswipe. No victor would be named on Thursday, Dale already knew. The judgment of Paris would be delayed until the safeguards were in place for layoffs to commence, and delivered under telephonic cover. Indeed, this had been *his* recommendation to Prudence Hyman. It was getting harder and harder not to see the fraud workshop for what it was—a fraud. One with real consequences, with people's livelihoods on the line—defrauding antifraud professionals out of their jobs. Framed as an epic clash, Dale was less than proud of the side he was on. He looked to Diana for some telepathic reassurance before his thoughts could get too entangled in the metaphor, but her attention was lightly focused on Eric in the kind of platonic flirtation in which she engaged when she had already succeeded in collecting someone.

*That was what she did.* Diana collected people the way Vivien collected things, carefully choosing those most flattering to her, tucking them in her drawer like scarves from Hermès. In this moment of self-doubt, Dale wondered if he was just another trinket. But no, even as he indulged himself, decorating his burrow of pity, Dale knew it wasn't true. There was nothing light or platonic about his relationship with Diana. Their interactions were loaded with heavy artillery and real danger. Dale knew he gave her pause in her decision to marry so young—knew, and reveled in it, reveled in presenting the same torturous cognitive possibility, however distant, of an alternative life that she reveled in presenting to him. The magic of their connection was established in its equal footing, and his ego urgently sought some new validating sign of it. The next time she turned toward him, Dale held her gaze with rapt seriousness until she returned it with greater avidity, touching the very extremity of appropriateness. Dale wanted to rip her dress off right there. But how could he? They were in the back of a taxi with Eric Hashimoto.

The Merchantes offices occupied the third to sixth floors of a Lutetian limestone building, yes, but a far sparer, more modernly designed one than an American might hope to find. It was nowhere as nice as Olympia inside—all mid-tier office furniture and industrial blue carpet. But when you looked out the window, down the side streets, or across the vista of rooftops, you knew you were in Paris. She was right there, all the more alluring for her proximity, just out of reach. A prison, certainly, but the kind of prison you would choose. A prison with an Instagrammable view.

# XIX.

**SELECT USPS MAIL ACTIVITY (RESORTED, BY POSTAGE CLASS, WEIGHT), VIVIEN FLORIS AND DALE S. MCBRIDE (XXXX WALNUT ST, PHILADELPHIA, PA 19103), RETRIEVED BY VIVIEN FLORIS, THURSDAY, JULY 2, 2015.**

**1. FIRST CLASS PACKAGE SERVICE**

**Exterior:**

**[MAILING ADDRESS]**
**Ms. Vivien Floris**
**XXXX Walnut St.**
**Philadelphia, PA 19103**

**[RETURN ADDRESS]**
**Knotty Little Letterpress**
**XXX Grant Ave.**
**San Francisco, CA 94108**

**[POSTMARK]**
**June 30, 2015**

**Contents:**

**Signature 2-ply Letterpress Wedding Invitation in Bone, 250 count [SAMPLE 1 REPRODUCED BELOW]**
**Signature 2-ply Letterpress Program (single page) in Bone, 250 count [SAMPLE 2 REPRODUCED BELOW]**
**Signature 2-ply Letterpress . . . *&c.***
**Customer Receipt, Total (Paid: American Express): $5,435.22 on June 20, 2015**

[SAMPLE 1]

[Monogrammed Logo]

DR. & MRS. ALTON ANDREW FLORIS
REQUEST THE PLEASURE OF YOUR COMPANY
AT THE MARRIAGE OF THEIR DAUGHTER

VIVIEN CHRISTINA
TO
DALE SEATON MCBRIDE

ON SATURDAY, THE FIFTH OF SEPTEMBER
TWO THOUSAND AND FIFTEEN
AT HALF PAST SIX O'CLOCK IN THE EVENING

WHIPPLEPOOL COUNTRY CLUB
VILLANOVA, PENNSYLVANIA

DINNER AND DANCING TO FOLLOW

BLACK TIE

[SAMPLE 2—FRONT]

[MONOGRAMMED LOGO]

VIVIEN + DALE
SEPTEMBER 5, 2015

— THE CEREMONY —

PRELUDE
"YOU ONLY LIVE TWICE," FROM *YOU ONLY LIVE TWICE*

SEATING OF THE MOTHERS
"LOVE THEME," FROM *CINEMA PARADISO*

PROCESSIONAL
"ORCHARD HOUSE," FROM *LITTLE WOMEN*

OFFICIANT'S GREETING

READINGS
FROM THE *METAMORPHOSES*, OVID
FROM "THE PHOENIX AND THE TURTLE," SHAKESPEARE

EXCHANGE OF VOWS & RINGS

PRONOUNCEMENT OF MARRIAGE

RECESSIONAL
EXCERPT FROM *VIOLIN CONCERTO IN D, OP. 77,*
*I. ALLEGRO NON TROPPO*, BRAHMS

**[SAMPLE 2—BACK]**

OFFICIANT
FATHER BENEDICT HUMMEL

PARENTS OF THE BRIDE
ALTON & KIKI FLORIS

PARENTS OF THE GROOM
MATTHEW MCBRIDE & PENELOPE SEATON

MAID OF HONOR | GRACE CHO
BRIDESMAIDS | JACQUELINE DARBY, AUDREY WIMBERLY

BEST MAN | GAGE THOMPSON
GROOMSMEN | SEBASTIAN FLORIS, HARRISON SINCLAIR

READERS | PAIGE SINCLAIR, ANDERSON GREGORY

MUSIC | THE VIOLENT VIOLINS

THANK YOU TO OUR DEAR FAMILY AND FRIENDS
FOR JOINING US ON THIS EXTRAORDINARY DAY
ALL LOVE, DALE + VIVIEN

#KISSTHEMCBRIDE

**2. FIRST CLASS MAIL LETTER**

**Exterior:**

**[MAILING ADDRESS]**
**Mr. Dale McBride and Ms. Vivien Floris**
**XXXX Walnut St.**
**Philadelphia, PA 19103**

**[RETURN ADDRESS]**
**St. Joseph's Episcopal Church**
**XX Ardmore Ave.**
**Ardmore, PA 19003**

**[POSTMARK]**
**June 29, 2015**

**Contents:**

**Tri-fold letter, typed, hand-signed [REPRODUCED BELOW]**

**[TRI-FOLD LETTER]**

**FATHER BENEDICT R. HUMMEL**
**ST. JOSEPH'S EPISCOPAL CHURCH**

June 19, 2015

Dear Ms. Floris and Mr. McBride,

As I am sure you are aware, we have been trying to organize a congregational service trip to Nepal since April's earthquake—an intention made all the more urgent by the devastating aftershock in May. Thanks to the compassion of our dear community (including the generosity of your wonderful parents, Vivien), we have reached our funding goal even sooner than anticipated, and I will be leading a group of fourteen volunteers to spend six months in Kathmandu. Our plans were finalized yesterday and we leave July 13.

Alas, just as there is a blessing embedded in every sacrifice, there is a sacrifice in every blessing, and the collateral impact of the dates above can scarcely have failed to register for you. I am, truly, deeply sorry not to be able to officiate your wedding. It has been my great pleasure getting to know you as a couple, and I was very much looking forward to the joyous event. Your commitment to one another, your patience, and the seriousness with which you are taking this step is a testament to fidelity, and an honor to God.

I know your thoughts and prayers, like mine, rest first and foremost with the thousands dead and millions left homeless in Nepal. But I am also aware that Christian priorities do not solve for the problem of a missing officiant. Father Clements is unfortunately already scheduled to perform another wedding the same day as yours, but has assured me he will be available to assist you in finding another suitable Episcopal Priest in the coming weeks.

Again, my sincerest apologies, and thank you for the grace and perspective with which I know you both will take this news.

Best Regards,

[SIGNATURE]

Father Benedict R. Hummel
St. Joseph's Episcopal Church

**3. NONPROFIT POSTCARD**

**Exterior:**

**[MAILING ADDRESS]**
**Ms. Vivien Floris**
**1000 Fifth Avenue**
**New York, NY 10028**

**FORWARDED**

**Ms. Vivien Floris**
**XXXX Walnut St.**
**Philadelphia, PA 19103**

**[RETURN ADDRESS]**
**THE METROPOLITAN MUSEUM OF ART**
**1000 Fifth Avenue**
**New York, NY 10028**

**[POSTMARK]**
**June 8, 2015**

**Contents:**

**Event invitation, Ninth Annual Young Members' Party**
**[REPRODUCED BELOW]**

[EVENT INVITATION]

[CELEBRATORY GRAPHICS]

THE METROPOLITAN MUSEUM OF ART
CORDIALLY INVITES YOU TO THE
NINTH ANNUAL

*Young Members' Party*

THURSDAY, JULY 9, 2015
8:00–11:00 P.M.

DRINKS, DANCING, HORS D'OEUVRES, AND ART

FEATURED EXHIBITIONS:
CHINA: THROUGH THE LOOKING GLASS
ART & MYTH: OVID'S HEIRS
THE ROOF GARDEN COMMISSION: PIERRE HUYGHE

MUSIC:
DJ ME-J

COCKTAIL ATTIRE

THIS EVENT IS MADE POSSIBLE BY CONDÉ NAST
AND MERCURY INCORPORATED.

**4. RETAIL GROUND POSTCARD**

**Front:**

[GRAPHIC FEATURING TWO STYLIZED SILHOUETTE PORTRAITS, ON THE LEFT A DOG, ON THE RIGHT A CAT, EMBEDDED IN A GEOMETRICALLY PERFECT HEART, SYMMETRICALLY FACING INWARD Toward ITS Y-AXIS BISECTION]

**Back:**

[NOTE FROM POSTAL SERVICE]
ATTENTION! MAILING ADDRESS NAME DOES NOT MATCH RESIDENT ON FILE

Dear DIANA WHALEN,

We hope that DALE has fully recovered from his little mishap, and is back to his rambunctious self!

At Best Friends, we know how important you and DALE are to each other—that he's your "special" friend. That's why for a limited time we're offering 15% off future visits when you register with us online as your primary provider of furry care.

Thanks for choosing Best Friends, and we hope to see you and DALE again soon!

**[RETURN ADDRESS]**
**Best Friends**
**XXX Arch St.**
**Philadelphia, PA 19103**

**[MAILING ADDRESS]**
**Ms. Diana Whalen**
**XXXX Walnut St.**
**Philadelphia, PA 19103**

**[POSTMARK]**
**July 1, 2015**

## XX.

THE MENDELSSOHN VIOLIN CONCERTO OPENS WITH THE SOLOIST, WITH the concerto's ultra-urgent signature melody at its very most urgent, an E-minor imperative statement, the one that ran through Mendelssohn's head prior to composition and gave him "no peace." It is a notably innovative break from the classical tradition, musically speaking, where it is customary to let the orchestra give a formal introduction—and yet, more broadly, nothing could be more classical than beginning in medias res, a Dionysian euphoria underlying the soloist's Apollonian control. As the nineteenth-century virtuoso violinist Joseph Joachim put it, "The Germans have four violin concertos. The greatest, most uncompromising is Beethoven's. The one by Brahms vies with it in seriousness. The richest, the most seductive, was written by Max Bruch. But the most inward, the heart's jewel, is Mendelssohn's." The Mendelssohn is technical and ruthless and disciplined—famously a favorite of prodigies—and yet there is an audible warmth there, a bridled romance, a tender youth and insecurity. You can hear the human blood under its skin, pulsing from protruding veins, trying in vain to escape. The soloist seems to play twice as many notes as two violins combined, and still its cadenzas, while extraordinary—perfect, even—are also insufficient, as if some inexpressible, achingly ungraspable joie de vivre is just out of reach. It is a thoroughly German concerto, but with a repressed French soul.

Perhaps that was why it was playing in the lobby of the Westin Paris Vendôme, where Dale McBride sat with agitation in a brocade silver chair. Look at him, closely now. He has obviously showered. His skin still has that just-showered warmth and humidity. His hair still wet, but combed. The air-conditioning is normalizing the room to a patriarchal 20 degrees centigrade, and yet there is a distinct possibility he will sweat through his windowpane dress shirt, resemblant in both pattern and texture of a fine Japanese graph paper. The hurry has hindered his ability to appear effortless, a side effect that would have gone unnoticed had the rest of the team appeared bubbling with excitement around the same time. But they were all late, and his E-minor adrenaline was boiling rapidly into the cortisol-laden anxiety of eagerness, that particular eagerness not to appear eager, even before Diana W. Whalen came into view.

*Presto.*

He stood up instinctively. Nothing in the weeks of petite-Madeline-type shift dresses could have remotely prepared him for the little white shorts she was wearing. An arpeggio-like flutter of nerves manifested somewhere south of Dale's sternum, a trill of a thrill. The voluminous asymmetry of her matching blouse allowed for an uninterrupted stretch of skin all the way up her left arm, all the way to the ear, behind which she had tucked severely straightened strands of hair. Her normally nymphesque physiognomy had been obscured by smoldering eye makeup; she glowed golden-pink all over. Diana had transformed, all right. She looked less like a nymph than a goddess.

Dale's expression hovered between a smile and a wince. It wasn't so much that she looked the way she did. Frankly it almost hurt to look at her like this, dressed to the nines, and on some level Dale probably would have preferred her unadulterated appearance. But Diana's effort also felt like an exhilarating sort of admission, a pointed gift, if not a form of surrender. An illusion, but an awfully nice one—and that he'd compelled her to concoct it had the distinct flavor of a personal accomplishment. That is, at least until Diana's perceptive smile quietly acknowledged the chinks in his own armor of nonchalance.

—Apparently the others left already and will meet us there, she said casually, in lieu of *hello*, as if to undermine her unprecedented sartorial effort.

—Really? How could I have missed them? . . . Oh, shit, my Wi-Fi isn't working. We better go, then . . . uh . . . let's hope they let you into the restaurant . . .

—Excuse me? Diana balked.

He motioned vaguely in the direction of her shorts, fully earning the playful smack to his shoulder and nasty look he craved. Diana turned on her heels in mock offense, strutting toward the door with such hauteur that Dale had to jog a step or two to catch up.

*Prestissimo.*

—What? Dale laughed, quite inadvertently reaching for her arm and catalyzing an about-face. It's just that this, er, *ensemble* . . . it's not exactly *Whalenesque*.

—You don't think it suits me?

—I did not say that.

—You don't say a lot of things, she said with quiet precision.

*Grand pause.*

—Well, there's a lot to be said for negative space.

—Please don't . . .

—Whatever you're telling me not to do, he assured her, is not something that I'm doing.

—Well, stop it, then!

—Stop what?

—Whatever you're "not doing."

— . . .

Diana evaluated Dale's expression, looking for signs of her own sense of urgency, the kind that tends to appear when relationships of short duration but high intensity imminently push toward their natural, predetermined expiration date. Dale returned her gaze; she could feel him intensely analyzing her face. She wasn't imagining it. Yes, he wanted her, certainly. She knew it. Precisely the way she wanted him. This scene of her metamorphosis was one Diana had been working up the courage to initiate for some time, and it was playing out so cinematically, so entirely to her satisfaction, that Diana's immediate desire for its escalation rendered her helplessly, torturously unsatisfied. There were only a few weeks left on the project, and there wasn't likely to be an extension. The workshops had proceeded exactly as anticipated. All that was left for Portmanteau to do was pretty-up and package the deliverables. Thus the future opportunities for such private exchanges were dwindling rapidly. And it was their last night in Paris.

The restaurant was only a few blocks away in the Eighth Arrondissement. Tucked into a side street just off L'avenue de New York, L'Autre Miroir was the sort of place that at first glance does not appear especially grand, but once inside it seems to expand into a vast array of plush period rooms. Upon entry, Dale swiftly realized it was one of those fancy old French restaurants where the menu is basically set, only the gentleman's includes prices, and small gamey portions of every variety get interspersed with, like, shot glasses of chili-pepper sorbet and egg-yolk puree sipped from the shell. It was the kind of experiential, ultra-expensive, three-hour-dinner type place Vivien always wanted to go to and post on Instagram; the kind of place that appealed to Dale himself in the abstract, but invariably made him oppressively uncomfortable once there. It was of the genre, in short, that Eric Hashimoto probably should not have booked for a boisterous group of American consultants to expense. As they followed the maître d' through the labyrinthine maze of velvet, Dale looked for him around every corner in the hope of conveying his stern disapproval.

—*Votre table, Monsieur, Madame*, said the maître d'.

It was a table for two, with no sign of the team anywhere.

—Oh, I'm sorry, there must be some mistake, Diana said before Dale could respond in French. There are six of us.

—No mistake, Madame. The others, they send the regrets. They have asked me to give this to you—

It was a note, in Eric's unmistakably neat, even hand:

*Dear Mom and Dad,*

*Sorry to pull a fast one on you like this, but we all thought you could use a night alone without the kids. You seem to really like hanging out with each other, and we thought this would be a nice way for us to say "thank you." The food here is supposed to be superb; it gets tremendous reviews on Yelp. Besides, the rest of us really wanted to go out tonight, to a place that definitely involves velvet ropes. We're just going to get burgers beforehand, so the expenses should even out.*

*Bonsoir,*
*Raj, Rich, Megan, and Eric*

*PS—There's a speakeasy downstairs that will probably be more your speed after dinner.*

Diana let out a wide-eyed sigh and surrendered the note to Dale. He squinted to read it in the soft, crimson light. Champagne in ornate crystal flutes arrived at the table almost as soon as they sat down. The romance of the place was so pronounced that it was embarrassing, as situational accuracy so often is. There was nothing to do but go along with it. Their faux debates on the merits versus pomp of a Full Windsor and whether to get a bottle of Margaux or Châteauneuf-du-Pape turned into real ones, and Diana's loose sense of etiquette and Oliver Twist appetite eased Dale's usual anxieties over propriety that he felt in such establishments with Vivien.

Chili-pepper ices and egg-yolk concoctions flew on and off the table. Dale lost track of the plates, and Diana lost track of the glasses of wine.

—Have you finished *Anna Karenina* yet? he asked over the cheese course. It's required reading before my novel, you know.

—What novel? You mean the unwritten one?

—Yes, yes, but it's all in my head now; a modern rerendering of *Anna Karenina.*

—How are you rerendering it?

—She resists Vronsky. Stays with her husband.

—Sounds boring, Diana said with a dry smile. Do you know how you're going to end it?

—I'm thinking my Anna will probably kill herself anyway.

—Ugh, that's so sexist. Why not have your Vronsky kill himself instead?

Dale laughed.

—I'll keep it under advisement.

—Or—I know—have your *Karenin* kill himself, and end it with a wedding.

—A wedding? Don't be ridiculous. No one ends novels with weddings anymore.

Diana was just sober enough to imprint a memory of the speakeasy scene: the warmth of Dale's enormous, frontier-shifting smile, the way he leaned forward in conspiracy—her mind's camera zooming in on his every witticism, his appreciation of a good return, the intermittent sips of his highball overwhelming her field of vision until she saw only his mouth, transforming close up and in slow motion into a laughing white beam, the slightly asymmetrical perfection of his bottom teeth teasing her like a wink.

When a few other couples got up to dance to an especially pretty French song, Dale offered her his hand.

—Our team is rather observant, aren't they? Dale said after another drink.

—Yes. They've clearly mastered the art of data-driven decision-making.

There was a serious note to her tone, like the foreboding transition from a major to a minor key.

—I wasn't talking about work, Diana.

—Neither was I.

Dale held his breath. He looked at her, analytically. He said it almost in a whisper:

—Do you want to go back to the hotel?

—I do.

Dale and Diana had both thought too much and too critically about the theoretical possibilities embedded in such an evening to be truly said to be "caught up in the moment," and yet it was impossible not to be caught up in it a little bit. The no-background bar theory was on shaky ground, Diana noted wryly. And Dale had to admit it. Paris isn't Philadelphia, and the Schuylkill isn't the Seine. The city of light flickered under the Pont Alexandre III. Even the Louvre, for all its austere grandiosity, felt strange and dreamlike from the far west side of the Tuileries. The gardens rustled in the warm breeze, blurry and impatient.

—I love the music they play in here, Diana declared when they reentered the Westin lobby. Doesn't it sound like Tom Hanks is about to uncover a centuries-old secret of the Illuminati?

—It certainly does not! Dale countered with playful derision. You can't possibly have mistaken this for some B-movie soundtrack.

—First of all, *The Da Vinci Code* totally held my attent—

—Diana, this is the first movement of the Mendelssohn Violin Concerto.

—That sounds like something you just made up.

—Shazam it.

—Fuck, seriously?

She gave him one of her epic eye rolls, the kind that Dale had come to recognize, in certain circumstances, as a supreme if begrudging sort of compliment. He shrugged impishly.

—I told you, I'm hideously cultured, he said.

—You have to stop saying that. You're offending my dignity.

—From time to time, your dignity needs to be offended.

Diana burst open, indulging in the kind of full-body laughter that conceivably requires a nearby perch for support. Dale's arm was larger but softer than Wes's, and Diana could not help but think it had a pleasing, gentle sort of heft. Dale wrapped it around her back to steady her, encircling her waist, calling the elevator without ever looking at the button. The tenor of the moment again shifted into seriousness.

—What floor are you on? Dale ventured, cautiously.

—I forget.

—Do you have a view of the Eiffel Tower?

—No! she exclaimed, bright again. Do you?

—Yes. It so happens I got upgraded to a suite.

—*What*? And you haven't shown me all week? I thought we were friends, Dale.

—We are friends.

—Are we, though?

—We're not *not* friends.

—Sounds pretty knotty to me.

—Very naughty.

— . . .

They stood parallel, eyes in perfect alignment, no more moving than marble statues. They were inches apart and willing each other to lean closer still, longing to kiss the image before them, but each deferring to the other. A kiss might be blameless, so long as it was the other person doing the leaning. Was it your fault, really, if someone else kissed you? They longed for at least that much: one kiss, one moment of *de minimus* elevator intensity—if not twenty-seven seconds then at least seven or eight—without guilt or shame of any kind. Just a proper data point of indication as to whether it was worth throwing another self, another life away.

They said nothing, but the importance of this moment was brutally self-evident. From a sheer human perspective, you didn't need a lick of background information to see it with trembling validity: that here were two people most certainly in love, and yet there was something holding each of them back.

The elevator dinged and, recalling himself, Dale motioned politely for her to exit first, which she did, stopping again just outside, waiting to follow his lead. Dale's suite was at the far end of the corridor, and she followed him inside. The television was set to the post-housekeeping-service default hotel channel, extolling the exclusive membership benefits available only to Starwood Preferred Guests.

—That's not obnoxious or anything, Dale said nervously as he fumbled with the remote. Um, you can see the Eiffel Tower from just over there.

Diana paced toward the view and assumed the absorbed, craning body language of one who is seriously considering it. But inside, every fiber of her being not already engaged in detoxifying alcohol was hard at work sensing Dale's unseen presence behind her as he futzed with his iPhone playlist. A beautiful aria started to play. Diana was in crisis. The action required to cinematize the scene would destroy the movie she'd so deliberately crafted into a life. When Dale joined her at the window, he could see that she was crying.

—Diana? What is it? What's wrong?

But of course he knew. Dale, too, had mustered a greater kind of alcohol-induced James Bond sexual assurance at various points in the evening than he was entirely certain he possessed. The realization that he was only himself came as a devastating relief. Diana wiped the tears hastily from her cheeks, and frantically scoured her handbag for Maximum Strength Visine.

—Ugh, I'm sorry, she said, obviously angry with herself. It's just that I—I . . .

—It's okay—it's okay, Diana. I know. You don't have to say it. Let's not say it.

—Yes, right—okay, of course you'd rather we just continue to delude ourselves—keep playing this pathetic little game. Don't you ever want to acknowledge reality for, like, eight fucking seconds?

—Diana—

—No, I'm serious! And I don't care if this means that you "win" or whatever, by the way. The really, totally fucked up thing about this is—it's that I—I—

Diana took a step forward. She gave him the kind of look that lives are rearranged around, the kind that film directors invariably interpret as a smoldering half-pout, but in reality conceive their attractiveness from something other than aesthetics. Diana's visage had the florid splotchiness of true human supplication, of total and complete transparency and misery and powerlessness.

Dale did not feel victorious. Quite unconsciously, even against his will, he was experiencing the radical discomfort of considering this scene from her perspective; he was experiencing Diana's pain as *her pain,* rather than in its similarity to his own. He wanted to embrace her, yes, but not because he wanted to embrace her. He wanted to embrace her because it was what he deeply, truly felt that *she* wanted—because it was the only thing he could think to do to comfort her. Had Dale been more readily acquainted with this disorienting sensation, he might have properly identified it as love.

Unthinkingly closing the remaining space between them, Dale wrapped his arms around her protectively, hushing her sobs, stroking her hair.

—*Don't touch me!* Diana wailed, far louder and more aggressively than the situation merited, and quite in opposition to her own intention.

She regretted her words practically as she was saying them. Alarmed—frightened even—Dale had released her instantaneously, gradually continuing his subsequent retreat. The heat of embarrassment rushed to Diana's face and neck, momentarily overshadowing her remorse. The aria ended and gave way to an orchestra. It was that same concerto from the lobby. Four minutes earlier, it would have been a delicious inside joke. Now it was searingly painful.

*Prestississimo.*

—I have to go, she said, brushing at her tears again, turning and exiting the room before Dale could process what was happening, before Diana could process it herself.

The heavy hotel door did not accommodate reconsideration. There was a petrifying finality embedded in the sound of its closure. Why had she reacted like that, Diana asked herself—and to a gesture so precisely in line with her greatest want? And then why had she made it worse by leaving? The first truly honest interaction they'd ever had—why had she spoiled it? She inched back toward the door, freezing again right in front of it, willing it to open. Open. *Open!* Was he waiting for her to knock? She should knock. But if he wanted her to knock, why did he not just open the door?

Dale was less than three feet away on the other side, waiting for her to knock. He could sense her unseen presence, still haunting the hallway. Why wasn't she knocking? After what had just happened—was she seriously waiting for him to just—to just open it? Absent the visual of Diana's tearstained face, a paralyzing thought wormed its way into his brain: that the ultimate act of power isn't getting what you want, but rather sacrificing it willingly. Because that is an act of power over yourself, of power over *power*. And what kind of mortal has that?

# PART THREE

# XXI.

Julian Pappas-Fidicia had a great many grievances concerning the Hamptons. The traffic was outrageous. Everyone knew his lily-white skin did not fare well in the sun. He found bathing suits categorically unflattering and difficult to accessorize. The cultural milieu was lacking, and seemed engineered expressly to attract the most vapid, insufferable individuals from within several—and even radically oppositional—demographic segments. It was harder to get a bartender's attention at Cyril's than to become a certified investor with the Securities and Exchange Commission. To Julian's thinking, it was the worst way to spend the Fourth of July, except for all the others.

Out of some nostalgic collegial habit to economize combined with an unspoken compassion for the underpaid creatives involved, the group from Penn he went with every year invariably sacrificed space for aesthetics when choosing a house—and Julian did indeed almost always have to share a room. This had been inconvenient enough back when it was a genuine budgetary necessity. In the dark ages, 2007–2010, there had always been a diving board and yet he'd rarely been given a bed. From 2011 to 2013, he'd bunked with Harry Sinclair, who was only marginally less obnoxious prior to graduating from Harvard Law and starting to sleep with a CPAP machine. The emergence of Harry's girlfriend (now wife) Paige had ushered in the 2014 reign of Grace Cho, who spent an interminable amount of time in what would have otherwise been—given Julian's chronically sensitive bowels—a game-changing en suite bath. The news of Grace's new beau last fall had initially triggered some concern that Julian would have to share with Jackie Darby, but even Jackie had finally experienced some professional success this year, published a collection of poems, and promptly shacked up with her editor. Gage Thompson—the semi-official Montauk Master of Ceremonies, who had always presented more like a Doctors Without Borders pediatrician than a board-certified plastic surgeon (increasingly renowned across the isle of Manhattan for breast augmentation, and privately, Julian suspected, the artist behind Grace Cho)—was either too kind or too spineless ever to say no, and Jackie's editor now had to be accommodated in the share house, too.

Picture him, then, Julian, a "discerning consumer of luxury travel services"—in his words—a "veritable living legend of the Trip Advisor review community," learning that the nature of his accommodation this year would disappoint even his own harshest expectations. Picture him relegated not only to a *bunk bed*, not only to the *top bunk* of a bunk bed, but to *the twin-size top bunk hovering over a full-size lower bunk bed.* It was a situation "inappropriate to a gentleman [of his] stature"; one guaranteed to double his customary number of roommates, "already 100% over [his] quota." As the twosome with the longest tenure, known well to all principal attendees of this perennial American freedom fest, the honor of sharing a room with Julian had been bestowed on Vivien Floris and Dale S. McBride.

We find Julian waddling into this "godforsaken" room now, frowning from behind his round tortoiseshell prescription sunglasses, little beads of sweat collecting on his brow, demanding of Gage Thompson where exactly he is expected to drop the mélange of monogrammed tote bags—known by Gage to be Julian's "long weekend" tote bags—dangling from his forearms.

—I can't be expected to put them way up on my bunk, and I can't very well put them below on someone else's.

—Just put them anywhere, Julian! Dale and Viv won't care. You worry too much. Have you seen the pool yet? There's an inflatable swan.

—Am I expected to delight in an ornithologically inaccurate floatation device at the expense of my personal comfort? Julian barked. I anticipate that next year you'll want me to sleep in it!

Gage laughed and relieved Julian of two of his tote bags, setting them down gently in the corner of the room. Julian released the remainder with a dramatic huff, as if to assure his old friend that this gesture was performed under legitimate protest.

—There, good. That's better, right? Gage asked, coaxing Julian out of the room and downstairs. So, how are you, what's new?

—It's been an eventful summer thus far, thank you for asking. I found the perfect pair of white gabardine pants and saw *Ex Machina* twice. Oh, and I ran the J. P. Morgan Challenge. I'll have you know that is a 5K race. All of my coworkers thought I couldn't do it, but they didn't realize what I could accomplish motivated by pure spite.

—I thought your boss was a friend, said Gage, sliding the back door open for Julian.

—Oh, I hate Wes, but he's a super-nice guy and we get along, Julian explained. He doesn't make me fill out time sheets or anything, which as you know is a critical factor in my employee satisfaction.

At first glance the scene behind the house was something of a Slim Aarons photograph, or a latter-day landscape out of Henry James: it was a seat of ease, indeed of luxury, telling of arrangements subtly studied and refinements frankly proclaimed. The pool seemed to flow organically from the cedar-shingled picturesqueness of the house and down into a kind of bay, a lair of sorts for the inflatable swan. White loungers sporting crisp striped beach towels lined the northeast arc, on which the afternoon sun cast long shadows. But it was perhaps the disorder more than the order that made this image so attractive: what might have been an architectural digest of pristine sterility was rendered supremely inviting by the glistening human being fixed in the scene, reading a book on the second lounger from the right, partially obscured by a very wide-brimmed hat.

Vivien Floris endeavored to comfort herself with this scene and the illusion she imagined herself creating from the perspective of her friends. For under the hat, things felt anything but glamorous. She was a veritable ball of nerves, *Middlemarch* proving nowhere close to an adequate distraction. How about that photogenic glisten? Personally experienced as the sticky, pungent mix of sunscreen and sweat. For all its distant beauty, Vivien's was a physical state of marked discomfort, hardly benefitted by the offhand mention of the name Wes.

There is a well-documented medical link between the human body and mind, a continuous feedback loop known to Hippocrates and rediscovered by modern medicine, whereby a psychosomatic reaction triggers a somatopsychic response, which in turn reinforces the original psychosomatic reaction, further exacerbating the somatopsychic response. Vivien's mind and body had been so thoroughly ravaged by this phenomenological loop in the past twenty-four hours that this casual auditory development threatened to expose a whole new level of anxiety. The surge in her blood pressure and heart rate was momentarily incapacitating, only compounded by the concern that she'd exhibited an incriminatingly delayed response to Julian's greeting. He at least allayed this secondary fear:

—Oh, no—no need to get up, it would wreck the tableau. Far be it from me to disturb your studies.

—Vivien's studies aren't very deep, said Gage, slumping into a nearby lounger. She's only reading a novel.

—What do you know about depth? scoffed Julian. You're a fucking plastic surgeon.

—Who better than an expert in superficiality to judge depth?

—I don't know, maybe an expert in depth?

—You want to be an expert in depth? Gage teased, sitting up and threatening to push Julian into the deep end.

—Don't even think about it. Gage! These loafers are bespoke!

Vivien laughed, or rather, instructed herself to laugh, thumbing compulsively at her bookmark.

It was right there. Tucked between pages 102 and 103: the strange postcard that had arrived yesterday, whose mysterious dark properties Vivien was still in the process of investigating. Keeping it so close at hand, she recognized, amounted to a sort of penance, encasing a pathetically brazen plea—almost as if she wanted Dale to find it, which, on some level, perhaps she did. There is, after all, a certain kind of freedom, a perverse sense of relief, experienced when an uncertain dread actually comes to pass. The nature of uncertainty in human minds is frustratingly illogical like that: for uncertainty itself often produces anxieties far in excess of the worst possible outcome, wrapping around even the most innocuous thoughts and impressions, infecting them with the vast poison of wanting things to be—or not to be—a certain way. The possibility that Dale was embroiled in some sort of freaky bestial affair with Wes Range's perfect wife was ghastly, yes. It needled Vivien's every insecurity; it practically germinated and reproduced them. She'd thought the only thing worse than losing Wes would be losing Dale, too, but that wasn't the half of it. The worse possible outcome was for *someone else* to have both of them. That Diana might have been in Paris with Dale, while Wes waited patiently for her stateside? This was definitional torture. Diana's employment status at Portmanteau had been a well-known fact to Vivien, and yet somehow, prior to yesterday, the likelihood of Dale's knowing her had categorically failed to register. Portmanteau was such a large firm, and Diana was based in New York. Moreover, in retrospect Vivien at least partially recognized the irrationality of her expectation here: that Dale should have somehow intuited that *meeting Diana Whalen* was an occasion of which Vivien should be immediately made aware. As if Vivien had ever mentioned Wes!

It would be a gross understatement to say that the inkling of Dale's extramarital guilt had forcefully resurrected Vivien's own. Absent those six or seven hours in May, there would have been an obvious course of action here. She would have confronted him casually, almost offhand, flipping him the postcard as if she fully expected a reasonable explanation. On the off chance he had one, Vivien would have sought corroborating evidence, and if his story checked out, let it go. This was the best-case scenario. But the alternative would have been almost as good: the right of indignation, the unimaginable grace and equanimity with which she might have assumed the high-dramatic role of Woman Wronged. Vivien could almost see herself, extracting long-term concessions without appearing to extract long-term concessions, finally offering her forgiveness with the serenity of the Pietà.

But unfortunately for Vivien, her fiancé was uncertainly guilty of an undefined crime, and thus the cruelest, most precipitous uncertainty at play lay in her moral position to judge him for it. And for Vivien, for whom clear, good personal judgment was nothing short of a self-defining feature, such uncertainty with herself was, in and of itself, a scathing judgment on her person.

—So, where's Dale? Julian asked, looking around.

How sharply the thoughts she'd been able to quash with some dry cleaning and a few mental gymnastics had resurfaced. And in a far more virulent strain. The hard, now inescapable certainty of her own actions made the potentiality that Dale *wasn't* having an affair with Diana Whalen almost worse.

—Flying into JFK, said Vivien, a bit too cheerfully, checking the time on her phone. He, ah, had a work trip. Probably landing any minute now.

—Oh, he didn't come with you? Where's he flying from?

—*Paris*, said Gage emphatically, before Vivien could answer.

There was, Vivien thought, a perceptible shift in Julian's facial expression, primarily discernible in the secondary overcorrection to the initial shift.

—You don't say, Julian said. And . . . how are the wedding preparations coming along?

There was something pointy about this question too, but Vivien felt a surge of gratitude for it nevertheless. It helped to redirect at least her superficial consciousness back to the comfort of smaller concerns.

—So everything was going fine until yesterday when—and you're not going to believe this—our officiant backed out. He's going on a mission trip and I can't possibly be upset about it—I mean, it's for such a good cause—but . . . I'd already had the programs printed, you know? Obviously I don't blame Father Hummel or anything . . . but it just would have been really, really helpful to know this was a possibility sooner, so we could have chosen someone else in the first place. Or even if he could have, say, emailed instead of mailing a letter . . . it'll be fine, but we have to find someone by Monday in order to have the programs reprinted in time.

—I could do it, Julian offered nonchalantly.

—What do you mean?

—I'm a Universal Life minister. Turns out, this is a fairly straightforward accreditation to obtain online. I got it a few years ago to officiate another wedding—Wes's wedding, actually, so feel free to call him as a reference.

For those skeptical of the psychosomatic-somatopsychic cycle, consider, for a moment, the blush. Vivien hoped she had already overheated sufficiently to mask her body's unwitting crimson confession, sharper than a sunburn, staining her cheeks with shame.

—Julian, that is so kind of you to offer! I'll have to—to talk to Dale, of course—but, I mean, I can't think he'd object.

—No pressure.

—Don't be ridiculous! We'd be indebted to you.

—Excellent. I much prefer people to be indebted to me.

Dale did not find the postcard when he arrived poolside some two hours later. He did not find it that night, nor the following morning, when it sat, still nestled in Vivien's book, inches from his head on the cramped little nightstand. Far more vexing to Vivien was that in the twenty-four hours following Dale's arrival, she could discern no fault whatsoever in his behavior. Indeed, he'd been as close to the perfect weekend companion as she could imagine. He was affable and humorous, sparring with Gage and Julian and Harry, making light small talk with Grace and Jackie and their boyfriends. He understood the tenor of each moment and drank the socially correct quantity of alcohol: two over Gage, a notorious prude—but several behind Harry Sinclair, who had twice already pantomimed elaborate fornication scenes with the swan. On the afternoon of the Fourth, Vivien was painfully delighted to discover that Dale hadn't neglected to pack appropriate attire for Gage's parents' club: a white polo and needlepoint belt atop gracefully frayed khakis that didn't quite fit, but didn't quite fit in just the right way. She had molded him so well, so painstakingly, that he'd just about hidden her art—hidden it even from her. When they crossed the threshold of the Montauk Yacht Club, she clutched his arm with a surge of bittersweet pride. They looked like its founding members.

The lawn was teeming with booze and patriotism. Flags and streamers hung from every conceivable surface; the music was set to a merry volume. The raw bar overflowed with fish and with people, edging one another out to dig in.

—Oh my god, Vivien *Floris*?

Despite the tail-end upward inflection, the voice behind her sounded more like an accusation than a question—a genre of greeting with which Vivien was acutely familiar. It belonged to Kate Manningham. Vivien probably hadn't seen her in a decade, and they had never been remotely close, but that hardly mattered. There was a strict salutatory protocol for unexpected encounters with fellow Sill alumnae: two or three impassioned hugs, animated reiteration of "how *are* you" without ever answering the question, and the introduction of all members of your present party with the appropriate modifiers to convey their socio-economic importance, sexual availability, and degree of relation to you. It turned out that Kate was accompanied by Ainsley Cooper, also of Sill repute—and this process was promptly repeated. *What was new?* They both lived in New York, although Ainsley was "imminently" moving to Los Angeles. No, she didn't know *exactly* when. And this was Kate's boyfriend, Hugh Winslow. *How* did they not know Vivien was working at the Met this summer? They were all going to the Young Members' Party next week. This was more than enough common ground to merit a group expedition to the ladies' room. Hugh Winslow, meanwhile, was ushered into conversation with Dale, Gage, and Julian.

—That's the problem with hedge funds, though, Hugh was saying, slurping down an oyster—too short-term focused. We only do private equity. It's a totally different approach to high finance.

Hugh pronounced *finance* with an ultra-soft "i," and Julian's eyes lunged into a roll:

—What, because leveraged buyouts have such a history of iron-clad ethics?

—Bro, this isn't 1985. We don't do LBOs. YW is a fund-of-funds; we only invest in other PE firms.

Hugh picked a bit of oyster from his teeth.

—So you're limiting your exposure to one PE fund by offsetting it with another, Julian ventured, not taking kindly to being called "bro."

—Sure, I guess you could say that.

—Sounds awfully like a hedge fund.

—Quick, get some champagne, said Dale.

—Good idea, said Gage, turning toward the bar.

—Yes, good idea, Dale, said Julian. You really know how to defuse a situation.

—Alcohol is always the answer, Hugh said.

—Until it's the problem, said Julian.

Hugh broke into a hooty laugh and clapped Julian on the back, as if he had been the one to burn Julian.

—Thanks, said Hugh, accepting a glass. Last one, though. Then I have to go load the fireworks into my boat.

—Oh, that's great, said Julian. Drinks, fireworks, and boating. What a winning combination.

—To America! Hugh cheered, ignoring Julian's sarcasm, downing his champagne in a swig, and heading to the dock in a relaxed sort of jog.

—He makes me want to be European, said Gage.

Dale had been mid-sip as he said this, and promptly aspirated on his Veuve Clicquot.

—Why, Gage, how uncharacteristically astute of you! said Julian. Thank you. Thank you for saying something.

—Are you okay? Vivien asked Dale, reappearing with a hand on his back.

He nodded and waved her off.

—Vivien, your friends are vile, said Julian. This is why I hate the Hamptons.

—Montauk's not the Hamptons, Gage corrected him.

—I barely know those girls, said Vivien. And I'm sure you had a great deal of fun at his expense. I have so little sympathy for you right now.

—And I have so much sympathy for myself.

—Try not to drown in it, Julian, said Dale. They're liable to blow themselves up with those fireworks anyway.

—Oh, I certainly hope not! Julian exclaimed. That would absolutely ruin the party. No, they have to go home and live their lives. That's the punishment for them.

Vivien wondered if this was not, perhaps, the punishment for her, too.

It was not Dale but Julian Pappas-Fidicia who ultimately found the postcard, when, on the late Sunday morning descent from his bunk, he missed a rung and sent the little nightstand flying. While entirely unhurt, he was predisposed to call downstairs in a rage—until he saw the addressee—and stopped to examine the curious artifact.

## XXII.

IF YOU WERE INCLINED TO FORECAST A METAPHORICAL COLD FRONT blowing into Philadelphia on Monday, July 6, 2015, please remember it is with good reason that resisting temptation does not have the reputation for quelling it. Indeed, there is nothing like the increasing seriousness of things to fertilize a landscape for jokes. The fifty-second-floor conference room that morning was, shall we say, well fertilized in this regard, and a palpable, prefrontal-cortical heat radiated from their enhanced imperative. The authenticity of the feelings at play had metamorphosed what might have been a Parisian anticlimax into a blood-boiling raising of stakes. The pressure to be witty had taken on the focused glare of Olympic competition. If the rest of the team didn't think they were romantically involved already, they certainly did then. Dale and Diana were more viciously flirtatious than ever.

It had been a breathy relief to enjoy their weekends with easy conscience, but it was an even greater one to learn that nothing had been permanently spoiled between them. To the extent there had been any fundamental sort of shift, it was more like a pattering barometer—vague and future-oriented; indicative, rather than prophetic. A lulling, homelike sense of security belied their escalating tensions; there was a comforting normalcy to them, almost—to all that anticipation and possibility, hanging thickly in the air once again.

When Prudence Hyman entered the conference room around half past eleven, she stifled a little cough before summoning Dale to her office alongside Parker Remington. Horace yapped when they stood up, and seemed, Dale thought, to be judging him over Prudence's shoulder as they made their way down the hall.

—I've been instructed to invite you to an event, Prudence said, in the least inviting way possible.

She closed the door to her office and bid them to sit.

—It's on Thursday, in New York, Prudence continued. Something called the Young Members' Party at the Metropolitan Museum of Art. I daresay you won't want to go, and I apologize for the late notice, but Jack was insistent. Mercury's sponsoring it.

Enshrined behind her massive desk with Horace sitting in her lap, Prudence Hyman produced an effect hovering somewhere between an authoritarian Catholic school nun and Austin Powers's nemesis, Dr. Evil.

—Oh, no need to apologize. What a lovely invitation; we'd be delighted, Parker answered, without conferring with Dale.

—Delighted, Dale echoed, less delightedly, but I should let you know that, coincidentally, I already have a ticket. My fiancée's a visiting curator there; she curated one of the feature exhibitions, actually.

Prudence rubbed at the sides of her mouth and gave Dale a squinty look, as if she was disappointed to learn he had any semblance of a personal life. This would have undoubtedly concerned Dale more if his attention hadn't been otherwise consumed by Horace—who began to lick his genitals ferociously.

—Okay, give it to Diana, then, Prudence directed. She's based in New York, isn't she? You know what? That's even better. We need all the Millennials we can get. That's why we're sponsoring this ridiculous bacchanal anyway. To "win the war for Millennial talent," whatever that means.

—It means shoddy T-shirts and free LaCroix at work, Dale said lightly.

—What is LaCroix?

Dale cleared his throat, reneging on any attempt at humor. He tried not to look at Horace, who had pivoted his attention to Prudence. To her utter oblivion, the Pomeranian now gnawed at the bunching fly of her pantsuit.

—It's, uh, canned sparkling water.

Prudence rubbed at the sides of her mouth again, her blood-red manicure lending a certain extra deliberateness to the gesture. She picked up the phone and called over to the conference room. Two minutes later, Diana was standing behind Dale. At some point during Diana's acceptance of her invitation, Prudence finally noticed Horace's undue attention to her fly and whapped him on the nose with a curt little *stop it*. Diana paused in accommodation, as if the rebuke were meant for her. At this moment, perhaps more than any other before it, Dale felt a powerful, almost Orphean longing for the briefest glimpse of her face. But he didn't dare turn around.

There would have been few parties inclined to pique Diana Whalen's interest more than one that Vivien soon-to-be McBride was certain to attend, but its setting at the Met—the opportunity to see Vivien in her natural habitat—this made the prospect of the Young Members' Party almost too delicious. Vivien would be, if not a sort of host, then at least a star of the show. To be nestled in the audience, Diana knew, would be a distinct advantage: she'd be free to observe Vivien while remaining unobserved. Diana could control the moment of introduction and the tone of engagement, scripting her first few lines and the modifier qualifying their connection. These were valuable options to preserve when you wanted someone to like you. And make no mistake, this was Diana's goal: for Vivien to like her—to like her very, very much.

Was there not also some prospective twinge of fear, of pain? Sure, but she tried not to picture it: Dale's arm encircling Vivien's waist, all casually and whatnot, in that dear, tasteful manner of appropriate public intimacy. How brutally unfair—that such a touch was not only to be allowed, but very likely necessary. Diana recalled the way he'd steadied her in Paris by the elevator, the passion and intensity with which his hand had arced around *her—that* was the form of such an act, of which this new imagined version, even if precisely realized, could never escape the realm of simulacra. Cruel, inferior gesture! The idea of witnessing its flaunted materiality—as if that meant it was the real true thing—was too, too horrible. *All the more reason to find her alone first, to independently impress her.* In certain instances, there is no better remedy for rising above one's torrid, circling horrors than to look certifiably hot.

As every woman knows, impressing another woman is a far more taxing enterprise than impressing a man. Unlike their basic counterparts, advanced bitches were unfazed by designer labels, let alone perky breasts. Such properties were not assets, they were assumptions. Diana needed to introduce Vivien to that illusory *New York Times* version of herself—and that wasn't about the clothes or the shoes or hair or makeup or even the jewelry—*even* the engagement ring and wedding band. It was about the subtle underlying message that the amalgamation of these things conveyed. And yet it went beyond style too. *Aura* would be closer. Her posture and movements, facial expressions, word choice and elocution—if even one of these elements was awry it would render the quality of a silk or the length of a leg line irrelevant. There was a thin, fragile balance to preserve between self-control and nonchalance. And with the slightest indication of inauthenticity, the spell would be broken.

Diana calculated the optimal ratios of simplicity and interest, classicism and trend, sex appeal and understatement, avant-garde art show and after-work business function, and the results brought her to the Theory boutique in Center City. It was a white dress that caught her eye, deliberately oversized but with a plunging neckline and pockets. The kind of garment that few men understand but women tend to deeply appreciate—to envy, even—especially from the position of entrapment in a beautiful, uncomfortable dress. Diana tried it on to ensure it wasn't *too* tentlike and bought it without looking at the tag. Shoes were next, and these were harder. Diana had the impression Vivien was on the tall side, or at least taller than she was. She needed the maximal height she could walk in with the impression of ease, and they couldn't be some ultra-chunky wedge where this calculus would be obvious. Stylistically, they had to be nothing short of show-stopping. The simplicity of the dress required it.

Four stores later and with every other shop closed, Diana found them at Nordstrom Rack. Technically they were the wrong season—navy velvet, with a festive holidayesque bow on the back, but they were open toe at least, and a high-quality Italian brand. Most importantly, the heel fell somewhere between a wedge and a stiletto, and even though they were probably four inches high, she seemed to be able to walk in them. Their comfort would surely deteriorate over the course of the evening—but once she had cemented her initial imprint and they'd all had a few drinks, it hardly mattered if she switched into flip-flops. By that point, such disorder in dress might even impart a poetic appeal.

Back in her hotel room, Diana evaluated the overall effect, and could find no fault. The mechanism of her self-distraction had succeeded twofold. And it was an appropriate museum ensemble, not so much in the sense that she looked like a work of art as in that she might fade nicely into an architecturally nuanced background. *Negative space*, Diana whispered to herself with an impish half smile, disrobing and falling promptly into a glorious, dreamless sleep.

Less than ten blocks away on Walnut Street, Dale's repose was marked by considerably greater agitation and ambivalence. The prospect of introducing Diana to Vivien had the potential to be thrilling: his fiancée would be, he was quite sure, at the very height of her wiles on Thursday evening, and it would be satisfying to show her off—not in the sense of a trophy wife, but in that of the modern, enviably equal one. And yet, for all of Vivien's cunning sophistication, Dale could not shake the notion that Diana would be impervious to her subtle brand of social one-upmanship. His fear wasn't that Diana wouldn't be jealous, but that she would too freely acknowledge her jealousy—that she would deconstruct

Vivien's charms with such astute precision that they'd cease to sound charming, overshadowed by the charm of Diana's astute deconstruction. Never having met Wes, Dale would have little recourse for an apropos counterattack. The scenario presented a fundamental lopsidedness that Dale would be powerless to correct. Then there was the larger fear, looming on the border of his consciousness: that Diana—or worse, Dale himself—would somehow betray the intimacy of their relationship in a manner that, to any outside party, would seem impossibly incongruent with sustained physical chastity. Had he expressed this fear to Diana, she would have summarily labeled it *guilty-seeming innocence*. But the fully subconscious truth went deeper, as fully subconscious truths tend to do, its genesis springing from contentment's ultimate killer: comparison. The metaphysical intimacy Dale shared with Diana outshone any connection with his future wife. That this fact amounted to an existential threat did not prevent it from being true, and Dale was overwhelmed by fatigue from the effort of hiding such a secret from himself.

And so, not quite knowing why, Dale left the Clock bar early on Tuesday. By Wednesday he felt so physically ill that he was forced to forgo a night out with Diana entirely, the dread of failing to equal her surmounting even his craving for her presence. Dale felt so improved on Thursday morning that he chastised himself for the habitual sleep deprivation he was now accustomed to tolerating for those wee hours together. It wasn't healthy. His wedding was in less than two months. Still, when he arrived at Olympia, Dale's newfound refreshment was immediately channeled into banter with Diana. Indeed, within the space of a few exchanges, their badinage began to seem the overarching raison d'être for feeling refreshed. There was a new-looking garment bag hanging in the corner of the fifty-second-floor conference room, and Dale itched to see Diana in whatever it contained.

—Oh my god, I *love* your dress, Megan gushed when Diana emerged from the ladies' room a little after 3:00 p.m.

Eric's jaw hovered no more than a few inches above the floor.

—Mom, you do *not* look like a mom.

Diana brushed him off, but Dale had to agree—even if her sartorial choices all paled in comparison to a certain pair of white shorts. It wasn't like she could've worn anything in the vicinity of her Parisian getup to an event that, however superficially glamorous, essentially boiled down to a client function. She was already pushing it with that neckline, Dale assured himself. When she bent down to lift her tote and affix it to the top of her suitcase, he caught a sliver of lacy bralette through the exaggerated armhole and had to actively redirect his thoughts.

It had been previously determined that Parker, Dale, and Diana would ride in the car arranged for Prudence and her deputies. It was a large SUV, but at full capacity, and with Diana wedged between her male colleagues in the back row, it was not a comfortable drive. Diana's body sidled up against Dale's, yet with the utmost prohibition of touch. When he looked at her to nourish his wretched passion, he found the heat wasting him away. There were several polite calls to turn up the air-conditioning.

# XXIII.

WES RANGE LEFT HIS UBER AND BRISKLY ASCENDED THE FRONT STEPS of the Metropolitan Museum of Art, squinting absently at his growing reflection in the glass of the revolving door. His mind was already inside the building, his first interaction with Jack Howard crystallizing with third-person omniscience: all warm smiles and complimentary platitudes and good-old-boy physical affirmations coming together like abstract snippets of future recollections. Only occasionally were these impressions interspersed with pictures from another exhibition—with actual, if conveniently altered, Mental Catalogue memories. Wes had prepared himself for this, too; for the déjà vu of this hallowed venue and the strong possibility of reencountering Vivien Floris in the flesh. He corrected his windswept hair, as if preemptively dusting off something buried in his brain beneath it. *There it was.* That trusty old heuristic: *polite brevity*. Wes's ring and watch caught the declining sun and flashed off the revolving door into his eyes. *No flash, please!* He entered the Great Hall.

—Welcome to the Young Members' Party! said a pretty young greeter in a bright yellow dress. Last name A through M on your left, N through Z on your right.

Wes gave her a half-smile nod of thanks to which she seemed disturbingly invulnerable, already employed in welcoming the next patron. He retrieved his ticket from another pretty young woman behind the right-hand desk, only to immediately hand it back to a different museum official, yet another pretty young woman guarding entry into what struck Wes as a high-end yet poorly attended nineteenth-century disco club.

—The VIP preparty is on the roof, the third girl explained, reading Wes's confusion. The main party down here won't get started until later.

—Ah, got it, thanks.

She smiled bashfully, almost less with her mouth than her shoulders, and Wes felt a revitalizing burst of confidence. He passed the sign for *Art & Myth* without incident on his way to the Roof Garden elevator.

Even partially obscured behind Pierre Huyghe's giant-rock-in-a-fish-tank installation, it was impossible not to spot Julian. He was wearing his signature round tortoiseshell glasses, a light blue-and-white striped button-down dress shirt, an orange-and-navy rep bow tie, and what Wes could only assume were the infamous white gabardine pants. He would have seemed fussily groomed even in isolation, but in animated gesticulation next to the generically businesslike gentlemen who were presumably Jack Howard and a high-level associate, Julian looked like a Charleston wedding guest poised to give an impromptu lecture on supply-side economics. Wes shook his head to himself, worrying that the latter half of this observation would turn out not to be a metaphor.

But no, mercifully—Julian was merely recounting the creation myth that was his version of Ecco's branding journey. The conversation paused to welcome Wes, and much to his relief, Jack's smile and handshake fell well within a standard deviation on the normal curve of his anticipated greeting. The second gentleman, Wes learned, was Mercury's chief marketing officer, Greg Templeton.

—I was just about to tell Julian how important branding has been for our business too, Jack segued—you have to understand, in the early 1990s, no one would have ever expected a payment-switching company to become a household name.

—And when he says *no one*, he means *no one*, emphasized Greg.

—I remember it well, Wes exaggerated, relying mostly on the research he'd done over the past two weeks. The "pay like a god" commercials. They were hilarious.

—Thank you, the humor was indeed an important aspect, said Jack. That the conceit seemed tongue-in-cheek camouflaged how serious we were about tying our product to divine power. I think the reason it was so successful, financially speaking, was because we were able to—we were able to tap into this genuine sense of immortality in our customers at the prospect of opening their wallets. And, look, we knew we had a great product. Once the association was made, the convenience of plastic made it easy to retrigger and reinforce the feeling.

—A brand is, after all, the promise of a repeatable experience, added Greg Templeton glibly.

—I would argue, Julian countered, that the best brands are actually the promise of a recursive experience.

Jack Howard looked intrigued.

—What do you mean by that?

—I mean they become embedded inside you, inextricably woven into the tapestry of your consciousness in a way that mirrors their presence in the broader tapestry of our collective cultural one. Think about it: how many people at this party would be unable to link *pay like a god* to MercuryCard? More people would have trouble identifying Barack Obama as the president of the United States, I assure you. It has become one of those seemingly random, seemingly incidental pieces of knowledge that it is nearly impossible *not* to know. If you can't establish the same mental connections that everyone else does when there's talk of *paying like a god* or *saving fifteen percent or more on car insurance* or *breaking off a piece of that Kit Kat bar* or whatever it is, you are fundamentally hindered in your ability to participate in contemporary American life. This is why I have such bullish expectations for Ecco's brand equity. Power is persuasive, addictive even, sure, but please tell me—what could be stickier than the recursive experience of recursion itself?

It was a favorite riff of Julian's, one Wes had heard versions of before and tried to convince him to tone down a bit. Three deep vertical creases had pooled in Jack's forehead. Greg looked hopelessly confused. But before Wes could temper Julian's rhetoric, Jack jumped in:

—I think it's brilliant, he said flatly.

—You do? said Wes and Greg, wide-eyed, simultaneously.

Julian looked terrifically haughty.

—Yes; this is exactly the kind of disruptive thinking I've been talking about, Greg, Jack said before turning to Wes. It's clear you have a visionary running your operations. Very little could reflect better on you as a young executive. Enough small talk. If you don't let me buy your company, I'm going to have to steal your chief operating officer. So, what's it going to take?

—Six glasses of champagne, Parker Remington demanded at the bar in the Great Hall.

—Sorry, sir, but this bar isn't open yet—you'll want to head up to the Roof Garden.

—I'll meet you all up there, Diana announced to the group, excusing herself to the ladies' room.

The others made their way to the elevator, hopping aboard with a pair of pretty young museum employees.

—Um, excuse me, ma'am, one of them addressed Prudence. I'm sorry, but pets are not permitted in the museum.

—He's not a pet, he's my service animal.

The girls looked at each other skeptically, but were powerless to question her. This was one of the benefits of being Prudence Hyman, Dale thought. Cloaked in the guise of a victim, she had unchecked power to oppress. He smiled at the girls sympathetically, hoping to soften the blow. Not too sympathetically, though—for all Dale knew, these were friends of Vivien.

From the moment he'd ascended the front steps of the Metropolitan Museum of Art, Dale had been sharply on the lookout for signs of his fiancée. He'd primed himself for her to appear unexpectedly, instructed himself to act as if she were perpetually standing just behind him. He would not be caught off guard, let alone in some seemingly compromising position with Diana. If there was to be a surprise encounter, it would at least be a predictable one. Or so Dale thought, until he spied Julian Pappas-Fidicia in earnest conversation with Jack Howard and Greg Templeton and—yes—yes, there was no mistaking it. There was only one person who that person next to Greg could be: Charles Wesley Range IV.

Dale nearly tripped on the uneven surface of Huyghe's ground installation. It was like coming face to face with a celebrity or, closer still, a character from a novel—the kind, frankly, he would have liked to have written. There was this misplaced yet powerful sense of familiarity, kinship even, known to be false but felt to be true. This sensation itself was a familiar one. To Dale's uncomfortable recollection, Wes Range engendered precisely the same sort of first impression as Diana Whalen.

—Ah ha, Parker, glad you could make it, Jack Howard addressed his old friend first. Prudence, thanks for coming; I want you to meet Wes Range and Julian from Ecco. Wes, Julian, this is Prudence Hyman, Mercury's chief information officer, and—er—

Even Jack Howard's well-oiled extraversion stumbled on how to introduce a dog.

—And this is Horace, Prudence helped him.

—It's a pleasure to meet you. May I? Wes asked amiably before petting Horace.

—Oh sure, he loves the attention, she said, significantly undercutting his "service animal" status.

To Dale's shock, Horace did love the attention. *Ugh, Horace would like Wes Range.*

—Julian Pappas-Fidicia, nice to meet you, Julian inserted himself. Tell me, Prudence, is Horace an . . . orange Pomeranian by chance?

—That's correct.

—Interesting, said Julian, making no similar move to touch the creature. Notoriously resilient breed, right, Dale? Great to see you, by the way.

—You two know each other? Jack asked, holding out his hand to Dale.

—I should hope so, Jack, said Dale, shaking it, actively ignoring Julian's odd introduction. He'll be officiating my wedding in September. We're old college friends.

—No kidding! Small world. Do you and Wes know each other then too?

—I don't believe I've had the pleasure, started Wes with an open, sociable smile.

Julian interrupted him with relish:

—Perhaps not, but you *have* had the pleasure of meeting Dale's fiancée.

—Oh really? Who's your fiancée, Dale?

Wes's inquiry came in that particular tone of loose, amiable curiosity reserved for playing the name game. Dale felt a nervous shiver run up his back that was utterly incompatible with it.

—You know Vivien? Vivien Floris?

—Vivien Floris! Wes exclaimed quietly, Ah, yes—but not well, I'm afraid—we went to the same high school, yes, but she was a couple of years ahead of me.

Jack Howard had been observing this interaction with waning interest and increasingly at a distance, having leaned into an aside with Parker Remington that was now approaching a full-blown separate discussion.

—Oh, so you went to Sill, Dale said, feeling a sense of relief at the distance of removal, moderated by the minor resentment of Wes's primacy in the history of his fiancée's life.

—The Sill School in Connecticut? Greg Templeton verified. You don't say! My daughter is going into her fifth-form year there.

Everyone's faces lit up with the same inflated expression of giving a shit and made the appropriate nods of vague undeserved congratulation, attempting to hide the extent to which they were now more interested in the contents of Jack and Parker's private conversation. The frustration of having to socially perform had been exacerbated by the departure of the primary audience of import. The only follow-up questions Dale wanted to ask in present company were all for Wes, and squarely prohibited within the social mores of a business conversation, not to mention by his personal sense of pride and dignity. No, he must appear entirely apathetic to Wes's casual acquaintance with Vivien. It could not possibly be more intimate, Dale assured himself, than the relationship he shared with Wes's wife. The close association with Diana that Dale had previously sought to downplay and even hide he now looked rather forward to highlighting. *She'll be here any minute now*, Dale mused smugly, wondering if Wes even knew she wasn't in Philadelphia. *Probably not.* Diana certainly had no idea her husband would be here. Unexpectedly having the benefit of asymmetric information tip in his favor felt like a kind of triumph over their marriage, and Dale basked in the anticipation of Wes's—not to mention Diana's—surprise.

Only one nettlesome thought gave him pause: *notoriously resilient breed, right, Dale?* Julian Pappas-Fidicia might be accused of many personal failings, but linguistic imprecision was not among them. Perhaps Wes had no idea that Dale knew Diana, but Julian certainly had an inkling—more than an inkling, it sounded like. Dale had never mentioned anything about Horace's brush with death to him, but Diana well might have. If so, and knowing that they both worked at Portmanteau, Dale's arrival with Horace would have been enough inferential information: Julian loved drama so much that if anything, it would be his tendency to over-infer. As much as Dale generally preferred to leave the choice of topic to others in competitive circular social clusters, in this instance it was essential he steer the conversation clear of any mention of Diana before she could present herself. But Prudence jumped in before he had the chance:

—That's sensible of you to send your daughter away to school, Greg. I'm sure it'll make it easier for her to accept your divorce.

Several eyebrows involuntarily popped up, but Julian Pappas-Fidicia's were joined by the sides of his lips. You wouldn't have thought it to look at her, but Prudence Hyman was his kind of woman.

## XXIV.

—OKA-A-Y, INTONED VIVIEN FLORIS, BECKONING HER AUDIENCE AWAY from the towering mirror and toward Nicolas Poussin's *Narcissus Lamented by Echo and Eros.*

She should have realized this would be a particularly avid group of selfie-ists: such an assemblage of privileged, well-educated American Millennials, all looking their personal best. Even those whose feet brought them toward the Poussin weren't paying attention to it. Their eyes were locked on their smartphones, evaluating which of the fifteen or twenty hyper-mimetic images they'd just taken was most suitable for social media, tagging @imetovidsheirs, tagging Vivien herself even. In her curatorial quest to demonstrate Ovid's outsized contemporary cultural relevance, this was precisely the behavior she had knowingly, expressly incentivized, but even Vivien had been unprepared for just how well her conceit would work. That was always the problem with incentives, though. Not that they didn't work, but that they worked only too well. Vivien enlisted her most resonant voice again:

—*Why try to catch an always fleeting image, poor credulous youngster? What you seek is nowhere, and if you turn away, you will take with you the boy you love. The vision is only shadow, only reflection, lacking any substance. It comes with you, it stays with you, it goes away with you, if you can go away.* If you can look up from your phones now, you'll see firsthand the fate of those who can't. Here, in Poussin's painting from 1630, generously loaned to us by the Louvre, we find Narcissus captured at a later moment in the story—just after the first-ever "death-by-selfie," if you will.

This turn of phrase garnered a few chortles, and several guests moved to get a closer look at the painting. Vivien stepped to the side and smoothed her dress: a short-sleeved mini in geometric white lace, sheer at the shoulder and fitted through the hip, blossoming at the hem into a controlled, peplumesque flare. It was from her new favorite label, a rising upmarket contemporary brand called Self-Portrait, whose distinctive blend of militaristic precision and ultra-feminine detailing had acutely appealed to Vivien even before she'd discovered its oh-so-apropos name.

—It's a challenging ask of Poussin, to visually communicate death and beauty at the same time, and he navigates it flawlessly. Yes, please, get closer. The details are just gorgeous. Look at Narcissus, bare-chested, his garment torn in grief, as Ovid tells us. He appears as if living in death; if you look carefully, you can see the narcissus flowers already sprouting at his head, his metamorphosis under way. And what about Echo? Look at the way she fades into the rock with escalating transparence; see the detail of her ribbony shoes, left empty.

Vivien pointed out these little flourishes avidly; half-turning toward the painting, obviously tickled by its beauty herself. As her audience cycled through their turns to scrutinize the picture, Vivien turned to scrutinize her audience. The colorful varieties in toilette and plumage collectively painted a pleasingly uniform tableau. There was one exception, however. An outlier. She was very young, but between the overprocessed blond hair and simple white shift dress possessed the aesthetic overlay of someone far older. Vivien looked attentively at this simple dress. She knew what such simplicity meant and what money was paid for it. The girl hadn't been there at the start of the tour—Vivien would have noticed. There was something unplaceably familiar about her, Vivien thought, and an arresting intensity to her gaze. After examining the Poussin, the young woman turned and focused the same unblinking gaze, framed by its giant dark eyebrows, squarely on Vivien, as if she herself had been a painting. There was the suggestion, if not the actual formation, of a smile. Vivien returned it with deliberate placidity, and continued her talk:

—Despite the way Narcissus treated her, Echo is filled with pathos for him in Ovid's final scene: *She was sorry for him now*, he says, *though angry still, remembering; you could hear her answer "Alas!" in pity, when Narcissus cried out "Alas!" You could hear her own hands beating her breast when he beat his. "Farewell, dear boy, beloved in vain!" were his last words, and Echo called the same words to him.*

Vivien paused dramatically.

—*Farewell, dear boy, beloved in vain!* For those of you who are dating, by the way, this is a great line to use when someone is ghosting you over text.

Many laughs, but the girl in white was immutable, and Vivien blushed.

—Anyway, even within such a story of solipsism, fundamentally about negating and negated love, there is this remarkable shadow strain of genuine feeling—of, dare I say it, unselfishness: Narcissus grieves for—he laments—the death of the boy in the pool, just as Echo laments him. This idea of *lamentation* is central to Poussin's painting. Recall that we still haven't talked about the third figure in the scene. That's right, Cupid. Iconographically speaking, he's the most important. Cupid's presence in the composition, flanking Narcissus on the other side of Echo, joining her in mourning him, uncannily mirrors another lamentation painting, one from a century earlier by Paris Bordone, which you can see at the Palazzo Ducale in Venice. Bordone's painting isn't of Narcissus, though. It's of Jesus Christ.

Many raised eyebrows, but the girl in white's dropped lower. She was precariously close to smiling.

—Bordone's Jesus lies prone in precisely the same position and state of undress as Narcissus here, with two grieving angels, *one at the head, the other at the feet*, as described *not* by Ovid, but in the biblical book of John. The two paintings are similar enough that in another era, Bordone might have been inclined to sue for copyright infringement. You laugh, but I assure you the enlightened elite of Poussin's own time would have easily made the association—and understood the audacity of the symbolism. Namely this: that Narcissus, a fatally flawed human being, is worthy of Christ-level lamentation; that is, that mortal and divine tragedy exist on the same plane, and should be awarded the same pathos. If anything, Poussin is trying to one-up Bordone, to give Narcissus an even grander funeral. Please keep in mind here, Cupid may look like an angel, with those precious little wings—but Cupid is a *god*. This painting depicts nothing short of a god mourning a human; specifically, a god mourning the "father of painting"; a god mourning not just any human, but a god mourning an artist. You'll notice Poussin's implication here is a pretty self-serving one: that art offers a mortal path to immortality to be revered even by immortals, and as the creator of a painting such as this one, this path logically extends to Poussin himself. Thus the artistic apotheosis—the deification—that Narcissus achieves in this scene is mirrored by Poussin's own in depicting it. As with Caravaggio's *Narcissus*, the conceit within and outside of the painting is the same. There is an echo here and now, in physical space—and we the viewers play no small part in it. Because really, what greater proof could there be of Poussin's mortal immortality than the fact that almost four centuries after his death, we're all still standing here in awe of his work? Is there anything that the bright individualistic ego—mortal or immortal—craves more?

—Caviar blini? the server offered, holding out the tray of hors d'oeuvres to the group on the terrace.

—Oh, yes please, Julian replied, leering over the tray, his deliberating fingers wavering to select the choicest morsel. And then, before the server could abscond, another.

—In my view, he continued, you can never have too much caviar.

• • •

—If you think this view is a stretch, said Vivien down in the gallery, consider that Poussin painted Narcissus not one, but four times. In addition to this picture there's a scene from earlier in Ovid's narrative in private collection and, in Dresden, *The Realm of Flora*, a thematic painting, where Narcissus appears centrally, surrounded by other characters who undergo similar floral metamorphoses elsewhere in the poem. Then here in the US, at the Fogg Museum in Cambridge, Massachusetts, you can see *The Birth of Bacchus*—a strange tableau, and one that again grants Narcissus exalted status by juxtaposing his death with the birth of a god. There are facsimiles of all of these images in the section label to your right, and I encourage you to look at them after the tour, but the main points I want to emphasize in relation to his lamentation are these: first, that Narcissus was, if not an obsession, then at least a keenly fascinating subject for Poussin; and second, that Poussin's symbolic insistence on redemptive mortal-immortal artistic metamorphosis persists across his works. This theme is consistent with Ovid's text as well: *Even in Hell*, Ovid says, *Narcissus found a pool to gaze in, watching his image in the Stygian water, while in the world above, his naiad sisters mourned him, and dryads wept for him, and Echo mourned as they did, and wept with them.* Even the immortal shadow of Narcissus clearly hasn't learned his lesson, and yet still he is worthy of pathos, of redemption, even from those whom he has harmed most. I guess you could say that if Narcissus ends up more a devil than a god, he's at least the kind of devil with whom you'd sympathize.

—Deviled egg, anyone? asked another server on the roof.

—Don't mind if I do, said Julian, carefully transferring the lamb lollipop he was in the process of consuming to his other hand, failing to account for its new proximity to Horace.

—No! Horace, no! Bad boy! Prudence chastised the dog, whose tiny jaws had managed to swipe a not insubstantial bite.

—Gracious, Prudence continued as the gristled bone fell. I'm terribly sorry, Julian.

—No apology necessary, said Julian promptly, surprisingly unfazed, as the damage had been borne entirely by a crevasse in Huyghe's floor installation, to the salvation of Julian's pristine white pants.

—You're a clever little thing, aren't you! Wes exclaimed.

He rubbed Horace's head fondly, laughing with enough good nature that Prudence couldn't resent him for it, but not quite enough for Dale not to.

—We can get Julian another little lamb lollipop, can't we?

—Still, I'm not sure what's gotten into him, Prudence insisted apologetically. He knows better than do be so rude. Don't you, Horace?

Horace did not immediately respond for comment.

—He has a strong survival instinct, Julian assured her. Honestly? I can respect that. I'm almost inclined to admire his tenacity—

—you're almost inclined to admire his tenacity, continued Vivien. At least Narcissus is consistent, pursuing his vainglorious folly even in hell like that. There's something about the depiction of love, I think—even in its most dysfunctional varieties—that inclines us toward generosity, toward empathy, even. I hung this painting across from Gérôme's *Pygmalion and Galatea* to illustrate this point: they're mirror images. The myth of Pygmalion, of a great artist coaxing his marble sculpture into flesh and blood, is, remember, a birthing story—of idyllic "true love" bringing art to life. The death of Narcissus, meanwhile, illustrates precisely the opposite metamorphosis, where the dysfunctional, fatally flawed love of a metaphorical artist nevertheless has the power to transform life into art.

Vivien made metered eye contact with her audience, forcing herself not to linger on the girl in white, even as she felt the girl's eyes linger on her.

—Ironically, it's this inverted narrative that hits on the more fundamentally human desire. Forget the stunning frequency with which

Narcissus is depicted in the history of art. If you pay attention, you can spot echoes of the myth everywhere in our society today. It has been inextricably woven into the tapestry of our Western cultural consciousness, ingrained so seamlessly that we often fail to notice it. Poussin couldn't have predicted the "selfie" per se, but I can promise you he would have understood its appeal. For he, too, longed to render the impermanent permanent, the mortal immortal; from life: art. He would have understood the selfie, yes—he would have loved and been afraid of it. With that, I'll leave you free to snap a few more of your own, if you dare. Thank you very much for your attention and for your support of the Metropolitan Museum of Art; I do hope you enjoyed the tour, and bid you an evening to remember.

Diana Whalen held her position after the audience dispersed, allowing two other patrons to ask Vivien questions, listening with her eyes to the curator's replies, studying her body, the musculature of her limbs, the movement of her dress as she gestured, the overwhelming sophistication of its delicate strength. Vivien Floris was the sort of woman who seemed so perfect she almost failed to pass the Turing test, the most impressive aspect of her algorithm being her apparent unconsciousness of her algorithm's effect. It was an art so well practiced, Diana recognized, that it had crossed into second nature.

—What a powerful exhibition, Diana declared, by way of introduction. You make it look effortless now, but I'm sure it required a great deal of work to actualize.

Vivien blushed prettily as the two women stepped toward each other, coming face to face. With Diana in heels and Vivien in flats, they were just about the same height.

—*The best art, they say, is that which conceals art*, Vivien purred in an intimate mezzo piano. It's the best compliment, too, so thank you. And you're right—it did. Require a great deal of work to actualize, that is. When you're talking about two Caravaggios, a Bernini, and a Poussin, the negotiations get complicated. Any one of them might command a solo tour.

—Who is the "they" you're referring to there—the "they" that says *the best art conceals art*? Ovid?

—Very close. The entire line is from Ovid, but he doesn't actually specify who the "they" is.

—Perhaps the "they" is "us," suggested Diana.

—You've been paying attention—or . . . forgive me, but you look so familiar—have we met? Did you go to Penn? Were you in the Art History department?

—No, I didn't go to Penn.

—My mistake; there's just something about your manner, I guess

—We all see ourselves in other people, said Diana impishly. It's generally the chief thing that we like about them.

—Aha! Too true. You should do my next tour for me.

—Oh, I'm hardly qualified for that; art history isn't my thing—though I must say, I do understand why you so love the Poussin.

—Yes, Vivien said, turning fondly toward the painting. He's my second-favorite Narcissus.

—Only your second-favorite?

Vivien gestured toward the Caravaggio, or rather, toward the mirror image of the Caravaggio.

—You did give him prime real estate in here, Diana said. And don't get me wrong, I understand the decision. He's beautiful. So lifelike.

Vivien nodded knowingly.

—He seems, I've always thought, to surpass life in its imitation.

—Yes, that's just it! Diana concurred, excitedly. He's such a real man that he's more real than any real man can be. This may seem like a non sequitur, but have you read *Anna Karenina*? I just finished it, and the Caravaggio makes me feel like Levin, looking at the portrait of Anna. Still, I have to say, I'm surprised *you* don't prefer the Poussin.

—Why is that?

—Because Poussin's Narcissus is a dead ringer for your fiancé.

Vivien's face was a pool of confusion. Diana, after waiting as long as she thought she could get away with it, smacked her forehead apologetically.

—I just realized I never introduced myself, she said with a boisterous, almost lurid laugh. How strange that must have sounded to you! I work with Dale; that's why I'm here tonight, actually. I'm sorry, I guess it must have felt like I knew you already, too—because I've—I've just heard so much about you. Anyway, it's a pleasure to finally meet you in person: I'm Diana Whalen.

It was the blond that threw her off, but of course Vivien saw it now, saw it all too clearly. She breathed deeply and smiled, projecting the appropriate degree of name recognition for a colleague of your future husband whom he has casually, asexually mentioned on an appropriate number of occasions, and firmly accepted her outstretched hand.

—Diana, Vivien echoed, the vowels rolling off her tongue, *goddess of the hunt*. The pleasure, I assure you, is all mine—

It was with great deliberation that, still firmly pressing Diana's hand, she continued:

—and was Wes able to join you this evening?

Vivien smiled beatifically as she said it, her face belying the sharpness with which she was scanning Diana's for any change of expression. The latter cocked her head, making no attempt, it seemed, to hide her astonishment. There was almost a note of perceived flattery to the gesture.

—No—he's still at work, unfortunately. . . . So, Dale's mentioned my husband?

—Oh—no, said Vivien lightly. Wes has mentioned his wife.

## XXV.

**SELECT INSTAGRAM ACTIVITY (RESORTED, CHRONOLOGICAL), ACCOUNT OF "OVERHEARD UPTOWN" (@overhearduptown), THURSDAY, JULY 9, 2015.**

**overhearduptown**
The Metropolitan Museum of Art

---

"There is an art to throwing a party. You want people to be loose enough to make bad decisions, yet keep it together enough not to ruin the furniture."

Liked by **imetovidsheirs**, **vivienfloris**, and **3,476 others**

**overheard uptown** ***WE WILL BE POSTING LIVE TONIGHT FROM THE METROPOLITAN MUSEUM OF ART YOUNG MEMBERS PARTY*** DM us your submissions from #YMP2015 for insta-gratification
Bartender, Great Hall.
Overheard by @overhearduptown
@metmuseum #ChinaLookingGlass @imetovidsheirs #IMETOvidsHeirs #PierreHuyghe

View all 95 comments

**imetovidsheirs** @overhearduptown we're excited you're here! Enjoy the party [confetti ball emoji]
**vivienfloris** @dsmcbride @grace_cho07 @audreywim @doctorgage @harrisonjsinclair @jackiedarby
**grace_cho07** @vivienfloris YAASSSSSSS
**audreywim** @vivienfloris @grace_cho07 XOXO gossip girl
JULY 9

**overhearduptown**
The Metropolitan Museum of Art

---

"You've only been out twice and she bought your ticket for tonight? Ugh, people in New York love giving their money to the charitable organizations least in need of it."

"Are you talking about the Met or about me?"

Liked by **vivienfloris**, **jdorset** and **1,673 others**
**overhearduptown** You, bro.
Two men, check-in desk.
Overheard by Anonymous
#YMP2015 @metmuseum #charitycase

View all 24 comments
JULY 9

**overhearduptown**
The Metropolitan Museum of Art

---

"OMG do you see how old that guy is? I can't believe they're letting him in."

"Lauren, that's Bill Cunningham."

Liked by **kmanningham**, **vivienfloris**, and **2,669 others**
**overhearduptown** Kiss goodbye any chance of a feature in the style section, ladies.
Two women, check-in desk.
Overheard by @kmanningham
#YMP2015 @metmuseum @nytimes @nytfashion #guestlist

View all 166 comments
**lauren_coddington** @kmanningham I hate you
**kmanningham** [face with tears of joy emoji]
**mdavenport** omg @kmanningham savage
**vivienfloris** @kmanningham so glad you made it tonight
**kmanningham** @vivienfloris can't wait to see your show [face blowing a kiss emoji]

**vivienfloris** @grace_cho07 @audreywim

**grace_cho07** @vivienfloris I am going to be so jealous when you're all over the NYT tomorrow

JULY 9

**overhearduptown**

The Metropolitan Museum of Art

---

"Wait, *you* drove *yourself* here?"

"You didn't?"

"Um, *no*. This is New *York*."

Liked by **dianawhalen**, **vivienfloris**, and **2,678 others**

**overhearduptown** Okay, who let in the bridge & tunnel crowd?

Man and woman, Great Hall.

Overheard by Anonymous

#YMP2015

View all 59 comments

**dianawhalen** omg @wesrangeiv this has to be our main man

JULY 9

**overhearduptown**
The Metropolitan Museum of Art

---

**Man:** "Do you think she'll be here tonight?"

**Woman:** "Who?"

**Man:** "Chyna"

**Woman:** "Please tell me you didn't think *China Through the Looking Glass* was about the female wrestler."

Liked by **vivienfloris**, **dsmcbride**, and **4,953 others**
**overhearduptown** Someone's not getting ready to rumble tonight.
Couple, China Through the Looking Glass.
Overheard by @doctorgage
#YMP2015 #ChinaLookingGlass #guestlist

View all 250 comments
**doctorgage** a little inspo for your next expo @vivienfloris
**vivienfloris** @doctorgage you made this up . . .
**doctorgage** @vivienfloris I would never! Back me up here @grace_cho07
**grace_cho07** @doctorgage it's legit @vivienfloris but your follow-up expo is a better fit for the Philly Museum—they love sculptures of wrestlers IMO
**doctorgage** @grace_cho07 so, Rocky was a boxer . . .

**grace_cho07** @doctorgage whatever
**doctorgage** @grace_cho07 @vivienfloris "Rocky vs. Chyna: Punching Through the Glass Ceiling" cc: @dsmcbride @jpappasfidicia
**jpappasfidicia** @doctorgage dear god, you are such a mediocre wit. I submit "Rocky vs. Chyna: Eye of the Crouching Tiger Hidden Dragon" for your consideration @vivienfloris @grace_cho07 @dsmcbride
**vivenfloris** @jpappasfidicia [face with tears of joy emoji]
JULY 9

**overhearduptown**
The Metropolitan Museum of Art

---

"Babe, get a photo of me taking my selfie."

Liked by **imetovidsheirs**, **vivienfloris**, and **6,762 others**

**overheardutown** Woman to boyfriend. Art & Myth: Ovid's Heirs.
Overheard by Anonymous
#YMP2015 @imetovidsheirs #IMETOvidsHeirs

View all 92 comments

**jpappasfidicia** @vivienfloris did someone really say this? The authenticity of overheard uptown and its sources is of tantamount importance to me

**vivienfloris** @jpappasfidicia . . . yes

**jpappasfidicia** @vivienfloris please point this couple out to me

**vivienfloris** @jpappasfidicia sorry, but my exhibition is a selfie safe space

JULY 9

**overheardutown**
The Metropolitan Museum of Art

---

**Man 1:** "That Adnan guy seems guilty as hell."

**Man 2:** "Oh, I thought you said you hadn't listened to *Serial*."

**Man 1:** "You don't have to listen to *Serial* to have an opinion about it."

Liked by **dianawhalen**, **vivienfloris**, and **4,512 others**
**overhearduptown** I prefer good podcast criticism.
Two men. Roof Garden.
Overheard by @overhearduptown
#YMP2015 #PierreHuyghe #serial

View all 85 comments
**dianawhalen** @jpappasfidicia
**jpappasfidicia** LOLOLOL @wesrangeiv @dsmcbride overheard uptown is in our midst!
**jpappasfidicia** @dianawhalen funny enough, I am at the met right now, and I witnessed this interchange firsthand, and "Man 2" is your husband
**dianawhalen** @jpappasfidicia what?
JULY 9

**overhearduptown**
The Metropolitan Museum of Art

---

**Man 2:** "Wow, you're like a character out of a Whit Stillman film."

**Man 1:** "Is that a compliment?"

**Snide Friend:** "Does it matter? You're going to take it as one either way."

Liked by **wesrangeiv**, **vivienfloris**, and **4,381 others**
**overhearduptown** Same two men discussing Serial, plus snide friend. Roof Garden.
Overheard by @overhearduptown
#YMP2015 #pierrehuyghe #serial #whitstillman

View all 80 comments
**wesrangeiv** @jpappasfidicia "snide friend" hahahahahaha
**jpappasfidicia** @wesrangeiv like you come out of this looking so attractive
**wesrangeiv** @jpappasfidicia relatively, I believe I do
**wesrangeiv** For the record @dsmcbride, it was a compliment
**dsmcbride** @wesrangeiv I took it as one, thank you
JULY 9

**overhearduptown**
The Metropolitan Museum of Art

---

"Will I see you again before I move to LA?"

"Probably. You've been imminently moving to LA for 6 years."

Liked by **mdavenport**, **hughwinslow**, and **4,944 others**
**overhearduptown** It's good to have goals.
Two women, Great Hall.
Overheard by @kmanningham
#YMP2015 @metmuseum #losangeles @overheardLA

View all 224 comments
**ainsleyc09** @kmanningham @mdavenport @lauren_coddington BUT I AM
**kmanningham** @ainsleyc09 sorry we'll believe it when we see it
**mdavenport** @kmanningham on a rollllllll
**kmanningham** @mdavenport you all make it too easy
**doctorgage** @dsmcbride @jpappasfidicia we've met this girl

**jpappasfidicia** @doctorgage and as such, I think her position is eminently reasonable. If you had her friends, wouldn't you want to move to LA too?
JULY 9

**overhearduptown**
The Metropolitan Museum of Art

---

**Woman:** "Excuse me, I'd like to buy that Chinese bathrobe."

**Security Guard:** "Miss, this is a museum, not a Dress Barn."

Liked by **dianawhalen**, **dsmcbride**, and **7,239 others**
**overhearduptown** China Through the Looking Glass. Overheard by Anonymous
#YMP2015 #ChinaLookingGlass

View all 347 comments
**dianawhalen** @dsmcbride did you submit this?
**dsmcbride** @dianawhalen lol I wish. Dying. Where did you abscond to?

**dianawhalen** @jpappasfidicia did you submit this? Also, what did you mean about Man 2 being Wes?
**dianawhalen** @dsmcbride I'm by the million dollar bathrobes
**jpappasfidicia** @dianawhalen no, I did not submit this. Dress barn is not an attractive name. It's like shoegasm. Who wants to buy anything at shoegasm? It just sounds wet and gross. Dress barn implies that it's designed for cows and pigs, which, as I understand it, is not an effective way to sell clothes to women. Damnit, now I am going to think about dress barn all the time.
JULY 9

**overhearduptown**
The Metropolitan Museum of Art

---

**Man:** "Tiramisu is a bullshit dessert."

**Cater Waiter:** "Why?"

**Man:** "I don't know—because it's served at the Olive Garden?"

Liked by **jpappasfidicia**, **doctorgage**, and **2,974 others**
**overheearduptown** When Instagram served me an ad for unlimited breadsticks I reported it as offensive content.
Great Hall Balcony.
Overheard by @overhearduptown
#YMP2015 #tiramisu @olivegarden

View all 113 comments
**dianawhalen** but is it served at the one on Mount Olympus @hashimotoe ? @dsmcbride
**dsmcbride** @dianawhalen @hashimotoe oh, definitely—goes straight to the neck cleavage
**hashimotoe** @dianawhalen @dsmcbride [man facepalming emoji]
**hashimotoe** @dianawhalen @dsmcbride so I take it you guys are having fun then
**dianawhalen** @hashimotoe mainly at your expense [winking face emoji] @dsmcbride
**hashimotoe** @dianawhalen @dsmcbride wish I was there
**dsmcbride** @hashimotoe sorry @dianawhalen and I will have a piece of Tiramisu for you
JULY 9

**overhearduptown**
The Metropolitan Museum of Art

---

"Are you going to Harry's after this?"

"I'm going to assume that's a rhetorical question."

Liked by **vivienfloris**, **harrisonjsinclair** and **4,099 others**
**overhearduptown** If you don't end up at Lord Henry's, did you even go to the Young Members' Party? (Hint: we'll see you there.)
Two women, Great Hall.
Overheard by Anonymous
#YMP2015 @lordhenrysnyc

View all 735 comments
**kmanningham** @hughwinslow
**hughwinslow** @ainsleyc09
**ainsleyc09** @doctorgage
**doctorgage** @grace_cho07
**grace_cho07** @harrisonjsinclair
**harrisonjsinclair** @jpappasfidicia

**jpappasfidicia** @dianawhalen
**dianawhalen** @dsmcbride
**dsmcbride** @vivienfloris
**vivienfloris** @wesrangeiv
JULY 9

## XXVI.

THERE WAS A VERY SPECIFIC, OBSERVABLE MODE OF OPERATION EXHIBited by Parker Remington when he was close to making a sale. You could feel him trying to temper his excitement; all of his gestures became small and precise. His forehead would freeze, eyebrows up, as if his eyes were stuck on their widest setting. He started leaning hard on the word *absolutely*. Even before Parker pulled him aside, Dale knew the private conversation with Jack Howard had been more than idle chitchat; that if Parker hadn't closed a big deal, he was about to. The question was what kind of deal it was, how much he had overpromised, and to what extent he had committed Dale to delivering on his overpromises without consulting him.

—I have your next project, Remington said on cue, pausing briefly to order a pair of G and Ts from the rooftop bar. Six weeks. Reporting to Jack directly. Starts ASAP—it's time you got some experience managing multiple projects. Haven't talked hard numbers yet, but it'll be high margin for sure.

Parker's expression indicated that it was time for Dale to express blind gratitude.

—Great news, said Dale, hoping to satisfy Parker's ego without technically committing himself to anything.

—Great news—absolutely, Parker echoed, testing his drink. Especially with your passion for M&A. Those guys back there, Wes and

Julian? Jack wants to buy them out. I'm still unclear on what exactly they do, but it's a techy B2B startup of some sort . . .

Dale had hoped Ecco's invitation to the Young Members' Party was in consequence of some matter of smaller import, but he had already been forced to consider this possibility. His annoyance was tempered by the comfort of knowing definitively. The project was even tempting to a certain extent, though for none of the reasons Parker thought it would be. The prestige of running due diligence was hardly worth the extra hours it required, and the potentially stratospheric boon to Wes's fortunes obviously mired Dale in envy. But since this train was moving anyway, it was far better to be aboard than under it. The prospect of dissecting Ecco's financials appealed to Dale's curiosity, and possessed the metonymic flavor of dissecting Wes himself. There was something deeply comforting in the thought of personally reducing Wes to a number—even if that number turned out to be depressingly high. A clear valuation offered either schadenfreude or luxuriant levels of self-pity. And is it not human nature to gravitate toward yardsticks of our own making?

—Techy stuff, absolutely, Parker repeated, but nothing Diana won't be able to figure out.

*—Diana?*

Parker looked confused by Dale's confusion.

—Look, it's not a knock against you, but we absolutely need an architect to lead the technical diligence. Don't worry, you'll have full autonomy on the financial side.

Dale was about to correct Parker's error, to explain that he wasn't threatened by the prospect of an enterprise architect encroaching on his managerial authority, simply surprised that Parker—Mr. Scrupulous himself—had named Diana, given her obvious conflict of interest. Then he remembered that he (Dale) wasn't supposed to be able to make the marital connection either. It was getting exhausting, trying to remember what everyone around him knew, and didn't know, and didn't know that he knew. Parker didn't wait for a reply.

—Speaking of Diana—where is she, anyway?

—I have no idea, said Dale.

—Go find her, will you?

Dale took a swig of his gin and tonic.

—*Absolutely.*

It had been Diana's idea to get a drink in the Great Hall. Vivien reminded herself of this over and over. The quid pro quo move to reveal her independent connection to Wes had seemed so clever, so failsafe in the moment, like she'd flipped Diana's script, doling out maximal shock with minimal personal exposure. Having gone to the same high school was, after all, such a powerfully innocuous bond, being not just incidental, but ancient. What bothered Vivien wasn't that she'd failed to throw Diana for a loop, but how readily Diana had admitted it. *Those were her exact words*, Vivien remembered: "You've thrown me for a loop." Diana had "so many questions about Wes at Sill," and wouldn't Vivien join her for a drink in the Great Hall?

In retrospect, this was when Vivien should have excused herself, pled some curatorial obligation, and declined. Not because Diana's company was unpleasant to her—far from it. Affair or not, she was undeniably *charmante*. To say that Diana was clever, animated, refreshingly frank—these were apt, but also insufficient. Her surface had a shiny, stylized quality, to be sure, but there was an underlying honesty of effort, an honesty almost unheard of in privileged circles. There was an implicit social risk in trying too hard, and a kind of bravery in it, in deliberate rebellion from manufactured nonchalance. And yet there was a nonchalant air to this very rebellion. Was not such honesty part of her gambit? The truth was such a foreign concept, it had its own kind of affectation. How easy Diana made it to let down your guard in order to join her—to try to impress *her* with *your* wit. For while Vivien could not quite say that she liked Diana, she couldn't shake the sensation that it was of the utmost importance for Diana to like her. Oh yes, the root of her charm was more layered, buried deep in the well of reflection. It wasn't Diana's cleverness that Vivien had found so alluring, it was her own. Diana possessed the cleverest sort of cleverness: the cleverness of making others feel clever. That Vivien understood this phenomenon did not entirely discount its effect. It was only after she did finally excuse herself—several drinks later—that Vivien realized they'd hardly spoken of Wes; that the conversation had expanded and contracted with a new focal point, narrowing in on Vivien herself. Glamoured by her own repartée, Vivien had disclosed far more data than she'd intended. Had she really not learned her lesson with regard to self-control? Vivien's powers were drawn not from cleverness but restraint. She thought of that scene in *The Princess Bride*, the battle of wits between the Man in Black and Wallace Shawn's character. It didn't matter if Vivien switched the cups: both drinks were poisoned—with a substance to which Diana had built an immunity. *Inconceivable!* No matter how successfully Vivien had returned volley, she'd been playing Diana's game.

Their meeting had been less an introduction than an ambush, and Vivien was convinced that Diana Whalen had some deliberate end in mind. The question was what kind of end, and to how many levels, exactly, the hierarchy of her cleverness extended. Heretofore, Vivien's anxieties had circled primarily around the lingering mystery of the postcard and the true nature of Diana's relationship with Dale. But what if Vivien's counterrevelation hadn't been a revelation to Diana at all? Prior knowledge is, ironically, all that is necessary to feign surprise. *Could Wes have told her?* Or worse, *could she have learned on her own?* A cold shame crept up Vivien's legs and under the peplumesque skirt as she walked, a little too briskly, toward the Roof Garden elevator. Vivien had objectively wronged this clever, clever woman. This woman with unfettered access—*powerfully innocuous* unfettered access—to her own fiancé. In the Medieval galleries, all of the baby Jesuses, with their lurid halos and warped adult features, seemed to be harshly judging her. When she spied Victor Barlett in Petrie Court, she pathetically ducked behind Perseus until he passed. How she might have impressed him! Vivien knew everything about Canova. But she was in no condition to converse with her boss right now. Vivien's job was the only remaining aspect of her life over which Diana Whalen did not seem to possess total control. *Would she dare to use it?* Something told Vivien that Diana at least had the capacity. She thought back to Diana's parting words. "Oh, you'll find Dale on the roof," Diana had told her. It was a final indignity so subtle that at the time, Vivien's embarrassment felt silly even in her mind. But now—that Diana Whalen had superior knowledge of Dale's whereabouts within the building? This seemed to validate every prong of her tortured analysis.

Vivien was still several steps away from the elevator when she saw its doors were beginning to close. She had to find Dale immediately, to reassure herself that nothing was amiss. In a tellingly uncharacteristic series of gestures, Vivien forced the elevator doors back open, briefly met the exasperated looks of her fellow passengers, tucked her body around into the last sliver of space, and buried her face in her phone.

When the doors reopened thirty seconds later, Vivien was in such a hurry that she nearly barreled into the first person queueing to descend. When her eyes rose up from Instagram, it took Vivien half a second to register that the object of this near collision was Charles Wesley Range IV.

The crowning glory of *China: Through the Looking Glass* was not, as it turned out, one of the "million-dollar bathrobes," but a contemporary evening gown by the couturier Guo Pei known as *Daijin*, or *Magnificent Gold*. Heavy vertical panels of highly structured, impossibly ornate embroidered silk taper at the bodice and expand at the skirt, fanning into an opulent, almost peacockian train with undulating geometric regularity. It is exquisite; a masterpiece of mathematical precision;

almost more a sculpture than a dress. Several patrons encircled it in admiration: not so many that the room felt crowded, but enough to engender a Gatsbyesque privacy. It was among this gently rotating group of admirers that Dale McBride spotted Diana Whalen.

—Certainly not, suffice it to say, something you would find at a Dress Barn, Dale whispered to Diana, sneaking up from behind to join her study.

—Certainly not.

She said it with a wry smile but without turning her head to greet him. It amounted to a willful sort of antigesture that forced him to begin again.

—Parker's looking for you.

—Is he? That's nice.

Dale could feel a trap coming. The veiled annoyance in her voice had that distinctive marital twinge to it, and Dale found himself circling toward a familiar form of anxiety: the one that overtook him when he expected to be accused of some unanticipatable peccadillo by Vivien. Dale had predicted some degree of annoyance on Diana's part once he revealed that her husband was here at the museum, here to shop Ecco to Mercury, no less—Diana being the sort of woman, Dale knew, disinclined to forgive such an omission, even in the context of a potential windfall that would benefit her, too. But this presaged perturbation had piqued Dale's interest precisely because its object was irrefutably *not* him, but rather—

—*Wes*, Vivien blushed.

She was in a state of agitation that could not be hidden, even by good taste: flustered and emotive and smiling larger than usual in overcompensation. Wes could feel the heat emanating off of her; a messy, red-blooded intensity that was very un-Vivien, but not without its appeal. For all his preparation to run into her, Wes could not have predicted this. He'd steeled himself against controlled politeness and cool regret, not passion—not big, scared eyes pleading for normalcy. That the predication for her disquiet at least partially rested on some unrelated impetus prior to their encounter made it less personally worrisome, and thus all the more sympathetic. This was no primordial temptress. She was not some siren, luring him to death for the sport of it. Vivien Floris, who time and self-interest had transformed from an object of devotion into a vessel of ridicule, was, in reality, neither. Behind her personage there was a person, a real woman on whom the Mental Catalogue was based, but insufficiently replicated. Her present expression, by contrast, seemed to capture the real Vivien. Wes determined this new, realistic portrait to be much her best. Somehow humanization had sharpened her attractiveness, and he felt a twinge of resentment for Dale McBride.

—I—I didn't know you'd be here, she stammered.

—Yes, he said, in that peculiar pitch of voice which makes the word half a negative, but only for work. I'm sorry; I should have told you.

—No, no, it's—

—really wonderful to see you, Wes interrupted with his signature warmth, that unimpeachable tone, rich in its history of wooing without seeming to woo.

Vivien's smile relaxed a little, and he felt further emboldened, flush with the freedom of the already guilty.

—You look . . .

She tensed up again, glancing down, as if concerned she'd spilled something on herself.

—I look what?

—Just stunningly—

—beautiful. Isn't it? Diana said, still laser-focused on *Magnificent Gold*. Do you know who recommended making the effort to come see it?

—Overheard Uptown?

Diana laughed, and turned toward him. The eye contact felt like a kind of reward, and Dale relaxed a little. Perhaps a little too much.

—*Vivien*, she hissed.

This was, to Dale's recollection, the first time Diana had ever said her name. Not that they didn't talk about her; they talked about her regularly. Hell, at this point Diana likely knew more about his relationship than anyone save Vivien herself. But Dale realized now that Diana had previously only referred to her indirectly, as, say, *your wife-to-be*, or *your fiancée*. It was a vocabular shift declaring a new frame of reference—though, he reminded himself, not an advantage he was unable to match. After all, he had met Wes. He enjoyed, moreover, the benefit of her erroneous assumption that it was she who firmly held the upper hand on this score. Her supercilious expression amounted less to an admission than a boast. Diana's move had been premeditated. He was almost tickled by her gumption.

—So that's what you've been up to, Dale said lightly.

Diana returned her gaze to the *Daijin*.

—There's something about it reminiscent of the dress Vivien's wearing tonight, don't you think? Not literally, of course, but conceptually, thematically. It's that princely, armor-like quality, I think. Like, delicacy aside, both have something impenetrable about them.

—I haven't seen Vivien's dress yet.

—*Oh*, Diana said, with a show of superiority.

—I suppose you'd like me to be annoyed, but I'm afraid I'm rather impressed.

—Thank you, said Vivien, reddening again.

—Your fiancé is a lucky man. I've just met him this evening, actually. Julian introduced us . . .

His tone was gentle, kindly—calibrated to reassure. He'd been discreet, she had no doubt—there had been no awkwardness.

—I explained we were old school acquaintances.

He said this last bit with great self-assurance, she thought, as if to convince her—or maybe himself—that it genuinely provided an adequate summary.

—You've met Dale.

—I have.

Vivien emitted her most florid blush yet, scanning the terrace.

—Um, do you know where he is now, by chance?

—Only that he's not up here. He excused himself like twenty minutes ago to find some coworker.

—Some coworker?

—That's what he said, said Wes.

—You do realize—

—something fishy is going on between Dale and Diana Whalen, Julian Pappas-Fidicia declared, waving his fork at Gage Thompson in between bites of galette.

Julian, too, had left the Roof Garden, having it on good authority they were serving dessert on the Great Hall Balcony. Of secondary interest was tracking down Gage to posit his theory concerning their mutual friend.

—Who's Diana Whalen? Gage asked.

—Sorry, minor detail there. Diana is Wes's wife. What? Do I have galette on my bow tie? Why are you looking at me like that?

—Because, said Gage, you have a tendency to confuse "something fishy" with how much you enjoy fishing.

—I do my best swimming against the current, Diana shrugged. And guess what else I learned?

—What?

—*She knows Wes.* You never told me Vivien went to the Sill School; Wes did, too. I can't believe we never put it together. What's more surprising is that he never fucked her.

She said this last sentence quietly, flatly, reveling in her tonal disconnect with such inflammatory content. Dale could tell she was enjoying herself. How strange it was, that instead of having been forced to reveal his own intel, he had succeeded, almost by chance, in wresting this report from Diana! That he knew her enjoyment to be misplaced only added to his own.

—Wes had a tendency to date the pretty girls, Diana explained.

Dale obliged her with the astonished expression she sought, and she threw back her head, celebrating her perceived victory with Maximum Strength Visine:

—Relax. It's not like he's a womanizer or anything. Besides, Vivien's name's never come up.

—Excuse me, miss, the disembodied voice of a security guard called from somewhere. You can't use that in here.

—Sorry! Diana acknowledged, quickly spritzing the other eye. Come on, let's go to the Great Hall. I need a—

—gin and soda, heavy on the gin, with lemon juice and simple syrup—um, a bit more syrup than that, Julian instructed the balcony bartender. Yes, that's good, thank you.

Gage gave the bartender an apologetic shrug.

—Just a regular Tom Collins, please, he said, turning back to his friend with a twitchy shake of the head that Julian misinterpreted as another affront to his theory.

—First of all, they both work at Portmanteau, Julian said, marshaling evidence as he polished off the last bite of galette.

—A lot of people work at Portmanteau, Julian. It's, like, the size of a small country.

—And did everyone from this small country have contemporaneous business trips to Paris last week?

Gage tipped the bartender and followed Julian to an open spot overlooking the Great Hall.

—So, maybe they're on the—

• • •

—same project, said Vivien urgently.

Wes knit his eyebrows together.

—What makes you think that?

—*Nothing* makes me think it, I know it. She told me herself.

—What? What do you mean? You've met Diana? When? Where?

—Downstairs. Just a few minutes ago . . .

—No, Wes shook his head. She's at a work event tonight.

—She said the same thing about you, Vivien said with a derisive exasperation he'd never seen in her before. *This* is *her* work event, too. She's here with Dale; she snuck onto my VIP tour and introduced herself after. We got drinks and talked for like an hour. Wes: "some coworker" is your wife.

It was the way she said "some coworker" that bothered him most, as if she had good reason to suspect that wasn't all they were. Wes wanted Vivien to be wrong, for her fizzy insecurities to have been pinned in error, but of course he knew she was right. Even as he'd contradicted her, the texts were coming back to him, the fight he'd had with Diana over her client's serv—

—ice animal, Julian explained. I mean, how many people bring an orange Pomeranian to work with them? Please do not tell me this is a coincidence. Prudence Hyman is not to be mistaken for someone else.

—*Prudence Hyman?* Seriously? Is that her real name?

—Not the point!

—No? So far you've only convinced me Dale and Diana work together and their client is a Looney Toon. I don't see how that makes *them* "fishy."

—Diana was dodgy about the Paris trip at brunch. And I found this bizarre veterinary postcard in Montauk. And you should have seen the look on Dale's face tonight when I met Prudence and her dog. It was like he could sense I was putting it together. He looked guilty.

Julian's implication was unmistakable.

—Get real, Julian. No guy would cheat on Vivien. You're just going to have to trust me on this one.

—Excuse me, but I'm gay, not blind. And for the record, you've never met—

Diana Whalen ordered another pair of drinks from the Great Hall bar.

—The only way I can think to adequately describe her is like a candid glamour shot, she said, still extolling Vivien's virtues. Except also with sound. Have you been on her tour? She's, like, a born raconteur. I expected her to be cultured and tasteful and smart and knowledgeable about art and all, but that's not what impressed me. It was more her voice and mannerisms. She managed to be authoritative and utterly nonthreatening at the same time. It's not easy to make people feel smart while you're teaching them something, but that's—that's precisely what she does. She lures you into finding yourself as cultured and tasteful as she is.

Dale said nothing. Diana grabbed a handful of bar snacks, and examined him critically.

—She really is too good for you.

—I'm well aware of it, said Dale.

—But, Diana equivocated, retrieving their drinks from the bar, pausing, exhaling, and beginning again, a wicked twinge in her eyes.

She took a long draught.

—But it's just that she isn't—

—with him *right now*! Julian smacked Gage's shoulder and gestured largely to the Great Hall bar below them. Look! Do you not see Dale? That's Diana, the bottle blonde handing him a drink!

Julian watched Gage watch Diana clink glasses with Dale in a wanton lean. They moseyed across the Great Hall together, and Gage's eyes followed them, until they were out of sight down the Greco-Roman wing.

—She's striking, Gage admitted, I'll give you that, but she's no—

• • •

—Vivien Floris—er, Dale's fiancée, said Wes, introducing her to Jack, Parker, Greg, Prudence, and Horace, who had entered the little Roof Garden elevator vestibule on their way downstairs.

—Great to meet you.

—Pleasure.

—Pleasure.

—Hi, Vivien.

—Arruff!

they all said, pressing her hand.

—She's also a curator here, Wes added.

—Visiting curator, Vivien corrected him modestly.

Nonetheless, they wanted to know what, in her professional opinion, they should make it a priority to see. When Vivien recommended *Magnificent Gold*, Wes objected:

—But surely, they must see your show, Vivien. Vivien curated the one about Ovid.

—*Art & Myth*? Jack confirmed. That was actually the one I was most excited about.

—Absolutely, said Parker, sensing an opportunity. If there is any chance you could give us a little tour . . .

*It would do great things for your fiancé's career*, he implied. Vivien smiled serenely.

—Oh, I'd be happy to—but—I have to run and grab something from my office first. Shall we meet at the exhibition in, say, fifteen, twenty minutes?

—The party is supposed to be over by then, said Prudence, much to Parker's consternation.

Vivien reassured them:

—It'll be fine if you're with—

—me, Diana said, rounding a Grecian urn to face the entrance to *Art & Myth*. She's not *me*.

## XXVII.

THE EXHIBITION DESIGN OF *ART & MYTH* MAY HAVE CENTERED AROUND the revelatory reflection of Caravaggio's *Narcissus*, but this configuration came with a literal side benefit. Past the entrance, you were forced into a near-immediate left, onto a corridor paralleling the main Narcissus room. A section label introducing the vast mythography of Medusa the Gorgon greeted you at the turn, describing the various writhing narrative and iconographic threads springing from its most enduring features: her hair, a tangle of live snakes; her gaze, turning those who would look upon her face to stone; her death, at the hands of the great hero Perseus, wielding his shield as a mirror. But it wasn't until you were halfway down the dim corridor, standing between two apses awash in a reverent glow, that it became clear just what Vivien had accomplished. Caravaggio's *Head of Medusa*, rendered on a circular shield, filled one apse, across from Gian Lorenzo Bernini's marble bust of the Gorgon. As if the painting were a mirror reflecting the sculpture, and the sculpture the head of Medusa herself, turned to stone by her own reflection.

Dale watched Diana follow this path and pause between the apses, just as Vivien mandated. From Diana's vantage point, studying the Caravaggio, the viewer became Vivien's final flourish, caught like Perseus between Medusa and mirror. You became the hero-murderer responsible for that indelible, lucid, phantasmagorical shriek—seen in front of, but heard behind you. Venturing toward her, Dale had the distinct premonition of walking into a trap: the kind Great Men bring about precisely in their efforts to avoid them. But he and Diana were alone in the corridor, all offstage-like and intimate, the party roaring toward its apex in the Great Hall.

—He's not *me* either, you know, Dale ventured with a false levity, that bedrock tone of psychological self-defense.

Diana opened her mouth, panting inaudibly, a savage rejoinder suspended on her parching tongue.

It is only upon closer inspection of these two objets d'art that one realizes they may not, in fact, depict the same person. The shield isn't even identifiably female, and some argue it's a self-portrait—a disturbing thought when you consider Caravaggio chose to capture that haunting split second between fatal impact and primary flaccidity that cannot be properly categorized as belonging to life or death alone. The Bernini's marble neck remains intact; she merely winces. Her face is a different brand of distraught entirely—not to mention classically symmetrical. She's the lovely nymph raped by Neptune in Minerva's temple and punished for "her offense"; glimpses of her former tresses, like grown-out roots, are still visible under her vengeful mane.

These discrepancies between the two Medusas did nothing to undermine Vivien's overarching curatorial design. On the contrary, hers was a thesis cemented by its cracks. For who among us, when we look in the mirror, is inclined to see what is actually there? Do not fail to underestimate the protean power of light and shadow—of *chiaroscuro*, *tenebroso*. If our reflections remain recognizable, it is not because they do not change. Medusa prays upon this much-worshipped prismic effect: of ineluctable identity, yet plurality of self. *Originally apotropaic, her image has come to symbolize everything from Nietzschean nihilism to feminist rage, and adorn objects from Archaic terra-cotta vases to the logo of the fashion house Versace*, the section label neatly summarized. *She has, perhaps, become the ultimate symbol of metamorphosis itself: a symbol able to metamorphose into whatever you want her to symbolize.*

Dale looked at Diana expectantly, his forehead burning, but the savage rejoinder never materialized. She swiveled in the other direction with a sigh, her face covered in shadow, but exposing her neck from the side. When Dale caught her eyes again, they were no longer haughty, but beseeching, her mouth slightly ajar—as if pulled down by the weight of unsaid things.

—Nothing is ever going to happen between us, she said softly, with a clipped sort of sadness.

—No, he said softly, in agreement.

She inhaled, brimming with that stoic brand of confidence strangely born of resignation. For the orchestration of this literal accord emboldened the exploration of its closet precarity. Having formerly rejected each other on explicit terms, new possibilities could emerge in the corners of self-awareness where their uncertain egos had formerly pressed.

—That doesn't mean we're not in love, Diana said, choosing her syntax carefully.

Dale clung to the double negative, not unmindful of building syntactic advantage himself:

—We can't exclude it from the realm of possibility, given everything that hasn't happened.

—Tell me you don't think of me, when we're not together.

—I can't—

—*Then why are you marrying her!*

He fought to resist her tonal pull, not to reflect it, and hated himself for the bitter edge his voice betrayed:

—I don't see you leaving Wes.

—That's different; I was already married.

—Are you seriously going to stand on the piece of paper? As if you have some biblical reverence for marital sanctity. Such hypocrisy is beneath you, Diana. Let's not pretend we haven't been equally complicit in this little charade.

There was something furious, even mad, building in her demeanor now that Dale struggled not to label "feminine hysteria."

—*Little charade?* Is that what this is to you? No, no, you know what? This is good, I'm glad you said that, that makes this easier for me. Because either you're deluding yourself, even now, because you still want to win, or the shared wavelength that has underpinned, like, my greatest self-doubt and unhappiness was founded on a fraud. Perhaps I've made a grave mistake, mistaking your thoughts for my own. And if that's the case, please let me be the first to apologize for my rampant inappropriateness—oh, and also, to tell you to go fuck yourself, because you could have saved me a lot of pain.

—Diana, please—

—Do *not* tell me to calm down—

—What? Why would you say that? I didn't; I wasn't going to. You're not mistaken, Diana. We may not fit into each other's lives, but you're not mistaken. You're—an outlier.

—And you're just a liar, Diana said.

She took a step back from him, down the corridor toward the Narcissus room.

—I'm not aware of ever having lied to you.

—Not to me, Dale.

—Discipline isn't the same as lying. I think it's a marker of maturity, to deprive one's self of what one wants.

—Oh, please. It's like your blind spot's in the center of the mirror. The truth is, you get off on self-denial.

Dale had too much respect for his opponent to refute this. It was a point so undeniably salient that Dale's only option was to concede in such a manner where he might claim some small share of her success.

—I mean, you do have to admit there's a weird sort of pleasure in it, he said.

—Well, duh!

It was a return concession, a form of détente, rebalancing the relational elements that allow for certain rivals to be, also, the closest of co-conspirators.

—See? said Dale, with just enough irony as to maintain plausible deniability. This is why I love you. You have just the right amount of contempt for me.

—The contempt is mutual, she said, overflowing with restraint, her words wielding all the gravity and power of *I love you, too*.

Diana trailed off, unsure how to end an affair that didn't technically exist. The silence, replete with cognitive dissonance and the phenomenological awareness of cognitive dissonance, and its total crumbling unsolvability and whatnot, seemed to expand, this tension, its seductive chastity, into unheard melodies, shared. *Thou still unravish'd McBride of quietness!* Their faces were less than six inches apart, but moved no closer. He understood, and she understood; she knew he understood, he knew she understood. He knew she knew he understood, and she knew he knew she knew he understood. They understood each other, perfectly. Dale asked if they were still friends. They were very good friends, Diana said.

—Maybe best?

—The kind that bare their souls, and tell the most appalling secrets.

Dale nodded gravely. He wanted to touch her, if only in some small way. A meaningful goodbye. Some proof they were different from little black and earthen figures etched into a pot. He raised his hand and, as if approaching a wild doe, tenderly reached forward, tucking a loose strand of hair behind her ear. Dale felt Diana's palm before he saw it, resting quietly on the back of his hand, stilling it there. As her fingers curled between his thumb and index finger, tears welled in his eyes.

—*What's this?* Vivien Floris gasped, turning onto the corridor.

How could he have forgotten the number-one rule of Museums: *Do Not Touch*.

—*Dale?*

The conundrum with this triangular form of encounter, for which there is both great historical and literary precedent, is that the natural phraseology arising from attempts to convey faithfulness has literally come to form the model argot of adultery. You've heard these Janus lines before, perhaps many times, to the point of contronymic cliché. *It's not what it looks like, There's nothing going on here, I swear we're just friends, &c.*—cringeworthy adjacencies to the holy grail of the genre, at least Millennially speaking, popularized by Shaggy's immortal refrain: *It wasn't me.* Over time and through significant misuse, these apologies have developed a mean, raveling transparency, inclining them to register as statements of contrition, even when uttered as legitimate defense. For all their formal education and social enlightenment, Dale and Diana still couldn't quite escape them.

—Do you think I'm an idiot? Vivien demanded, as most people in her position are inclined to do.

She rifled through her lecture notes and papers, fighting tears, biting her lips furiously, as if, in the absence of such an effort, her words might prematurely escape:

—How do you explain this, then? she said, flinging something at them, a small piece of paper, a postcard, which landed on the floor, a few steps from Dale's feet.

He picked it up, Diana reading over his shoulder. They looked, for a moment, genuinely perplexed by it. Recognition reached Diana first, at which point she emitted, loudly, a laugh so lightheartedly relieved it seemed almost unselfconscious.

—What kind of freak show—

—Vivien—Diana stopped her, reconciliatory, physically collapsing the space between them.

Vivien strode pointedly past her, past Dale, too, and her reverent apses—past the Caravaggio, the Bernini—moving into the space that Diana had, until a moment earlier, occupied herself. Diana circled back again persistently, imploring her to listen.

—Vivien, please, you've misunderstood things—I promise, you're mistaken. If you give us the chance to—it's really quite funny, you'll see. We have this ridiculous client, Prudence Hyman. I know, I know, but seriously, that's her real name . . .

Diana spared no detail; if she could be accused of anything, it was hyperbole. Her facial impression of Horace during his transfer from the conference room floor into her bag was particularly obscene, around which point in the story Vivien became visibly reactive, her own facial features all gaping prettily. Interpreting this as an encouraging sign, Diana redoubled her narrative efforts, taking even fewer pauses and greater creative license with ever-expanding animation and flourish.

—you have to know how devastatingly sorry I am about the postcard, Vivien, she concluded. I mean, I can only imagine what a mind fuck that was for you out of context. But you have to admit, it's pretty funny now, right?

—Hilarious, pronounced a cold, disembodied voice behind her, echoed by a panty little bark.

Even if you are Perseus, it's a frightening prospect, standing between Medusa and mirror. For as you shift your position slightly, your gaze, as is natural, fully locks on those murderous, Caravaggian eyes. You freeze. For the eyes have that quality more commonly associated with another masterpiece of portraiture, a living woman as calm and serene as the monster before you is defiant. *Uncooperative.* From your physical position, caught between shield and bust, blocking their reflective connection, you understand. It is the mirror, not the sword, that is the true weapon. Whose eyes follow yours in the mirror? That's right. You are the catalyst of your own destruction; these horrible eyes are yours.

Diana inhaled, blinking. She turned bravely toward Prudence:

—What a great relief it is, to know you see it that way, she said, taking Prudence at face value, mulishly ignoring her tone.

—*Diana?* A familiar voice called to her.

He was standing behind Prudence, fettered between Parker and Jack Howard.

—*Wes?*

—Do you know this woman? Prudence demanded.

—You could say that, Wes said. She's my wife.

—Well, your wife is fired.

—Oh, come on now, Prudence, Diana coaxed.

—Save it, said Prudence as Horace grew increasingly antsy in her arms, his little body writhing under all that opulent fur. Jack, if you still want to wheel and deal with the husband, that's your business, but—

She turned to Parker:

—I better not see her at Olympia again. You'll have to find some other way to complete your deliverables.

—I understand, Parker said, making no move to defend Diana. Absolutely.

—Parker, just let me—

—I think you've said enough, Diana.

—Oh, well, *absolutely*.

Wes's eyes blazed in embarrassment for her. He suggested they go. By this point Horace was howling, begging for release from his Prudential cage.

—No, Wes, you know what? Diana hissed. You stay. *I'll* go. It's not like I have the faintest idea what you're doing here, anyway.

She retucked an errant strand of hair and smoothed her dress elegantly, proudly, the way she'd seen Vivien do earlier.

—Congratulations on your masterful exhibition, Diana said to her, taking her leave with an acerbic courtesy both impolite and impossible to fault.

She flung herself past the corridor and through the Narcissus room, bisecting it on the diagonal with locomotive efficiency. The gilded mirror stood in front of her, Narcissus's reflection hovering overhead. With only the briefest passing glance, her eyes met Dale's in that other gallery, that other well-lit world, filled as it was with radiance and umbrage, deception—incandescence—her gaze gone before he could begin to process its presence. She fixed her pooling eyes on some harsher light, and exited through the gift shop forever.

Wes excused himself apologetically to Jack, and followed in the wake of his wife, all but ignoring the present and future McBrides and giving Horace the out-and-out fantods to the point that the rascal managed to escape Prudence's embrace, falling remarkably catlike to the floor and cantering devotedly after Wes. But though his little legs moved quickly, alas, they were very short, and poor Horace could not outpace the heavy gift shop door, which trapped him in the Narcissus room, powerless to follow Wes beyond its glass. Bearing this rejection with considerably less grace than many (many) suitors had before him, Horace promptly went berserk. There was a general commotion as Vivien and Dale, Prudence, Parker, Greg, and even Jack tried in vain to trap the little beast, his pathetic cries echoing maniacally in the cavernous space, pining for Wes at the door, running away from it in unpredictable circles, through various arms and legs, frantic to avoid pursuit. In one particularly vexing tangle, Greg inadvertently backed into his boss, sending Jack, to everyone's mutual horror, flying onto his ass. This new spectacle diverted the attention of everyone save Horace, who promptly laid claim to the center of the room and settled down to take a delicate little Pomeranian shit. A violent hush replaced the cacophony. Everyone except for Vivien turned wide-eyed, mouths agape. The curator, meanwhile, merely winced, motionless, her hair disheveled, fallen eyes empty, her marble skin aglow.

—So, said Julian Pappas-Fidicia, appearing at the end of the corridor, sliding his glasses up the bridge of his nose, what did I miss?

# PART FOUR

## XXVIII.

One of the less touted but not insubstantial benefits to being a management consultant is that it is very possible to be summarily fired by a client, yet not to lose one's job. Indeed, with the notable exception of data and security breaches, most violations—and nearly all of those stemming from client complaints of indecorous behavior—carry few if any lasting consequences to the offending consultant. The market for skilled labor capable of communicating sophisticated analyses at a fifth-grade reading level and willing to travel four days a week is simply too robust. These people are expensive to hire, expensive to train. Besides, most partners have encountered enough client caprice of their own not to be terribly invested in punishments, especially in the case of first offenses. Thus standard operating procedure when a client expresses unremitting displeasure with someone is to grovel conspicuously on the spot but internally chalk it up to "a bad fit," throw her back in the staffing pool, and, say, a week or two later, present her on a pedestal to a different client.

Diana's dismissal from Mercury was sufficiently incendiary to catalyze a deluge of additional unpleasant administrative niceties, but for the most part, this systemic advantage held true. Sure, there was a tepid internal investigation. Reports and counterreports. Lengthy HR interviews with mommy-track part-timers with extensive empathy training and *I-want-to-speak-to-the-manager* haircuts. The real point of contention, it became clear, had nothing to do with Horace, but rather Diana's perceived undisclosed conflict of interest re: Ecco and its "business impact" on the Portmanteau sales pipeline (needless to say, Jack hired another firm to run the due diligence). Parker wouldn't speak to her, not that it mattered much to Diana. She'd been fond of him, but there's only so much loyalty one can muster for a leader whose own extends solely to the point of self-interest. Besides, other partners were already clamoring to hire her. Diana scheduled a vacation for early August, making her effectively unstaffable in the meantime, and readied herself to enjoy a largely subsidized month on Nantucket.

Dale was considerably less fortunate, as the unfired souls left with an angry client tend to be. While he and Eric Hashimoto only bore Prudence Hyman's indirect wrath, they bore it at exponentially closer proximity, and there was no shortage of long nights spent in the fifty-second-floor conference room during those last few weeks. Such stretches can sometimes really galvanize a team, whipped into the addicting conflation of type-A stress with teleologic (*ontologic?*) significance, but the dynamic without Diana just felt forced and bleak, like the illusionless morning after a one-night stand, awkwardly formal in compensation for the prior show of intimacy. The work itself lost any remaining pretense. The impending layoffs just seemed pedestrian and sad. Eric was inconsolably desolate, and particularly pitiable when he developed a head cold in the height of summer's heat. Dale picked up the slack himself, conscious that the rest of the team, though no one ever said anything, felt rather hard done by, caught in the crosshairs of Olympian conflicts that were none of their concern and above their pay grade. It was just as well. The few waking hours Dale spent outside work were consumed by the ever-elastic exercise of planning for his wedding.

With some conspicuous groveling, Vivien had "forgiven" him almost immediately. Dale understood this quote-unquote forgiveness to carry contingencies, that it was more like a tacit probationary agreement, whereby Vivien would not mention his conduct with regard to Diana Whalen in exchange for the authority to command him as she pleased.

This was the form his atonement took: wedding vendor management, support of various last-minute "upgrades," validation (*only* validation) of aesthetic minutiae, more-than-cursory participation in seating arrangement analyses. It should be noted that the actual procession of their union had never been in serious jeopardy. Dale's compliance with his fiancée's terms were tied closer to a quotidian path of least resistance than any sort of essential relationship-saving. Even if Vivien's worst suspicions had been true, Dale didn't think she would have gone so far as to call off the wedding. The invitations had already gone out. And more subtly: she exhibited far too much evidence, however neatly disguised, of that mounting febrile desire most women her age (even if they refused to acknowledge it, even if they themselves found it bizarre or disturbing or even sexist) were on some level consumed by. The great irony was, rather, that the terms of his subjugation realized precisely those daily unpleasantries he'd resisted a textbook affair to avoid in the first place.

As the summer weeks waned, Vivien showed few signs of winnowing reparative expectations. The more accustomed you become to getting what you want, the more it loses its luster, and at the same time needles all the more in those rare instances when you do not. This is a feature of privilege in general, but especially of beautiful, rich young women in the days leading up to their weddings. No one could have credibly used the word *Bridezilla*, of course. Vivien's desires were far too refined, and she expressed them with calmness and precision. That she made herself above reproach was part of Dale's mounting vexation. He began to get the sense she was leveraging her temporary power explicitly in the service of its permanent installation, like a spousal sort of gerrymandering, or a clever wisher, wishing for more wishes. Hints of irritation started creeping into his acts of compliance. At first Vivien either didn't or pretended not to notice. She was still traveling to New York during the week. But as his resentment grew more manifest, she began, ever subtly, to tug at the veil covering their original agreement. Dale became consciously aggrieved, feeling he'd done quite enough penance for a fundamentally innocent party. Their relationship became increasingly transactional. A wafting malaise enveloped the town house, one no amount of busyness and prenuptial logistics could quite paper over. It was under these curling corners of obligation, in the fractional slits of negative space, that Dale's mind came to rest newly on Diana Whalen.

He knew she still worked at Portmanteau. He'd been contacted by the internal investigation shortly after the Young Members' Party, as had Eric Hashimoto. *No, I have no reason to believe Ms. Whalen had any prior knowledge of Mercury's interest in acquiring Ecco; Yes, I have every confidence that at another client, she would succeed.* If Diana had been terminated, her E-IM status would have changed to the ominous *Presence Unknown* weeks ago, whereas she was mostly just *Offline* or *Away*, with a little yellow dot next to her photo. On the rare occasions Dale saw it flash green, he could feel the physiological stress response, the moistening glandular anticipation that *maybe she would ping him*, which he both worked strenuously to quell and seemed unable to resist exacerbating—rolling his mouse over her picture, her name; hesitating, clicking on it, bringing up a little blank window, watching it glow whitely. He thought about typing many things, sometimes going so far as to actually type them, but sent nothing. Still, these little actions, the shifting pixels on the screen, seen by no one else, were the subject of great pleasure and defiance, of torment and somatopsychic anxiety. Sometimes, minutes after she'd gone offline, his stilted inhalations still uneven, his fingers still hovering above the keys, it would hit him. The sheer magnitude with which he missed her. This isn't to say he experienced regret proper, or even the disinterested sense he might have acted differently. A part of what continued to so arouse him was, indeed, the memory of his own resistance, of which his unsent missives cut a crude facsimile.

He came to covet her E-IM photo, that particular photo specifically. It was an oldish portrait, from before Dale had known her at least. Her hair was still long, natural—gorgeous and collegiately unruly. If Dale had to put a date on it, he would have guessed 2012 or '13. Technically, it was an appropriate corporate headshot—blue background, wide smile, conservative neckline; a professional photo taken explicitly for use in a professional setting. And yet there was something distinctly improper about it, Dale thought. It seemed to reveal too much of her. It seemed to contain, in a single image, all possible versions of her—an inchoate galaxy you had to know her to see—though Dale had never seen it aside from in the photo. *It's been retouched*, he told himself, *it's just Photoshop*. Still, the avatar's special beauty, while surpassing the real Diana's, recalled her with such emotional fidelity that sometimes, away from his computer, he wasn't sure whether it was the real Diana or the little portrait with whom he longed to speak.

In mid-August, during his final week at Olympia, Dale's itch to make contact hit a fever pitch when he overheard the conversation of two young men, nearly indistinguishable in fleece vests and double-monk-strap shoes, hands wedged into the pockets of dark chinos, sauntering toward the forty-ninth-floor elevator with postprandial ease. They were from the rival consulting firm hired to vet Ecco, the little vest logos declared, and it was clear enough from their discussion that Mercury would not be proceeding. When Dale googled it, he found a frothy M&A blog was reporting the same, citing not only *inadequate synergies* and *Ecco's resistance to Philadelphian relocation*, but rumors of a more personal scandal *not un*related to Jack Howard's *strange failure to rehire Portmanteau, which is usually his go-to advisory—as well as the employer of Range's wife, Diana Whalen* . . . There was an incendiary story circling, the article went on, about a Pomeranian at the Metropolitan Museum of Art. The author only got about half the details right, and mercifully did not mention Dale or Vivien by name, but he'd held his breath reading it—twice, just to be sure.

—Was the point to make us look like tech douchebags? Yes, and they were eminently successful, Julian complained over the phone when Dale called him a few days later, at Vivien's behest.

—It just sounded like a bad fit, Julian, honestly. Besides, *Murgers & Hackquisitions* isn't exactly a heralded publication. It's practically a tabloid.

Dale could hear Julian rolling his eyes.

—That's part of the problem, though, isn't it? I cannot believe I'm saying this, let alone in the crumbling wake of my brand and prestige—may it Rest in Peace—but I almost feel sorry for Wes. You know, given his history with salacious press.

But Dale did not know, and so said.

—Really? Diana never told you about Wes's father?

—No? Why would she?

—Interesting, Julian said, ultra-syllabically. I guess I had assumed you two were closer.

Dale sensed a loosening conviction on Julian's part that he was keen not to retighten.

—Anyway, do you have a navy bow tie? Vivien wants to know.

—Obviously I do.

—She wants you to wear it to the rehearsal dinner.

—Oh, goodie. That will complement my boater hat nicely; its grosgrain ribbon is the same shade of navy. I've been looking for excuses to wear it all summer, you know. It's hard to establish a new affectation, when I already have so many. Please do thank her for me.

—Yeah. Will do.

They hung up, but Julian's words echoed in his mind. *I guess I had assumed you two were closer.* When, click by click, Dale learned the extent of Charlie Range's crimes, Diana's failure ever to mention them seemed not just odd and curious and wounding but *inconceivable*. All those lunches in the Underworld, evenings in the backgroundless bar—Paris—where they'd spoken at such great lengths of their spouses, their families, even their in-laws? Of novels and *Anna Karenina* and the very topic of suicide? It didn't compute, and the incomputability irked him. It seemed both to mock and intensify his misery, and in the void once filled by her dazzling repartee, his mind searched simultaneously for how to forget and punish her. Dale reflected on their conversations, and imagined new, hypothetical ones. He saw her, too, alone, without him. He imagined, from Diana's perspective, the critical acclaim of his unwritten novel, concocting ever more gratifying scenarios with rising degrees of fantasy. There she was, in her cold apartment, reading it. Then learning it was to become an HBO miniseries. With schadenfreude and compassion, he felt her swallow a cocktail of emotions—literally swallowing himself, in imitation of his own imaginings, at turns gratified and touched by her pride and rue, her identification, her insecurity. She could see there was a character drawn in her likeness, yes, and was chuffed by the inclusion, to have had some effect on one of her generation's literary luminaries. And yet she also found it distressing. It seemed unfair to hold no commercial share of his success, to have to watch his work—*their* intimacy—taken so readily by fawning TV hosts as the brilliant conjurings of fiction. When Katie Couric asked for his inspiration, he'd only said *Tolstoy and Melville and Wilde and James*. Though Diana would have been embarrassed, too, to be recognized. She was unable to shake the impression it was not the most flattering portrait.

It has been said, and will be said again, that passion makes one think in a circle. Certainly with hideous iteration Dale shaped and reshaped these visions, so pleasing and torturous, with their potential and unreality, until they came to seem a sort of plan, if not a foretold destiny. Dale exhumed a black Moleskine from his bag, made a few notes, and put it back again.

—What will you do for the next two weeks, before the wedding? Eric asked Dale the next day, twirling his suitcase past the white Chesterfield benches for the last time.

—Whatever Vivien tells me to, he said blithely.

## XXIX.

In the May 7, 2013, issue of the *New Yorker* there appeared a 629-word satirical essay by Emma Rathbone, written from the perspective of a bride addressing a stylist, describing her vision for her wedding hair. "I've got something kind of specific in mind," the bride admits, before launching into a series of crisp extended metaphors for the tousled up-do vibe she is going for—sexy *Little House on the Prairie*, Georgia O'Keeffe–ish sophisticate, your young mom on moving day, who, everyone agrees, "looks prettier when she doesn't even try." Vivien loved the piece for its humor, but even more for its breathtaking accuracy. It might have been written expressly for any number of her friends, and its memory served as a catty beacon of solace on the wedding circuit prior to her own engagement. After Dale proposed, she dug up the dog-eared issue again, approaching it with the kind of hip irony that permits one to simultaneously be a part of something and make fun of it without contradiction. When she quoted it to her stylist at her own trial appointment, they'd laughed together—and the stylist understood precisely what Vivien had in mind.

At half past eleven on the morning of her wedding, Vivien sat at her mother's vanity in a monogrammed white robe and holding a mimosa, studying with controlled anxiety the hands of her stylist as they sectioned and curled and teased according to plan. The spacious, neutral bedroom had been outfitted attractively for the occasion. Vivien's wedding dress hung in the picturesque bank of farmhouse windows. Across the room, a colorful spread of refreshments had been set up next to the beige linen settee. There were precisely the right number of flower arrangements to convey a general sense of tasteful festivity. Vivien's bridesmaids—also wearing monogrammed robes, but of a pale blue—distributed themselves about leisurely, looking like the subjects of a late Renoir. They approached the vanity in between bites of gourmet bagel and their own hair and makeup services to pay tribute with compliments so effusively heaping and indiscriminate that Vivien scarcely trusted and largely ignored them, preferring to critically evaluate each step in her bridal metamorphosis for herself. Still, Vivien was glad to have them there, in their pretty matching robes. An equipage is not complete without staff in correct attire.

—A little more volume on top, I think, Vivien told the stylist. More, you know, windswept.

—It already looks perfect, Vivien, Grace Cho declared, licking a globule of cream cheese from her fingers and sinking into the battalion of decorative pillows on Vivien's parents' bed.

—Yeah, you look like Kate Middleton, said Jackie Darby.

—Vivien's prettier than Kate Middleton, Audrey Wimberly corrected her, not to be outdone.

Vivien studied the faces of her bridesmaids in the glass, then she studied her own. She'd lost three pounds in the preceding weeks, and even before contouring, her face and neck had a gratifying angularity that was undeniably Kate-like, enhanced by the softness of its dark, textural frame. Glancing again at her bridesmaids, Vivien decided that while they were being disingenuous, they were also correct.

—Thanks, she said with equanimity—but I'm going more for, like, 1994 Wynona Ryder in *Little Women*—

—Oh, my god, I *love* that movie.

—Me too.

—Me *too*.

—And Winona is so pretty in it.

—*So* pretty.

—Vivien's a total Jo, don't you think?

—*Totally.*

—I always wanted to be a Jo, but I'm more of an Amy, Grace Cho lamented.

—Jackie's a Meg, Audrey said.

—I am *not* a Meg.

—Who is Meg then—who is *Beth*?

—Gr-*ace*! Beth *dies*, Jackie protested.

—Yah, but *she's Claire Danes*.

—None of us are Beth, Audrey said diplomatically.

Vivien caught her stylist's eye in the mirror and gestured to the swoop on the long side of her part.

—Just a little more volume, she instructed her quietly.

Downstairs in the sunroom, Dale and his groomsmen performed their concomitant prenuptial rites. While the requisite images of them donning bow ties and cufflinks were photographed for posterity, these mainly revolved around nursing their hangovers by sipping single-barrel bourbon, punctuated by the occasional shot. In contrast to—or, perhaps better stated, *on account of* the previous evening—the drinking was markedly uncompetitive. Set under twinkle lights in the dimming garden of the Rodin Museum, Dale and Vivien's rehearsal dinner and welcome reception had created the kind of atmosphere that inclines the elite to drink in quantities that in the absence of privilege would probably be labeled alcoholism, and even with it generated euphemistic whispers that so-and-so (but generally, Harry Sinclair) was having "rather too good a time." Mercifully no one had done anything so inappropriate as to spoil Vivien's enjoyment, but they'd all been overserved, and into the early afternoon both Harry and Sebastian were visibly wrecked. The groomsmen's alpha impulses were thus relegated to lightly roasting Dale, showering him with insults that a disinterested observer might note had more in common than not with Vivien's bridesmaids' flattery.

Only in the very final stages of grooming did the conversation veer toward the unironic. There was a lot of "you look good, man" and back-clapping. *Was it time to go?* No, the photographer had returned to the ladies. "Getting-ready photos," the wedding planner explained, were only focused on the actual process of getting ready for the groom. The bride's were often restaged at the end, so she and her maids might be fully powdered not just for the posed photos in their matching robes but also the "candids," the makeup artist pretending to dust an already-painted face. It was fully another hour before the wedding planner reappeared in the sunroom to announce it was time to head to the club for the couple's "first look" in the library and formal photographs, which would last approximately two hours.

—*Two hours?* objected Sebastian.

—Two hours *before the ceremony*, clarified the wedding planner—we'll reconvene after for more shots on the lawn, when the natural light is best.

—See? Not so bad, Dale said with brother-in-lawly affection—you're all about Natty Light, right?

Everyone laughed, even the wedding planner, and Dale couldn't help but wonder why he didn't feel better about it. Their reaction had been instantaneous and authentic; he hadn't caught the slightest whiff of sycophancy. Normally, in such moments, he keenly felt the warm swell of praise. It was not the particular exchange, but the absence of this swell, that, on the most important day of his life, still tingled in Dale's mind forty-five minutes later as he posed artfully next to the ponderous library ladder supporting his bride.

Vivien looked stunningly—*stunningly*—beautiful. Dale didn't have the textile vocabulary to personally express it, but he very much liked the tulle of her gown, how the skirt seemed to float in cloudlike layers, the way it wrapped the slim nip of her waist and gathered to create a diaphanous illusion neckline. She hadn't gone overboard with the rouge either, as brides so often did. He *loved* her hair. When she'd first seen him, she'd glowingly beamed—and so had he. But then he noticed the videographer, and felt awkward. Vivien reminded him to take care as he kissed her, so as not to disturb her makeup, and it seemed only thirty seconds later he was being told where to stand and how to position his chin.

The editorial series in the library was followed shortly by portraits in the conservatory, traditional photos in the ballroom, and an illustrative shoot on the terrace. Family members and the wedding party were cycled in and out for the group shots in what seemed to Dale every possible permutation, as if they were the Duke and Duchess of Cambridge or something. It was such a production Dale almost felt compelled to apologize to his parents, for whom signifiers of great wealth always held an air of ostentation, even when executed with graciousness.

Shortly before the guests started to arrive, Dale and Vivien were again led to separate quarters, as if to preserve the illusion—Dale was not quite sure for who—that when Vivien walked down the aisle he would be witnessing her nubile splendor for the first time. The groom's room was small and smelled of sandalwood and primogeniture; the first movement of the Bruch Violin Concerto played at low volume. It had the air of a matrimonial bullpen, the lingering anxiety of previous grooms mixing uncomfortably with Dale's own. This compounding anxiety of cliché might well have been stronger had Dale seemed to himself more like "a groom" than merely an imposter. There is often a certain surrealism to events of great anticipation, but never before had Dale felt more like an echo of someone else's music, the actor of a part that had not been written for him.

The now-familiar click of the wedding planner's sensible heels could be heard on the other side of the door.

—Hurry up please it's time.

—Are you ready? said Gage reflexively, because it was the thing your best man was supposed to say.

How to answer such a question? *You know, Gage, I'm really not sure. I don't feel like myself; it's hard to believe that what is happening right now is actually happening to* me. *So you could say I have conflicting thoughts in regard to the state of my readiness. In many ways I felt readier yesterday. Maybe months ago, too.* That certainly wouldn't do. He cringed at the thought of a canned response, though, at *Definitely!* or *Ready as I'll ever be!* But his modulated off-script options all sounded even more fraudulent in his mind; the solemn ones were too grim, the nonchalant too flippant. He feared his voice would crack in any case. For while Dale wasn't sure whether or not he was "ready," there was genuine emotion in his wavering. And so he remained silent, nodding tensely with a tense little smile.

The Whipplepool Country Club was the kind of property irresistible to Veblenite brides. Its winding entry drive was marked by little more than a weathered sign reading PRIVATE PROPERTY, and was so overgrown with thickets as to resolutely deter those unfamiliar with the subtle signifiers of exclusion. The steep wilderness persisted for a little over a mile before a lush, sportive paradise presented itself, all the more beautiful in contrast to the nettled drive. The club's immediate grounds had been landscaped in the Anglo-American manner of much pecuniary emulation, the green so thoroughly and sympathetically integrated with the natural environment as to suggest that the smooth, dense turf regularly mowed itself. The Greek Revival clubhouse, imposing and symmetrical, seemed to exacerbate this impression, its sharp white lines throwing the verdurous hills in relief. The stateliest view, and indeed, the vantage point that, if the weather was fine, nearly all couples chose for their ceremony (Dale and Vivien included) was the front terrace, creating an aisle from the two-storied columnar facade to a floral arbor overlooking the golf course, as though a window gave upon the sylvan scene.

Dale straightened his dinner jacket in the shade of the arbor, his eyes fixed back on the facade with its French doors, its soaring balcony windows reflecting the evening sky. His groomsmen fanned out like matryoshka replicas to his left, standing arranged by height in that distinctive three-quarter turn to the side. To Dale's right presided Julian Pappas-Fidicia, who, between the sumptuous clerical stole draped over his navy tuxedo and the velvet slippers with embroidered emerald-eyed tigers on them, looked less like a traditional wedding officiant than a preppy Liberace. Dale's parents had already been seated in the first row, as had Vivien's mother and the readers. The chamber group concluded one cinematic piece and began another. Two-hundred-some necks turned in unison with the music's swelling cue. The French doors opened. There was Audrey; Jacqueline; Grace. The opening thematic melody fell into false retreat with the countersubject's introduction as the bridesmaids made their way to the arbor, mirroring the stance of the groomsmen. Julian pushed his round tortoiseshell glasses up the bridge of his nose with ecclesiastical majesty. As the returning crescendo of the main theme approached its climax, Vivien crossed the threshold on her father's arm. There were audible gasps. It didn't hurt that it was the sort of music so inherently moving it had the ability to override even mediocre dramatics. In the context of Vivien's touchingly nervous aesthetic radiance, the sensory effect was overwhelming to the point of disorientation. For the briefest of moments, blinking his eyes, Dale thought she was someone else.

Julian's welcome remarks were both warmer and more professional than Dale might have imagined, his characteristic wit and pomp adapting surprisingly well to ritual appropriateness and genuine formality. If Julian hadn't so charmingly and with remarkably little reference to himself elucidated the nature of his personal association with the couple, Dale was certain their guests would have thought he had officiated weddings before—*which*, Dale remembered, with poorly timed and unwelcome memory, *he had. Wes and—*

The aposiopesis hung in his mind by sheer force of will. But thinking about not thinking about a person is merely another way of thinking about her, and while Dale may have successfully refused to allow the progression of vowels and consonants that composed her name to enter his inner monologue, he could not suppress the associated sentiment. Paige Sinclair finished reading from the story of Pygmalion (the only brief excerpt from the *Metamorphoses* Vivien could find even tangentially fit for a modern wedding). As Anderson Gregory took Paige's place and began the second reading, Dale's gaze floated past him, back up to the soaring balcony—

*So they lov'd, as love in twain*
*Had the essence but in one;*
*Two distincts, division none:*
*Number there in love was slain.*

*Hearts remote, yet not asunder;*
*Distance and no space was seen*
*'Twixt this Turtle and his queen:*
*But in them it were a wonder.*

There—there was a *person* up there. A *woman*—

*So between them love did shine*
*That the Turtle saw his right*
*Flaming in the Phoenix' sight:*
*Either was the other's mine.*

*Property was thus appalled*
*That the self was not the same;*
*Single nature's double name*
*Neither two nor one was called.*

The sensation of hyperarousal was so intense it threatened to shut down Dale's entire sympathetic nervous system. He imagined Diana on the balcony, frantic but beautiful—*windswept*—wondering if she'd made it in time, screaming his name with desperation. He imagined his own steps, slow at first, measured, his feet wary of obeying him, then breaking into a run to join her, racing through the French doors as she flew down the stairs to meet him, the pair of them toppling some flowers or a Ming vase or something in the foyer as a gaggle of guests chased after them—

*Reason, in itself confounded,*
*Saw division grow together,*
*To themselves yet either neither,*
*Simple were so well compounded;*

*That it cried, "How true a twain*
*Seemeth this concordant one!*
*Love has reason, reason none,*
*If what parts can so remain."*

Dale recomposed himself with Herculean concentration, hoping the tsunami under his arms hadn't seeped through to the outermost layer of his dinner jacket. At Julian's instruction, Dale turned toward Vivien and managed to clasp her hands. The woman on the balcony raised a six-thousand-dollar camera, to capture the picture in panorama.

# XXX.

Much has been said of the tendency for hardship to reveal the true nature of a person. Political turmoil, economic strife, war—times when the precarity of life, or at least the precarity of life as we know it, hangs in the balance tend to foster the honesty of urgency, stripping away pretense and affectation, neutralizing the will to dissimulation, exposing who we are at the core. As an old dog once observed: *adversity has the effect of eliciting talents, which in prosperous circumstances would have lain dormant*. The same might be said of eliciting cowardice or monstrosity. The broader point is rather that whatever lies beneath becomes difficult to mask. But, when for years the leader of the free world has been a measured, responsible adult of the progressive enterprise, realizing incremental gains and emblematic of more significant ones, this urgency, particularly for fundamentally comfortable people, has the tendency to dissipate. It is a notable feature of peaceable times that the face is considered secondarily to the mask. Even to ourselves it becomes an abstract kind of hieroglyph. The literature surrounding this phenomenon is almost as well documented as its opposite. To quote one of the great poet-philosophers of our own time, *what am I 'posed to do when the club lights come on? It's easy to be Puff, but it's harder to be Sean.*

It would be a mistake to channel the relevance of this reflection in Dale's direction alone. For all her pride and care in the outward presentation of her hymeneal rites, Vivien had her own underlying misgivings about becoming a McBride. The name itself, for starters. She didn't love it. She never considered keeping her own, because doing so would have felt like an exposition of disappointment, and besides, made far too much of a "feminist statement" for her taste. But she couldn't quite relieve her mind of the impression that *McBride* didn't have the ring of *Kennedy* or *Rockefeller* or *Vanderbilt*, or *Range*. Why Diana had hung on to *Whalen* Vivien could not understand, beyond the assumption that people must call her Mrs. Range often enough anyway, and the pleasure of correcting them—of conspicuously throwing away such an advantage as if it were nothing—seemed, while obnoxious if you really dissected it, superficially symbolic of equality and independence and that sort of overtly liberal general wokeness Diana Whalen *would* deem consistent with her personal brand.

Vivien's more serious reservation only developed in the aftermath of the Young Members' fiasco. Not that she still suspected Dale of any hanky panky reaching farther than his own imagination. The explanation of the postcard was too ridiculous not to be true, and Vivien continued discreetly punishing him for it mainly for purposes of precedent. No, it wasn't the inciting image of Dale's red hand that lingered with Vivien from that night, but of Wes, chasing after Diana—the single-mindedness of his gait, the unilateral devotion scripted on his fucking Fibonacci face. In the ensuing weeks Vivien scolded herself for ever worrying he'd told Diana anything, and yet it was worse, somehow, to think he'd been so thoroughly unfazed by their tryst. This new lens of anxiety proved a remarkable motivator for embellishing her wedding, though. She wanted Wes to tangentially see all the pictures of it on Instagram, and decompose in regret.

Not until the ceremony itself did Vivien begin to internalize the fantastical folly with which she had been filtering so genuinely momentous an occasion. Vivien had prepared herself for her nuptials as one prepares for a performance, almost the same way she would have prepared for a curatorial lecture, and was entirely blindsided by the raw, emotional vulnerability Dale displayed. Once it became clear he wasn't *actually* going to faint, Vivien was highly touched by the threat of it. As he pronounced his vows, there were tears in his eyes. Vivien saw herself through these tears, and tried to suppress her guilt that she was not exactly the same woman Dale was seeing. It occurred to Vivien how obliging he'd been in the actualization of her wedding vision, that he'd styled himself to her specifications, that he looked straight out of *GQ*. He was precisely the groom she had always imagined, in every way save one.

—Eek! the wedding planner squealed in overwrought delight after Dale and Vivien signed their marriage certificate. It's official-official now! Yay! Okay, time to head to the lawn—

—Oh, forget the staged lawn photos, Vivien said, almost spontaneously. We should go enjoy the cocktail hour. I want to have a good time.

Vivien smiled sweetly at her husband, and his show of gratitude stirred something in Vivien as they returned to the terrace. Not romantic love exactly, no, but a pleasant sense of mutual understanding, of social relief; a marital shelter, almost, which was not without its psychological benefits. Dale clasped Vivien's hand and squeezed it tight.

—My beautiful bride, ladies and gentlemen! He introduced her triumphantly, crossing the threshold to thunderous applause, chaotic and choreographed in equal measure.

He jolted his wife's hand in the air in the manner of a referee with a victorious prizefighter. Vivien smiled extra-wide, iconically, imagining the photojournalist-style image of her iconic, extra-wide smile, glossily smiling again at all of her friends from the cover of their first Christmas card.

Dale and Vivien had limited further interaction as the sun sank behind the green, bathing the terrace in oblong, crepuscular light. Not that they were avoiding each other intentionally; they were merely too caught up in the canons of decency associated with being a bride and a groom—of greeting and thanking, of air-kissing, selfie-taking—though from a distance Dale could see that Vivien was indeed having a good time.

She had that characteristic flush precipitated by others' unmistakable admiration, which no development in the history of cosmetics has quite been able to emulate. She allowed herself a second glass of champagne, and he could sense even her will to aesthetic control dissipating amidst her merriment. She still coached him clinically through their first dance, but when Dale muffed one of the moves anyway, Vivien laughed it off with generous nonchalance. Julian was somewhat less charitable.

—Congratulations, he said, leaning over to Dale as Vivien danced with her father, on making it through that.

—How bad was I?

—Somewhere between Gage the summer he tore his ACL and white girls in the hip-hop class at Equinox.

—You don't go to Equinox.

—*Au contraire*, said Julian. Equinox is my favorite place to go to the bathroom. Their bathrooms alone are worth the membership fees. I'm serious! They're that nice. Not to mention how hard it is to find a bathroom in New York City. But Equinoxes are everywhere.

—I was gonna say, I can't exactly see you doing extensive squats.

—I should think not. I'm not training to give birth in a third-world country.

Audrey Wimberly looked aghast, and Dale was almost grateful to receive the band's peremptory summons to dance with his mother. By the time he made it back through the throng of well-wishing side conversations and returned to his seat, the caterers had already cleared the first course, though Dale couldn't remember having eaten anything. Vivien's father and Grace and Gage gave heartfelt toasts, the last of which was shockingly well constructed and reminded Dale how much he genuinely liked him. ("Obviously I helped him with it," Julian boasted later.) As the dinner began to break apart at the margins, the band reannounced itself at tempo with that Bruno Mars wedding song, the one about spontaneous elopement that immediately gained obligatory playlist status at weddings carefully planned well in advance. Its impossibly catchy xylophone cut through the twinkle of conversations and cutlery in a way that made even Dale's extremities tingle with the urge to dance. He gamely drew Vivien to the floor, but she migrated into a throng of her girlfriends somewhere during the next song, and they lost track of each other again in the whirling circles of convivial activity until it was time to cut the cake.

—Don't get any on my face, okay? Vivien reminded him.

—No, no—of course not.

There must have been two or three unstructured celebratory hours thereafter, but they passed with dreamlike brevity, as if he'd only read the abridged versions of them, the conversations and alcoholic beverages refracting to the point of perceptual cliché. Dale could recall crouching on the ground to *(Shout) a little bit softer now-ow*, and Julian launching into an unexpected panegyric on the thoroughly mediocre romantic comedy *Something Borrowed* and how it "actually changed [his] life," but these were not the sort of recalcitrant memories Dale had anticipated forming at his wedding, and when the band signaled that the next song would be the last song, and the wedding planner retrieved him from the dance floor to collect his personal articles from the sandalwood waiting room so that they might be preloaded into the Jaguar, an empty feeling, a sort of loss almost, overcame him. The penultimate song for everyone else had been the ultimate for him, and he hadn't realized it.

It was purely on an abstract, conceptual level that Dale understood himself to be the same living human person who led Vivien McBride through a shrieking colonnade of sparklers as they blurred in pointillistic streaks through the starry, starry night; the same person who kissed her like the sailor in Times Square returning from World War II—or, if not actually *like* him, then at least mirroring the pose. Because wasn't it impossible now, really, for a man to kiss a woman like that? Even when you set aside, like, issues of consent and heteronormativity. Did not the picture's ubiquitous existence preclude its ability to be repeated with the same wild joyous utter lack of reference? Yes? Yes? . . . No?

• • •

Dale opened the door to the Mark V for his bride and rounded the car to climb in beside her, saddling up close to join her in waving goodbye. The chauffeur drove forward gently at first, eliciting a new flurry of cheers that, as they accelerated further, sank precipitously into the diminuendo of time and distance and, as they turned off the golf course path and onto the proper thoroughfare, lingered for a moment longer in their minds before it was quiet. The car grew extravagantly still. Dale moved to undo his bow tie, only to realize he'd already untied it. Vivien's bottom lip began to quiver.

—It was such a beautiful wedding, she said.

—Yes, it was.

Dale's words echoed in the wells of silence. Not the loaded, unsaid kind, but the truly empty silence of having nothing to say.

—Such a beautiful wedding, Vivien said again, but almost as if its beauty was regrettable.

The next morning over breakfast, Wes and Diana read all about it in the *New York Times*.

**THE END**

# ACKNOWLEDGMENTS

For readers interested in learning more about Ovidian art, I highly recommend the books of Paul Barolsky. *Ovid and the Metamorphoses of Modern Art from Botticelli to Picasso* (Yale University Press, 2014) in particular recalls the "Art and Myth" seminar he taught for many years at the University of Virginia, which inspired Vivien's exhibition. Paul: thank you for introducing me to Ovid and his heirs, for illuminating the architecture of my mind in the specter of their exquisite self-reflexivity.

I'm also grateful to the catalyst of my misery and the love of my life, Michael McDuffie; to our darling son, Dorian; to my parents, Natalie Thorington and Nicholas Joukovsky; to my wonderful friends who were early readers and supporters—Jessica Hirschey, Tara Singh Carlson, Jia Tolentino, Defne Gunay, Blake Edwards, Sid Pailla, Josh Cincinnati, Kyle O'Connor and the rest of RyukTV; to my brilliant agent, Sarah Fuentes and Fletcher & Company; to Alyson Sinclair and Nectar Literary; and to my editor, Chelsea Cutchens—I am so deeply honored that of all the potential books that cross your desk, you chose to make mine a reality. Thank you and the whole Abrams/Overlook team—Jessica Focht, Andrew Gibeley, Devin Grosz, Sarah Masterson Hally, Kimberly Lew, Lisa Silverman, Mamie VanLangen, Jessica Wiener, John McGhee, and Janine Barlow—for publishing *The Portrait of a Mirror*, for publishing it so gorgeously. For making it a work of art, too.

The last word here is reserved for the incomparable Evan S. Thomas, to whom this book is dedicated. To those who loved Evan as I did: I hope you will look on the character of Julian Pappas-Fidicia fondly. To say that Julian was "based" on Evan feels inadequate. My goal was nothing short of resurrection.

# APPENDIX A
## Anxieties of Influence

### Novels & Novellas

*A Portrait of the Artist as a Young Man* | James Joyce
*À rebours* | Joris-Karl Huysmans
*American Psycho* | Bret Easton Ellis
*Anna Karenina* | Leo Tolstoy
*Atonement* | Ian McEwan
*Brideshead Revisited* | Evelyn Waugh
*Changing Places* | David Lodge
Complete Works | Jane Austen
*Infinite Jest* | David Foster Wallace
*Madame Bovary* | Gustave Flaubert
*Middlemarch* | George Eliot
*Moby-Dick* | Herman Melville
*Nightmare Abbey* | Thomas Love Peacock
*On the Road* | Jack Kerouac
*Small World* | David Lodge
*The Age of Innocence* | Edith Wharton
*The Corrections* | Jonathan Franzen
*The Great Gatsby* | F. Scott Fitzgerald
*The Metamorphosis* | Franz Kafka
*The Picture of Dorian Gray* | Oscar Wilde
*The Portrait of a Lady* | Henry James
*The Secret History* | Donna Tartt
*Ulysses* | James Joyce

**Poetry**

*Aeneid* | Virgil
"Delight in Disorder" | Robert Herrick
*Divine Comedy* | Dante Alighieri
"Kubla Khan" | Samuel Taylor Coleridge
*Metamorphoses* | Ovid
"Ode on a Grecian Urn" | John Keats
*Odes* | Horace
*Odyssey* | Homer
*Paradise Lost* | John Milton
"The Phoenix and the Turtle" | William Shakespeare
*The Waste Land* | T. S. Eliot

**Philosophy, Nonfiction, Humor, Essays & Criticism**

*Bernini* | Howard Hibbard
*Caravaggio* | Howard Hibbard
*Legend, Myth, and Magic in the Image of the Artist* | Ernst Kris and Otto Kurz
*Michael and Natasha: The Life and Love of Michael II, the Last of the Romanov Tsars* | Rosemary & Donald Crawford
"My Wedding Hair" | Emma Rathbone
"On Painting" | Leon Battista Alberti
*Ovid and the Metamorphoses of Modern Art from Botticelli to Picasso* | Paul Barolsky
*The Anxiety of Influence: A Theory of Poetry* | Harold Bloom
*The Book of the Courtier* | Baldassare Castiglione
*The Birth of Tragedy* | Friedrich Nietzsche
*The Power of Glamour* | Virginia Postrel
*The Theory of the Leisure Class* | Thorstein Veblen
"Tradition and the Individual Talent" | T. S. Eliot
"Ulysses, Order, and Myth" | T. S. Eliot

### Plays & Musicals

*A Midsummer Night's Dream* | William Shakespeare
*Antigone* | Sophocles
*Evita* | Andrew Lloyd Webber & Tim Rice
*Faust* | Johann Wolfgang von Goethe
*Hamlet* | William Shakespeare
*Macbeth* | William Shakespeare

### Film & Television

*A Beautiful Mind* | Ron Howard, Akiva Goldsman, and Sylvia Nasar
*Chocolat* | Lasse Halström and Robert Nelson Jacobs
*Cinema Paradiso* | Giuseppe Tornatore
*Citizen Kane* | Orson Welles and Herman J. Mankiewicz
*Dead Poets Society* | Peter Weir and Tom Schulman
*Ex Machina* | Alex Garland
*Family Guy* | Seth MacFarlane
*Law & Order: SVU* | Dick Wolf
*Little Women* | Gillian Armstrong, Robin Swicord, and Louisa May Alcott
*Match Point* | Woody Allen
*Metropolitan* | Whit Stillman
*St. Elmo's Fire* | Joel Schumacher and Carl Kurlander
*The Da Vinci Code* | Ron Howard, Akiva Goldsman, and Dan Brown
*The Graduate* | Mike Nichols, Calder Willingham, and Buck Henry
*The Imitation Game* | Morton Tyldum, Graham Moore, and Andrew Hodges
*The Princess Bride* | Rob Reiner and William Goldman
*The Social Network* | David Fincher and Aaron Sorkin
*You Only Live Twice* | Lewis Gilbert, Roald Dahl, and Ian Fleming
"Sympathy for the Devil" | The Rolling Stones
"Caught by the River" | Doves
"I Heard It Through the Grapevine" | Marvin Gaye
"Diane Young" | Vampire Weekend

## APPENDIX B
### Soundtrack Supplement

“Video Games” | Lana Del Rey
“We Used to Wait” | Arcade Fire
“Welcome Home, Son” | Radical Face
“I’ll Be Your Mirror” | The Velvet Underground
“Sprawl II (Mountains Beyond Mountains)” | Arcade Fire
“Caravane” | Raphaël
“I Can Only Imagine” | David Guetta feat. Chris Brown and Lil Wayne
“You’re So Vain” | Carly Simon
“Reflektor” | Arcade Fire
“Reflections” | MisterWives
“Torn” | Natalie Imbruglia
“Locomotion” | Carole King
“Lost in My Mind” | The Head and the Heart
“The Sound of Silence” | Simon & Garfunkel
“Pompeii” | Bastille
“Mirror Master” | Young the Giant

# APPENDIX C

## Select Artifacts

Antonio Canova, *Perseus with the Head of Medusa*,
marble, ca. 1800, The Metropolitan Museum of Art, New York.

Credit: The Metropolitan Museum of Art

Michelangelo Merisi da Caravaggio, *Medusa*,
oil on canvas mounted on wood, ca. 1597, Galleria degli Uffizi, Florence.

Credit: Uffizi Gallery/Google Cultural Institute

Gian Lorenzo Bernini, *Medusa*,
marble, 1638–1648, Musei Capitolini, Rome.

Credit: Livioandronico2013/Wikimedia Commons

Michelangelo Merisi da Caravaggio, *Narcissus*,
oil on canvas, 1597–1599, Galleria Nazionale d'Arte Antica, Rome.

Credit: Wikimedia Commons

Salvador Dalí, *Metamorphosis of Narcissus*,
oil on canvas, 1937, Gala–Salvador Dalí Foundation/DACS, London.

Credit: © 2020 Salvador Dalí, Fundació Gala-Salvador Dalí, Artists Rights Society

Nicolas Poussin, *Echo and Narcissus*,
oil on canvas, ca. 1630, Musée du Louvre, Paris.

Credit: Wikimedia Commons

Jean-Léon Gérôme, *Pygmalion and Galatea*, 1890,
oil on canvas, The Metropolitan Museum of Art, New York.

Credit: The Metropolitan Museum of Art/Wikimedia Commons

Guo Pei, *Daijin* (*Magnificent Gold*),
gown embroidered with wire and silk-, 24-karat gold-
and silver-spun thread, and embellished with Swarovski-sequin
accessories, 2006, shown in the "China: Through the Looking Glass"
exhibition, The Metropolitan Museum of Art, New York.

Credit: lydia_x_liu/Flickr